the
darkest
lies

ALSO BY BARBARA COPPERTHWAITE

Invisible
Flowers for the Dead

the darkest lies

BARBARA COPPERTHWAITE

bookouture

Published by Bookouture
An imprint of StoryFire Ltd.
23 Sussex Road, Ickenham, UB10 8PN
United Kingdom
www.bookouture.com

ISBN: 978-1-78681-181-3
eBook ISBN: 978-1-78681-180-6

This book is a work of fiction. Names, characters, businesses,
organizations, places and events other than those clearly in the
public domain, are either the product of the author's imagination
or are used fictitiously. Any resemblance to actual persons, living or
dead, events or locales is entirely coincidental.

To Paul. You know why.

And Mum, my greatest cheerleader. You never gave up hoping, even when at times I did.

PROLOGUE

The cry for help is ragged and desperate, the voice hitching. There is no one to hear it.

A moon hangs so fat it oozes an aura into the sky that almost blots out the stars surrounding it. It looks down on land as flat as an open palm, and as unforgiving as a clenched fist, and gives no answer to the screams of fear and rage that float up to it.

This is the wind's playground. It races across the North Sea and hits the land full force. There is nothing to slow it; no hills, few trees or hedges here on land reclaimed from the water to create the marshes and fertile flats of Lincolnshire. It screams ecstatically, punching the handful of houses it comes across, revelling in its unfettered freedom as it rattles windows. On its journey it picks up the entreaties for help that are echoing into the sky. Hurls them across the landscape, as gleeful as a toddler with a toy.

'Help me! Please! Help!'

There is no one to catch the words.

No one, except a lone figure, turning, walking away towards lights in the far-off distance.

CHAPTER 1

Beth chewed at her thumbnail as she stared at the clothes that were carefully folded in the bottom of the rucksack. Was she doing the right thing? Yes; there'd be no harm done, and no one need ever find out. This was not a big deal. Still she gnawed, worrying at the nail.

The thirteen-year-old suddenly yanked her thumb from her mouth. She must remember not to chew it tonight; it looked as if she was sucking it, like a baby. Tonight, she needed to show that she was grown-up, no longer a little girl.

Right, had she remembered everything? Yep, it looked like it.

It had taken ages to choose both her outfits. One for her parents; one for her secret. She slipped a jumper on and smoothed down the Minnie Mouse picture on the front. It was a firm favourite of her mum's so it was the obvious choice, even though she didn't like the childish top herself any more. Everything was perfect for tonight – and her parents would never guess in a million years.

A huge grin on her face, Beth glugged a glass of milk and set it down on her dressing table. Then called out: 'Mu-um. You ready to go?'

A laugh floated up from downstairs. 'Isn't it normally me asking you that?'

Beth hurried downstairs with her rucksack, her dad making the usual joke about 'a herd of elephants'. She gave him a peck on the cheek and a big hug, which he returned, but peered around her at the television.

'Ooh, offside,' he groaned.

'See you tomorrow.'

'Have a nice night, Beans.' He grinned as he used her nickname, but continued watching the football, casting her only a sidelong glance.

Minutes later, Beth and her mum were wrapped in their hats and coats, and striding along with Wiggins by their side. The russet cocker spaniel held his nose high, tail swishing casually from side to side, catching various scents on the cold January air.

'Hey, wouldn't it be amazing if we could smell things the way Wiggins does? We could follow scent trails!' Beth said.

She linked arms with her mum as they took the left-hand lane from the village crossroads on which they lived, towards the home of Beth's best friend, Chloe.

'Like a superhero? You could be called Dog Girl,' her mum joked.

Beth wrinkled her nose. 'Yeah, on second thoughts... The name's not great, is it?'

'What other superpowers would Dog Girl have?'

'Well, okay, she could take all sorts of things from nature. Like, she could have echo-location, like a bat, so she could find her way in the dark. That'd be handy now!'

They giggled.

'What are you up to with Chloe tonight, anyway? Pamper night? Watching a film?'

'Yeah, we'll probably watch a film. Not sure about the pampering – Chloe might not have any face packs.'

'We could nip back and get some. There's a couple in the bathroom cabinet.'

'No. It's fine. We'll probably watch a film and eat a lot of chocolate.'

'Want some money for a pizza? It's a Friday night, you might as well treat yourselves.'

'Ooh, great!'

Her mum stopped abruptly, waving the tenner at the sky before handing it over. 'Look how big the moon is tonight.'

'Is it a supermoon?' Beth asked, gazing upward too. There had been one a few months earlier, and her dad had told her about how it was special, being closer to the earth and bringing bigger tides. That had been really cool.

'Don't think so, but it's beautiful, isn't it?'

She nodded. 'I can see the man in the moon ever so clearly.'

Given that they had stopped, it seemed as good a time as any to try…

'So, I might as well walk the rest of the way alone.'

'No, I'll walk you to the door. It's dark, Beth.'

She gave her mum her very best puppy dog eyes look. If the plan were to work, her mum couldn't take her to Chloe's house. Despite her parents thinking she'd be spending the night there, she had no intention of setting foot inside the place.

'I'm a teenager. I'm not a baby. Pur-lease, Mum!'

After a second or two, there came a reluctant nod. 'Be careful.'

'I will!'

'I love you to bits and whole again,' Mum added.

Beth felt her nose prickle with guilty tears. They had been saying that to each other since she was about four. She remembered it vividly, being cuddled on her mum's lap; her feet tucked under Dad's legs to keep them extra toasty warm. One hand twirling a piece of hair round and round and round her fingers as Dad read to them. She'd loved to hear the sound of his voice, but no matter how hard she'd fought, her eyelids had grown heavier and heavier and…

The sensation of weightlessness had woken her, as Dad carried her upstairs. When he'd tucked her in, he had stroked her face and kissed her forehead.

'Sleep tight, Beans. I love you to the moon and back,' he had murmured.

Beth had stirred sleepily. 'To the moon? That's a really, really, really long way.'

'It is, but I love you so much that it would easily stretch all the way there and back again – and more.'

The next day her mum had walked her across the road to school, holding her hand. As Beth slipped from her grasp, her mum had pulled her back, into a bear hug.

'Love you to bits,' she'd whispered.

Beth had paused in her squirming. 'To bits and back?' she'd checked.

Her mum had laughed. 'Er, yes, I suppose. To bits and whole again.'

Ever since, that saying had stuck. Hearing her mum use it now, Beth wanted to call a halt to her plan. To throw her arms around her and confess everything. She wanted to go home. She wanted to curl up and watch telly with Mum and Dad, while Wiggins did sneaky trumps that they all tried to blame on each other, laughing, even though they knew it was the dog. She wanted to tell her mum she'd love her forever and ever and ever, to bits and whole again.

Instead, she grinned cheekily, turned and skipped away like a little girl. Taking the mickey was easier than trying to articulate all of those feelings.

The wind plucked at her ponytail as she flew from sparse light pool to light pool between lamp posts until they ran out completely. The darkness swallowed her. Ahead she could feel her fate waiting for her and she rushed towards it eagerly. Tonight was going to be a big night.

CHAPTER 2

MELANIE
SATURDAY 23 JANUARY

The hysteria I had been trying to keep at bay bubbled up again as his name came up on my mobile phone. I pressed dial. The words needing to be said crammed into my mouth, clogging it like dry crackers, but I didn't stop running. Eyes darting everywhere, but seeing nothing.

Ringing. Ringing. Come on!

'Hello?'

'Jacob, she's gone. She's gone!' My voice quivered and cracked, face crumpling. 'What if someone's got her? What if she's hurt? Maybe she's run away?'

'Calm down.' Your father sounded firm and certain, Beth. It was exactly what I needed. 'What's happened?'

'No one knows where Beth is. She never arrived at Chloe's house last night. I only found out just now, when I called to see when she'd be home. Her mobile is switched off…'

'Don't panic, it's going to be okay. I'll come home; we'll look together. Just breathe.'

Calm. It's going to be okay. Breathe.

Hearing it said out loud, I believed it. I believed that you weren't really missing, Beth. That you would soon be home, with some silly excuse as to why you hadn't been where you had said you would be and your phone was switched off.

Yet even while telling myself that, I hadn't stopped running. My chest still felt as if it would burst.

'I'm coming to the house now. Stay where you are,' said Jacob. The line went dead.

I should have turned back to meet him at home, but knew he would be twenty minutes or so, and panic urged my legs on. There was nothing to be calm about.

My little girl was missing. My baby. My world.

I shouldn't have let you make your own way to your friend's house. But you are thirteen, Beth; old enough to be trusted. Aren't you? And Fenmere is a village where nothing ever happens. The most exciting thing to have occurred recently was when neighbours Bob Thornby and Phyllis Blakecroft fell out over Bob's untrimmed garden hedge narrowing Phyllis's driveway. Do you remember the hoo-ha over that?

So again, I repeated Jacob's words silently… *Calm down. It's going to be okay.*

I looked at my watch. Noon. No one had seen you since I'd dropped you off at the bottom of Holders Lane; Chloe's house is at the top. That was at 7 p.m., seventeen hours ago.

Seventeen hours! What had happened between that wave goodbye and Chloe's front door?

Anything. Anything could have happened in that time.

I cursed myself; I should never have let you out of my sight. I should have insisted on delivering you right to the front door. But you had begged to be allowed to walk alone.

'I'm a teenager now,' you had insisted. 'I'm not a baby.'

Not stroppy. You had been pleading. The breeze blowing across the fields of cabbages had plucked at your hair, creating a halo that made you look younger than you were. Still, I had relented because, despite my urge to wrap you in cotton wool, the slow, painful process of giving my daughter responsibility had to start at some point. That had seemed as good a time as any.

Now I reached Holders Lane again, deeply regretting my decision. Chloe's home was the lone building far off at a right-angle corner of the road. It was painted a soft shade of lilac, so stood out easily from the patchwork fields of cabbages and warm brown fallow earth topped with white frost. On either side of the lane ran large ditches, for drainage. Looking at them, a horrible idea formed in my mind.

Hands curled tight in my pockets to fight the tension roiling through my stomach, I forced myself to peer over the edge and focus my panic-blinded eyes.

Twisted limbs. My little girl's body broken on impact by a car bonnet, then flung aside by a hit-and-run driver. So much blood.

That was what I expected to see. Instead, there was coarse grass, mud and a smear of frozen brown water.

Every step I took made my heart jolt. Maybe this would be the step when my worst fears came true. The adrenaline coursing through me screamed *hurry, hurry, hurry.* My mind forced me to slow down. I couldn't risk rushing and missing you. Progress was painfully plodding.

When I finished one side, I crossed and searched the drainage ditch on the other side.

Despite my measured gait, by the time I was done I panted as if I'd run a marathon, the cold hitting the back of my throat and making me cough.

If you weren't here, where were you, Beth?

Once again I started to run. Shouted your name, tears streaming, taking in only snapshots of houses, gardens, hedges, the playing field. The low winter sun in my eyes making everything sparkle cheerily in the frost. Soon I was back in the centre of Fenmere, where most of the village's houses were huddled. At the main crossroads was our house, along with the church, primary school, general store, café and the most popular of the two pubs, The Poacher.

'Melanie!'

Someone shouting my name made me whirl round. Jill Young stood in the doorway of the Picky Person's Pop In, Fenmere's general store. The 'c' had fallen from Picky some months earlier, making it close enough to 'pikey' that villagers had sniggered guiltily until it was rapidly fixed.

'All right?' asked Jill. The owner showed the economy of language that marked out true villagers from incomers. Why use twenty words when one sufficed?

'Have you seen Beth? She's been missing since last night.' Saying the words again ripped something in my soul.

Jill's mouth set. Her squat body reflected the flat fens; she was a woman of horizontal lines: frown, mouth, folded arms.

'I'll spread the word. Get the lads out looking.'

Relief spread through me. Jill knew everything that happened in Fenmere. Her network of informants would put MI5 to shame. A woman in her sixties, she ruled her family with a rod of iron, and still called her four forty-something sons 'the lads', despite some of them having families of their own.

If anyone could discover what had happened to you, it was Jill Young.

'Thank you. You've got my number?'

When she nodded, I pushed off again. Chest hurting, throat burning. I was not a gym bunny, and my legs were resisting my urge to run. Gathering what little breath was left, I stood in the middle of the village and screamed your name.

Curtains twitched. People appeared in doorways, then gravitated towards me. Everyone talking, but with nothing useful to say.

'You called the police?' It was Martin Young, one of Jill's lads. A farmer as no-nonsense as his mother, but with his late father's dark hair, dark eyes and swarthy skin. Chunky, capable and balding beneath the woollen hat he wore almost permanently.

I shook my head, unable to speak.

'Get home.' His head jerked back the way I'd come. 'We'll look, you sort that.'

It made sense. But I stood still, head turning this way and that. Torn.

'Go on, Melanie. We'll find her.' Martin's voice softened but remained insistent.

He was right, I had to go home. You would be there, I was suddenly sure. I would tear a strip off you for scaring me, for making me look stupid in front of the whole village, for panicking over nothing.

Your father's car pulled into the drive as I crossed the hundred yards or so from store to house. He jumped out, looking at me expectantly. Chin down, eyes serious.

'Any sign?' he called.

An impatient shake of my head as I strode past him and pushed the front door open, hoping, hoping. 'Beth? Beth! Are you here?'

The only reply was the scrabble of claws racing across hardwood floors. Wiggins appeared, wagging his tail. He reared on his back legs, placing his front paws on my thighs. I pushed him down impatiently, calling for you again, my daughter.

'Melanie…' Jacob trailed off. His face reflected my fear.

Standing in the hallway at the bottom of the stairs, all the pounding adrenaline, the fluttering panic for you solidified into something new. Something worse.

'Someone's taken her, Jacob.'

Wiggins jumped up again. I pushed him down. He jumped up and your dad grabbed his collar.

'Who? Come on, we just need to call some friends—'

'I called everyone. I phoned all her friends. She's disappeared.'

'What about our parents?'

Damn, I should have thought of that myself. Perhaps you'd got it into your head to catch the bus to see one or other set of grandparents. It would be the first time you'd ever done it, but you were, after all, at that age where you were starting to want to push the boundaries. No longer a child, not yet a young adult.

We both made the calls round family, me on my mobile, your dad on his. Brief conversations that lanced the hope that had risen in us. We both signed off with the same thing: 'Call us on the landline if you hear anything.'

Jacob looked at me, his usually clear blue eyes looking dangerously pink.

'I think it's time to call the police,' he said, voice thick.

I nodded. Hung onto his arm, toddler-like, as he dialled 999.

'Shit. Okay, umm, I want to report a missing person. My, my daughter appears to be missing,' he said, reluctant to say the words that would make this nightmare a reality.

A faint reply could be heard from the other end of the line. Jacob spoke again. 'I was at work when my wife called and told me. I told her not to be hysterical.' He gave an embarrassed laugh – you know how he always does when under real pressure. I squeezed his bicep, let him know we were in this together.

More questions and answers. Listening to the one-sided conversation was frustrating.

'What's going on? Why don't they send someone?' I stage-whispered.

Jacob frowned, shaking his head at me, and started giving a physical description of you.

'For goodness' sake,' I hissed.

'Just get off the phone and send someone!' Jacob sounded agitated now, so unlike his usual calm self. If he was worried, that made me all the more worried. Extricating his arm from my grip, he ran a hand over the blond stubble of his closely cropped head. Frowned again. 'What, outside now?'

My head shot up. I ran to the front door, flung it open expecting to see you, Beth. A squad car was pulling up. Jacob stood beside me, phone still in his hand, hanging loosely at his side. A faint voice came from it. I took it from him and hung up.

Uniformed officers stepped from their car and started up the garden path. But with every footfall, the strength that had carried me this far seemed to erode.

This was actually happening. To me. To my beautiful daughter. To my perfect, happy family.

The world began to narrow into a dark tunnel. My knees gave way, as if someone had kicked me at the back of the joint. A shout from the police and they rushed forward, hands reaching as I fainted.

CHAPTER 3

They were guarding me, I realised. Jacob beside me on the sofa, his fingers woven with mine, studying me intently. With no fat on his face the muscles and bone structure showed clearly, and the clenching and unclenching of his jaw could be seen by all. Wiggins was on the other side of me; ears back, tail tucked firmly down, body pressed up tight against mine. Man and dog equally worried since I had fainted.

Two police officers sat in front of me now, their uniforms making them strangely anonymous, drawing my eyes away from their faces. Five minutes after meeting them, their names were forgotten. Nothing mattered, except them finding you.

'We'd like to take some details from you, if you feel up to it,' one officer said.

'Of course.' I nodded forcefully to show I was up to the task.

'How old is your daughter?'

'Beth's thirteen,' Jacob replied. 'She went to stay with a friend last night, but didn't arrive. We only discovered this morning. Someone must have taken her.'

'Could she have stayed with another friend?'

'No. No, she'd have told us. We've called round friends and our family. No one has seen her.'

'Why do you think she was abducted?'

'I have no idea. When we woke up this morning everything was normal, then my wife realised she wasn't at Chloe Clarke's. I... we looked everywhere. Beth wouldn't just go off on her own, she'd tell us… She tells us everything, we're very close. Something must have happened.'

'Okay, how tall is she?'

'Umm, she's, what, about an inch shorter than you, Mel?'

'About that. About five two.'

One officer asked all the questions; the other scribbled notes. 'Right, so she's about five feet two inches. And is this the most recent photo of her that you have?'

I leaned forward, instantly the proud parent despite the circumstances. 'Yes, this was taken at Christmas. It shows her eyes, they're a beautiful colour – grey with a hint of green to them, like the sea. She gets her hair from both of us.' My gesture took in Jacob and myself. 'But it's much paler. Like spun gold, with just a touch of strawberry blonde.'

I could almost see you rolling your eyes at my description, Beth, furious with embarrassment. The officer seemed to agree, repeating only: 'Green eyes. Long blonde hair.' You wanted to have your long hair cut, but so far I had resisted your entreaties. I wanted to keep my little girl for a bit longer.

The constable took the photo back from me. 'Okay. You say she's about five feet two inches tall. Do you know how much she weighs?'

Jacob and I exchanged a helpless glance. 'Uh, probably, I believe she was… I don't know. I'm not sure. She's slim. Very slender,' he offered.

'She's only about seven stone,' I guessed.

'Right. Do you remember what she was wearing last night when you last saw her?'

'Uh, before she went out I believe she was wearing blue jeans and a red jumper?' Jacob's voice went up at the end of the sentence, unsure.

'Yes, a red jumper with Minnie Mouse on the front.'

'You believe?' The policeman had picked up Jacob's uncertainty too.

'No, we're sure,' I confirmed. 'She had her winter jacket on, too – it's black, padded and has a reflective strip in the shape of a chevron front and back. It's quite distinctive.'

Scribble, scribble, scribble, it all went down in the notebook. 'Are there any friends you might not know about? Has she ever run away before?'

'No, Beth's a good girl.' We talked over each other, saying the same thing. Jacob nodded at me, giving me the go-ahead.

'She tells us everything. She's a joker sometimes, but she's also caring, sensitive, sensible; she would never let us worry like this.'

Then we both explained the last time we had seen you. My voice caught as I told how Jacob had been watching football, so I'd walked you part of the way to your best friend's house. In the morning, I'd only called Chloe's house because I had wanted to go food-shopping and had wondered if you'd want to come, or stay a bit longer with Chloe. I'd spoken to Chloe's mum, Ursula.

'When it became clear Beth had never arrived…' My whole body convulsed as the tears came again. Jacob clutched my hand, staring at me so fiercely, as if trying to absorb my pain. After a minute, I managed to get myself together again. 'When it became clear she'd never arrived, I called Jacob. And then we called you.'

'This is just a routine question,' the officer apologised, 'but where were you both last night?'

'Here. Together. All night,' said Jacob.

I opened my mouth, but the constable's next question blew all thoughts away.

'Can you think of anyone who would want to hurt your daughter?'

'Good grief, no! No way!'

'Okay. Could we have a list of your daughter's friends?'

We compiled the list, then another of our friends, family members, pretty much everyone we came into contact with. We had already got in touch with them all, but the police insisted they needed it anyway.

'What about hobbies? I'm just trying to get a clearer picture of what Beth is like.'

'Nature. She's nature-mad.' The officer waited, clearly wanting more. 'You know, watching wildlife, all that kind of thing. She loves going to the woods to look for signs of badgers and foxes, or to the marsh to watch birds. She wants to work in conservation when she grows up.'

I couldn't hide the pride in my voice.

'Could she have gone out into the countryside to do some nature-watching? Or to play alone?'

'No.' I shook my head, certain.

'I think we have everything we need for now. Thank you.' The officers stood in unison at some unspoken sign.

We were left alone, uncertain of what to do next.

Not for long, though. A knock on the door came. Then another and another. The house soon filled. Family, friends, villagers, all coming together to help the search for you, our missing girl. In a small community such as Fenmere we all know each other, and are always there for one another in times of trouble. It heartened me; surely it wouldn't be long until you were found.

A Family Liaison Officer was assigned by the police, too, making sympathetic noises and trying to explain what was happening. She introduced herself as Britney Cooper. She seemed nice enough, but I couldn't take her seriously. Not with a name like Britney. And she was so young! Only in her early twenties, with round eyes that seemed to match her round face. Her ginger bob accentuated her childlike features too. I wanted someone with gravitas. Someone I knew had the skill and experience to find you. Not a child.

With every second that passed you seemed to slip further and further from me. I couldn't take in a word anyone said to me. They were the whirlwind; I was the still centre, sitting on the sofa, crying.

My own mum, your Granny Heather, enveloped me in a trembling hug that did nothing to soothe me. I didn't want my mother's tears, and didn't want to use valuable strength fighting irritation. After longing for the police questioning to be over, now I felt redundant. I stared at the thick woollen rug, my eyes following the twisting strands; the previously homely and warming deep orange colour looked like a warning sign. The air felt too thick to breathe properly, and our home was too hot, with the radiators on full and so many people crammed inside. A pressure built inside me. Any minute I might explode.

Boom.

It propelled me from my seat and my mum's arms, across the room full of people huddled together, having conversations in low voices, and into the kitchen.

Now what?

At a loss, I put the kettle on. I didn't want a drink, but other people might and it gave me something to occupy myself. Mum bustled in behind me, clearly loath to leave me alone.

'Want a hand?' Her face was so soft with concern that it hurt me to look at it.

'Could you ask who wants what, please? Tea, coffee, whatever.' The excuse to get rid of her came in a flash.

Alone at last. I leaned against the counter and sighed. The corkboard in the kitchen was opposite me, full of important appointment cards, invites to birthday parties for you, bills to pay for me and your dad, silly notes to one another, drawings and photographs. It was a huge thing, yet still crammed, and each pin held so many bits of paper that the points were not driven in far, everything precarious. Peeling back the layers would have been an archaeologist's journey back in time.

The reminder to pay for your guitar lessons was most prominent. You had only started them a couple of months before, as an early Christmas present, and were just coming down from your initial enthusiasm. Your dad and I weren't sure if you would do them for much longer. When we asked about them, you just shrugged.

A note from your dad to us stood out too. Do you remember it? It started with him saying he was nipping into town, so not to worry that he wasn't around, and ended with him going on about how much he loved us. You had scrawled *Sloppy devil. Love you loads too!* at the bottom, and approximately a hundred kisses.

Below it was a photo of you and your dad, faces smushed together, pulling silly expressions at the camera. That had been taken on Saturday, exactly a week ago.

'We have a perfect life together. Untroubled, full of laughter. We are not the kind of family this sort of thing happens to: police, drama, worry, this isn't us. We're close, have no secrets,' I said out loud to myself. A mantra against what was happening.

Closing my eyes, my mind's eye burrowed deeper into the detritus of the noticeboard, into the precious memories hidden beneath the surface.

The drawing you had done of a ballerina when you were six. That had gone down in the annals of family history, a source now of much hilarity. The ballerina doing impossible splits; her thighs weirdly lumpy where the green felt-tip pen had wobbled in inexperienced hands; her face, unintentionally, a grimace of shock; her smile more of a round 'o'. Every time we looked at it we all laughed, your own giggles always giving permission to mine and Jacob's. You didn't like to take yourself too seriously.

I bit my lip, though, remembering how proud you had been when you first drew it, jumping down from your seat at the kitchen table and running over to me, holding the picture high like a streamer. I had lifted you up, so tiny, so light in my arms, and given you the biggest hug.

Please God, let you be okay. Please let us find you quickly. I can't cope...

CHAPTER 4

Grief crushed my chest. I needed air. Stumbled to the back door, threw it open and dragged in lungfuls. The late January cold felt like a slap in the face, clearing me of hysteria.

I clutched the door frame, not to keep myself upright but because it was something solid in a world suddenly as unreliable as a mirage shimmering in a desert heat haze. Looking to my left, over the low fence that ran along the side of the drive, I saw movement. Police in high-vis vests strode around the village, breathless, urgent. I shifted to get a clearer view. They trampled down the four lanes our home sat on, through long grasses, going up to their ankles in muddy sections of drainage dykes.

I couldn't tear my eyes away. Not even when a warm arm came around my cold shoulders.

'Come on, duck. Melanie... Sit down. Dad and John have gone to join the search,' said Mum.

John? I hadn't even realised my brother had been at the house, but didn't acknowledge Mum's words. Couldn't engage my brain, too intent on staring at the police, willing them to find something. Dreading in case they did.

Come on, Beth, call home. Breeze through the door with an excuse. Any excuse. I won't be angry.

The officers called out to villagers they came across: 'Have you seen a teenage girl on your travels? Possibly distressed?'

'I'll keep an eye out,' came the repeated reply. 'I'm joining the search now.'

'I should get out there again, look for her,' I decided.

Mum's gentle touch restrained me.

'Why don't you stay here, eh? Don't want Beth coming back to an empty house, do we?' She spoke in that over-bright voice adults use on young children.

'Has Jacob gone with Dad and John?'

'No, love. He wanted to but the police persuaded him to stay here. You know, he's in a bit of a state, like you… Might do more harm than good.'

How the hell was it possible to do more harm than good in this situation? But I'd no strength to argue; it took everything I had to keep myself together. Poor Jacob, being overruled by the police, though. No chance of anything stopping my dad – your Grandpa Mick – or your Uncle John; they were both so stubborn. That was where you got it from, I supposed, though I wasn't like that at all. Too soft for my own good. As for Jacob, he was a gentle man; artistic, kind, sensitive. Stubborn, in his own way, but only on matters such as family coming first, fidelity; the things that count to a good man – the ideologies that someone should be immovable on.

How long had I been standing there? How long had you been missing? A hole had been ripped in my heart, and I couldn't seem to breathe. I wrapped my arms around myself, trying to hold myself together. Turned to speak to my mum, but she had slipped away, perhaps some time ago.

A *thwump, thwump, thwump* that had been so far distant I hadn't noticed it now became impossible to ignore. Squinting in the low winter sun, I found the culprit. A helicopter crawling across the limitless sky like a blue and yellow beetle.

Where are you, Beth? Come home. Please, baby, come home.

A scream ripped through the silence – Mum, making a sound I wouldn't have thought her capable of. I shivered, turning slowly for fear of what I might see. She walked towards me, careful as a bomb disposal expert.

'Your dad called. They've found Beth.'

CHAPTER 5

They had found you, Beth! Thank God!

'It's bad. They don't want anyone down there,' Mum added.

It was bad; okay, I could deal with bad. I disregarded your gran's scream from moments earlier, shoved aside the shock on her ghostly face. I concentrated on the positive – because it was all I could deal with, Beth; there was no other option. You must have changed your mind, started walking home last night after all, perhaps by a different route. Got hit by a car and injured, but you would be fine.

Unless...

Headlines ripped from newspapers flew across my mind.

'Teenage Girl's Rape Horror!'
'Tortured Then Left for Dead!'
'Drugged & Abused in Frenzied Attack!'

Anything could have happened to you. 'It's bad,' Mum had said. You could be barely alive. Every bone broken. Unspeakable things done to you at knifepoint. Your beautiful skin slashed and gouged.

No! No! No!

Just a few hours earlier, everything had been fine. I'd thought you were safe at your best friend's house, and had called Ursula to see if you fancied coming shopping with me in Wapentake.

'Beth? She's not here. She didn't come over last night,' Ursula had said.

I'd almost smiled through my first shot of fear, convinced she'd come back, laughing, at discovering you in Chloe's room. I'd heard her calling up to her daughter, checking with her.

At the sullen 'no' my stomach had plummeted. I'd insisted on speaking with Chloe.

'You didn't see her last night?'

'No, no, she didn't come round last night,' she said.

The terror had been a lump cutting off my oxygen.

'She must have done! Where is she? What's happened?'

Chloe started to reply, but I slammed the phone down, biting back screams of frustration. My hand shook as I dialled your mobile. It went straight to answerphone.

'Sweetheart, call me as soon as you get this message. It's urgent.' I made my voice stern but calm.

Maybe I'd got the wrong friend? Maybe you hadn't said you'd be staying with Chloe. No, that made no sense; you and I had walked virtually up to her front door. Still, I called your other pals, but no one knew anything. Repeat-dialled your mobile, but it never rang out.

Even as my head whirled in panic, I tried to convince myself I was overreacting.

Snatching up my mobile, I'd run from the house. You had disappeared on Holders Lane, on your way to your best friend's house, so that was the obvious place to start looking for you. That's when I'd called your dad. That's when this nightmare had begun.

At least you had been found now. Mum stared at me, eyes wide and wary. 'It's bad,' she had said. I needed to stop imagining and see for myself exactly what had happened. Surely nothing could be as bad as what was going on in my head.

'I… I need to get to the hospital.'

'Just… just wait a little bit.' Mum's restraining hand was once again on my arm.

'I need to see my daughter.'

'Let's have a cup of tea first, let the police sort a couple of things out.'

'No, I need to see her now.' I pulled away from your Granny Heather's grasp as tyres crunched on the drive. My dad's car pulled up. But he didn't get out. I saw him put a hand on my brother's shoulder. John was crying.

Big brothers don't cry. Your Uncle John was a tough fireman, and I hadn't seen him shed a tear since he'd broken his collarbone when he was ten, after showing off jumping from a tree.

So there was only one explanation for his tears. You were dead, Beth. You were exactly two weeks short of your fourteenth birthday.

Another scream ripped through the air. This time, it was mine.

CHAPTER 6

My triumph, the moment I committed murder, was a film in my head I revisited. I knew it so well that it could be fast-forwarded through the dull bits and rewound to watch the interesting bits over and over again.

The sound of the girl's head being hit was like a watermelon smashing open. That wasn't a metaphor, because when the thought first occurred to me I bought a watermelon to compare the sounds. It gave me a rush to hear it, and so I'd done that again and again too.

Of course, the watermelon didn't make the helpless little huff of breath that she had given. Remembering that was one of my favourite parts.

The real highlight had been watching her skin turn from a pink glow to a corned beef mottle to grey then finally blue. That was amazing, and each time I replayed the memory I felt a warm glow of satisfaction.

CHAPTER 7

I felt a touch on my shoulder, but I didn't look up. I stayed curled on the floor of the hallway, Wiggins whining and trying to get to my face to lick away my tears.

You were dead. My daughter was gone.

My chest tightened horribly. I couldn't breathe. Maybe I'd die. That would be good.

Voices surrounded me; Mum, Dad and John hunched over me. Jacob's voice broke through, pulling people away. A strong hand under my chin forced my face up to meet his.

White face. Wide eyes. Pupils like bottomless wells. He was as stricken as me. I stood and threw my arms around him, clinging on, a drowning woman to a life preserver.

Not a word was uttered between us. Just pain screaming silently.

Everyone stood back, watching, hands over mouths. In a separate world to us now. Mum's hands fluttered around us, weak as butterfly wings in a gale.

Jacob cradled my head in one hand, protecting me and holding me safe against him as he turned and looked at someone.

'Mick, what happened?' His voice rumbled through his chest against my ear, distorted, as he questioned my dad.

'There's CID on their way. We should wait for them. The new lead officer, Detective Sergeant Devonport, she'll be able to explain things better,' said a muffled voice. A woman's. Must be that Family Liaison Officer, Britney.

'Mick.' Jacob's urging tickled my ear. I buried my face further into his jumper. Wanting to escape. Desperate to hear.

'We were on the marsh.' My dad spoke, his voice uncharacteristically unsteady. 'We, er, we heard a shout. Saw police running.'

'Yeah, everyone ran,' John confirmed.

My fingers dug further into Jacob's jumper, feeling the taut muscles of his back.

'We ran too. Jill's youngest, Davy, was pointing at something. There…' Dad's voice broke. 'Beth was there. Floating in a mere.'

'No. I don't want to hear.' Jacob pulled me tighter as he protested, trembling against me.

But I raised my head.

'I do.'

Dad looked at me, shocked. Shaking his head. But I didn't agree with Jacob. I needed to know what had happened to my daughter, no matter how hard it was. I had to do it for you, Beth.

He and John looked helpless, but John took a deep breath, carried on speaking. 'Right, so… the, umm, the one officer felt for a pulse. And shook his head.'

Seismic shocks ran through Jacob's body. I held him close, each of us stopping the other from falling apart. There was something that had to be asked…

'What did she look like, Dad? What had happened to her?'

'I didn't see too close, duck. I don't know. Pale. She looked very pale. I didn't really see anything else.'

'What was she doing on the marsh?'

My question went unanswered, along with a million others. Perhaps you had gone there in the dark to do some bird-spotting. Slipped and hurt yourself. Had hypothermia killed you? Or had you hit your head when you fell? Why the hell were you there in the first place?

Jacob and I were too stunned to cry. Wiggins pressed against us, trembling, because he knew something was terribly wrong, the way animals always do.

'Love, love, let's get you onto the sofa,' sniffed Mum, her own face wet with tears.

I nodded. Because what else could I do? I let myself be urged gently along, supported, to the living room. Murmured talk. A hot drink pressed into my hand, which was held only because I couldn't think of anything else to do with it. More staring at the carpet.

I wouldn't get to hold my daughter again. You loved your cuddles. As a youngster you'd asked for them so often that I'd even had to stop in the middle of washing up, suds dripping on the floor as we'd hugged. Do you remember, Beth? You hadn't changed a bit; even as a teenager you were always asking for a hug.

Another knock at the door. I didn't move. More voices; this time urgent.

'Mr and Mrs Oak.' A woman with a low, calm voice but with such authority that my head rose in spite of itself.

'Mr and Mrs Oak,' she repeated, to be certain she had our attention. 'My name is Detective Sergeant Ellen Devonport. I have an urgent update about your daughter.'

'We know.' Call herself a detective? I shrugged helplessly at the scene in front of her.

'I believe you're aware that Beth has been found on a section of marsh a couple of miles from the village boundary. An officer couldn't find a pulse—'

'We know.' Jacob spoke to the floor, head in his hands. Voice dead.

'What you don't know is that a paramedic *did* detect a faint pulse.'

What! Invisible strings jerked everyone to their feet. We all stared at the CID officer.

'She's alive? Beth's alive?' I demanded.

Jacob's nervous laugh sounded.

DS Devonport gave a cautious hint of a smile. 'She's being taken right now by air ambulance to St James's Hospital in Leeds.'

'But she's all right? She's alive?' I had been drowning and now rushed up to the surface, dizzy, gasping, euphoric. 'Can we see her?'

'We can drive you to Leeds now, if you'd like.'

Jacob and I clung onto each other, grinning.

'You must understand: Beth is very poorly,' DS Devonport added.

But we barely heard, too busy celebrating. Your Grandpa Mick gave a whoop of relief, and clapped Uncle John on the back. Granny Heather looked as if she couldn't decide between dancing and fainting.

You were back from the dead, Beth. Our miracle girl.

CHAPTER 8

Alien bleeping sounds, a spaghetti of wires, odd machinery and crisp white sheets: I had entered a different world. And in the middle of it all lay you, my love. You were as pale as the bedding, a breathing tube crammed down your throat and a device forcing air into your lungs and out again.

'So that's breathing for her?' I checked.

The machine hissed, and your chest rose. A bitter taste of bile hit the back of my throat.

'That's right. Beth is in an induced coma to help her heal,' said the consultant. It was the third time he'd explained that bit. This was all so hard to take in, I'd asked for a bit of paper and a pen to make notes. A string of incomprehensible words had been jotted down.

The Family Liaison Officer, Britney, had driven us to St James's Hospital, Leeds. The two-and-a-half-hour journey had been a blur of elation that you were alive, Beth. You probably don't know, but that's a really famous hospital. People call it Jimmy's because they love it so much – it even had a television programme devoted to it years ago. You're too young to remember that, of course. But it's a centre of excellence in the treatment of head injuries, so your dad and I had been pleased knowing you were in such capable hands.

Until we'd seen you. Hope had rapidly been replaced with fear again. Beth, you looked like something from a horror film.

A moan escaped through the fingers covering my mouth. I clamped them down harder as I made myself look at you.

Your beautiful long blonde hair had been completely shaved off on the right side, and a tube came out of your skull. The sight of it made me feel faint. Your temple and eye were swollen and blackened, distorting your delicate features so that you didn't look like you.

Always as slender as a fairy, now you looked insubstantial in the hospital bed. Someone could whisk you away with the bedding, screw you up and toss you to one side without noticing.

This was not my daughter.

You were always rushing about. Hiding round corners and jumping out: 'Boo!' Laughing like a loony at the look on your dad's or my face. You even did it to the dog, who would look at you full of reproach, then leap forward and pin you down for a thorough licking, so the pair of you formed a tumbling, giggling, barking mass of fun.

You would talk in a breathless stream about nature, about working in conservation one day and saving the world. You had an opinion on everything. Like me, you read voraciously – the only time you were quiet was when you had your head stuck in a book. You sang, played guitar. Thundered down the stairs making more noise than was surely possible for one tiny teenager.

Now you just lay there. Dead but not dead. In limbo. I could not equate the empty shell with the lively daughter. Your soul seemed to have fled.

I peered at you, trying to see a spark of life. Something that looked like an inflatable Li-lo covered your body for some strange reason. Then I remembered, I'd been told about it. Something about it keeping you cold to aid healing.

I shuffled even closer, taking in the terrible dark circles beneath your eyes. No, it was smudged make-up. Odd. You never wore cosmetics, and certainly hadn't had any on when you left the house.

The thought was snatched away by the other doctor speaking, the one who wasn't a consultant but a neurosurgeon. Yes, you had a team looking after you, Beth.

'For now, the most important thing to understand is that we have stopped the bleed on your daughter's brain. That's good news,' she said. The blue of the scrubs set off her eyes, which confidently met first mine, then Jacob's. We moved our heads like nodding dogs.

'Right now, it's too soon to say how profound Beth's injuries are. We won't have any idea until she wakes up – if she wakes up.'

'If?' Jacob's voice sounded scratchy and thick.

'The injury to her brain is significant. The blow was to her temple, and caused an epidural haematoma – a bleed to the brain. Although we have stopped it, you need to be prepared for the worst. Beth may not wake up, and if she does, her injuries may be profound.'

'Wait.' I flapped my hands as if to shoo away what she had said. 'You mean Beth might die?'

'I'm going to do everything in my power to stop that happening. But yes.'

'I'm going to be sick.'

The doctor grabbed a kidney-shaped cardboard bowl and pushed it under my mouth as my stomach heaved. Just in time.

'Nurse,' she called.

One had already appeared with a larger bowl. I heaved again, my whole body rejecting what was happening to my daughter.

CHAPTER 9

As she walked down the lane that crisp Friday night, Beth had a spring in her step, only slightly burdened with guilt. She had fooled her mum, and the plan was working a treat. But if her parents ever found out the truth they would totally freak out.

Lying wasn't something the teenager was good at, but lately she seemed to be getting a lot of practice. So many secrets weighed down on her; and not only her own. She needed this night to let her hair down and have some fun.

Beth checked over her shoulder. Her mum wasn't watching her progress towards Chloe's house; in fact, she had disappeared. Good.

No one saw Beth change direction and slip away to her real destination.

CHAPTER 10

Jacob and I sat side by side, holding each other's hand and yours too. The machines were a constant percussion.

'Come on, love,' I whispered. 'You can do this. Come back to us.'

Those hours were the worst of my life. I held your hand, willing my strength into you. Wishing I could swap places. Jacob sat beside me, doing the exact same; silently, fearfully, fervently.

Each second that ticked by was an achievement. *She's held on for this long. She's made it this far. That has to be a good sign.*

The conviction that you would wake any second kept us beside your bed well past the point of our own exhaustion. I stood, stretched, my back giving a twinge, then walked around a bit and yawned. A nurse bustled in, chubby hands checking the read-outs from the bits of machinery. Quick eyes running over me, then Jacob.

'There are private family rooms on the other side of the hospital. You should go there, get some sleep,' she said. Brisk, efficient, well-meaning.

'Yes, your colleagues have mentioned it.' *About a thousand times*, I silently added. 'But I have to be here when she wakes, no matter when that is.'

You would be scared, confused, and you'd want your parents there to hold you and tell you everything would be all right. And then you could tell us who had done this to you. Because the more I thought about it, the more I realised it had to be someone local

– strangers stood out a mile in our little village, where everyone knew everyone else so well they could quote their lineage or even their favourite breakfast cereal. Besides, you've had stranger danger drummed into you since you were so high, and are far too sensible to disregard it – aren't you? Which meant someone we knew had done this.

They must have lured you into their car on a pretext, then whisked you to the marsh and hurt you. It couldn't have been for money, so… My stomach lurched. Sex?

Your fingers were digging into my palm; I uncurled my hand from the fist I'd unconsciously made, afraid I'd inadvertently hurt you. But the anger remained balled inside me as I tried to make a list of people you would trust to get into a car with. It consisted of pretty much the entire village.

A strangled sob came from beside me. Jacob wiped furiously at his face, but couldn't hide the tears.

'I didn't say goodbye to her properly last night,' he croaked. 'Too busy watching football, I barely even looked at her. She must have thought I didn't care.'

'She knows how much you love her,' I soothed.

But despite the calm of my voice, I couldn't tamp down my growing anger. Whoever had hurt our daughter, they were going to pay.

CHAPTER 11

I swayed on my feet as I walked from the car to the front door, beyond exhausted after the last seventy-two hours or so. Dad and I hadn't left your side since you had been found on Saturday, not even to return home to get a change of clothes. We didn't dare, willing you to cling on – and by a miracle you had.

Now it was Tuesday afternoon, and my mum and dad were sitting with you, having previously been dog-sitting for us. Wiggins would be having a great time running round the big garden of their house on the far edge of Fenmere, so at least I didn't need to worry about him. Between them all – John and Dad's parents, your Grandpa Isaac and Granny Julia, and Grandpa Mick and Granny Heather – they were sorting out a rota to cover for the times your dad and I couldn't be at the hospital. Your Aunt Tricia was in bits, so she couldn't help, but with her living in America it wasn't really an option.

No matter when you woke, the first thing you would see would be a person you loved.

The Family Liaison Officer had brought us back from hospital. Unable to remember her name, which Jacob kept reminding me was Britney, in my head I referred to her as Flo, because it was the initials of her job title. She had been great over the last three days, barely leaving our side, giving us updates on how the police were sweeping the area for clues and interviewing villagers. It all sounded really positive, and freed your dad and me to concentrate on you. Flo had even offered to come into the house when she dropped us off, and make us some food. We refused. We wanted to be alone for a while, at home. Get our heads together, then gather bits and bobs for you, Beth, to make the hospital room more 'you'.

Our family home had a stale, disused air to it after being empty for three days.

'Cup of tea?' Jacob called as he strode into the kitchen. I shook my head, trailing after him.

'Knackered.' I threw a piece of paper onto the kitchen table to look at later. Jacob glanced at it. 'It's a list of some of the phrases chucked at us earlier. Thought I'd look them up.'

'They've told us,' he said over the sound of the running tap as he filled the kettle.

'You know me.'

'Always have to find stuff out yourself, yep.'

Typical journalist, always making notes and sniffing out information. Well, would-be journalist. Once upon a time I'd wanted to become one, but had given up my place at university after falling pregnant. Still, I'd never lost that basic instinct to find things out.

Now my head spun with medical information overload.

Epidural haematoma. Traumatic brain injury. Pressure in the intracranial space. Hypertension. Bradycardia. Irregular respiration. Suddenly these words were my world; it was too important not to find out more about them.

I hugged myself to keep the shivering at bay. Every muscle aching from being constantly tense; even my jaw hurt. Being in the house wouldn't help me relax, though. It felt strange and empty without you and Wiggins. No singing, shouting, barking, no herd of elephants running down the stairs. No laughter. Just Jacob and me, rattling around.

It wasn't simply the atmosphere; the missing pieces of our family had a physical impact too. Every noise the two of us made sounded different. Louder. More echoing. Lonely.

Someone had torn our world apart. Who would hurt you, Beth? Why?

Once again, my instinct told me it was someone we knew. Statistically, the most likely suspects were our own family, but my brain rebelled at the thought of my brother or husband as the attacker.

'Can we go to bed?' I asked suddenly. 'I need a hug and some sleep.'

Tea abandoned, minutes later we were curled up together, even though it was only just gone three thirty. Beneath the covers, the smell of Jacob's bare chest comforted me; the sweet odour of wood resin permeated his skin from hours working at the local handmade furniture factory. Something reliable in a world gone mad, its odour carried me into a dreamless sleep and fleeting respite.

Something dragged me from sleep. My eyelids felt heavy as they lifted with some effort.

A knock at the door. Gentle, apologetic, but enough to disturb my slumber. I felt groggy.

I slipped from Jacob's side just as he groaned and turned over, his face crinkled from the pillow. As I pulled on my jeans, he sat upright.

'What is it? Has something happened?'

'Someone's at the door,' I called, hurrying from the room and down the stairs.

He was right behind me, top half-naked.

We almost fell out of the front door in our haste. Was it the police, with news of an arrest? Someone sent round to give us terrible news from the hospital?

Your best friend's mum, Ursula Clarke, stood on the step. She held up a casserole dish. The first of no doubt many visitors we would get now we were finally home. Kind, but my heart sank,

Beth – I didn't want to see anyone or answer any questions. I didn't have the strength.

'Oh! I was about to leave this for you. Sorry, I didn't want to disturb you... I've been so worried. When I heard what had happened... well, I feel so helpless, and wanted you to know that we're all thinking of you. If there's anything I can do to help...'

She looked as perfectly made-up as ever. Not a curl of her peroxide-blonde hair out of place. Perish the thought that the village bombshell should let herself go, even in a time of crisis. But despite the way she looked, the barrage of words illustrated Ursula's nerves at what state she'd find us in, bless her.

She held the casserole out to me again.

'That was kind of you,' I said, touched.

I took the heavy dish, even though the thought of food made me feel sick, and passed it straight to Jacob. How long had it been since I'd eaten a solid meal? Mum and Dad had bought us sandwiches at the hospital, but I'd only had a little nibble before putting it down, fearing I'd vomit again. I'd managed a banana not long before leaving the hospital. Was that all? I should have been ravenous.

'How, umm, how is Beth?' Ursula asked, head on one side. She used the sort of hushed tone more usually associated with people talking of the recently deceased.

'She's... Ursula, would you like to come in?'

'Well, I'd better get back to Chloe. She's upset by what's happened, understandably.'

'Of course, of course. I just wondered if Chloe had any idea why Beth was on the marsh in the middle of the night.'

'I've asked, believe me. But she doesn't have a clue.'

Of course she didn't have a clue. Your best friend wasn't exactly blessed in the brains department, was she, Beth? I know you two had been inseparable since nursery school, but she didn't understand half of what you said these days. Her idea of a deep conversation was discussing what the Kardashians had been up to. Why did it have to be you lying in that hospital bed, fighting for your life, when you had so much potential compared to her?

Are you shocked that I could think that way, Beth? I was. Fear and exhaustion were making me feel out of character. As soon as your attacker was arrested, and you had come round, I'd be back to my old self. We all would.

Suddenly, a thought occurred…

CHAPTER 12

I frowned. It didn't take a psychic to work out my thoughts, and Ursula soon twigged. 'Melanie, I believe her. She's not hiding anything – she knows how serious this is.'

'Of course, sorry. But you know what best friends are like at that age. They share everything. I just… I just hoped.'

'We're desperate for answers,' interjected Jacob.

'Of course you are. I'd be exactly the same.'

Ursula reached out and hugged me. Taken by surprise, I hugged her back.

We'd grown up together, living in the same village, but as kids the fact that she'd been four years older than me had put her in a different sphere. As we'd got older things had changed, of course. We'd made mutual friends, and then when our daughters had become best friends at nursery we'd got to know each other much better. But she and I had never been close. Ursula was the kind of person who wore her heart on her sleeve, but could be a little superficial. She always had to look perfect, get perfect marks in school, have the perfect wedding, buy perfect furniture. Now she was thirty-seven, it was easy to imagine her becoming one of those women who tried to cling to their youth by having Botox and dressing identically to her daughter.

You know me, Beth, I couldn't give a toss about my looks or what people think. I'd always been comfortable in my own skin, doing my own thing. People thought I was mad for giving up a place at university after falling pregnant with you, and that I was too young to raise a family. There had been plenty of gossiping and judging going on about me. So what? The timing may not have been ideal, but you were a gift that I'd never, even for a moment, regretted.

When Ursula and I pulled apart she gave me a watery smile. 'So, how *is* Beth doing?'

'As well as can be expected. It's all too soon to tell,' replied Jacob.

'She's in a coma. An induced coma. The doctors have told us to prepare for the worst… but she's clung on, so we're hopeful.'

'They don't know what type of injuries she'll have when she wakes, though.'

'It's bad. Pretty much as bad as it can get.'

Ursula's head moved back and forth between us as Jacob and I played fact tennis about your prognosis. Her face paled as she heard the news, and she grabbed my hand.

'I'm so sorry. I mean it – if there is anything I can do, please let me know. And, could I ask a huge favour from you? Could you let me know if there's any change in Beth? Anything at all? Chloe is going out of her mind.'

'Of course,' I promised. 'And if she does think of something, anything at all, that might help the police figure who did this, or why, or—'

'I'll let you know. It goes without saying.'

We said our goodbyes, tears in our eyes. It meant a lot that everyone in the village had rallied round us.

Jacob lifted the casserole dish and sniffed it.

'Smells good. Steak stew. Do you want some?'

'Umm, maybe a little bit.'

As he walked through the lounge and into the kitchen with it, I walked after him. 'But only a tiny bit, Jacob.'

Even then, he gave me more than I wanted. I'd known he would, of course, hoping that my appetite would kick in once I started eating.

'We've got to keep our strength up for Beth. She'll be coming round soon, and I don't want her worrying about us,' he reminded me.

True. You were a sensitive girl, Beth. Always worrying about others, and taking in injured birds and wild animals, trying to fix them. When one died – as they so often did – you were always heartbroken. The thought of you fretting about me instead of concentrating on getting yourself better made me force down a mouthful. But the food seemed to stick in my throat, then sit heavy in my stomach. Ursula was a great cook – after all, she ran the village café and did the catering in the pavilion for the cricket matches every summer. But my stomach was churning too much for anything to seem appetising.

Lack of sleep was making me feel sick too. We'd only snatched an hour before Ursula had woken us. I wasn't sure how much longer I could keep going. My eyes felt gritty. They started to droop as Jacob launched into his second bowl of casserole, mopping up the gravy with a slice of bread.

Another knock at the door.

For a second we stared at each other. Then jumped up and ran to the door, Jacob still clutching the dripping bread.

It was Jill Young, armed with what looked like a huge lasagne. Her frizzy, steel-grey hair was pulled into a high ponytail, as usual, and bobbed up and down as she nodded her greeting. It always seemed strangely girlish compared to her flat shoes and sensible clothes.

But Jill's hair wasn't what caught my attention at that moment; it was who was behind her. A car was pulling up, and inside was DS Ellen Devonport.

CHAPTER 13

This was my first chance to look properly at the detective sergeant. Last time had been too much of a rush. There had been so much to take in, having gone from thinking you were dead to discovering you were alive.

Now Ellen Devonport sat in an armchair in front of me and I had the time to study her, as she studied me. The glossy curtain of dark brown hair pulled back into a low ponytail. A thick, blunt fringe cut across her eyebrows. No sign of grey, but the start of fine lines around her eyes and mouth showed her to be in her early thirties, like me.

Her face seemed familiar, but that was the thing about living in this area: everyone knew everyone, even if only by sight.

In the armchair opposite her sat a younger man who seemed to take in every detail with his intense eyes, but he barely spoke a word. This, Jacob and I had been informed, was Detective Constable Alan Musgrove, whose shirt was slightly crumpled, as if he had grabbed the first one to come to hand that morning. It looked all the more noticeable because his colleague was so crisp.

Flo hovered in the background. Her chubby little face looked a bit intimidated by the detective sergeant. She hurried into the kitchen to make us all a brew, robbing me of my job. Jacob helped her carry the steaming mugs.

DS Devonport gave a smile, just a little too tight to be genuine. Smoothed the tweed material of her trousers before placing her folded hands there. Leaned forward at an angle that seemed to have been carefully calculated to look sympathetic. Her perfection in the face of the chaos since your attack seemed so at odds that it rankled with me. But no matter what my personal feelings were, she was our best bet for discovering what had happened to you.

'I want you to be assured that we are treating this case seriously.' She had one of those low, husky voices that men find sexy. It didn't quite seem appropriate for this situation. 'Beth suffered a serious assault, and we are doing our utmost to find the perpetrator. We've put together an appeal for information which we've released to the press, so be prepared if you do watch television.'

Great; it made me feel better knowing we were going to be getting maximum publicity. It meant that what had happened to you would be looked into properly. Hopefully someone would come forward with information, and the culprit would be caught quickly.

'I would like to get a little more detail from you, though, and double-check a few things.'

Jacob and I held hands and agreed in unison.

'What time did you last see Beth?'

Good grief. 'Don't you already have all this?'

'We do, yes, but as I said, I'd like to go over it again, if I may.'

I bit my tongue. The police knew what they were doing, and arguing with them would slow things up. 'I'm sorry. Whatever it takes to find out who did this to Beth, I'll do it. Even if it means saying the same thing a million times over.'

A gentler, more genuine smile came from DS Devonport this time.

We went over everything again. It was exhausting, and seemed a nonsense, but what did I know about detective work?

'After she left, you both stayed home?'

'That's correct,' Jacob confirmed.

'And what clothes was Beth wearing?'

'Blue skinny jeans, a red Mini Mouse jumper, flat black ankle boots and her black winter coat,' I replied dutifully.

'Do you recognise these?'

The silent DC Musgrove passed me a series of photographs of clothing. A filthy white crop top with three-quarter-length sleeves. A black miniskirt. Thick black tights. I turned the photographs this way and that, as if changing the perspective would make clear the reason we were being shown these things. Passed them on to Jacob, who took them, a curious look on his face. We both shrugged. You had clothes like that, but so did lots of girls.

A final set of photographs was handed over. From varying angles they showed a pair of black suede ankle boots with a thick platform sole, high heel and silver metal down the back, like a seam. I gasped.

'Let me check something.' I pushed away from the sofa and walked upstairs, quick, full of purpose.

Into your bedroom. Refused to be distracted by the sight of a glass you had left on the side, a thin film of milk misting its insides, which made it look as though you were coming straight back from wherever you had nipped to. I marched right past it and flung open the wardrobe. Dug around in the bottom. There was the shoebox.

When I opened it, it was empty.

I ran downstairs.

'Those are Beth's. But she definitely wasn't wearing them when she left the house.'

You'd begged for those ridiculously expensive and totally impractical boots. I hadn't approved of the huge heel, which added a good six inches to your height. How you were supposed to walk in them was beyond me, and besides, I'd thought them too grown-up for you. But you'd been determined – and whether I liked it or not, my little girl was no longer so very little. As it was Christmas, I had given in. Despite my misgivings, the look on your face when you had opened that present had been worth every penny.

'She hasn't worn them yet. So where were they?'

'Mr and Mrs Oak, the boots and the outfit photographed are what Beth was wearing when she was found. There is no trace of the clothing you described to us.'

'I don't understand,' Jacob said. Exchanged a look with me, as if I could explain. We were as confused as each other.

'We also spoke with Chloe Clarke and her mother. Both say that your daughter hadn't planned to stay at their home that night.'

'No, Beth told me. I walked her virtually up to the door,' I whispered. You wouldn't lie, so... 'They're lying. When I spoke to them, they didn't say that.'

I ran the conversation over in my head. It was confused, garbled; panic seemed to have erased most of it. But when I'd phoned I'd been calm at first, just thinking you were running late.

'Any sign of them stirring from their beds? What time will Beth be home?' I'd asked, all breezy.

'Beth? She's not here. She didn't come round last night,' Ursula had said. She'd called up to Chloe, spoken with her to check, then I had insisted on speaking with her.

'You didn't see her last night?'

'No, no she didn't come round last night,' Chloe had said.

At no point had either of them made it clear that they hadn't expected you to be there with Chloe, Beth. I had assumed, in my panic, that they'd known you were coming. Assumed, not asked. That explained why they hadn't called to alert me or Dad that you hadn't arrived. Even when speaking with Ursula just now I hadn't thought to check.

'Beth lied to me,' I croaked.

Admitting it hurt like hell. I couldn't get my head round it. Your betrayal gripped me – then anger with myself for wanting to tell you off when you were fighting for your life. A sob escaped. I hid my face in my hands, trying to rub away the confusion of emotions.

'Mrs Oak, did Beth have a boyfriend she might have been meeting?'

I shook my head, unable to tear my hands away. Too ashamed. Why had you lied to me? Surely you knew you could tell me anything. But these clothes, the smudged make-up… they hinted at a whole other life, hidden from me.

Then again, it was natural for teens to have some secrets from their parents. I'd kept some from my own mum. Nothing very exciting in the grand scheme of things, but enough to have shocked her or got a lecture if she'd found out at the time. Perhaps I'd been naive thinking that you and I were different.

I realised I was hugging the photograph of the boots. Those stupid boots you had loved so much.

'Umm, can we have the boots back, please? They were a present,' I explained.

'We need to keep them for now. Evidence. I wonder if we could take a look in your daughter's room while we're here?'

Jacob and I exchanged uneasy glances. 'Umm, why… ?'

'It really would be helpful.'

You wouldn't be happy about a stranger in your room, but what choice did I have, Beth?

CHAPTER 14

It felt utterly wrong to enter your room with two people who didn't know you. You would have been so embarrassed, I know. In the last few months you had got very protective of your personal space – yet another little sign you were growing up.

Clothes decorated the floor as though the wardrobe had recently exploded.

'Sorry for the mess,' I apologised. 'Typical teenager, eh?'

I bent to pick the things up, but DS Devonport stopped me with a gentle hand.

'Don't worry, Mrs Oak. We won't be long.'

She wanted me to leave her and DC Musgrove alone; I could tell by the way she angled her body, inviting me to go through the door. I hovered, uncertain. Torn between my desire to do everything possible to help the police and my urge to protect your privacy, because you weren't here.

I could just imagine your reaction when you found out people had been through your things, Beth. First, you'd go red, colour mottling your cheeks and your neck. Then you would put your hands on your hips and start lecturing about how people should respect your personal space. If you were really annoyed, you might even start talking about your human rights being invaded.

'We could go back to the living room and I'll make a cuppa, eh?' Flo suggested brightly.

I shook my head, stubborn.

Instead of going downstairs, I waited at the threshold, your dad behind me with his hands on my shoulders. Watched as the detectives stood in the middle of the room, simply looking at first. DS Devonport picked up a notebook on your bedside cabinet and flipped through it. Casual and cold. I lurched forward at the violation, but Jacob's hands steadied me. The tremble in them gave away his own feelings on the matter.

Flo brought up two cups of tea. Neither of us wanted them, so she stood awkwardly holding both. No one could take their eyes off the detectives.

The pair of them peered at books, photographs, inside your wardrobe, under the bed… They leafed through papers on your desk and pulled open drawers to glance inside. I bit my lip to stop the cries of protest and stem my guilty tears.

The police were searching your room for a reason, Beth, a good reason. I had to let them.

Finally, they seemed to be satisfied. DC Musgrove picked up your laptop and iPad, but it was his superior who spoke.

'We need to take these away to check the contents.'

'Yes, of course,' I said. Because, despite it being yet another assault on your privacy, it would be worth it if the attacker were discovered. Jacob's fingers massaged my shoulders, trying to comfort me.

At the front door, DS Devonport paused.

'Don't forget, we're going to put an appeal out on the local news. Prepare yourselves to see that, should you put the telly on. It can be upsetting.'

Jacob and I nodded. Numb. Dumb.

'Well, I think we have everything we need for now. Thank you.' She inclined her head again, giving another small, practised smile. 'We'll let ourselves out.'

Then she and her colleagues left, leaving us to the ticking of the grandfather clock in one corner of the living room. It shaved the present into manageable pieces for us as we tried to work out what the hell had happened to us in the last three days.

You had lied, Beth.

You had been secretly meeting with someone.

Someone we knew – because we knew everyone in your life.

A thought occurred to me unexpectedly. I turned to Jacob, frowning.

'Why did you say we were together all night when Beth was attacked?'

CHAPTER 15

The plan itself had worked a dream, but the execution could have been better. The more I watched the attack in my mind's eye, the more silly mistakes revealed themselves.

'Next time,' I found myself thinking. 'Next time will be perfect.'

But it was too soon to undertake another just yet. The risk of discovery would be too great – even stupid people could put two and two together sometimes. No, my time must be bided for a little longer. My alibi would hold, of that I was confident; it was tighter than cling film over a mouth struggling for breath.

Still, there was an itch growing, one that simply must be scratched. I needed to kill. Smashing watermelons, remembering the thrill of snuffing out a life, wasn't doing it for me any more – I needed someone's pain to feed off.

CHAPTER 16

Your dad stood in front of me, his arms open wide in apology. 'It was just… it wasn't supposed to be a big deal. Think what the police would make of it, if they found out.'

'You bloody idiot. It's bound to come out! And when it does, it's going to look a lot worse than if you'd told the truth.'

I hissed the words, furious. Jacob and I never rowed. Ever. We disagreed, discussed, but never usually rowed.

'And I'll tell you something else – I'm not lying for you. Why the hell should I give you an alibi? You're a complete and utter idiot. If I hadn't been in such a state I'd never have gone along with it, but with so much else going on I'd not even thought about it until now.'

With so much on my mind, it was only now that I had remembered Jacob telling the police twice we had stayed in together all night. But we hadn't, Beth.

'Look, take an hour or so to think about it before you make a decision,' he begged. 'It's not worth me getting into trouble over.'

'The truth will come out.'

'Maybe. But it's not relevant, anyway. If people find out about this, though, they'll make judgements, they'll—'

'Jake, if they find out you're lying about something like this, it might make them suspect you of bigger lies. Like hurting your own daughter.'

His head snapped back at the verbal blow. 'You think?'

'Come on, it's always the family people suspect first.'

'Oh! The news – it's time!'

The change of subject gave me mental whiplash. Jacob gestured urgently towards the television.

'It's six thirty; time for the local news! Beth's appeal!'

Of course. Our discussion suspended for the time being only, Jacob put the telly on. We both flopped onto our squishy brown corduroy sofa and I grabbed a cushion to hug. Instead of putting his feet up on the chunky wooden coffee table, like he generally did, Jacob sat forward, eager, elbows resting on knees. Hopefully loads of people would see the news report, and information would come pouring in.

But no. The news was all about a murder that had happened over in Nottingham. It was a terrible thing, but I couldn't help feeling angry. That attack had happened months ago – 27 September, according to reports – and the family had had their share of publicity.

'Police now believe that Tiffany was lured out by her killer in the middle of the night. Her phone was found this week, discarded under bushes near where her body was discovered. Messages described as being of a suspicious nature were on it. If anyone saw anything, they should call the number at the bottom of the screen.'

I knew exactly what I was doing that night, 27 September 2015. Like many people, the three of us had spent much of it gazing up at the super blood moon, two stunning lunar events coinciding so that the moon looked massive and shone red. Remember? You inherited my, and your dad's, amateur interest in stargazing, and we'd all been fascinated by the event.

Even on the night of your attack, remember, Beth, you and I had been looking at the full moon as we walked. My throat caught thinking about how, only four nights ago, you had been so bursting with life as you laughed, then skipped away from me.

We hadn't even hugged, I realised, tears prickling.

You had to get better, Beth. And your attacker had to be caught. Why weren't you important enough to appear on the news? I could imagine all too well this other mother's pain, but this report needed to stop and the one about my own daughter's attack to start.

It was eventually replaced with a story about the Duchess of Cambridge visiting a drugs charity in the area. Then another on immigration and Brexit. Finally, it was time for the weather. I turned the telly off, stunned.

We were now in competition for publicity, and we were losing. Our daughter's attack was less headline-grabbing than a murder, and there were no salacious details to give out. On a slow press day you would have got some coverage: a pretty white teenage girl found seemingly lifeless on a marsh. But not that day. Of course, I knew, in theory, that was how things worked in journalism; after all, I was employed as receptionist at the local weekly newspaper office, the *Wapentake Investigator*. But to be on the receiving end of it was awful. It made me glad that being a receptionist was as far as I'd got to becoming a journalist.

University had been put on hold only temporarily when I'd fallen pregnant with you, Beth, at eighteen. But somehow, despite Jacob insisting he'd support me, and with my parents and his parents vowing to help out, it had never felt the right time to leave my little family – to leave you – to study. I was happy with my life.

The receptionist job had been a handy halfway house, though, making me feel I was still half-living my dream. The editor, Finn, was certain to give your attack good coverage; a thought that lifted my spirits. He was a good bloke, and let me type up the minutes from local council meetings, or the obituary and wedding forms. It was a fun challenge finding a unique angle and turning them into something interesting. Even Finn admitted that I had a good eye for a story.

A good story… If the truth got out about Jacob, we'd definitely be in the news…

CHAPTER 17

With blurry eyes I glanced at the clock: 5.03 a.m. Damn. My brain was working overtime, my body keyed up. No more sleep for me.

Holding back a sigh, because it might disturb Jacob, I did a sort of horizontal limbo dance, sliding inch by careful inch from under the duvet and onto the floor.

Still not daring to straighten fully, I crept across the light-less room, cautious of the bedroom equivalent of landmines: discarded shoes, jeans tossed aside in a tangle, the sharp point of a belt buckle.

Free of the bedroom at last, and able to breathe normally, I stood in the darkness of the landing trying to decide what to do with myself. Go to your bedroom, maybe? Five seconds later my fingers rested lightly on the doorknob, the cold brass warming under my touch. I couldn't move.

I couldn't face it, Beth. The house was bad enough without you. Too quiet, too empty. A husk of itself. It was ten times worse in your bedroom. Each time I entered it seemed to get harder. The night before, while the police had searched it, the bedroom had felt as if it was in suspended animation, waiting for your return. The glass with its film of milk. The clothes discarded as if you'd be back any second.

The thought of going back in there made me shiver. I longed to be somewhere I could feel close to you, but your bedroom wasn't it. Besides, it reminded me of your lies. The wardrobe door gaped open to reveal the empty shoebox your boots should have been in.

Instead of your bedroom, I decided to go downstairs, stepping to the right to avoid the creaking bit of stair three down from the top. Your poor dad was shattered, so the last thing he needed was me waking him. Let him escape his pain in dreams for a while; I wished I could.

But what should I do? After two hours, sitting alone in the darkness held no appeal. My brain whirled with everything that had happened; my body longed to be on the move, to be doing something. I wanted to jump in the car and be at the hospital with you again. I couldn't even pour my heart out to Wiggins, because he was still with your grandparents.

According to the grandfather clock striking noisily, it was 7 a.m. There was about an hour until dawn. That suited the plan forming in my mind perfectly.

Still not daring to put the light on for fear of waking your dad, I crept through the darkness to the hall. The slippery, cool feel of waterproof material helped identify my coat among the others hanging up, along with the familiar density of its padded thermal filling and the faux fur trim around the hood. I blindly pulled it on over my pyjamas, the pale blue brushed cotton ones you had bought me for Christmas, Beth.

The wellies were harder to differentiate in the darkness, but I shoved my feet into them all until I'd found both parts of the pair that fitted. A woolly hat and scarf were put on, along with the thick gloves that had been sitting in my pocket, waiting patiently for their next expedition. The last time I'd worn them had been to walk you to Chloe's on Friday night, just three days and one lifetime ago.

*

Outside, I scurried along, my footsteps echoing through Fenmere and making me wince. I didn't want to be seen, couldn't face having a conversation with people, even though they would only be asking about you because they cared. The orange glow of the street lights didn't feel comforting; they made me feel spotlit, like an escaping prisoner highlighted by guards in a watchtower.

A scraping noise came from the Picky Person's Pop In. Jill would just have opened up, after getting the delivery of newspapers. That woman was one hard grafter. Thinking of newspapers, it suddenly occurred to me that your attack would be front page news for the *Wapentake Investigator*. Finn had been great when we had spoken, calling me to show support after the lack of coverage on last night's news. Brilliant – at least we'd get some publicity for you.

Hunched against the cold, I hurried away from the shop and street lights towards the darkness that would soon swallow me up, my breath a pulsating pale orange halo hanging before me, whipped by a soft breeze.

The final building for me to pass was The Malt Shovel. Huddled on the edge of the village, the pub faces it, with its back to the marsh and the sea. Like all the older buildings in the area, it has a long, gently sloping roof one side and a more steeply pitched, shorter one on the other. Incomers assume it's simply a design quirk popular to the area. Locals know it's far more practical: they are aerodynamic. Sea breezes that are vicious enough anywhere else along the coast take on new meaning here, on the flat fens of Lincolnshire just a handful of miles away from the famously bracing resort of Skegness. With nothing to break that wind – no hills, few hedges, just coarse grass – even a mild breeze can inflict an impressive punch. The gentle side of the area's roofs breaks the force of the winds, the steep pitch getting rid of it as quickly as possible before it tears off the tiles.

I stepped from the shelter of the buildings and the gentle breeze grew to a bluster. But I've spent my entire life here, so I was braced for it and sank my gloved hands deeper into my pockets.

Within a minute came a sharp right off the main road. Sea Lane, although tarmacked, was only wide enough for one car to pass down at a time. The sky began to grey, dawn approaching, enabling me, just about, to see where I was going without a torch as the village's lights were left behind.

There was no sign of anyone around, not even a tractor working a distant field.

The single-track lane ran straight and true for two miles, with no change in direction or level to give a clue to the distance travelled. Not many people came to the marsh, apart from the occasional dog-walker or birdwatcher – and as an avid nature-watcher, you had often begged me to drive you here. It felt strange walking the route, and seemed to take forever, but it made me far more aware of the subtle changes of smell as the landscape slowly altered. First, the cabbages in the fields, fading to a rich, earthy scent, finally joined by the sharp ozone and brine of the sea.

A sudden steep rise in the road obscured the view immediately ahead. That was the sea bank, an ancient man-made defence against nature which ran perpendicular to the lane and parallel with the horizon. Over I went, and the lane dropped back down then stopped abruptly in a small, permanently empty car park. It had taken forty minutes to get there, but at last the marsh lay before me. It was so lacking in undulation that it seemed to be squeezed into a couple of inches, the rest of the view taken up solely by a huge sky streaked with dawn's first hints of pink and orange.

The olive-green marshland was covered in weird and wonderful plants hardy enough to survive the harsh, salty conditions. I tried to remember some of the names you had told me: sea aster, purslane, sea-blite, couch grass. A flock of brent geese gabbled gently and constantly, like gossipy old women, as they breakfasted among the meres, the shallow saltwater ponds. Although I couldn't see them, you and I know that dangerously hidden beneath the springy undergrowth further in were meandering tidal creeks several feet deep. They made their sluggish way to the shallow, silt-filled beginnings of the North Sea. Across the other side of

The Wash, far in the distance, Hunstanton hunkered down on Norfolk's coast.

What the hell would a thirteen-year-old girl be doing here in the middle of nowhere, in the middle of the night, Beth? Someone must have abducted you, brought you here against your will.

Searching for answers, I made a ninety-degree turn and trudged along the mud track at the top of the sea bank. Frozen puddles gave way beneath me with a crunch and splash.

After ten minutes, with the sun sitting fully above the horizon, I could see white tape that cordoned off a distant area. As I grew closer, the wind making the rectangle bulge convex then concave, the tape no longer seemed pure white, but blue and white. Closer again and words became distinct: 'POLICE: DO NOT CROSS'. They shivered in the wind, meaningless, now that the authorities had collected all the forensic evidence they needed from the scene.

That was where my daughter was dumped like a piece of rubbish. It had taken me over fifteen minutes to walk there from the car park. Surely someone couldn't have carried you all this way? But you weighed almost nothing, and if the man were strong, it would have been easy enough.

I quivered like the police tape as an image flared in my mind. *You, thrown over a powerful shoulder. Unconscious and bleeding. Your head lolling and bobbing in time with your attacker's step.*

On my right was the mere you had been floating in. My imagination kicked in again. *You were walking alone, engrossed in watching a fox or badger or some such. You tripped. Stumbled in the darkness. Hit your head and rolled, unconscious, into the mere. Is that what happened?*

No. Not in those clothes, those ridiculous boots. And you had been wearing make-up. You'd clearly dressed up for someone and met them elsewhere, then been brought here by them – you wouldn't have come to the marshes in those clothes.

Who brought you here, Beth? Who knows these marshes? Villagers? But they barely come here, because there's nothing to see for miles.

I looked around, hoping to find some clue: something, anything that would explain what had happened. Something the police had missed and only a mother would spot. In the distance the skeleton of a young sperm whale that had been stranded and died stood out against the skyline. You had been so upset at its death. The local authorities had no choice but to leave it to rot as the mudflats were too dangerous for a vehicle. Nearby there was a single sycamore tree, twisting away from the sea and reaching towards Fenmere as if imploring someone to stop the wind from bullying it and warping its growth. Neither the whale nor the tree offered any clues as to what had happened to you.

At the sycamore's base sat a teddy bear and a couple of bunches of flowers.

A shrine to you, Beth.

My stomach flipped. I wasn't sure how I felt about that. It was as though you were dead. But you were alive. You were going to be fine.

I was being silly. It was nice, really, and kind of people to be so thoughtful. I forced myself over to it and read the notes. The Clarkes, of course; the teddy was from them.

Miss you, read the note.

Jill Young and her brood: *Thinking of You*.

The Jachowski family had left no note, simply their names on a card tucked among the blooms. Huh, that was unexpected. The Polish family had moved to the village about a year before. They seemed nice enough, but the most we'd ever said to one another was 'hello'. Do they know you, Beth?

Finally, I turned to leave. And as I did, something plucked at my clothes. I gasped. Looked around wildly. It was only the wind.

Just the wind. But it had felt exactly like you were tugging at me for attention, the way you had when you were little.

I pulled my hood up and ran, stumbling, back along the sea bank. The wind playfully tugged at me again, pulling my hood down and… Was that a person, watching me? I turned, squinting. Yes, someone in the distance. A man. Even at that remove, it was possible to tell from the way the person stood, and their stocky build and tall frame, that my watcher was male.

I ran again. This time the wind pushed me on, seeming to want to help.

CHAPTER 18

By the time I'd reached the main road, after a hurried forty minutes of speed-walking to get away from the person watching me, I'd calmed down and silently scolded myself for getting so spooked. Despite constantly looking over my shoulder, he had not followed me. But something more practical worried at me: what if, when Jacob's secret came out, the police decided to try to pin your attack on him?

I'd have to find the real culprit.

The most obvious place to begin was Chloe. Surely she knew something about what you had been up to that night? I refused to believe you hadn't confided in your best friend. She might not want to break confidence, though – particularly to the police.

I'd talk with her, make her understand.

Once across to the other side of the village, silly nerves kicked in. Fiddling with one of the toggles on my coat, as I always did when fretting, I knocked on the Clarkes' door. The toggle popped off just as the front door swung open to reveal me bent over. I straightened quickly, and Ursula, understandably, looked surprised to see me doing a jack-in-the-box impression.

'Melanie! Is everything all right? Is Beth okay?'

'She's fine, yes. Well, no change.'

Her face tightened, clearly unsure of what to say. Her platinum hair fell in waves to her shoulders and framed her chunky face. She was made-up perfectly, with thick eyeliner and hot-pink lipstick. I stopped playing with the broken toggle of my coat.

'No news is good news, eh?' she managed finally.

We looked at each other. Her hand still rested on the door, blocking my way.

'Umm, may I come in? I was wondering if I could have a quick chat with Chloe.'

'Now isn't a good time. I'm about to drive her to school – we're horribly late. Then I've got to open the café.'

'Yes, I can appreciate it's not a good time. I'm not having such a great time myself.' My voice was brittle.

Her eyes widened, and she hurried me in, apologising.

She left me standing awkwardly in the immaculate lounge – everything cream, apart from a pillar-box-red sofa and scarlet picture frames – and as I sat down I suddenly realised I was still in my pyjamas. I decided to keep my coat on in case they thought I was a lunatic.

When Ursula and Chloe emerged a few minutes later, the teen gave a half-smile and a little wave of her hand. With her long limbs and already impressive chest, she was turning into a mini-me version of her mum. She'd also inherited Ursula's lack of waist, her body square rather than curvy, despite Ursula seeming to consider herself Fenmere's answer to Marilyn Monroe. In a bid to look different from her mother, Chloe had recently dyed her long hair a strange shade of burgundy. It clashed nastily with the red leather sofa as she sat beside me.

Her navy-blue uniform was neat and tidy and her school bag lay at her feet, ready to go at any moment. Still, she made herself comfortable by pulling up her feet, while Ursula perched next to her on the arm of the sofa.

'How are you doing?' I asked.

'I'm okay…'

'You're not in trouble.' I smiled gently. 'But I need to ask: is there anything you know about that can help me find out who hurt Beth?'

Chloe shrugged. Her mum's fingers twitched on her shoulder, giving it a reassuring squeeze.

'Was there ever a plan that she'd stay here on Friday, the night she got attacked?'

'No, she'd never meant to stay,' said Ursula.

I bit down my frustration. 'Chloe?'

'No, Mum's right. Beth never asked to stay here that night.'

'Steve was away on a business trip, you see – well, an excuse to go golfing, really,' added Ursula. 'So we had a lovely girlie night in together, didn't we? We'd been looking forward to it ever since Dad said he'd go away, eh?'

Chloe nodded. 'Sorry. I do want to help, Mrs Oak.'

'I know. It's not your fault. Look, did Beth have a secret boy-friend? Or a crush? Someone who was interested in her? Maybe someone who fancied her, but she wasn't interested in him?'

The questions tumbled from me, even as I warned myself not to overwhelm Chloe. She looked calm, though. Her maturity impressed me.

'Right, I think Beth did fancy someone,' she admitted. Her fingers played with the strap of her bag as she spoke. 'But she wouldn't tell me who. So I kept teasing her about it, and she'd blush and get mad at me. It was funny.'

'Any idea who?'

Another shrug. 'Aleksy Jachowski had started talking to us on the bus to school, like. I think he fancied Beth, but she told me she wasn't interested in him.'

'Could she have been meeting him?' I pressed, remembering the flowers from the Jachowski family left at the shrine on the marsh.

'I don't know. I… I just, like, so can't believe this has happened… How is she? I'm sorry, Mrs Oak, but I've told you and the police all I know.'

'Everything? Come on, I know what I was like at your age. My best friend and I told each other all kinds of things, and nothing would have made me give up one of our secrets to an adult.'

'I'm not a child. I do understand how important this is, you know. Is… is she going to be all right?'

Being upbraided by a kid I'd known since she was knee-high stung me. 'She'll be fine. But until you have kids yourself, you won't understand what I'm going through. Please, who was Beth meeting that night? You must have some idea.'

Ursula stood abruptly. 'That's enough. We'd love to help you, but Chloe's tired, she's upset and has to go to school now. She doesn't have anything else to say.'

'Ursula, please. Just a few minutes more.' I leaned round her to look at Chloe.

'This is so important. The tiniest thing could make a difference. Were there any new friends Beth had made lately, boys or girls? Any reason at all why she'd be on the marsh? Anyone she might have met who'd take her there?'

My voice grew louder as frustration and desperation took hold.

'Melanie, leave her be. Chloe's had enough.'

'So have I! So has Beth!'

'Look, me and her dad are splitting up.'

That stopped me in my tracks.

Ursula sighed. Chloe stared at the floor, fingers clutching the bag strap. 'I know it's nothing compared to what you're going through, but between that and what's happened to Beth… It's a lot for someone to deal with at Chloe's age. You have to understand: I must protect my daughter.'

'I… Yes, of course, I understand that.'

That's what I'd failed to do: protect *my* daughter. That was the thought that brought tears to my eyes, calling quick apologies over my shoulder as I fled the house.

But at least there was a name now – Aleksy Jachowski, the seventeen-year-old son of Polish immigrants. Him, and the sinister figure who had been watching me on the marsh.

CHAPTER 19

Beth shivered as she quickly got changed in the freezing cricket pavilion. Her fingers were numb as she backcombed her hair. Stuffing her rucksack out of sight behind a tangle of practice nets, she hesitated, then pulled her coat back on. It ruined the look of the fashionable little outfit she wore, but she was too sensible to face the cold without it.

Besides, she wouldn't be wearing her coat for too long, hopefully. As soon as she got where she was going, she'd slip out of it.

The goosebumps she got at that moment had nothing to do with the temperature and everything to do with excitement. This was it: the night her relationship changed forever. She couldn't wait to take things to the next level. When her friends at school found out, they'd be so totally green.

'Ready?' whispered a voice in the semi-darkness.

'I was born ready,' Beth said, sounding far more confident than her flipping stomach would let her feel.

CHAPTER 20

The front door had barely closed before Jacob threw himself at me.

'Where have you been?' he gasped, squeezing me in a bear hug until every sinew in his body pressed against me. 'I've been worried sick. You didn't take your mobile with you.'

'God, I'm so sorry. I needed some fresh air.'

'Anything could have happened to you,' he said, bursting into tears.

Good job he didn't know I'd been on the marsh, or he'd have been even more worried. I decided to keep shtum about everything – including my visit to Chloe Clarke.

'Hey, it's okay. I'm okay,' I replied gently. 'But... now we have to go to the police station and tell them the truth about you.'

He ran his hand over the blond stubble of his head fretfully. His face had aged over the past week, new lines appearing around his tragic blue eyes. We had both been pushed beyond endurance. He heaved a sigh.

'Look, it's not worth it, Mel. It's got nothing to do with what happened, and I'll just get into trouble.'

'It's "not worth it"? Telling the truth about the night our daughter was attacked "isn't worth it"?'

'Don't be like that.'

'Like what?' My words cracked like a whip. 'We've already discussed this. When this comes out – and it will – people are going to suspect you of lying about everything. They'll think you had something to do with Beth's attack, unless you come clean now.'

'But…'

'It's always the family people suspect first.'

'You might be right. Let me think—'

'You're not thinking, Jacob; you're doing it. If you don't, I will. You've got the time it takes me to pack Beth's things for hospital to agree with me.'

I couldn't believe your dad was being such a coward, Beth. He and I had always tried to set you a good example about doing the right thing. What a joke.

In a fury, I stomped up the stairs to your room. And stopped. All emotion drained from me, leaving only terror behind. Who was I to talk of your father's cowardice when I was so scared of your bedroom, Beth?

Do you want to know a secret? It took every single ounce of courage, squeezed up tight into a ball, to turn the doorknob and step into your room, Beth. I tiptoed across the dirty clothes strewn on the floor, feeling guilty for picking them up and putting them into your wash basket as I went. I was another person invading your privacy, coming into your room without asking. At least I left untouched the clothes across that uncomfortable pink chair. I stood in the middle of your room, taking in the posters of wildlife and pop stars. Breathed in your perfume, Daisy, that hung in the air – another Christmas present you had begged me for. Guilt punched me.

I should have kept you safe. I had failed you.

Hunched over in pain, I snatched up random bits and bobs you might like with you in hospital. Pulling down a favourite poster to take, and swearing at the rip I made in your wallpaper. Ran out, crying, slamming the door behind me.

Overnight bag packed, I forced myself upright, wiped away the tears and came down the stairs.

'We'll go straight to Leeds,' I said. Jacob's face relaxed, relief spreading over it. 'From the police station,' I added firmly.

It was time for the truth finally to come out.

CHAPTER 21

Fifteen minutes or so later we parked at Wapentake police station. The ugly five-storey creation of concrete slabs had been pebble-dashed in an attempt to soften the harsh rectangle, which also incorporated the magistrates' court. Stairs outside led up to the reception on the first floor, where Jacob asked to speak to DS Devonport.

As soon as he made his confession, the pair of us were separated. The small room they put me in was windowless, cell-like and painted a pale grey. I sat on an orange plastic chair, instantly feeling guilty for no reason. I would never make a master criminal, I decided.

'Mrs Oak, can you talk us through events on the night of your daughter's disappearance?' asked Detective Constable Alan Musgrove.

So I told him again about you asking to stay at Chloe's house. About me not bothering to check whether or not this was true because it happened so often. Lately I'd simply got out of the habit – you two lived in each other's pockets, and besides, you and Chloe were growing up and I'd thought you could both be trusted. That's what you'd been relying on, wasn't it, Beth? Habit and trust making me lazy. You had taken advantage of that to lie and manipulate me. Why?

What time we set off. Our conversation about superheroes inspired by wildlife. You skipping away from me. Once again, I went over those painful last moments of seeing you truly alive and vital. I hadn't imagined for a second that the next time I saw you, my daughter, you'd be lying lifeless in a hospital bed.

They quizzed me about your clothes, of course. About whether or not you were carrying a bag.

'For the hundredth time, yes, she was. I'd thought it contained her overnight things to stay with Chloe. In fact, it must have been her make-up and clothes for some kind of night out. Have you found Beth's rucksack yet? Or her coat?'

'Not yet. She wasn't wearing make-up when she left the house?' the detective checked.

'No, none at all. I'd have commented on it. She had just started experimenting with make-up but I wasn't a big fan of it; although, to be honest, I might have let her wear it as I'd have thought she was simply dressing up for a girls' night in with her pal. Chloe sometimes stays with us, and the two of them have started messing about with each other's hair and stuff.'

'So, Mrs Oak, at what time did your husband leave the house?'

Ah, now we were getting to the real reason for the grilling. I certainly didn't blame the police for this. I laid my hands flat on the pale grey Formica table.

'Umm, he left at about 9 p.m. I'm not certain of the time, but it was straight after the football match on the television ended. He came home at one-ish. I was sleeping and barely registered his arrival.'

'So it could have been later than that?'

'Well, maybe, but he's not much of a night owl, so I very much doubt it. And he doesn't like to be late because he knows I'll worry.'

'But you weren't worrying on this occasion?'

'No,' I admitted, reluctantly. My fingers started to drum.

'Why was that?'

'Don't know. I was knackered. Fell asleep. It wasn't a big deal. It wasn't an unusual night. I didn't know my daughter was being attacked.' My voice started to break. No more drumming; I clenched my fists, trying to fight the tears. 'If I'd realised what was going to happen, I'd never have let Beth out of the house, much less worry about what my husband was up to!'

'And what was he up to, Mrs Oak?'

'Oh, for goodness' sake, you know what he was doing. He's just given you a statement telling you. He was smoking dope with a friend. He doesn't do it often, and I don't really approve, but, well, it's not the end of the world.'

There, Beth, I'd said it. Your dad sometimes smoked a spliff. After all the anti-drugs talks we gave you. But we all have secrets, don't we?

'Why did you lie to us? You knew you were giving him a false alibi.'

'It… it wasn't that simple. My worry for Beth blotted out every other thought. When Jacob said he was with me all night I barely took it in. I didn't actually agree or disagree; I did nothing. It was only much later I thought of it.'

'Mrs Oak, are you certain that your husband was where he said he was? The initial 999 call shows a lack of commitment and urgency.'

'What?' *Where had that change of tack come from?*

'When Mr Oak spoke to the emergency services, he said: "I want to report a missing person". It's interesting that he didn't use Beth's name; it shows he's distancing himself. Here's the transcript of the call.'

I looked at the printout, confused. 'I don't need to read it, I was there.'

The officer leaned forward and tapped the page. 'See the use of "appears" there?'

My eyes flashed over Jacob's words: *My daughter appears to be missing.*

'That's interesting too. It isn't definitive and lacks conviction. There's no urgency. No use of "Send help!" In fact, all the way through, he barely uses Beth's name. It's depersonalising and distancing.'

'Depersonalising? Sorry, what exactly are you trying to say?'

'Here, he was asked: "Why do you think she was abducted?" Your husband replies: "I have no idea. When we woke up this morning everything was normal, then my wife realised. I… we looked everywhere". See, "I have no idea" addresses the motivational aspect of why someone took her, rather than saying why he believes that she was taken. Also notice this change of pronouns: "I… we looked everywhere" – wording such as this is frequently associated with deception.'

'Are you insane?' It seemed the only explanation.

The officer ignored me and read out another bit of the transcript. The bit where Jacob laughed.

'Look, he always laughs when he's worried or nervous.'

'It's inappropriate behaviour.'

'Inappropriate, yes. An indicator of him hurting his daughter? No.' It was unbelievable; I had to say it.

'Has he ever hit Beth in the past?'

'No!' The urge to stand up and walk out grew stronger. But it would probably convince the police that we were both guilty of hiding something. I forced my voice down from a shout. 'Jacob is one of the most sensitive, gentle men in the world. He would never, ever raise his hand to anyone, much less his daughter.'

The officer leaned back in his chair. 'All right, Mrs Oak. We're going to leave things there for now. Thank you for your time.'

The sudden suspension of hostilities left me confused but relieved. Okay, families were always the first under the microscope when something happened, but in our case, we genuinely were as innocent as we seemed.

Your dad came out at the same time as me, looking pale and shaken. Part of me wanted to slap him. Most of me wanted a hug.

'I'm sorry, I'm an idiot,' he muttered, kissing me. 'Come on, let's get out of here.'

Hand in hand we hurried to the car, only letting go to get inside. Before he turned the key in the ignition he looked at me, grabbing my hand again.

'Forgive me?'

I hesitated. *Depersonalised. Distancing. Lying.*

The police's crazy suspicions could not be allowed to drive a wedge between us.

'It was a bloody stupid thing to do, but of course I forgive you. Come on, let's get back to Beth.'

During the whole drive to Leeds I thought once again about who could have hurt you, Beth. If the police were concentrating on us, the real attacker could get away.

The real attacker, who we almost certainly knew well. A stranger always attracted notice, so someone would have come forward by now if they had spotted an unknown person in the area on the day of your attack. Besides, the marsh was so isolated, the lanes to it so small, that it was unlikely anyone without local knowledge would go there.

The problem was that every time I considered a villager as a possible suspect, a childhood memory flooded back. I'd gone to the village primary school, then on to the secondary school in Wapentake with everyone around my age; their parents knew my parents and our kids were all friends. Generations of bonding. One of my earliest memories was of Jill Young, her expression inscrutable even in an act of kindness, giving me a lollipop for being brave after falling over and skinning my knee right outside her shop. It had dried my tears faster than Mum's magic rub. People like that would never hurt me or mine; they were virtually family.

Then Aleksy Jachowski popped into my head again. He and his family were newcomers, didn't have the links the rest of us had.

But they had settled in well, apart from some muttering about 'Polish vermin' among a certain section of villagers. He and his little sister seemed to get on with the other kids their age in the village.

Perhaps it was one of the occasional birders who came to see migrant waders on the mudflats. Remembering the stranger who had been looking at me made me shudder. Maybe it had been him or someone like him. Watching you from afar with huge binoculars, stalking you.

CHAPTER 22

Even though we'd only been away from you for one night, it felt like forever by the time we arrived at lunchtime. We rushed through the hospital's labyrinthine corridors to the paediatric ICU ward. Washing our hands before we entered your room seemed to take an eternity; I hopped from foot to foot, as if that were going to make me wash faster. I needed to be by your side again, Beth.

Bursting into your room, hope rose. *Your cheeks would be pinker. You'd squeeze my hand. You'd open your eyes.*

Instead, you simply lay there, head slumped to one side on your plumped pillows.

'Any change?' I asked your Uncle John, who was sitting with you.

'Nothing so far. Although I think her eyes flickered earlier.'

My heart hammered. Jacob and I peered at you. No reaction. No improvement. Disappointment settled as heavy as lead.

'How are you feeling today, Beans?' asked Jacob. He used the teasing nickname he had for you, perhaps hoping to get a reaction.

You generally pretended to be furious when he used it, but he meant it with love. You've heard the story a hundred times, but I can't resist telling it again, Beth. The very first time he held you, he was overwhelmed. He'd teared up – and so had I at the sight of his hand dwarfing your head as he cradled it. We were both so exhausted, so proud and so terrified of you and the endless love we already felt, despite you being just minutes old. He'd told you how perfect you were and lifted you to his face to kiss you, and at that moment you had opened your eyes and seemed to look straight into his soul.

Then you had broken wind. The sound was incredible. That such a tiny, gorgeous newborn could produce something like that had had us in stitches. Your dad'd had to put you down in your crib, terrified he was going to drop you, he was laughing so much.

Since then, Jacob has called you Beans. Much to your chagrin.

You didn't react that day, though. Not so much as a fluctuation in the readings on the machines surrounding you.

'Well, we've brought lots of things from home for you, to cheer this place up,' I said brightly. 'The nurses have said we can put some posters up, so we've brought that one of the mountain gorillas. Hope you don't mind me taking it from your room, but I thought you'd like to see it here. Oh, and we've got you… Ta-da! A new Justin Bieber poster. Think I preferred him with his old hair and fewer tattoos.'

'Did you bring her speakers? Yes, we've brought your speakers, too, so you can listen to Justin to your heart's content. Lucky us, eh?' your dad joked.

'And because you can't cuddle up to Justin, here's Jesus.'

For some odd reason, that was what you called the now tatty teddy Jacob had bought for you when you were born. You've never been able to explain why you chose that name; it has been rather embarrassing for us, at times. Now, the blue bear nestled beside you on your pillow.

After putting everything in its place, including throwing a colour-ful home-made patchwork counterpane over your bed to cheer it up, the room looked a little better. But you looked the same, Beth. Tubes coming out of your nose and throat, your shaved head. Some of the swelling had gone down a little, but the bruising was the deep black and purple of storm clouds. I took hold of your hand, careful to avoid the arterial cannula, which measured your blood pressure, and told myself that at least things couldn't get any worse.

That night, there was one improvement: the local news covered your attack. It was a quick one-minute segment on the television, with your photo, then footage of the police combing the marsh and DS Devonport asking anyone with information to come forward.

Fingers crossed.

CHAPTER 23

'COMA GIRL'S FATHER QUESTIONED: DOING DRUGS WHILE HIS DAUGHTER FOUGHT FOR HER LIFE.'

I stood in my kitchen and read and reread the headline of Friday's edition of the *Wapentake Investigator*. It didn't change, no matter how much I glared at it.

'Bloody Finn. I'll kill him!'

'Maybe he's just printing what everyone else has,' offered Jacob miserably.

Oh, the naive fool.

'Jacob, Finn's the one who has sold this story to all the nationals. The story broke with them today – and our local paper came out today too. There is no way that could have happened unless he was the one who flogged it to them.'

My voice had started out quiet and sympathetic, but began to speed up again with the tempo of my heart.

'Finn's a small-time reporter who likes to imagine that his weekly rag full of school initiatives, town councillors congratulating one another and the occasional shed break-in or car theft will one day launch him into Fleet Street. He's seen what's happened to Beth not as a terrible thing for a colleague's family, but as a golden opportunity to show the big papers what he is capable of. Look!'

I stabbed my finger randomly at the page, but Jacob knew which paragraph I referred to. 'He's even quoted me about Beth's attack! He called me to offer support, then recorded the conversation and quoted me!'

The betrayal by a colleague of seven years was absolute. Your dad suffered the most at Finn's hands, though. Beth, Finn had made him sound like a junkie. A contact in the police must have tipped him off about Jacob's spliff confession. Then he had clearly seized his big opportunity and contacted everyone from *The Sun* to the *Daily Mail*. Each had run a variation of the story, with much added background 'colour' and even more sensational details of your attack.

I'd wanted what had happened to you to get publicity – but not like that. The article wasn't about raising awareness and uncovering the attacker; this was about crucifying a struggling family. The implication was clear: we were no-goods, and had let our daughter run riot in the middle of the night. Your injuries were our fault for being bad parents.

Maybe they were right.

I looked around the room in despair. The photo on the noticeboard of you and your dad caught my eye. We'd had such a giggle taking that. You had spent the morning in Decoy Wood, the small patch of Wildlife Trust land near the Daughtrey-Drews' big house. You were a little late, so I had been in your bedroom, looking out for you and mucking about with a camera your dad had just bought. He'd got a brilliant bridge camera with 60x optical zoom on it so you could use it for taking nature pictures, and I was focusing on the Picky Person's Pop In, a couple of doors down, impressed with the zoom function. Then I had spotted you, in such a hurry to get home that you bumped right into Alison Daughtrey-Drew as she came out of the shop.

The woman's handbag had flown from her shoulder, spilling its contents as it dropped to the ground. You both scrambled to pick everything up. A packet of cigarettes, a phone, a clear plastic bag stuffed with pastel-coloured sweeties. A quick exchange of pleasantries and you had scurried on, the front door slamming seconds later. Telling me breathlessly about the things you had seen.

'There were redwings and fieldfares, crows and starlings, as well as several robins. Not too bad a day. I lost track of time, though; sorry I'm a bit late.'

You had shrugged your coat off and hung it up. Kicked your shoes into the corner and chucked your bag on top of them, as usual, before flopping onto the sofa.

Usually nature-watching put you in a great mood, but that day you had seemed anxious. I had wondered, momentarily, if there had been more to the exchange with Alison than there had seemed. Perhaps she had been angry with you for knocking into her. But then your dad had showed you his new camera, and soon we'd all been laughing.

We were a happy family before this, weren't we, Beth? Was this our fault? Were the papers right?

Screwing up the newspaper, I threw it in the bin.

'Jacob, could we manage only on your wage? I don't see how I can go back to work after this.'

He was the foreman of a factory that made all kinds of wooden furniture. It was handmade, good-quality stuff. His wage wasn't too bad for the area, which was renowned for low pay.

'Yeah, we'll just tighten our belts. You want to call Finn now, or have a cup of tea and calm down a bit first?'

I loved that he didn't even hesitate in his support.

'Call first, then tea.' Why should Finn be spared my fury? I didn't get annoyed often, but when I did, the world needed to watch out.

*

'You using piece of Fleet Street wannabe scum,' I spat, the second Finn answered the phone. He spluttered, but I gave him no chance to reply, furious.

While I gave it to my now ex-boss with both barrels, Flo arrived.

'I'm so sorry about the press leak,' she told Jacob.

I stuffed a finger in my ear to block her out, and Finn took my moment of hesitation to speak.

'I'm sorry you feel—'

'How I *feel*?! Don't give me that,' I bellowed. 'You can't even say sorry properly, instead you do the "journalist apology" – can't admit liability, eh? You shouldn't be sorry about how I feel, Finn, you should be sorry that you betrayed me. We've worked together for seven bloody years!'

Flo's arrival was distracting me from my telephone rant, so Jacob took her out of the way, leading her into the kitchen.

*

By the time I'd finished the call, she'd gone.

Jacob popped the promised cuppa in front of me, along with some custard creams.

'To keep your strength up,' he said.

Bless him, he still fretted about my birdlike eating. I munched on one to give him some peace of mind, while he filled me in on Flo's promise of an internal inquiry into the leak to Finn.

'No need to ask what you said to Finn,' he added. 'The whole of Fenmere heard you, I reckon. Did he say who'd given him the tip-off?'

'No, the complete git. He gave me the spiel about how a journalist can't reveal their sources. That's when I told him to stick his job – although I think he'd probably guessed.' I savagely bit into a custard cream. 'Maybe this job thing is a godsend.'

Jacob cocked his head as he dipped his biscuit into his tea.

'I'm going to be at the hospital at lot, and once Beth comes round we don't know how long it will take to get her back to full strength. Without a job, I can concentrate on Beth, and we can bring her back that much faster. I can look after her here. Even…'

I trailed off, worried about voicing my fears. The thought had been tapping on my shoulder for a while now, though, begging to be articulated.

'Even if it's worst-case scenario stuff – you know, she has to learn to walk, talk, eat, all over again – it'll be better to do that here than at a hospital, if possible.'

'It's not going to come to that,' insisted Jacob.

'But if it does, then I'm ready for it.'

I'd taught you all that once; I could do it again. A vivid memory flashed: of you as a toddler, wiggling your nappy-covered bottom in time to something playing on the radio. Bare feet slapping on the wooden floor as you discovered the joy of dancing for the first time. Your giggle had been musical.

It was hard to keep talking through the gathering tears. 'Maybe I could research some homeschooling techniques too. Hopefully none of this will be necessary; Beth will come round, be fine and be out of hospital by, heck, Sunday.'

'And back at school Monday,' agreed Jacob.

'Exactly! But this way, we're prepared for every eventuality.'

As I wiped my face dry, we toasted our new-found positivity with tea.

Then I glanced at the clock, and couldn't help thinking that this time exactly one week earlier we'd had no idea our lives were balanced on a cliff edge.

One week ago you had been at school, happy and healthy.

One week ago you had come home as usual, chatting about homework, rushing around, laughing.

Until you'd lied to us, and gone out for the night. Then everything had changed.

Why, Beth? Why?

CHAPTER 24

It was inevitable that the police would trace the phone records eventually, but I felt confident they wouldn't ever tie them to me. I'd covered my tracks too well, and destroyed my burner mobile as soon as it had served its purpose.

No, it wasn't fear of discovery that was bothering me. It was that I was already starting to suffer withdrawal symptoms.

Like a drug addict, the high I experienced lessened each time the memory replayed in my mind. There simply wasn't the same thrill any more at reliving the moment of attack. The huff of breath the girl gave as I smashed at her skull didn't excite me; it was as dull as a pair of well-worn slippers. A crawling sensation under my skin made me so restless it couldn't be ignored for much longer. I needed a fix.

But I couldn't risk striking again. Not so soon. I would have to be patient, wait it out, plan things. It would happen again, though. Eventually. That thought was enough to ease the crawling skin for now, despite it being the equivalent of a junkie taking paracetamol.

One heroin hit was never enough, was it? And my particular drug was more addictive, more refined and harder to procure than heroin. Bloodshed was a drug for the elite, not the masses.

What I needed was a new supplier. And suddenly an idea leapt into my mind that made me chuckle out loud. A fresh person for me to target – or rather, an old one.

CHAPTER 25

As the days passed, Jacob and I kept ourselves busy, distracting ourselves from the fact that there was no change with you, Beth. We kept asking medics what was happening, when we would see an improvement, but were constantly told it was too soon to tell, that we had to be patient, that more tests were being run. Our frustrations ate away at us, but we determined to stay positive. I struggled with it, but Jacob was such a tower of strength that he inspired me whenever I felt low. Seeing you like this was killing him. Sometimes he would lock himself in the bathroom and cry quietly.

In front of you, though, he always remained strong. He fussed over your bed sheets, smoothed your hair, talked to you in a bright, chatty voice, never betraying how devastated he felt.

'We're going to stay over tonight. So that'll be nice, won't it? Maybe we can all watch a film together, one of your favourites, eh? *Frozen*? Or... something else?'

He gazed at you. Waiting.

When you didn't reply, he pulled something from his rucksack and randomly started spritzing perfume over your bed. The air filled with your scent.

You cuddling beside me on the sofa; me kissing the top of your head and taking in your smell. You hogging the bathroom, and emerging an hour and a half later on a cloud of scented steam. You breezing past me, waving goodbye as you skipped up the lane, cheeky grin on your face...

The memories punched me. With no time to brace for them, the tears welled. Yet Jacob's spritzing had no impact on you. We looked at each other, needing no words to convey our disappointment.

'We'll keep trying things,' Jacob said.

We'd done a lot of research into sensory stimulation in coma patients, and although you were in an induced coma we decided it might help your brain injuries to heal and bring you back to us. We'd checked with the doctors that it would be okay, and they'd given us the go-ahead. Talking wasn't enough; all the senses should be targeted. So as well as your perfume, over the following week we tried my perfume and Jacob's aftershave, and Mum found a bath bomb that smelled exactly like cut grass. Because you loved the outdoors so much, we were all excited as we wafted that under your nose. I stared at the read-out of your heartbeat, willing it to beep faster or slower. No change came.

Jacob also tried different types of materials. He gently stroked your skin with a feather, fake fur, a brush for a slightly prickly feeling, anything. We once even used a scrunched-up piece of tinfoil that had encased our sandwiches.

We talked constantly about happier times, sharing memories. Made plans for the future, once you got out.

'Maybe we could scrape up enough money to go away somewhere special. Whale-watching, or see the mountain gorillas or something,' I suggested, desperately, one day.

An idea that, days earlier, would have had you running around screaming with joy didn't elicit so much as a blink.

We played board games, with Jacob taking your turn as well as his own. And we played music constantly. I knew all the words to every single One Direction song.

Sometimes it all felt worryingly futile. As time passed, despair built in me of never hearing your voice again. But I pushed on with researching homeschooling. I also looked up exercises that we could do together to combat the muscle wastage you would be suffering after lack of movement for such an extended period.

Your dad and I spent every spare moment with you, Beth, but reality started to come knocking. Your dad had to return to work, which meant he often slept at the hospital then drove the two and a half hours straight to the factory, leaving me alone with you. I held your hand and talked until my throat hurt. Every. Single. Day.

You never reacted.

Despair closed in on me every time I saw your beautiful, animated face now empty. The sound of the machine filling your lungs with air made me want to scream. Being in the same room as you began to feel claustrophobic. My fingers twitched; I paced all the time. I wanted to run from the building, the tears, the pain, the guilt.

What could I do that would make things better? I offered every pact under the stars to God, the great They, whatever entity might be interested in taking me up on it.

Take me instead of her. Take me and Jacob – we don't mind.

But there was never any change.

At home, the steady flow of concerned visitors slowed to a trickle, a dribble, a drought. After the fuss of your dad's 'drugs revelation' in the newspapers, there had been no further coverage in the nationals and only a tiny update in the *Wapentake Investigator*. Posters around the village appealing for anyone with information to come forward were so shabbily made that they were peeling off street lights within a week. Yesterday's news, tomorrow's litter. Only the one in the window of the Picky Person's Pop In looked as fresh as the day it was printed.

Not that it did any good. Not a single person had come forward.

'Someone, somewhere must have seen something, surely?' I despaired to Jill one day, after popping in for some milk. 'There's about eight hundred people living here, give or take. They can't all have been at home with the curtains closed.'

Jill's eyes were full of pity, but her words were to the point as she handed me my change. 'Why not, duck? You were.'

It wasn't an accusation. Still I blushed – with guilt and anger. I turned to the handful of other villagers browsing the shelves.

'Please… have you heard a rumour even, of what might have happened? Any of you?'

They all suddenly found the floor interesting.

Outside, I spotted Ursula walking with Chloe. I called out. They turned, waved, but hurried on.

'Sorry, we've got to get home. I'll call tomorrow,' Ursula said, with a melancholy smile.

*

It was three days later before she did, then it was my turn to get away as quickly as possible because all she could give me were platitudes and news of how brave her own daughter was being.

All the time she talked, I wondered: *Why can't it be your daughter in hospital instead of mine?*

On Saturday 6 February, a fortnight after you had been found, your fourteenth birthday dawned. To treat the day like any other would have felt like a betrayal to you, Beans. It would have felt as though we were forgetting about you and weren't bothered enough to make an effort. So instead, the whole family gathered around your bed. We wore party hats, and opened presents in some twisted pass the parcel where no one wanted to rip off the paper because it should have been you doing it, Beth.

What do you buy the girl who can't move? New clothes; the latest iPad, to replace your old one; tickets to a wildlife exhibition? Jacob's present broke my heart. Using pale lime wood, he had carved your favourite bird, a little egret. You loved the way their brilliant white plumage made them appear almost ghostlike as they flew across the marsh. Dad had perfectly captured the bird's long-lined elegance, so like a heron's, and the 's' shape of its lithe neck as it lifted its wings ready to take flight. You would have adored it. But you weren't there to see it. Not really. Looking at you lying on the hospital bed, I felt a horrible disconnect, as if everything that made you my daughter had gone. All that was left was the shell.

The police still had no idea who had done this to you. Jacob's mate, Stuart (aka Stinky Stu, because he smoked so much dope he was permanently impregnated with the smell) had confirmed they had watched a marathon run of *Family Guy* and smoked a joint before Jacob walked the ten minutes home at just after midnight. The problem was, your dad hadn't arrived home until gone 1 a.m. He claimed he'd spent that time looking up at the stars – a distinct possibility given that he was mashed – but it meant there was an hour or more of that night for which he didn't have an alibi.

Officially it meant that Jacob still wasn't eliminated from the police's enquiries. We didn't see much of the investigating team, including the cool DS Devonport; all our information came through Flo, our Family Liaison Officer. And although they didn't seem to be investigating your dad further, no one else was in their crosshairs either. All Flo ever said when we asked was that the team were pursuing several lines of enquiry, but that it was too soon to tell us anything. Sounded like a load of excuses to me. Your dad was far more tolerant of Flo than I. Her constant visits grated, when she never had any news. I suspected she was keeping an eye on us, waiting for evidence to trip us up in a lie about your dad's missing hour. As my annoyance showed more and more, Jacob took over dealing with her, to spare my blood pressure.

Nothing was happening, Beth. Everything was in stasis. I wanted to smash down the walls I could feel closing in on me.

CHAPTER 26

Jacob's leg twitched then stilled. He lay slumped on the sofa, mouth slightly open, a gentle snore escaping every now and again. Zonked out in front of the television, bless him, despite it only being 6.30 p.m.

Hardly surprising. That morning, we'd had to get up ridiculously early to set off for home from the hospital, then poor Jacob had had to go straight to work.

Lack of sleep had become a way of life for me in the sixteen days since you were found. I'd gone through the stage where insanity felt likely because of it, and come out the other side. There was no point complaining about feeling permanently shattered, because no one could fix it.

Loath to wake Jacob, but unsure what to do with myself, I thought perhaps a walk was the solution. Wiggins stood at my movement, tail wagging hopefully. I beckoned him over and he let me pop his lead on.

A biting wind froze my cheeks the second we stepped outside. It flew gleefully over the rooftops, using the height to launch itself at me and stab through my clothing. Walking wouldn't be such a good idea after all. Besides, the tiny sliver of new moon hid behind banks of clouds, so the night seemed even darker than usual. I decided to nip over the road to The Poacher instead.

Inside the pub were only a handful of locals; typical for a Monday night. They looked at me briefly, nodded, then looked away. That had been happening to me a lot; since your attack, Beth, no one seemed able to look me directly in the eye. Perhaps they thought bad luck was catching. Perhaps they knew more than they were letting on.

Dale, the owner, scribbled answers on *The Sun*'s crossword. He was so engrossed that I had to clear my throat to get noticed, then realised I hadn't decided what I wanted.

'Umm, a glass of cabernet sauvignon, please.'

That would do.

To distract myself, I gazed around the pub I knew off by heart. Read the poster on the wall telling me to Keep Calm & Carry On. Scanned the old photographs of Fenmere from 1852, 1912, 1950… They all looked pretty much the same, except that the quality of shot improved and the angle changed slightly. There was a slight jump in the number of buildings in the 1984 photograph, when Joe Skendelby had built his place on the land between what was now our house and the general store. It was after his death, four years ago, that Ursula Clarke turned it into her café, the Seagull's Outlook.

My eyes followed the hairline crack that ran across the ceiling, down the wall and, ah, over to something different. A person tucked behind the table in the far corner, well away from the fire. A stranger. Interest flared in me, then disappeared like the glow of a cigarette end. It was probably a birdwatcher.

The stranger looked up.

'Melanie Ludlow?' A deep, quiet voice. 'It is, isn't it. Melanie Ludlow. You've not changed a bit. Don't you recognise me?'

He grinned, which transformed him from a slightly menacing hulk into a face I'd first seen at the village school when we were both four years old. The cheeks were as chubby as ever. He came over.

'Glenn Baker! You haven't changed much, either.' Apart from the tight curls of his hair dulling down from almost white blond to the colour of corn. They had thinned a bit, too.

'You do remember me, then?'

'Well, there weren't many people in the whole school, Glenn. 'Course I remember you. You always used to choose me to play on your football team.'

'Oh, yeah. You were nippy, that's why. Your ball skills were a bit lacking, mind.'

'Can't have been that bad. Seem to remember scoring a few times when I was against you.' Smiling. I was smiling. The second I realised, it slunk away, ashamed.

'Bet you couldn't do it now, though.'

'Probably not.'

If I said nothing else, the conversation would die. But… chatting felt good. Odd, but good. Talking about nonsense with someone who clearly knew nothing about my recent past. He looked me in the eye; no pity, no judgement, or fear that I may be contagious with bad luck. I didn't want to let that go yet.

'What are you doing back here? Visiting someone?'

'Nah. I'm back for good – to quote Gary Barlow.'

'He a hero of yours?' *Get that: banter. My first attempt at it since… Best not to think about that.*

'Oh yeah, Gary's my idol.' Glenn's blue eyes twinkled.

Funny how someone can look so exactly like the child they were, despite being six feet tall and broad. His ruddy, well-scrubbed cheeks added to the good nature that radiated from his round face. Although a little overweight, he looked strong. As he grasped his pint, I noticed his hands: the big, capable kind inherited by so many in an area whose ancestry was generations of farmworkers.

He took a slurp of his drink. 'Yeah, I've rented a place in Wapentake. Moved in the other week. Couldn't get anything here in the village, but hope to soon.'

'Well, it's only nine miles down the road, not the end of the world. But what brings you back after all these years?'

'Took redundancy a while back, spent some money travelling. Now it's time to get back to the real world and… Well, I could have settled anywhere, really, but all that travelling made me yearn for home.'

'And home is here? After all these years?' I tried to think back to the last time I had seen Glenn. Must have been just before I had you, Beth. 'You moved away when you were about, what, nineteen, or something?'

He nodded cautiously, busy with his beer. 'Never looked back. But now Fenmere is calling me. I miss it – no place like it, is there?'

True. Once you were used to Fenmere's open landscape, everything else felt hemmed in or cluttered with buildings and trees.

'I've applied for a job at the furniture company.' Glenn didn't need to say the name; Woodturners is the biggest employer in the immediate area, not counting farming. It's where your dad is a foreman.

'You married?'

'Was. Divorced. Twice. Heading for a third. Can't seem to make 'em stick with me.' His eyes flicked to one side, as though the thought had sparked a memory. Then they were right back on mine again. 'Look, I'm not going to lie… When I came over to chat, it was only because I recognised you from school. It was nice to see a familiar face again. But, well, I've just realised you're Melanie Oak now, not Ludlow, and…'

'And you've remembered the headlines.'

A single nod.

Taking a big slug of my wine made my eyes water. As soon as my vocal chords realised they weren't burned away, I spoke. 'Right. Nice chatting. Got to go.' Each word a bullet of sarcasm.

Wiggins stood, sensing we were leaving.

'I'm sorry for upsetting you, but I didn't want to lie.' Glenn still looked me in the eye. He still spoke to me as if I were human, not something fragile that might break. 'Stay. Have another drink.'

Oh, screw it, I thought. *Why not?*

*

Had I had three drinks, or four? Four. Or was it five? A warm glow wrapped me up, the thermals of which were pushing ajar the door in my mind that I tried to keep shut. The door that held my anger and resentment at bay.

'I don't want to talk about it.' I'd said it a couple of times, but it didn't seem to stop the words from leaking out. Why? Because it wasn't true. I did want to talk about you, Beth – but no one wanted to listen to me. At that moment there was a captive audience, though.

'No one outside family asks me about how Beth is doing now, you know? Because they know what the answer will be. They never ask about how I am; they avoid the subject. Avoid talking to me even.'

'Okay.' Glenn nodded. 'Well, if you do want to talk about it, I'm all ears.'

I cocked my head at him. He spoke softly, so I had to lean close to catch it. It gave even that most innocent of conversations an intimate feel.

'I'm a good listener. We used to be friends once,' he added.

That wasn't quite how I remembered it. As kids at primary school we had sometimes hung around together, and he'd always chosen me for his football team. When we moved up to secondary school in Wapentake we'd had nothing to do with each other, though, not even on the school bus. He had his friends, I had mine. Well, actually, he'd hung around a lot on his own or with his dad. But there had been sidelong glances from Glenn that had made me think he was working up to asking me out. He'd never got the courage, though. And, aged sixteen, I'd started dating your dad.

Whatever we had meant to each other then, I could definitely do with a friend now. Jacob had always been my best friend; I'd never needed anyone else. But now I didn't dare tell him some of the dark thoughts that were growing in my mind. My fears. The fact that I couldn't stand the thought of going to that hospital one more time and looking at you, Beth, knowing there was nothing I could do, no way of helping you…

'Another drink!' I shouted. Slapped my hand on the wooden bar a couple of times, even though Dale was out of his seat and grabbing a glass.

'Mel, keep it calm, eh?' he said.

'Keep your hair on. This place is like a graveyard. Ha, like Beth's hospital room. Ha.'

No one found that funny. Not even me.

I got the sudden urge to run away. Glenn seemed to sense it and patted my shoulder with his paw of a hand. Silence stretched between us as big as the sky outside, but Glenn didn't look away. My lids felt heavy as I blinked.

'It's such a tough time for you, Mel. It must be awful. But you and Jacob are getting through it together, right? You don't mind me asking… ?'

Jacob had been so strong, so amazing. It was hard for me to keep up with him. I felt weak in comparison. Negative.

My bottom lip wobbled pathetically as I shook my head.

'He doesn't want to hear that I imagine myself in Beth's place. That I feel as if, if I think hard enough, make the scene real enough, time will spool back and somehow I will be able to swap places. Better me dead than my daughter.'

I waited for Glenn to correct me. Say my daughter wasn't dead. But in my booze-filled haze, it suddenly seemed so clear that you were. The only thing that was keeping you alive was a machine.

I needed something to distract me.

'Another round, please.' The stool slid to one side beneath me, almost bucking me off, but I managed to recover before anyone noticed.

'You've not finished that one yet,' Glenn pointed out.

Oh. Yeah. 'Course.

'Cheers.' He downed the rest of his pint in one.

I did the same with my wine, and smiled a warm, slow smile that had nothing to do with humour.

'Thing is, Glenn,' I said in a deliberate stage whisper, 'I live in a village where nothing ever happens. Where everyone knows everything about each other. And yet no one knows anything about Beth. No one saw a single thing. Don't you think that's a bit suspicious?'

I held up a finger which seemed to waver in front of me like a candle flame. *Might need to slow down with the drinking*, I thought. Then turned and pointed at a poor unfortunate who happened to be standing closest.

'Ben Miller! I know that you sneak your rubbish into your neighbours' bins, and deny it to their faces.'

I pointed at someone else, who jumped back from my loaded finger. 'Colin Winston, when the village has charity collections or stages fundraisers, you always explain that the reason you don't donate is because you have standing orders for all the charities you wish to support. But your wife, Susan, admitted to me two years ago that that's a lie. You're just a tightwad!'

Glenn laughed and grabbed my weapon, forcing my hand down by my side, still grinning. 'Yep, I get the point.'

'See, we all know everything about each other. Yet no one knows who hurt Beth? I don't buy it!'

He looked at me seriously. 'If you really believe someone here knows something, why not find out the truth yourself?'

I looked at him for long seconds, taking in what he'd said. Made a decision.

'I need a wee.'

I turned and fell flat on my face.

CHAPTER 27

Chloe sat on the edge of Beth's bed, swinging one leg backward and forward, as the pair of them sang along to Taylor Swift. Beth stood suddenly and grabbed her hairbrush to use as a microphone. Chloe snatched up the blue teddy that had always lived on Beth's pillow, but which she'd recently downgraded to sitting on her desk instead. It was childish having him out, it had recently occurred to her, but she couldn't quite stand to put him away yet.

Her best friend started pulling at his arms, up and down, in and out. Making him do a jig.

'Hey, be careful of Jesus. Don't tear him.'

Chloe giggled. 'OMG, Beth, I'd forgotten he was called that. Why the fuck did you call him that anyway?'

She had started swearing a lot lately, though never in front of any parents. She thought it made her look older, tougher. Like she'd thought smoking would make her look more grown-up, until she had vomited after smoking three on the trot while showing off in front of Jason Salter a few months ago. He'd taken pictures and posted them on Instagram and Snapchat. It had taken her a while to live that one down.

Beth thought swearing was kind of pathetic, but kept quiet. She envied Chloe her confidence. Chloe acted as if from the moment she was born she'd known she would conquer the world. Beth was a lot less sure of herself when not in front of those she knew well.

'Earth calling Beth. Anyone there? Why the fuck did you call your teddy Jesus?'

Beth laughed. 'Because as a kid I thought all babies were called Jesus. You know, at Christmas it's always "the baby Jesus" that we're told about. This was my baby, so there was only one name for him.'

'Baby Jesus. Like, that's so hilarious!'

Chloe put the teddy back, then leapt onto the bed and rolled onto her stomach, legs waving in the air.

'So, how buff is Aleksy? He keeps sitting near us, have you noticed?'

Her eyes twinkled with mischief, but Beth refused to get drawn on that subject. No way.

'Ooh! Love this song,' she said instead, as Justin Bieber came on. They sang along, both giggling at the line about loving yourself.

At the end, Chloe sighed. 'So, you'll never guess what Mum's up to now. She's, like, so embarrassing.'

Beth's stomach dropped. This was it. Chloe would reveal she knew what Beth had already discovered. The secret would be out.

What Chloe told Beth stunned her even more. Because the revelation was nothing of the sort – it was simply that Ursula was looking into having a facelift.

'The Botox clearly isn't enough any more,' Chloe added, her eyebrows arched cattily.

Her best friend shook her head in despair and laughed.

'Pinkie-swear you won't tell anyone, though. It's meant to be a big secret. Like, maybe she'll tell people Dad beats her or something when they see her with bruises.' She cackled as she held out her crooked little finger.

'Pinkie-swear I'll stay quiet.'

Chloe knew Beth would keep her word. They had always kept one another's secrets, always told each other everything and trusted one another completely.

Always, until now.

Somehow Beth didn't feel comfortable telling Chloe about what she had been doing lately. She preferred to keep it her little secret. Just for the time being.

The secrets were stacking up, though, Beth worried as she gnawed on her thumb. Hers and the ones she held for other people. Sometimes she felt tempted to break her word and confide in someone.

She would wait until she was certain, though.

CHAPTER 28

My face pushed into the pillow. Couldn't breathe. Legs kicking, body bucking, fighting until…

Yes! I was free!

I rolled over on the mattress, panting after my exhaustive fight with the duvet. My head pounded; my mouth was full of fuzz and it hurt my throat to swallow, thanks to a raging thirst. Even my teeth felt weird. Best not to think about my stomach.

I closed my eyes and drifted back to sleep.

Waking the second time, I persuaded myself to sit up in the empty bed. Huh, Jacob must have got up for work without waking me. He must have put me to bed the night before; I certainly didn't remember doing it.

A memory burst through the darkness of alcohol amnesia. Me, pounding on the front door, demanding to be let in because the key refused to go into the lock.

I winced and swung my legs to the ground, my need for water winning over the weakness of the hangover. I still wore yesterday's clothes. With every wobbly step, guilt pounded through me. But why?

Another memory firework exploded. My finger, pointing at everyone. Falling over. Eurgh, then my voice, screaming, having a go at pretty much everyone in the pub and finding them all guilty of a cover-up of your attack, Beth. Shame fired my skin. These people were my friends, and I'd lost it with them. Hopefully they understood the strain I was under.

What else?

Heck, Glenn Baker carrying me out of the pub, then setting me down on the church wall opposite our house and talking to me. What had he said?

I veered towards the bathroom, stomach roiling. As I used the loo, another incendiary memory exploded.

If you really believe someone here knows something, why not find out the truth yourself?

Glenn had repeated that while propping me up on the church wall.

Why not find out for yourself?

My dismissive grunt echoed slightly in the bathroom. But… actually, it wasn't such a bad idea. I couldn't do a worse job than the police, that was for sure.

Find out the truth, Glenn had urged. *I'll help you.*

Shaky hands flushed the loo. Could I?

Lost in contemplation, I made my way downstairs and said good morning to Wiggins, who replied with copious licks on my hand. On the kitchen table stood a glass of juice, which had left a ring on the note it rested on.

Hey you,

Hope you're okay. Look after yourself! Drink plenty of OJ and eat a decent meal. I've gone to work. Hope you'll be well enough to come to the hospital tonight.

Love you!

Jxx

I drank the orange but couldn't face food yet. Instead, I filled up a reusable filter bottle with water and took Wiggins for a walk to blow away the cobwebs.

*

We ignored all the old places we used to go, and Wiggins knew now that there was only one place we'd be headed. The marsh. Haunting it was my guilty secret; Jacob had no idea. Instinctively I knew he wouldn't approve.

He wouldn't approve of Glenn's words, either, rolling around my head, gathering momentum as we trudged across the endless, recumbent landscape.

Find out the truth.

Jacob trusted the police to do their job. Or maybe he preferred the investigation to stall? *That missing hour. The police's insistence his reaction was distancing and depersonalising.* No, that wasn't fair. Jacob simply questioned everything less than I did. He had blind faith in the authorities. I was losing faith in them.

As I walked, the haunting *pe-pee-whit* call of lapwings in flight pierced my thoughts occasionally, or the gabbling of brent geese feeding on the coarse grass, their white rumps bright against their neat, dark grey bodies and black heads.

By the time Wiggins and I returned home, three hours later, my stomach was growling like a rabid dog. Stupid of me to walk so far on an empty stomach and hung-over. Wiggins had a drink then stepped into his basket, turned round three times and lay down with a contented sigh, glad to be home and out of the wind. He was too exhausted even to bother watching me as I made a peanut butter sandwich with shaky hands. I wolfed it down, along with a handful of Brazil nuts and a banana, disgusted with myself for needing to eat when you were being fed through a tube.

My body insisted on more food, though. I sipped a hot chocolate that both warmed me and filled me up, while Wiggins twisted onto his back and made little noises in his sleep, his legs twitching as he raced through a dream world.

No chance of rest for me. Glenn's words haunted me. I needed to see him again, check if he had meant what he'd said.

I headed upstairs and got changed. Nothing special; still jeans, but clean ones, and the blue-grey jumper you always liked. The one you said matched my eyes exactly, remember? It was size 14 and didn't fit as nicely as it used to, the shoulder seam hanging low down my arm because of my weight loss. The result was baggy and disappointing.

Silly, but there was no denying the drive to make a good impression on Glenn. If I wanted him to help me, I needed him to know I was together and sane, not the drunken slob I'd been the night before, sobbing like a child going through the terrible twos. I brushed my dark blonde hair, pulling it into a neat ponytail that had no stray hairs escaping from it. I even dug out some mascara from the bottom of my drawer and put it on. My eyes looked strangely large, dominating my pinched face. My naturally pale skin – the kind that never tans, just goes red then white again – was a blotchy grey. In desperation, I furiously scrubbed a blusher brush over my cheeks.

Great, now I looked feverish.

This was daft. What could I discover that the police hadn't? I decided to give Flo a call, see if there was an update.

'We're pursuing several—'

'Lines of enquiry. But, let me guess, you can't say any more than that at the present time?'

'I'm sorry.'

'Not as sorry as me,' I finished, hanging up.

That decided me once and for all.

Trembling, I walked over the crossroads, past the church and into The Poacher. There were a handful of customers inside already, and a group playing darts. The sound of the darts thudding into the board was strangely comforting. As I'd hoped, Glenn was leaning on the bar, but he didn't see me.

Dale spoke up.

'Melanie, look, we all know you've been through a lot. But I'm sorry, you're barred.'

I clenched my jaw, biting back the anger instantly surging because he couldn't bring himself to say what I'd been through, or ask how you were doing. Instead I made myself speak calmly, unlike my display the previous night.

'I've come here to apologise.'

Glenn turned to look at me.

Please be impressed with my humility.

'Mate, last night was my fault,' he said, putting his hand on his heart. 'It was me who kept buying Mel drinks, and asking her about what happened to Beth.'

He said your name as if it were the most natural thing in the world. I silently thanked him for that. No one else did any more, as though you had become a curse, like Macbeth.

'Come on. Blame it on the stupid newcomer. Don't blame Mel.'

Dale hesitated. Then the tension in his face and shoulders slid away. It was obvious he'd relented before he said the words.

'Go on, then. One more chance.'

Glenn held out his paw and the men shook on it.

'Stupid newcomer,' repeated Dale, laughing. Clapped Glenn on the back. 'Like our dads weren't best mates.'

That was the thing about Fenmere: we all knew each other, our families woven together for generations. Friendships forged through grandfathers working side by side, or enemies made because a great-grandfather cheated someone out of land. Our battle lines and alliances drawn up before we were born. All the villagers were my family.

Jacob and I weren't like that. Our families shared no history. He had moved to Wapentake, along with his elder brother and younger sister, from Leeds when he was fourteen. The fresh blood had caused quite a stir at school when he arrived, and all the girls had fancied him. He had gone through them like a hot knife through butter, dating them then casting them aside, no one lasting longer than a couple of months. When he'd asked me out, I had turned him down, not because I didn't fancy him but because I didn't trust him. So he had stopped asking and instead become my friend.

Later, he'd admitted that, while friendship was great, he had always hoped it would turn into more. He'd confessed on our first date, just a handful of days before I turned seventeen.

After that we'd been inseparable, our friendship the foundation that made us solid enough to last through anything. Even this.

Glenn waved a hand in front of my face to regain my attention.

'Drink?' I asked. 'I'm having an orange juice.'

'Yeah, the same.'

'What about you, Dale?'

He poured himself a pint, then wandered back to his stool and the day's crossword.

My stomach fluttered as I took a seat beside Glenn, and it had nothing to do with the final remnants of hangover. Well, not much, anyway.

'So, umm, sorry about last night…'

He held his hands up. 'Don't worry about it. Enough said.'

My mouth quirked up at the ends into a small smile. 'I've been thinking about what you said last night.'

'Surprised you can remember.'

'Yes… Did you mean it? About helping me find out what happened to Beth?'

He took a long sip of orange juice. Clearly buying time, trying to think of a way of letting me down that wouldn't turn me into the gibbering, tearful loony I had been the night before. I picked at the skin on the side of my thumb, bracing myself for the inevitable.

'Of course I'll help you. Not sure how, though.'

The relief!

'Just listen to me as I work through my mad theories,' I gushed. 'Two heads are better than one, and all that.'

Finally I'd found myself a purpose. After weeks of drifting helplessly, I grabbed onto the idea like a drowning woman clinging to flotsam. The tide was turning.

Even better, I had an ally in my plan to turn detective. Someone to listen to me, who I didn't have to be fearful of hurting, like I did with Jacob. Besides, Jacob had far too much to juggle with work and worrying about you. Glenn wasn't a stranger from out of the blue who had offered to help; he was a villager, someone I'd grown up with, but who, crucially, hadn't been around when you were attacked, so I could absolutely trust him.

'Where do we start?' he asked.

I studied him, trying to find doubt, or worse, amusement. He leaned forward, elbows on the small round wooden table, clearly keen to get on with the task. His pale blue eyes searched mine, as if testing my own resolve, and his strong, surprisingly dark eyebrows drew together in concentration.

'Umm, I don't know.' I blinked, trying to gather my thoughts.

'Did you find any clues in her room?'

'Oh, well, umm, I haven't. I can't face going in there for longer than a couple of seconds. And searching through her things feels like a huge betrayal of trust.'

'But it's the most obvious place to start,' Glenn said slowly. He looked stunned.

'I just can't, okay?' The room felt dead, like you looked dead when I visited you in hospital.

We stared at our glasses of orange juice as if somehow they would provide divine inspiration. This wasn't the most auspicious start to our detective work.

Suddenly Glenn sat upright, clicked his fingers. 'Got it! Scene of the crime.'

'What?'

'Yeah, it's perfect. We'll go to the scene of the crime. We don't know where to start or who to investigate, so let's look at where it happened.'

Downing our drinks, we hurried outside. Jumped into his white van, covered in mud splashes, and we were off. I felt hope for the first time in a while.

CHAPTER 29

Glenn glanced at me as he took the turning for the marsh. Through the driver's side window, a flock of redwing could be seen taking flight from the field. Their russet flashes showed clearly as they banked.

'Are you definitely all right with going there? Only it's suddenly occurred to me it's probably not a great idea… bit upsetting for you, and all that.'

I shook my head. No need for thought or doubt. 'I go there all the time. I know it sounds crazy, but it's the only place I feel close to Beth.'

He changed gear while nodding as though he understood. 'I s'pose so, but wouldn't you feel closer talking to her at the hospital? Or being at the house, surrounded by her things?'

'You'd think, wouldn't you? But it's…' I tried to choose the right words to explain. 'When I look at her, in the hospital bed, all I feel is bitterness. I want to shake her awake. I feel furious with her and everyone and everything. She just lies there! I'm terrified I'll never hear her voice again.

'When I'm in her bedroom it's like it's frozen in time, like her. It's not full of life, it's full of dust. Full of the slowly fading scent of her perfume. There's no life there. No meaning to it. That is not where she is.

'But I go to the marsh and, I don't know, it's quite an eerie, atmospheric place. I go there and can feel her. Yeah, it's where something dreadful happened to her, but it's also where she's been really happy. We used to go down there and spend hours together watching the birds, and she'd bang on about identifying an animal from a dropping we'd found. And you know, she'd be able to tell all sorts about it, how fresh it was, what the animal had eaten… just from a bit of poo.'

Glenn didn't say a word, but he listened intently. Encouraged, my words tumbled out.

'Half the time I didn't take it in, to be honest, but it was lovely to see her face. She glowed with enthusiasm, you know? She lit up from the inside. She was so passionate about nature that her whole body language changed when she spoke about it. It filled her up; she'd stand straighter and her head was lifted and her hands would gesticulate with larger movements, you know? To see that, to see what nature could do for her was incredible. So that's partly it.'

The words all came out in a rush, Beth. It was so lovely to talk about you as a girl full of life, rather than lying in a hospital bed. I couldn't speak to Jacob or anyone else in the family this way; they'd get too upset. Besides, we were always too busy talking about medical care, prognosis, medication…

Glenn nodded. 'Yeah, I kind of know what you mean about the marsh. I used to come with my dad sometimes. We loved the wildlife here. It's a place that's kind of empty but full of life, isn't it?'

'That's exactly it. Exactly!' Just like Beth, I sat up straighter, hands gesticulating. 'It's a place of bonding. And it feels isolated, but actually it's really, really full of life.'

Someone else got it the way we did, Beth! Time to take a chance. Before speaking, I studied him, keen to gauge his reaction to my confession.

'Thing is, Glenn, it's like I said, in hospital and at home everything feels devoid of life and I don't feel close to Beth at all. But out on the marsh, she's truly alive, still. She's on the wind; she's in the blades of grass; she's speeding through that great big sky with the birds, free. Sometimes I can almost feel her, almost hear her. If I can only concentrate hard enough I'll connect with her again; we'll find each other. That's where I'll find my Beth. That's where I'll get her back.'

Instead of answering, he shuffled forward in his seat to hunch over the steering wheel and beeped his horn twice, because we were about to go over the sudden rise in the lane. Everyone always honked their horn there, to let anyone on the other side know they were coming and avoid a crash on the single lane. As we crested the rise, the air freshener hanging from the rear-view mirror swung crazily from side to side, filling the van cab with faux pine freshness. I stared at Glenn. The slightest frown played on his face as he considered what I'd said.

He thought I was nuts, Beth. I'd taken a leap of faith sharing such a ridiculously intimate thought with him and fallen flat on my face.

'I think I know what you mean,' he said, finally, eyes still ahead. 'My mum used to be into all this spiritual stuff; you know, mediums and all that. Ghosts. Before she died.'

He pulled over, switched off the engine and turned to me. 'You know the sort I mean?'

I told him I did.

'Well, I'm not sure I believe in ghosts and stuff, but I think I sort of believe in energy, you know? When something happens, a lot of energy, maybe positive or negative, goes out into the world. And maybe stays there. What you're picking up is not so much Beth's spirit but more the force of what happened to her, all that good and bad energy, and that's why you feel closer to her here.'

'Maybe. Makes as much sense as anything.'

We both gave sad laughs. Sighed. Glenn rubbed his hands together and gestured across the windscreen. Before us lay the marsh, currently half-covered by the high tide, the calm, shallow sea scintillating every time the sun broke through the clouds. Faced with that, I understood perfectly why you loved it there so much.

'Ready?'

'Definitely.'

As I got out and turned to close the door, I realised I'd been sitting on his coat the entire time. 'Sorry,' I winced. 'Didn't notice it. It's all crumpled now.'

'Don't worry about it. I barely wear it anyway.'

I raised an eyebrow.

'I'm tough,' he joked.

True to his word, he carried the parka despite there being no warmth to the weak February sun. Personally, I was glad of my hat and gloves, let alone my thermal coat. Once again I was struck by how cold you must have been, Beth. Your coat had never been discovered, or your rucksack.

*

After twenty minutes we had walked to the place where you were found.

'Beth was dressed up, like she was going to meet someone,' I said, explaining how the police had shown us an outfit totally unlike the one you had left the house in. 'Police believe she was attacked here, then dragged into the mere and thrown in. As if she was nothing,' I explained. My stomach twisted like a rag being wrung out.

Despite everything, despite the fact that I thought I'd been over this so many times in my head that there were no feelings left; despite the fact that I thought I was hardened to everything now, a couple of tears escaped. I sniffed, but couldn't be bothered to wipe them away. But as I carried on talking I forced myself to stick to the facts and be businesslike.

'Whoever did it must have thought she would sink. They didn't weigh her down or anything. So she floated in the pond, face up, in her little outfit. I thought hypothermia would have killed her, but it was the freezing temperatures that saved her. Which is ironic, really, because she's always hated being cold.'

'The cold saved her?'

'Mmm. Apparently it's best to keep head injuries very cold as it lessens the damage done. Even in hospital, after her operation, Beth was kept under a special blanket that looked like a Li-lo on top of her – it had freezing air blown into it to keep her temperature down. Not that it seems to have helped.'

I turned away, unable to look any more, only to be confronted with the little shrine by the sycamore. The blue and white crime scene tape had been removed, and there were ribbons tied to the tree. They waved in the wind, defiantly bright against the muted tones of the land. Looking at them, hope replaced my despair: they were a symbol that you would overcome your injuries.

My little girl would get better. *You are a fighter*, I thought.

Glenn read the messages from friends and neighbours. Like the amateur sleuths we were, we searched around for dropped clues the police might have missed.

'I thought there might be some footprints we could follow,' Glenn shrugged apologetically, looking down at the mired trail of tracks from well-wishers, police and goodness knows who else. It was completely futile. I'd been kidding myself, thinking I could do a better job than the official investigation.

The cold made the pair of us sniff, our noses bright red. We turned and made our way back, while I filled Glenn in on the terrible moment I had first realised you were missing. The cold almost took my breath away, though, and Glenn even put his coat on. It was a blessed relief to jump back into the van.

*

Immediately, Glenn turned the ignition key and put the heater on full blast. The warmth made my fingers tingle almost painfully.

He began rooting through the door's side pocket.

'I've a pen and notebook in here. We should write everything down.'

I gave him a grim smile. 'You actually, genuinely want to do this? Find my daughter's attacker?'

'Well, yeah.' He looked down, embarrassed. 'If you don't want to, it's fine. I only want to help. It's awful – obviously – what's happened. There's not much I can do, but I'm quite good at solving puzzles.'

'Yeah, I remember you with that Rubik's Cube,' I said, taking the mickey. He had pulled off all the stickers in frustration and stuck them back on, insisting to anyone who would listen at school that he had solved it.

He pulled a face. 'I can certainly give this my best shot.'

Reaching out, he touched my hand. Squeezed it. I muttered a 'thank you', then pulled my hand away to crack open the steamed-up windows.

Finding a pen, Glenn opened a bright pink Moleskine notebook. Not the sort of thing I'd have thought he'd buy at all, given he lived in scruffy workmen's clothes, but each to their own.

The inside of the van was neater than expected too. No discarded food wrappers, very little mud – unlike the outside. The dashboard sparkled because it had recently been cleaned. It was clearly an old van, but well-loved; the gearstick so worn the numbers on it could barely be made out, and the steering wheel smoothed from hands constantly running over it.

'What have we learned from visiting the scene?' Glenn asked. 'Nothing?'

'No, come on, we've got to have learned something.' As he thought, his mouth formed a half-smile. 'Why was she on the marsh, dressed up? It's cold, it's muddy, it's bloody windy.'

As he spoke, he wrote those exact words in his little book.

'Well, right after the attack I spoke with Chloe. She said Aleksy had a crush on her.'

Glenn noted down the name, after I'd spelled Jachowski for him.

'So he fancies her… How well does Beth know this Aleksy?'

I shrugged. 'They get the same school bus. He's in his final year at Wapentake Secondary, doing his A levels, so they don't have much opportunity to socialise apart from the bus. Chloe told me they had been chatting on there sometimes, but that seems to be the full extent of his flirtation.'

'To have lured Beth to the marsh, it's got to have been somebody she knew, and knew well. Unless she was abducted and driven here from somewhere else.'

'I think her being picked up in the village and driven here is likeliest. Our FLO – Family Liaison Officer the police have given us – has told me there's no evidence of her getting the bus into Wapentake. No CCTV of her in the town, either.'

We went over the same ground I'd quizzed Chloe about. I couldn't think of anyone you fancied. But then, you clearly hadn't told me everything about your life, judging from the fact you had lied to me about where you were going the night you were attacked.

'What about hobbies? Could she have met someone through anything she did?'

'Beth didn't have much spare time. She was always busy with homework, or with Chloe, or with us as a family. She was into nature, so she and I would often come to the marsh – Jacob too. That was it. Oh, apart from guitar lessons with Mr Harvey.' A wave of despair crashed over me. 'Aleksy is looking like a stronger and stronger contender, isn't he? He's only a kid himself, though; surely he couldn't have done it?'

'What about the guitar tutor?'

'James Harvey? He's a nice bloke. In his early twenties. Twenty-four, I think.'

'Not that much of an age difference, then,' observed Glenn. There was excitement in his voice.

'Ten years! The police looked into him, anyway. He has a watertight alibi – he was with Alison Daughtrey-Drew on a date.'

'Blimey, the Daughtrey-Drews. There's a name I haven't heard for a good few years.'

Everyone knew the family. The Daughtrey-Drews were the area's equivalent of landed gentry.

'So, that James Harvey and the Daughtrey-Drew girl were on a date?'

'Think it was more of a one-off than a date, from what I hear.'

Glenn grunted in surprise. 'Really?'

'Alison isn't much like her parents – but not many twenty-year-olds are.' I smiled, despite myself. 'She's a bit of a tearaway. Last year she got pulled over by the police for speeding, and I heard that her parents had a word with some pal in the police force. As a result, she got off. They're always having to get her out of one scrape or another. But rumour has it she got chucked out of university a few months ago, and her parents are so furious that they're refusing to give her any money until she's got a job.'

Glenn gave a rich, deep chuckle. 'Bet they're embarrassed by that.'

'Just a bit. I think sleeping around is the least of Alison's troubles. Though I've always found her decent enough when I've spoken with her, even if she is a bit of a spoiled only child.'

'And that means James Harvey has an alibi.' Glenn crossed the name out on the page.

'Everyone has an alibi,' I said. 'Everyone in the entire village, according to our Family Liaison Officer.'

He frowned, clearly wanting me to explain further, but there was nothing else to say. 'Anyway, what about other men?'

'Beth's fourteen, Glenn. She doesn't have much to do with men.'

The silence became uncomfortable as it stretched out. He scratched his fingers through his blond curls. Cleared his throat, shifting in his seat.

'Okay, who found Beth? Was it the police, or someone else? Because that can be suspicious, can't it? There have been murders where the person who discovers the body is the one who did the deed.'

'It was Davy Young. He's not capable of harming a fly. And besides, he was with his mum the night Beth was injured.' The indomitable Jill Young would never lie to the police. Even the way she stood was trustworthy; it reminded me of that famous painting of Henry VIII, legs akimbo. She was solid, reliable, unmovable.

Still, Glenn was right – it was worth having a chat with Davy. Although I'd heard from my brother and Dad about the scene when you were found, it would be good to hear it from the horse's mouth.

I always felt a bit sorry for Davy. He wasn't necessarily the sharpest knife in the drawer, but all his life he had tried to play catch-up with his older brothers, who loved nothing better than telling embarrassing tales of him as a kid. He was dismissed by everyone as being a bit dim. It must have been particularly awful proving people right when his farm had failed and he'd ended up having to move back in with his mum again at the grand old age of thirty-nine. He was a lovely bloke, though, and I'd no doubt he'd be keen to help me get to the bottom of who had hurt you.

With that thought, I looked at my watch. Gasped. 'I've got to get back; Jacob will be home in half an hour! We're going straight to the hospital for the night. Umm, I don't want him to know what I'm doing. You don't mind keeping this secret, do you?'

''Course not.'

'Are you around tomorrow, or are you job-hunting?' I asked, hesitant but keen to get on, now we had made a start.

'I can be around if you want me to be.'

He smiled, and although I felt guilty for taking up his time, I also felt better because I was doing something useful at last. Something so much better than sitting by your side, watching you, helpless. I would get you justice so that when you woke you would know you were safe. I'd protect you, Beth.

Despite knowing there was nothing wrong and everything right with what we were doing, I got Glenn to drop me off at the top of the lane and walked home. Already I knew I wouldn't share any of this with Jacob. He had enough on his plate juggling work, our fears for your long-term health and money being tight now he was the only breadwinner. Best to keep quiet until I could tell him everything.

The secret was for the greater good, Beth. You understood that, didn't you?

CHAPTER 30

Death was a constant fascination for me. Even as a kid, I thought it the most beautiful thing in the world. I used to enjoy setting traps and seeing what I'd caught. I liked to watch the delicate birds flapping helplessly. The panic in their tiny, beady eyes right up until the point of death. If they froze and accepted their fate it was always a disappointment.

Best were the animals. Watching them pit their strength against my trap, trying and failing, striving for freedom and always falling short. I was a god, with power over their lives.

Seeing them twisting and pulling at the wire, it biting into their skin as they became more and more desperate; it did something for me that nothing else could. I felt truly alive in those moments. Sometimes they even chewed their own leg off. Seeing that took my breath away, and I'd laugh at their audacity.

Whatever they did, they never got away. Where would the fun have been in that?

People are just the same, I've discovered. When they are backed into a corner, fighting for their lives, some will snap and snarl. Others panic and lose themselves to fear, bowels opening, mouths screaming. Adults hold little appeal for me, though, with their dull, grey lives.

No, I have more refined taste.

I steal the most protected and precious things on this planet. Children. They are the little treasures of our world, and I am the god who can pilfer them from under their parents' noses. I've done it before; I'll do it again.

I am killing innocence. I am slaughtering purity. I am butchering potential.

There is no more powerful feeling than that.

CHAPTER 31

Jacob and I sat side by side. You lay on your hospital bed. I traced the pale blue veins of your eyelids. I listened to the machine breathing for you. I talked about a future with you, me and your dad that felt like a fairy tale. I went quietly mad with grief.

As arranged, Glenn and I met up outside the Picky Person's Pop In at 9.30 a.m. the next morning, on Wednesday, after Jacob had gone to work. He leaned against the low windowsill of the single-storey, cottage-style building, making some comment to the youngest Jachowski, Roza, about her bike. I waved, and he pushed himself off the sill, sauntering over to me, hands in his parka. Roza sped off, stick-thin legs pumping at the pedals, so that she soon reached the school on the other side of the road.

'She's late,' I observed.

'She had a dentist's appointment, apparently. Anyway, I was just finding out about her brother,' Glenn said.

He bent down and petted Wiggins, who leaned his head into my friend's hand to ensure his ear got a really good rub.

Guilt at using a seven-year-old child warred with curiosity. 'Anything interesting?'

A shrugged reply. 'Not particularly. Only that he likes to read her bedtime stories about princesses.'

Aleksy sounded like a good lad. My heart sank. At that moment, someone emerged from round the back of the shop.

'Davy! Hi, how are you?' I sounded so fake.

He gave me a strange, sidelong look. 'All right, Mel? How's, er, how's…'

'No change.' I was used to getting that reaction from people, but today I needed to put him at ease. So I made the effort to smile back, trying to make sure it reached my eyes, not just tug my mouth into a weird grimace. Smiling didn't come easy these days.

'You remember Glenn Baker, don't you?' Introductions proved the perfect icebreaker.

'Good to have people coming back to the village instead of leaving it,' Davy beamed. 'What brings you back here?'

His tiny little nose bobbled up and down as he talked with Glenn. It looked like a small new potato glued to his face, and had earned him the nickname Spud when he was younger. Not that it stopped him attracting women these days. He was all bulging biceps and six-pack. As a consequence, my private nickname for him was 'paper bag man' – put a paper bag over his head and he was gorgeous.

Davy was a good bloke, though. Not the brightest in the world, sadly. That was probably the reason why his own Brussels sprout smallholding had failed, and he was now reduced to working on the farm owned by his three elder brothers, Martin, Jon and Peter, who had pooled their resources to buy land.

As the pleasantries between he and Glenn petered out, I struck. 'I, uh, wondered if I could have a word, actually, Davy. About Beth.'

Instantly his open expression closed down.

'Melanie… I don't want to talk about it. It were upsetting.'

I touched his arm. 'Please, Davy, for me. For Beth.'

Shameless manipulation, but also true. A slow nod of the head conceded his defeat.

'Look, let's go to the café. We can sit comfortably there.'

'No, I don't really have time for that. What do you want to know?' As he talked, he shuffled a few steps away so we were no longer in front of the store's door.

'Well, how did you find Beth?'

He poked an index finger in his ear and wiggled it, thinking. 'There were a line of us. We were all just walking along, like the police had shown us. We'd all got our eyes down to the ground, looking for anything she might have dropped. I'd, er, I'd got a bit ahead of the line, and looked up and there she were. Floating, face up, in the water.'

'So there were lots of you there?'

He nodded furiously. 'Yeah, yeah, loads of us. The police were there too.'

He sounded so defensive, and I felt a stab of pity for him. Poor bloke had nothing to feel bad about.

'It's okay, I'm not accusing you of anything. I just, I don't know, I wondered if maybe you had seen something, or spotted any of the searchers looking shifty. Anything that might help us get Beth's attacker.'

'Mel, honest, I saw nothing.'

'Why were you ahead of the line?' asked Glenn.

'Dunno, just was,' Davy shrugged. He rolled his thumb and index finger together as he spoke. 'I didn't do nothing.'

'What's going on?'

We all jumped guiltily at this new voice. There stood Jill, her expression unreadable.

'We were chatting about when Davy found Beth,' I explained.

'He's told the police all he knows, Melanie. Going over and over it won't change things.'

She stood with her arms folded over her forest-green pinafore, her stance set in the powerful Henry VIII pose. Her mouth was as flat as usual, her eyes as steely and determined, though softened with pity. But her voice was faster than normal. I looked from her to her son and realised – they were worried, Beth. Twitchy. They knew something.

'Your brother and dad were there. They saw her with their own eyes,' added Davy.

He was right. Of course he was right. I was letting my imagination play tricks on me, desperate to get to the bottom of things.

But, judging from the slight frown, the angle of his head, Glenn was having the same thought as me.

Jill stepped back towards the door. 'Well, if you're done, Davy, there's some stock needs shifting. The boxes are too heavy for me.'

'Yes, Mum,' he said, dutifully.

It was only a few steps before they disappeared back inside. But in that time Davy had thrown a look over his shoulder that convinced me we needed to speak to him again. It would have to be without Jill, though. No mean feat, given that he lived with his mum – a woman who exerted a powerful hold not just over her sons, but over the entire village, thanks to her network of extended family. There was nothing that happened in the village that Jill didn't know about. Not usually, anyway…

CHAPTER 32

BETH
FRIDAY 22 JANUARY

Beth ran from SSG. Ran from the look in his eyes that made her stomach twist. She had thought she was being so grown-up; had congratulated herself at the way she was handling things. She was a keeper of secrets. She was going up in people's estimation, where before she had been invisible, too young to consider.

But she had just been playing at being a grown-up. She was no better than a little kid giving pretend tea parties. She was so out of her depth in this adult world.

She wanted to be back on the bus, chatting innocently with her best friend. She wanted to be home with Mum and Dad and Wiggins. She just wanted to be safe, in a world that had suddenly become very dangerous.

So she ran from SSG. Ran into the darkness.

CHAPTER 33

The sky was a uniform dove grey. Glenn, Wiggins and I had come to the marsh because it was easier to talk there than at the pub, but I felt antsy. For all the sky was vast, it felt claustrophobic, the air uncharacteristically still as we stood beside the van gathering our thoughts.

I yanked at my scarf impatiently, feeling stifled. Opened the passenger door and threw it onto Glenn's crumpled coat, which was chucked on the passenger seat as usual. Then I slammed the door shut again and leaned against it with a huff.

'That was weird, right? Tell me it's not my imagination.'

'Davy and Jill definitely seemed to be hiding something.'

'She's always been more protective of him than the others, but—'

''Cos he's thick like his dad.'

I nodded; it was cruel, but it was true. Jill had famously been the brains of her marriage. Everyone knew the store owner's life story – it was too juicy ever to die away. Villagers had apparently been scandalised when sixteen-year-old Jill, the daughter of an alcoholic prostitute on Wapentake docks, had married a forty-five-year-old pig farmer. After ten years of marriage, Bill Young had keeled over from a massive heart attack. Jill had been pregnant with Davy at the time, and had three boys under the age of ten to look after. But that hadn't slowed her; she'd sold the tiny farm and sunk the money into the Picky Person's Pop In. To be honest, Beth, I'd always admired her tenacity and business brain – but Davy definitely hadn't inherited those traits.

Glenn slipped his notebook out of his pocket and made a quick record of what had happened.

'What possessed you to buy a pink pad? It doesn't seem very you,' I snapped.

My gesture took in the van, which, thanks to mud and general road grime, looked more brown than white. It had a large penis drawn on the back by some comedian, along with the words: *I wish my girlfriend was this dirty.* Then I took a glance at Glenn himself. Big brown workmen's boots, dark jeans that were slightly tatty around the hem, a plain, dark blue sweatshirt with the cuff fraying lightly at the right wrist. Even the parka he barely ever wore was only just on the right side of grubby.

A myriad emotions flitted across Glenn's face. His small eyes flashed with hurt as he shrank away from me slightly. Instantly I regretted my words. I had overstepped the mark, taking my mood out on him.

A second later he turned to me again, his round face as open as ever. He gave a heartfelt sigh.

'Might as well tell you the truth. It's my daughter's notebook.'

'You have a daughter? But… why have you never mentioned her?'

He shrugged an apology. 'It's complicated. Her mum and me, we didn't exactly split amicably. Her mum – well, she uses my girl as a weapon against me. Basically, she's banned me from seeing her.'

Fury raced through me. How dare someone use their child like that? Glenn had a healthy daughter who he could talk to, spend time with, make new memories with. Things I was desperate to do with you, Beth, but couldn't. No one had the right to deprive a parent of their child.

'Why the hell did she do that?'

'Because she can, because she's a vindictive—' He bit off the retort and shrugged again. 'It's Marcie's way. She's spiteful, and she knows that the best way of hurting me is to keep me from my daughter.'

'What's her name?'

He was so upset that for a moment he couldn't speak. He swallowed hard. 'Katie. Her name is Katie. She's twelve.'

'Oh, Glenn, why didn't you say something? You've listened so patiently to my troubles.'

'Yeah, but what I'm going through is nothing compared to your situation. And it's one of the reasons why I'm helping you. If anyone hurt my daughter, I wouldn't be responsible for my actions.'

I felt dreadful for him, especially as I'd never asked him much about his life. I reached out and rubbed his arm, consoling.

'Tell me about her.' My words were gentle.

'I don't really want to talk about it. It hurts too much.' Glenn stepped away, as if distancing himself from his pain. 'Maybe I'll tell you everything one day, Melanie.'

For his sake, I changed the subject; started yattering about shared childhood memories and what people had been up to while he'd been away. Soon, any tension had disappeared.

'To be honest, not many people have moved away. It's not terribly adventurous of us, is it?'

'You been abroad much?'

I shook my head. 'Nowhere more far-flung than Spain; the usual holiday destinations. We prefer to stay in this country, especially since we got Wiggins.'

The russet dog looked up at the sound of his name and wagged his tail, before being distracted by a scent trail and hurrying off busily into the long grasses.

'I've been to a few places. Australia, Thailand, Borneo.'

'Really? Wow, you make me look so parochial.'

He swelled at the compliment. 'Yeah, when I split with Marcie in September I went to Australia for a month. It was good to get away. You should go some time.'

I raised an eyebrow and he blushed, clearly realising the mistake he'd made. No holidays for me until you woke up.

*

We walked past the stunted, twisted sycamore that marked your shrine, and the pond where you had floated. On we continued, towards the only other blip on the horizon: an old armed forces lookout tower, completely dwarfed by its vast surroundings. Anywhere else, the 1970s building would have looked massive and impressive, despite starting to look a little the worse for wear in places, having been battered for decades by the unforgiving wind.

'Do the RAF still own the building?' asked Glenn.

'No, they sold it. It's owned by Jill Young, actually,' I added after laughing at Wiggins. He had been jumping through the undergrowth of the marsh beside the firmer path, and looked as if he had springs for legs. I gave him a cuddle as he came back over to me, panting, then darted off again, nose down, tail up.

'Why the hell did she buy this place?'

'Reckon she'd watched one too many episodes of *Grand Designs* and thought she could do it up and make a killing. She bought it back in 2005, immediately before the credit crunch. As far as I know, she's done nothing with it since. Must be a bit of a millstone around her neck, really.'

'Serves her right for being greedy,' Glenn sniffed. 'Why doesn't she sell it? She might not make a killing now, but she'd get her money back, surely?'

'Well,' I leaned closer, simply gossiping now. And loving it. 'She tried to sell it at auction—'

'Probably hoping to get a sucker from down south to pay an overinflated price.'

'Exactly. And because it's such an unusual building the sale even got some national press mentions... but no bid met the reserve price, so that was that.'

Glenn huffed. Looked up, craning his neck and shielding his eyes from the glare of the milky sky that managed to be both overcast and bright at the same time. The five-storey tower was hexagonal in shape. Two of those storeys – the middle and the top – had windows wrapped all the way around, giving 360-degree views.

You know I'd always had a soft spot for the place, Beth. Although industrial-looking and mainly concrete, there was something pleasing about the shape. Remember the conversations we all had, picturing how it would be if we owned it? The lounge would be at the top so that we could fully appreciate the views as we sat. With land this flat, we could literally see for miles and miles. If we looked inland we could probably see right to the mighty cathedral-like church in the town of Wapentake. Facing the sea was even more dramatic, watching the weather fronts racing in, waiting for them to hit. It would be wonderful, exhilarating, far better than sitting in front of a widescreen television. We'd have full cinematic vision.

The building attached to the tower was the size of an industrial cattle shed. We'd fantasised about Jacob one day being able to run a woodcarving business from it. He was brilliant. You remember the beautiful I Will Always Love You plaque that hangs over our bed? And you saw the mirror he gave me for our most recent wedding anniversary, with the exquisite carved frame? Such a talent! Then, of course, there's the egret he carved for your birthday. But you haven't seen that yet…

Glenn cut through my thoughts. 'Cost a fortune to do it up and make it habitable. Mind you, I bet the view's great from the top.'

'A man after my own heart, clearly,' I said, forcing a smile.

He looked at me and smiled, too, bemused.

'God, I remember the fighter planes going over constantly, as a kid. The sounds of war, eh?' He chuckled.

'The bombs exploding in the distance, and the *rat-tat* of gunfire. Sometimes the windows would rattle!'

Funny, really, that in such a rural landscape Glenn and I had grown up used to the noise of war, thanks to the marsh being used as a practice bombing range. In the distance there could still be seen the rusting hulks of ships that had been towed there so they could be bombed repeatedly. Instead of the peace and quiet of the countryside, there had been the boom of jets breaking the sound barrier overhead. Now that former scene of violence was so peaceful, at last.

Maybe the fact that Glenn shared those ties of history was what made it so easy to open up to him.

'I've been thinking,' he said. 'You know what we were saying, about Beth dressing up because she may have been going on a date?'

I frowned, uncomfortable with thinking of my little girl this way: being interested in boys, growing up. But to deny it was ridiculously naive.

Glenn continued. 'So... do you reckon Davy might have been the one? I mean, he's a bit simple, so maybe a kid would be right up his street.'

'He's not the brightest spark, but he's definitely not simple.' I was appalled by the idea of him enticing you away. Davy was a nice guy; he wouldn't hurt a fly. Would he? 'I know it would explain why he was so twitchy, but I'd need some proof before I went accusing him. We'll talk to him again.'

'How are we going to get proof?'

I shrugged, playing with the toggle on my coat. I was not convinced by Davy being either Lothario or attacker, but how well do we ever know anyone? Glenn was right – you had got dolled up for a reason, and that reason had to be someone you fancied. It made sense that it was a person we knew, which meant everyone was a suspect.

I'd racked my own brains and come up with nothing as to who it might be. I'd quizzed family and friends and even tried to speak with Chloe and Ursula, and come up with a big fat zero. Of course, there was one completely obvious thing I hadn't done yet, Beth – have a thorough search of your room. I was still too afraid to spend more than five seconds at a time in it, because it felt so dead without you.

If only you would wake up and give us all the answers we needed. I missed your smile, your voice, your laughter, so much.

'We still need to talk to Aleksy, too.' I sighed.

Suddenly there came a high-pitched bark. A sound of distress.

'Where's Wiggins?' I looked around, but couldn't see him. 'Wiggins!'

There was no sign of him. Panic smashed into me, catapulting me back to the day you went missing. Searching, running, screaming, hoping, despairing. I couldn't breathe, the sky feeling as if it was tumbling in on me. Where was the dog?

I shouted his name. Another disconsolate bark came, more of a whine this time.

'Over there somewhere,' said Glenn, pointing to an area of marsh that looked exactly the same as the rest. It was right on the edge of the scrub, at the start of the mudflats.

Seagulls broke into the sky, making me glance further into the distance. The sea was a grey line on the horizon, flat and featureless and far away, for now. But the tide was coming in – and on land as flat as this, it came in lethally fast.

I started running.

CHAPTER 34

'Melanie! Wait!'

I didn't slow. Shouted over my shoulder: 'The tide, Glenn – don't you remember?'

'Oh God – it comes in fast, doesn't it—'

'Faster than a person can walk!'

That didn't sound too bad. But factor in hidden creeks that people would come across suddenly, which forced them to double back the way they had come and made them try another route, then another and another. It could take an age to get across the expanse of marshland. And the terrain made it almost impossible to run. It was full of hummocks, and unexpected bits of bog that looked firm but gave way instantly.

I couldn't lose your dog. Not after everything else. I hadn't been able to help you, Beth, but Wiggins was somewhere nearby. Surely I could save him.

'Wiggins!' Panic blinded me, like before. Another bark came, then another. Where was he?

'This way!' shouted Glenn. He jogged forward, but almost turned his ankle on a hummock. I went past him, hopping from one firm bit of land no bigger than my foot to the next. All the time spent on this marsh hadn't been wasted.

'Look for vegetation that's greyer,' I called, concentrating. 'The greener the vegetation, the more likely it's in a wet bit of land.'

The sea was closer. Damn it. Ahead of me the earth opened up like a crevice, and a few feet below ground level was water. A creek. It was narrow enough… I leapt across it, just managing to keep my footing on the other side.

Another whine from Wiggins. He was nearby, somewhere.

'Melanie, wait. Is it worth it? If you get caught by the tide, you'll drown,' shouted Glenn. He moved slowly, carefully.

'I can't leave him!' Tears gathered, but I forced them back. I had to keep my head. I had to save our dog. No way was I letting him die.

There! Another high-pitched bark. Desperate. Scared. This one from somewhere near my feet. I stopped, searching the ground. There must be another creek nearby. Picking my way slowly forward, I spotted him. Yes – he'd somehow got jammed into a narrow creek. Unable to go forward or back, he was stuck fast.

A quick glance at the water. The white crest was clearly visible. The land was so flat here that the tide didn't come in as a series of waves, but as one continuous motion, pushing forward, relentless and speedy. It was gaining on us.

I fell to my knees and started digging at the soft ground with my bare hands, all the time making soothing noises to Wiggins. Nails tore, my fingers hurt, but I kept digging.

I can't even keep your dog safe, let alone my daughter. I'm a Jonah. Better I keep away from you, Beth.

More mud flung to one side. Wiggins wriggled but stayed stuck fast. The creek started to fill, the water level rising rapidly. Now Wiggins was up to his chest. I risked a glance up. The sea was almost covering the mudflats, and only the top of the whale's vast skeleton could be seen.

Glenn crashed beside me, sinking to his knees and hauling great handfuls of muck away.

'Come on! Come on!' he urged, grunting with effort.

Wiggins gave another wriggle. Leapt forward and up in one movement, scrabbling into my arms. I fell back, laughing with relief. But we weren't out of danger yet.

'Come on, boy, stay with me.'

Then I was up, all three of us loping along, picking our way back to safety. Eyes always down, just briefly looking up to check we were going in the right direction. We could hear the sea clearly now. A low, rushing noise. Jumping across the first creek, now almost full. The land getting wetter, not drier. My feet slipping and splashing.

Then firmer ground. Smoother. Springy vegetation that came up to mid-calf. Now low, coarse grasses. Then soft, long grass. Finally we reached the sea bank.

I almost crawled up its steep side, my jeans clinging round my ankles where they had got wet. Gasping with exhaustion and relief, I lay on my back, a starfish. A shorelark wheeled above, then turned and headed into the field behind me. The sobs hit as the adrenaline drained away. Wiggins licked my face feverishly until I pushed him off and sat up. Glenn sat beside me, knees up, arms resting on them, panting.

'That was crazy. We almost died for a dog.'

I was too knackered to reply.

Thank goodness he had got stuck in a smaller creek, rather than one of the larger ones. The deeper creeks sometimes still had barbed wire, or rusting drums, in the bottom of them. I had once seen what looked like an ejected plane seat poking up from some gelatinous mud. If Wiggins had been caught on one of those, then I might never have got him free.

I cursed myself for getting so deep in conversation with Glenn that I hadn't kept a closer eye on Wiggins. He'd gone further and further away from me, exploring the marsh. This was all my fault.

Still, I'd saved him in the end. And as I lay there, catching my breath, I felt full of renewed determination. I would find your attacker, and you would get better. I would save you, Beth.

'I'm going to talk to the Jachowski boy,' I decided.

CHAPTER 35

BETH
FRIDAY 22 JANUARY

Beth was careful never to refer to him by his actual name. Instead, he was always SSG, because he *Smells So Good*.

He wasn't like the other lads she knew, the still-childish boys she had grown up with. He was older. More mature. He would protect her. Even though they had only been talking to each other for a couple of months, it felt, to Beth, as though she had been dreaming of kissing him all her life.

And now the moment was finally here.

As she wrapped her arms around his neck, she breathed in his cologne. Hmm, lush. Then they kissed. It felt incredible.

Until she saw the look on his face. Her stomach flipped as if she had smelled something sickeningly sour. She had made a terrible mistake.

CHAPTER 36

Glenn had been instructed to wait for me in The Poacher, while I talked to Aleksy alone. I didn't actually suspect the handsome seventeen-year-old. Not truly. But perhaps he could shed some light on what you had been up to.

The only time I ever saw Aleksy was when he waited in the morning for the school bus to Wapentake Secondary, and hopped off it in the late afternoon. He used the same stop as you, almost opposite our house. I'd never taken much notice of him. He was one of those beautiful boys who seemed painfully shy about his looks and spent most of his time hiding behind a long lick of hair over his eyes, although the rest of his dark locks were quite short. Hands permanently in pockets, his head always down and bobbing to the beat of whatever music he was listening to through his headphones.

I lurked in the lounge waiting for the bus to pull up. Your bedroom would, of course, have given me a better view in the failing light, but going in there was too much for me. Besides, it had become your dad's place to go and cry – mine was out on the marsh.

The bus was late. Light was fading.

I thought about when I was your age. I'd been a seething mass of insecurities about my looks, my personality, my future. Then I thought about what I was like at seventeen, Aleksy's age. What a world of difference! I'd been confident, happy, felt loved – and I'd been just a year or so away from falling pregnant with you. Would someone such as Aleksy, on the brink of manhood, be interested in a girl your age?

The bus pulled up, brakes squeaking gently. Ten minutes late. Typical.

I hurried from my lookout, trying to appear casual. 'Aleksy.'

He didn't hear, but caught sight of me as he crossed the road. 'Hi, Aleksy, isn't it?'

His dark brown eyes widened in confusion. A quick movement and he'd pulled off his headphones so the wires dangled down and swung against his chest. A tinny *tsk tsk tsk* escaped from them.

I'd never noticed before how tall he was, but he towered over me, the smell of his citrus body spray drifting over me. I cleared my throat. 'I'm Beth's mum. You know Beth? The girl who has been hurt on the marsh?'

With the universal wariness of teenagers faced with a questioning adult, he nodded, avoiding my eye.

'I'm chatting to anyone who had anything to do with her. Trying to find out a bit more about her life, you know?'

What was I doing? This was ridiculous, and worse, we were drawing attention – Martin Young had just come out of the shop and done a double take before heading into the pub.

'So I wondered, did you know her well? Did you ever speak with her?'

'Er, yeah. Sometimes.' His voice was surprisingly deep for such a skinny whippet of a lad; his legs looked like a couple of strings in his tight black jeans. There was no trace of a foreign accent in his speech.

'What sort of things did you talk about?'

Aleksy was built for the loose shrug he gave. His jacket looked like a wire coat hanger had been shoved inside it, rather than a body.

'School. Music. Dancing.'

'Dancing?'

His eyes darted to his house then floated across my face before drifting back to the narrow pavement we stood on. 'I better go.'

'What sort of dancing?' It was the would-be journalist in me that prompted the question. The untrained instinct that told me where the story was.

'Dunno. Just clubs. You know. Dancing.'

'But Beth has never been to a club.'

He shook his head while pulling awkwardly at the straps of his rucksack. 'Mum's expecting me.'

Why wouldn't he look at me? Was this your attacker?

'I heard you were a bit sweet on Beth. Is that right?' But I was addressing his back, and he didn't pause in his stride into the dusk.

'Did she meet you that night, Aleksy? Aleksy! Did you take her to a nightclub? Did something happen? Did something go wrong? How did she end up on the marsh, Aleksy?'

As he strode away, I felt more sure than ever that he knew something. But I had no earthly idea how I was going to find out what he knew about that night.

Wiggins gave me a hero's welcome when I came through the door. Jumping up, whole body wagging with his tail, as though we hadn't seen one another for hours rather than ten minutes. I pushed him down and flopped on the sofa, unsure of what to do. There was only one person who I could talk it through with: Glenn.

He answered my call within two rings, listening intently as I recounted what had happened.

'You're right; the kid may have taken Beth to a nightclub on a date, and somehow something went wrong.'

'But what on earth led to her being on the marsh?'

'God knows. But I think you should tell the police about this.'

I curled my fingers through Wiggins's fur, uncomfortable at the thought. 'I'm not sure. There's no proof, only my gut instinct.'

'Yeah, but if you tell them, then they can find the proof, can't they? That's their job, after all – not that you'd know it at the moment.'

'You're right. I'll do it now. They've been useless so far.'

I called DS Devonport, but couldn't get through. I left a terse message explaining that she needed to check if any cabs had been used by Aleksy and you that night.

'The Jachowski kid knows more than he is letting on,' I warned.

Exhausted, I slumped back and closed my eyes. Wiggins rested his head on one of the colourful patchwork cushions I had made to brighten up the brown corduroy sofa we'd bought in a sale a few years earlier and hated ever since. Within minutes, he was breathing heavily. Sleep didn't come for me, though, Beth.

Twenty minutes later, the door slammed shut, making me jump. The dog jumped up with an instinctive bark that turned into a yelp of joy when he saw Jacob.

'How's your day been?' I asked, getting up to give your dad a kiss.

He gave me a cursory peck, his stubble scraping my face – he hadn't even had time to shave that morning. 'All right. You ready to go to Leeds?'

'Just give me a minute to get some stuff together.'

'You're not ready? What have you been doing today?' Something sharp in his tone made it sound like an accusation.

'Not much, but—'

'No? I heard you spent the day with Glenn Baker. That you've been spending a lot of time with him, in fact.'

His jaw tightened. I blinked, confused. Then balled my fists.

'If you're accusing me of something, come right out with it.'

'Not accusing, asking. But the way you're reacting makes me wonder…'

'Oh, come off it! He's just moved back to the village, and he's been helping me with—'

'Helping you? If you need help, why not come to me? How much did he help you when you got drunk together the other night? You didn't tell me you'd been with him.'

We stepped closer, eyeballing each other.

'You didn't ask! Are you seriously accusing me of something?'

'Is there anything to accuse you of?'

'Jacob! Don't you think I have enough on my plate without adding an affair to the list?' *If he'd only shut up and let me explain…*

'What do you have on your plate? You don't work any more, and you've stopped going to the hospital during the day. Why's that? Have you stopped caring about what happens to Beth? 'Cos you only seem to go when I take you.'

How dare he! 'It's only been a couple of days, and I go every night with you. I don't see you spending any more time there than me.'

'I go to work, Mel! When I'm not working, I'm there, talking to our daughter. Letting her know she's loved, and that she needs to come back to us.'

'I do that too. I've been trying to work out who did this. That's what I've been doing with Glenn. I need to tell you something.'

Wiggins barked, interrupting me. Just as well, because Jacob was glaring as if I were mad.

'Quiet,' I ordered.

But Wiggins was right: there was a strange noise. Row temporarily suspended, Jacob and I looked at each other quizzically.

'Something's going on outside.'

We moved to the window and peered out, but couldn't make out much in the darkness of the winter night, lit only with pools of light from the street light in front of the school opposite, and the glow of the pub on our left and the store on the right.

There was definitely a lot of shouting, though. Sounded like quite a crowd too.

'What's happening?' I breathed.

*

All three of us went to the front door. Jacob told Wiggins to stay, and shut him in before we went down the garden path together. Jill strode towards us.

'I was just coming to get you. You need to come right now.'

Without explanation, she hurried away, walking full of purpose, arms swinging by the sides of her soft rectangle of a body. Her steel-grey ponytail bobbed jauntily. She was so used to everyone doing as she said that she didn't wait to check whether we were following, just assumed we were. And it didn't even enter our heads not to.

We hurried after her, bemused, but quickly saw where she was going. Beyond the café and the shop was a row of council houses that were now mostly privately owned – you know the ones I mean, Beth. Next to where Bob Thornby and Phyllis Blakecroft live; the neighbours who row about the overgrown hedge all the time. There, a crowd of villagers had gathered. Shouting. Angry. It seemed to be focused on the Jachowski family's house.

CHAPTER 37

I grabbed Jacob's arm, fearful and ashamed, pulling him back from the gate.

'I don't think we should get involved.'

He hesitated, looking from me to the crowd. Then we heard it. Your name, Beth. This was something to do with you. I blushed, wondering if somehow my confrontation with Aleksy had triggered it.

Snatches of some shouts became clearer over others as the calls rose and fell, as the wind picked them up and threw them in our direction.

'Cowards! Come out!'

'You'll hit a girl, but don't have the courage to tackle us lot, do you? Eh?'

'Go back to your own country!'

Jacob walked closer and I followed, reluctantly, hanging onto him still. When the crowd realised who had arrived, they didn't so much part for us as surround us. Bob Thornby was there, temporarily putting aside his feud with Phyllis Blakecroft. Ben Miller, Susan and Colin Winston and a lot of the Young clan, including Peter and Jon and their sons, who were adults themselves now. Half the village seemed to be there. Suddenly there was quiet. Expectation.

'What's going on?' Jacob demanded.

'The Polish kid hurt your Beth.' It was Martin Young who spoke. Jill glared at him, but he folded his arms, mirroring her pose.

Jacob gave a bark of a laugh, clearly more nervous than he appeared. 'Aleksy? How do you know this?'

A curtain twitched inside the Jachowski house. Someone peering outside to see if the crowd had dispersed.

'Is this true?' Jacob called to them.

That was the trigger for the mob to start again. A surge of insults. Pushing, shoving, faces twisting.

'I want nowt to do with their type.'

'They don't want owt to do with us! They don't integrate.'

Everyone moved forward. The breath was knocked out of me. Faces of friendly neighbours I'd known my whole life were transformed with hate. Spittle flew from lips.

'Bloody foreigners!' yelled Phyllis, apparently forgetting her daughter lived abroad with her Spanish husband.

'Taking our jobs. Taking over everything!' spat Colin.

'They only left the flowers on the marsh 'cos they had a guilty conscience.'

'He probably nicked 'em from work anyway – he works at the flower factory.'

My instinct told me Aleksy knew something. Maybe he was the one who had hurt you, Beth. Maybe this would scare the truth out of him.

But this baying mob felt wrong.

'What proof do you have?' I asked. I could barely be heard over the shouting.

'This village was always quiet. Suddenly they move here and a girl is attacked!' Ursula yelled, her perfect pout skewed in a sneer. 'Who will it be next?'

'Come on, they've been here for over a year, so you can't say that,' argued Jacob. But no one listened to your father. The mob's righteous indignation had somehow given them the right to be angrier than your own parents.

'What evidence have you got? Any?' I shouted.

'They've got different ways to us.' Universal nods to Bob Thornby's comment.

'They don't listen to the law. They've all been poaching,' added Peter.

'Well, I know for a fact that you go poaching sometimes, Peter Young, so that's a hell of a thing to accuse people of,' I shot back.

'I want to get the person who did this more than anyone, but we need proof,' said Jacob.

'So yeah, give us proof,' I added, hopefully.

Martin planted himself in front of me. His dark eyes bored into me. 'You're suspicious of Aleksy, though, aren't you?'

I hesitated. 'Well, yes, I think he's hiding something…'

He stooped, then picked up a rock from the Jachowskis' garden, trampling on a low shrub in the process.

I looked around for someone to stop this madness. Glenn was lurking in the churchyard, watching but not taking part. Clearly not wanting to get involved. Behind him, hovering in the pub's doorway, were Dale and your guitar teacher, Mr Harvey, who looked like a scared sheep. Sweeping past them was a police car.

The single whoop of a siren sounded a warning that it was pulling up. People scattered. That was all the officers seemed to want, as they stayed in the car. Eyeing everyone but not bothering to chase. Only Jacob and I remained, along with Jill.

'Hey, lady, this is your fault. Your questioning and finger-pointing has got the whole village at each other's throats. Happy now?' she snapped at me.

'Hold on a minute, I never encouraged this…'

She looked over at the police car as the door swung ponderously open. It was Flo, with a male colleague. Jill nodded at them as she walked away, slow and deliberate.

The two officers pulled their caps on and sauntered over to me and Jacob. Then stood with their hands on their hips. Alison Daughtrey-Drew cast a curious glance our way as she drove towards The Poacher.

'Jacob, Melanie… we've had reports of a disturbance. Is there a problem?' asked Flo.

'Not with us, no,' said Jacob, explaining that we had only come out when we heard the noise.

The curtain twitched again. Seconds later, Mr Jachowski appeared at the door. When he walked towards us he took small, hesitant steps, despite his rangy frame.

'My son didn't do anything,' he insisted. His accent was thick.

The male officer held up an admonishing hand, trying to keep him quiet. But Jacob got in first.

'We know. This was just racist nonsense. I'm sorry you've had to witness such an ugly thing.'

'Hang on a second – he is hiding something,' I cut in. 'You need to speak to Aleksy.'

'Melanie, we will find out who attacked Beth, but nothing is going to be achieved through mob rule.'

'Maybe if you did your job better, people wouldn't have to turn vigilante,' I hissed.

'Come on, Mel, that's not fair. I'm sure the police are doing all they can,' offered Jacob.

'It's not enough!' I looked from him to Flo to the other officer. It felt like they were on one side of a wall and I was on the other.

'Come on, let's get you home,' said Flo.

Fine, I'd leave. But DS Devonport would be talking to the Jachowski boy soon – and so would I. I had a feeling we'd both better get in quick, though, before the mob returned. It was inevitable they would be back at some point over the following days or weeks.

I didn't want things to get out of hand, or for anyone to get hurt. But, despite my guilt, if I'm honest, Beth, I didn't really mind what they did as long as they helped me find who had hurt you.

CHAPTER 38

From an early age I knew I was special. I've fooled people my entire life. No one knew the real me. No one even suspected – friends, family, all taken in. I walked among the rank and file, fitting right in as if I were merely normal; my mask of weakness was my strength. I had the power of a god. I was stronger than a hurricane, as inevitable as the incoming tide, as terrifying as a hawk swooping down on a quivering mouse. I had control over life and death, but these fools couldn't even see it.

Even when I got away with murder right under their noses, they couldn't see.

Only one person had ever suspected what I was, and they were no longer a problem.

It was time to have a little carefully planned fun.

I was the scientist; she was my lab rat. She had no idea how I was deceiving her, laying out breadcrumbs for her to gobble up until she hit her head against a brick wall. Again. And again. And again.

Dead end.

CHAPTER 39

The sense of trespass made my heart beat faster as I turned the brass doorknob. Even when the door swung open, I hesitated on the threshold, a vampire needing to be invited in or suffer dire consequences. But there was no one to say the words, of course. You weren't saying a word to anyone.

Holding my breath, I stepped inside your bedroom. Pale pink walls; glittery pens; a noticeboard devoted to smiling photos; a poster of a humpback whale breaching the ocean and surrounded by sea spray. They made my soul writhe in agony, the uninvited vampire suffering dire consequences indeed.

The thought of invading my daughter's privacy was hateful. We were a family who respected one another's space, who knocked before entering each other's bedroom rather than barging in. None of us would ever dream of reading a diary, or going through each other's mobile phones. But until you woke up, this was the only way to get hold of information you held, Beth. Hopefully, I had reasoned, once you realised the extreme circumstances, you could forgive me for this betrayal of trust.

Of course, I'd already given it a cursory search once, on that awful Saturday. The police had given it a more thorough going-over that day, too, but had come up with nothing. I hoped a mother's intuition would guide me to something. I'd checked your Facebook account, of course, but had known before starting that there was nothing to find on it, because we were Facebook friends. That had been my condition when you had begged me to let you open an account. I couldn't look at your private messages, of course, but the police had accessed them and found nothing worth investigating. The same with your Snapchat account, not that I understood that – it was something to do with sending friends silly photos that only lasted ten seconds, filtering your face to look like a cartoon dog or adding flowers in your hair. It made no sense, though I knew you'd tried to explain it to me several times, giving up with a dramatic sigh and a roll of your eyes each time.

So as soon as Jacob left for work at 8.10 a.m., I had gone to your room. I'd decided the night before, as your dad and I sat not side by side with you, but on opposite sides of your hospital bed. He wasn't speaking to me because on the drive up to Leeds I'd told him exactly what Glenn and I had been up to. Although it had assuaged his fears of an affair, he seemed even more furious with me that I was investigating on my own. Told me to stop immediately – *as if!* The last thing he had said to me was that I was 'being ridiculous'.

Ridiculous or not, I wasn't stopping.

Where to begin? The police had your phone and laptop, so I couldn't look through those. Instead, I got on my hands and knees and peered under the bed, despairing at the dustballs that had gathered there. Wiggins shoved his head and shoulders under alongside mine, then sneezed, sending the dust flying into the air. Spluttering, I pushed him away, then bent back down.

An old jumper that you had insisted was lost lurked alongside an odd sock. There were a couple of cardboard boxes pushed right up against the wall. I pulled them out. They were full of drawings of animals. You had never shown them to us – why, Beth? Was it because we had laughed at your ballerina all those years ago? My word, you had progressed since then. These sketches were amazing. The sweep of a wing, the movement of fur on a running animal, the glint in the eye; all beautifully captured.

I was eaten up with guilt that you had chosen to keep them private.

Halfway down the box lay a journal. My hands started to shake, almost too scared to open it. I had wanted secrets to be revealed, but was also terrified of what I might discover. Even finding those drawings had thrown me a little.

Your neat, round writing filled page after page. Qualms aside now, I eagerly read a section. Then read it again. What the…?

It was a list of nature sightings. Nothing more.

Maybe it was a code, my fevered imagination decided. I scanned it again, trying to decipher it, then realised this was crazy. Popping it back in the box carefully, so you would never know it had been looked at, I moved on.

Posters of animals and brightly coloured birds – and Justin Bieber – covered the walls. I found myself peeking behind them in case something was hidden. Of course there was nothing, and I grew more and more annoyed with my own paranoia.

Desperate, I pulled books from shelves and leafed through them. Then shook them. Nothing suspicious fluttered from their pages. Books on identifying animals, dragonflies, birdwatching, nature photography. All were pulled off and stacked on the floor until the shelf was empty. There weren't many fictional books, as you preferred to read on your tablet, but you always asked for your favourites in paperback too. *Twilight*, *The Fault in Our Stars*, *The Vampire Diaries*, *Divergent* – all books I'd never read but which you devoured.

I'd give anything to see you poring over a book again, Beth. Please, come back to me soon.

The force of longing for you made me sway. I had to steady myself against the bookcase for a moment. When I pulled myself together, I made a mental note to read aloud to you, and also buy some audiobooks for you. Perhaps you would like that, my love.

There was only one book left on the shelf: a well-thumbed copy of *The Little White Horse*. The room went blurry again at the sight of it, tears springing afresh. How you loved this book when we bought it for you! You were only eight, but already a bookworm. You had been so captivated by the description of the dog, Wiggins, at the start of the children's classic that you had read it aloud to Jacob and I, laughing at how conceited the dog was, how in love he was with his gorgeous looks. It was a brilliant piece of writing, and had reminded me so much of my own passion for words.

When we'd bought our own dog a few months later, you had been adamant about what to call him. You had taken one look at his shiny coat, the soft waves of fur cascading down his chest, and instantly been reminded of the character in the book. Our own dog had an utterly different personality, but from that moment on, he was tied to the fictional character.

He watched me from your bed now, as I opened up the wardrobe and went through your pockets. It felt grubby and wrong, and I only discovered a couple of receipts for chocolate and deodorant, along with an ancient, crispy tissue. I pulled a face and carried it to the bin, which the police had already gone through.

There was nothing, absolutely nothing in your room to help me. I'd even checked inside your shoes and boots, for goodness' sake.

I walked over to your wash basket, knowing I'd find nothing in there but desperate to smell you. I hadn't been able to bring myself to do any of your washing yet. Picking up an orange hoody of yours, I held it to my nose. Inhaled. It smelled wonderfully of you, in a way you no longer did in the hospital, where you were too full of chemicals and surrounded by disinfectant.

Tears were threatening to overtake me once more, and that couldn't be allowed. There was a job to do. Gasping like a marathon runner, I walked over to the window to escape the pain. From this vantage point I could see straight into the village primary school playground, with its painted wiggly lines. When you'd attended, I had often gone there, standing just a little back so that no one would see me watching my daughter play. Chase, tag, skipping, ball, racing around with your golden blonde hair streaming messily behind you, or in corners, whispering conspiratorially with your friends.

Oh, Beth, will I ever see you chatting again?

My despair was not simply an emotion; it was a physical being. It smothered and choked. It fogged my head, and sat on my chest until I could barely breathe. It weighed me down until I slumped over the windowsill.

I had to do something. I didn't know what, but if I didn't do something I would go mad. I had researched on the Internet, trying to find something doctors might have overlooked, some new breakthrough in treatment for your kind of injury. All I had discovered was that doctors at St James's Hospital genuinely were doing everything they could. Now the only option left was to keep pushing on with trying to find your attacker.

Full of purpose, I turned back to the room, ready to search again, and accidentally kicked the skirting board beneath the radiator at the window. A section clattered to the floor. Good grief. Like me, this place was falling apart.

I got on my hands and knees to pop it back. Was that… ? Yes, a notebook was pushed into a recess that was usually hidden by the board. A pink Moleskine, like Glenn's. They were identical. My heart was hammering like crazy as I eased it out and opened it up. The handwriting inside was instantly recognisable as yours, Beth.

When he kissed me… OMG, it was the most amazing thing in the world. My whole body tingled with it. All my worries about being a good enough kisser flew out of the window. I instinctively knew what to do.

God, I am so in love with SSG.

I dropped the notebook on the floor in horror.

Who the hell is SSG?

CHAPTER 40

I paced the bedroom, trying to work out what to do. I felt sick to my stomach – and furious. Ab-so-bloody-lutely furious.

Obviously, the police should be called. Of course. But if I could figure out who this SSG was first, then all the better. There was no one we knew with those initials, though. Not even close.

I forced myself to read more:

What is happiness? I think it's a really good book and a really nice boy to snuggle up to. I think a lot about boys. Someone who will look after me and protect me…

… I love to think about me and SSG kissing. That's because he's the right person for me. It shows how perfect we are together. I'd been so nervous, but he's experienced and that really helps. All my nerves fly out of the window when he touches me, strumming my body like a guitar. He's so special…

… It snowed today, and all the boys in my year had a snowball fight. I got three crumbled on my head, two on the back of my neck and one in my eye. They are such children. SSG is a man. Just imagine everyone's face when they realise I've got an older man. They'll be absolutely jell! Ha! Especially Chloe…

So this SSG was an older man. How old? Did you think of Aleksy as a man? He was almost eighteen, after all. What if this SSG was a paedophile who had been grooming you? The thought made me dizzy. A dirty old man with designs on my gorgeous, innocent little girl. What had the two of you done together? How far had this gone?

My stomach clenched and I ran to the loo. Fell onto my knees with my head bent over it. I wasn't sick, but it took several minutes before I felt in control enough to stand and face that notebook again.

I had to. I had to unmask this pervert.

SSG was so tender today. He makes me feel so safe. He told me how much he loved me. 'I want to spend the rest of my life with you,' he said. And he meant it. I could tell by the look in his eyes. I can't wait for us to get married. I'll be 14 soon, so we'll have to wait two years, but it will be worth it. I love being held by him. He just Smells So Good, lol!

The caps caught my eye. Clearly SSG weren't his initials, they stood for your nickname for him. So who was this Mr Smells So Good?

I closed my eyes and forced myself to take a deep breath. I needed to calm down if I was to think clearly.

I tried to think of men who wore aftershave. Not many men in the village did. Most were old-fashioned types who thought it was feminine and would probably beat up a bloke if they discovered he used moisturiser. So chances were this SSG was in his late teens or early twenties. Aleksy fitted that age range. And he used strong body spray. So it was Aleksy!

But another line was bugging me. I reread it. *Strumming my body.*

The answer hit me like a thunderbolt. Oh my God, I had never thought, never imagined… I'd trusted him with you, Beth.

I dialled DS Devonport's direct line, where it went to answerphone. So instead I called Flo. She answered within a couple of rings.

'I know who hurt my daughter,' I said. 'He groomed her, took advantage of her, then hurt her when he tried to take things further.'

CHAPTER 41

Things happened quickly after I'd notified the police. I called Jacob at work and told him everything. By the time he arrived home, Flo was knocking on the door with an update. Her hand, with well-scrubbed nails cut short and rounded like a child's, rested on my arm as she explained that your guitar teacher, James Harvey, was being questioned, following the shocking discovery of your diary.

'We'd like you to give permission for Beth to undergo a medical check, to see if she has been sexually assaulted,' Flo added. Her short ginger bob swayed as she spoke. She tucked both sides behind her ears, then looked at my clenched fists.

I couldn't uncurl them as I gave my consent.

'I always liked the bloke,' muttered Jacob, stunned.

My reply was a bitter bark of laughter. 'Me too. Liked him and felt for him. He always seemed a lovely man, but awkward; aware of every move he made, everything he said. Didn't seem to fit in around here. Now I know why. You know he's applied to do teacher training, don't you? So he can prey on more innocent girls.'

I'd always tried to put him at ease, and he'd seemed pitifully grateful for my efforts. How he must have laughed at us as he seduced you right under your parents' noses. The words in the diary haunted me.

All my nerves fly out of the window when he touches me.

'I could kill him for what he's done.'

'If he's guilty, we'll find the evidence to jail him,' assured Flo.

'If he's touched her…' I swallowed. Tried again. 'If he's touched her, I don't know—'

'Stop it, Mel!' shouted Jacob. 'I don't need to hear this. I don't want to think about… that. Christ, it's hard enough…' A ragged breath in, held, out. His cheeks reddened as if they had been slapped.

Pain constricted my throat but I forced the words out, desperate finally to voice what I'd been longing to say for so long. What Jacob didn't want to hear.

'When I'm on the marsh I can feel her, Jacob. She must have screamed for us. She must have cried for her mummy and daddy, and we weren't there.'

'Shut up! Shut up!'

Jacob stormed from the room, tears rolling down his face.

'Are you all right? Do you want to talk about this, Melanie?' asked Flo.

Throwing a glare her way, I stomped from the room too. Into the hall and up the stairs. If you had seen me, you might have laughed, Beth; my stomping reminded me of one of your strops.

I locked myself in the bathroom, trying to calm down. Jacob was right. I had to put my faith in justice. But it didn't stop how I felt. I'd always imagined myself to be a forgiving person, but a mother can never forgive someone who hurts her child. I wasn't a violent person; knew I would never carry out my threat, and yet that didn't make the feeling inside me any less real.

I wanted to kill James Harvey for hurting you. In just three weeks, the changes wrought in me were deep and permanent. I was losing myself. Bits of me were being scoured away and the dust of me blown in the wind, flying somewhere across the Lincolnshire fens. Soon there wouldn't be anything left that was recognisable.

Would you still recognise me, Beth?

We had been too happy. That was the problem. No one goes through life so untouched by pain.

Your dad and I had been childhood sweethearts. Friendship had given our relationship a good foundation – we genuinely were best friends. When I'd fallen pregnant unexpectedly, it hadn't been a trauma; there had been no heart-rending decision. Instead, we had sat down, talked about things sensibly and decided that, although the timing could have been better, we very much wanted to be parents. We were excited to see how you would turn out; a mixture of the two of us, physical proof of our love.

Our parents had been supportive, not disappointed, and we'd married because we'd wanted to do everything right. It had been a tiny wedding, but perfect. Full of love, laughter, family and friends – well, you have seen the photographs, Beth, seen the joy on our faces for yourself. As we had exchanged vows in Fenmere's church where I, and later you, had been baptised, I'd known I would spend the rest of my life with your dad.

The pregnancy had been smooth, the birth painful, but no worse than anyone else experiences. You, my beautiful daughter, were so perfect that the memory of the pain quickly faded. We had become a happy family, leading a small but relatively successful life. We had no desire to move away, branch out or take over the world.

You may not know this, Beth, but the only problem had been our assumption that other children would come along. Our only sorrow was that they never had. Even that had been taken in our stride, though. We had never bothered having tests to find out what was wrong; we simply accepted our lot. We were perfectly happy as a family of three, well, four if you counted our honorary second 'child', Wiggins.

Of course, over the years there had been arguments, strops and fallings-out. Since you'd become a teenager you had got a little sulkier, but nothing worrying.

Now, from out of the blue, we were dealing with *this*.

We had tempted fate with our happiness.

*

I splashed my face with water, then went downstairs to make peace with my husband. But then I saw him with Flo, their heads together, intimate.

They were kissing.

I backed up the stairs and sat at the top, hugging my trembling knees to my chest. How had I found myself in this nightmare?

I should have rushed downstairs, confronted them… but I didn't have the strength. It was taking everything to hold it together as it was. Perhaps it was a way of getting his own back for the 'affair' he thought I was having with Glenn. Perhaps it was the pressure of what was happening. Perhaps he simply didn't love me any more and had fallen for Flo.

Beth, we were crumbling without you.

CHAPTER 42

I couldn't settle. Jacob was the same. The family had gathered round, all waiting expectantly for news. Jumping at everything, sitting down then standing up again, often losing the thread of our conversation because all we could think of was you and James Harvey. Most of the time the only sound was the ticking of the grandfather clock we inherited from Jacob's grandparents, which stood in one corner of the lounge, beside the window. Fighting the urge to scream and shatter the silence made me visibly shudder, and I tensed all my muscles against it.

Flo kept trying to talk to me, but her calm sympathy annoyed me and made me itch to punch her. Jacob seemed to appreciate her words, though. Of course he did. All those times I'd been grateful he'd dealt with her, saving me the trouble, I'd been pushing them together.

By two o'clock I was going out of my mind. There were so many horrific scenarios running through my head, and I couldn't talk to anyone. Mum kept suggesting counselling. My dad and John were more your strong, silent types; good at practical things, bad at emotions. As for your dad, I was too scared of blurting out what I'd seen. A row at that moment might tear us apart for good.

So I sent a text to Glenn.

Something has happened. Fancy a walk on the marsh?

See you in 10 came his reply.

'I'm going to take Wiggins out,' I told Jacob.

He nodded weakly. 'Want some company?'

'You've barely got the strength to speak. Stay. Keep the relatives company.'

'Thanks, Mel. If you're sure.'

I was sure I couldn't be around him, and would use any excuse to get away. I kept thinking of him kissing Flo. *Why her? Why now?*

Why not? We had both been pushed beyond endurance.

Even though there was nothing untoward about my clandestine meeting with Glenn, guilt nibbled at me. Jacob would not be impressed if he knew, and I clung to his jealousy as a sign of hope that Flo was a fling and it was me he loved. I would not give up Glenn for him, though. Not when your dad had betrayed me when I needed him most. Not when Glenn had become such an indispensable friend in so short a time, and I needed someone to offload my pain with. Someone whose feelings didn't have to be tiptoed around.

For such a wide, open landscape, I felt strangely claustrophobic while waiting on the marsh for him. As if someone were watching me – your attacker, perhaps. I could be seen for miles in the daylight, and it made me uncomfortable. This was supposed to be a secret meeting, but anyone could happen across us. Still, it was a lot less public than the pub. Even if we'd met in Wapentake, the chances of us being spotted together were high; it wasn't exactly a great metropolis, boasting a population of around thirty thousand.

Despite my paranoia, there didn't seem to be another soul in sight, aside from the wading birds far in the distance, hurrying up and down the tideline for food. The wind slapped my face, trying to beat some sense into me, but I pulled my hood up, instantly comforted, like a child diving under a duvet to keep monsters at bay. But I missed the wind. Some people hated the constant breeze that haunted the fens. The area was so flat, it rarely ceased. Even in summer it could be fierce, and one gloriously sunny day a few years earlier I had got a huge blister on the top of my ear from windburn after hours of walking without a hat on. But even so, I loved the wind, especially now. It felt like a treasured companion: the one thing that could always be relied on in this uncertain world.

Screw it. I threw my hood back and turned my face to feel my cold February companion clawing and numbing my flesh. We revelled in one another's company.

'Beth? Are you here? Can you hear me?' I called softly.

The wind gentled, smoothing my clothes, soothing my skin with its caresses. It whispered in my ear, but I couldn't make out what it said. Was… was that you, Beth? I knew it was only wishful thinking, but wanted so much for it to be you. My arms ached, physically ached, to hold you.

'Melanie?'

I gave a little cry of shock, jumping. I'd been concentrating so hard on the wind that I had somehow missed the sound of Glenn's van pulling up in the car park, and him walking up behind me.

'What's happened? Have the police arrested someone? Are you okay?'

'It's Beth's guitar teacher, James Harvey! I found a diary Beth was keeping and…' Tears leaked from my eyes; I bullied them away. I started to walk along the sea bank, Glenn by my side, bringing him up to date on finding your diary and calling the police.

I had to speak up to be heard over the wind in our ears, but there was no one to listen in so I could speak freely. And I did.

My fears that you had been groomed… You being fooled by a clever, manipulative man… The things you hinted in your diary that you had done…

They were bad enough. But it was my reaction to those things I really needed to share. My pain. My fury. My fantasies of grabbing my sharp dressmaking scissors, which had lovingly snipped squares of fabric to make patchwork cushions and throws for my family. But which I now wanted to use to chop James Harvey's penis off.

I wanted to punch him, kick him, have him on the ground, bloodied and beaten and shown no mercy. I wanted to be as strong as a man, and reduce his handsome young face to jam for desecrating my daughter.

It took a lot to articulate these terrible thoughts. I didn't want to admit them to myself, let alone anyone else. But my biggest terror was that, if I didn't get them out of me and into the world, they would poison me into acting on them.

This was not your mother speaking, Beth. The woman who had nurtured you, taught you always to be kind. Who had kissed you better when you hurt yourself. This was not the woman your dad loved. It wasn't someone I wanted either of you ever to meet.

Glenn was wonderful. He didn't seem to mind my pain. The graphic scenarios. In fact, the only time he said anything was to probe a little deeper, to get me to open up further. I appreciated that.

As I spoke, my body quaked. Adrenaline rushing around even though I was lost only in memory. We went over my emotions again at discovering you were missing. My fears. How I had imagined your body broken and twisted by a car; the feelings that had swept through me when we had thought you were dead.

Glenn flushed at the impact of my words, clearly angry on my behalf. But he never once told me that he had had enough. He took verbal blow after blow.

I talked, too, of how hope faded for you as time went on.

'I'm betraying Beth for even thinking these things, let alone speaking them out loud. If Jacob knew…'

'Well, he won't hear from me. No one will.'

'Thank you.' My words were spoken so quietly, and were snatched away instantly by the tumbling air. I wasn't sure if Glenn heard. But other words were pushing forward, eager to be shared.

'I used to hold her hand all the time. I didn't want to let it go. Thought if I talked hard enough, prayed hard enough, begged her to come back, that it would happen. One night I held her hand and tried to *will* it to happen. You know? I mean, actually trembled with effort.'

I laughed at my stupidity and grabbed at my face. 'My cheeks were wobbling like this. Imagine! But magic doesn't work. There are no gods. There's no great *They* that will step in and do good works if you only believe hard enough.'

The wind skirled around us, and my sigh joined it. 'I'm so sorry for talking so much. If you don't want to hear me going on, I understand…'

'Hey.' He held his hands up. Those big, strong, practical hands, so different from Jacob's artistic, tapered fingers. 'I've told you I don't mind. I'm a good listener, remember.'

'The best. Aren't you cold?' I added, suddenly noticing that once again Glenn was carrying his coat instead of wearing it.

'Told you, I'm tough. Men don't feel the cold like women do. Even when we do, it's one more thing to fight against – I'm not going to get beaten by the cold, I'm going to win.'

'You know that's crazy, don't you? Why fight the cold when you can put a coat on and be warmer?'

He made a dismissive gesture, slowing to squeeze my shoulder, but quickly let his hand drop away. We were friends, nothing more, and I was grateful to him.

'How are you doing? You must miss Katie so much.'

His face was a careful blank. 'I'm fine.'

'Hey, you can talk to me, too, you know.'

Turning his back on me, he sighed. 'I'd say you had no idea, but you're one of the few people who knows exactly how I'm feeling – and you're going through something even worse.'

His voice was so gentle that I barely heard him. I stepped closer.

'Talk to me about it.'

When he turned, the pain etched on his face was a mirror of my own. 'What a pair, eh? Both grieving for our lost daughters. Please God, they'll come back to us soon.'

Beth, my heart went out to this father forced apart from his child. It was so unfair. I made up my mind there and then that if I could help him in any way to get back in touch with Katie, I would. I would track down his wife and persuade her to let this wonderful man see his family.

'Fancy a drink?' he said abruptly.

'Hell, yes!'

We laughed at my keenness, and went to The Malt Shovel rather than The Poacher, not because there was slightly less risk of us being seen together there, but because I needed a drink. Needed it immediately – and frankly didn't give a toss who saw me.

After a double vodka, things felt calmer. More focused. Glenn bought me another.

'For medicinal purposes.' He shrugged, smiling gently. 'You've been through so much.'

I nodded. Took a warming gulp of my drink.

'Better now?'

'Much. Thank you.'

A moment passed. Glenn checked his watch, then put his head on one side as if something had just occurred to him.

'What I don't understand is why Chloe didn't mention any of this business with Beth and James Harvey. I mean, surely at some point Beth confided in her? They're best friends, right? Maybe you should ask her. Have it out with her. Now that Harvey's been arrested, there's no point in her keeping quiet, is there? Maybe she'll finally tell the truth now.'

He was right. The more I thought about it, the more annoyed I grew. I didn't like this talk, though. It made me wonder what other secrets you had, Beth.

'Chloe's a kid, really,' I justified.

'Old enough to know the difference between right and wrong. Sorry, I'm getting all overprotective of you. But if she'd been a bit more honest, then maybe James could have been caught earlier. Not that it makes any real difference, does it?'

No, no difference at all. But I found myself swallowing down my drink quickly as I noticed what time it was.

'I'm, er, going to get off now.'

'Oh, right. Want a lift?'

I asked him to drop me off on the other side of the village from my house. He thought it was to avoid us being seen together. In reality I needed to be somewhere.

His words danced around, taunting as I pulled my hood up against the wind and walked towards a bus stop.

CHAPTER 43

The bus pulled up and I stepped aside to make room for the sole person getting off.

'Hello, Chloe. I'd like a word with you, if you don't mind.'

She looked confused, but nodded. 'Sure thing, Mrs Oak. Is Beth, er, is Beth getting any better?'

I closed my eyes for a second, fighting the urge to snap that she could go and visit you if she were that curious about your health. That would have been unfair of me; Chloe was fourteen, only four months older than you, Beth.

Old enough to know better. The words in my head taunted me.

'I wanted to ask you about James Harvey—' I began.

'Everyone's talking about his arrest!'

'You've heard already?' Word always spread fast around here, but this was impressive even by the village's usual standards.

'My mum's cousin saw him being led away in handcuffs from his flat in Wapentake, and she texted Mum. So Mum texted me at school, and my mate Sonya's best friend's auntie says we're not to tell anyone but that it is definitely true. She's a cleaner at the police station,' she added. 'Yes. It was a shock—'

'Was it?' The words shot out. 'Surely you must have known something was going on between them. Why didn't you say anything?'

It sounded like an accusation, but it was too late to take the words back.

'Mrs Oak, it didn't seem that big a deal…'

'It didn't… ? I'm flabbergasted. A man of twenty-four with a girl ten years his junior? Part of you must have known you should have told someone about what was going on.'

She seemed to be thinking.

'Chloe…'

Reached a decision. 'Mrs Oak, you're so right. I should have been honest. But Beth kept a lot of it secret from me too.'

Suddenly she started to cry. 'I'm sorry,' she sniffed, still looking me square in the eye as the tears poured down her face. 'I didn't know what to do, had no idea things had gone so far. Like, I mean, if the rumours are true that they slept together… well, Beth definitely didn't tell me that. And I… I'd have done anything, *anything* to stop what happened to her.'

She gave a huge sob. I wrapped her in my arms, consumed with guilt.

'It's not your responsibility to look after her. It's mine. I'm so sorry, I should never have spoken to you like this,' I apologised.

Chloe is taller than you, Beth – where you are as slim and lithe as a willow switch, she's sturdier, has a more womanly figure. But holding her reminded me so much of hugging my daughter that I was overwhelmed by loss. I missed you, Beth. Sitting by your seemingly lifeless form was torturous.

When will I hug you again and feel you hug me back?

We stood in the lane, a teenager and a grieving mum comforting each other, for several minutes. Finally, each sniffing, we broke apart.

'I'm so sorry,' she repeated.

'No, no, I should be apologising to you. Anyway, you'd better get home or you'll be late. I don't want your mum worrying.' I knew the horror of that worry all too well, and wouldn't wish it on anyone.

I watched her walk up the lane towards the lilac house, and didn't move until I saw her go up the garden path and let herself in. I would not let history repeat itself.

She waved before she closed the door.

CHAPTER 44

They stood side by side, waiting for the bus to pull away so that they could cross the road. Beth had never stood so close to Aleksy before. Wow, he was tall, she realised; she only came up to his chest.

The silence between them was awkward.

Aleksy, Chloe and she had been talking about music on the fifteen-minute bus journey home from school in Wapentake, but now it was just the two of them, it felt too intimate somehow to continue the conversation. Beth didn't want to give him the wrong impression. Sometimes his look was so intense it made her shiver. From the corner of her eye she saw him pulling nervously at his rucksack straps, hooking his thumbs beneath them.

A belch of black smoke and the bus lurched forward. Beth only had time to lift one foot to move before Aleksy spoke.

'Are you definitely going on Friday night, then? I'll see you there?'

'Um, yeah.' The reply was a squeak as Beth hurried off.

The next day at school Chloe kept nudging her and asking what Aleksy had said.

'I saw the two of you chatting as the bus pulled off,' she whispered during English. 'Come on, spill – what did he want?'

Beth put her finger to her lips then pointed to the teacher, who was bound to catch them talking.

Chloe wasn't giving up, though.

'Hey. Hey! Have you still got the hots for that guitar teacher as well? Shit, juggling two blokes! Look! You're blushing! You go bright red every time I mention his name. Beth fancies her teacher.' The last was in a sing-song whisper.

'Shut up! I do not!' Beth hissed.

She screwed up a piece of paper and threw it at her friend. It bounced off Chloe's head and landed on the floor. The teacher turned and frowned in their direction, clearly knowing something was going on but unsure what. When he went back to the whiteboard and started talking, Chloe and Beth began to giggle uncontrollably.

Then Chloe mouthed something to Beth.

'So what's the big secret?'

Beth felt like replying, 'Which one?'

CHAPTER 45

Before I went home following my chat with Chloe, I had another teenager to apologise to: Aleksy Jachowski. I nipped round to his home, feeling foolish. His father answered my rap on the blue door, and held it open just enough to be seen. Clearly he wasn't in a hospitable mood; no surprise there.

His son had inherited Mr Jachowski's sharp cheekbones and upward-slanting eyes. His high forehead, currently crinkled with a suspicious frown, gave a glimpse of the future for Aleksy – the handsome boy wouldn't be able to hide behind a fringe forever.

'I wanted to apologise for last night. That mob was—' I gave a helpless gesture. No words could describe how awful it must have been for his family, cowering in their home, terrified, while villagers screamed obscenities at them. 'I know it sounds hollow, but… Anyway, the police have arrested someone for Beth's attack, so everyone will know soon that Aleksy had nothing to do with it.'

Mr Jachowski said nothing, simply grunted. Nodded his head.

'But I did wonder if I could have a quick word with your son about—'

The door closed.

Well, that was as much as I could have expected, really, given what his family had been put through.

*

'All right, all right,' shouted Jacob, running to the front door. Wiggins barked enthusiastically, presumably running at his master's feet, as eager as Jacob to discover who was hammering to get in. From the bedroom I heard muffled conversation, voices rising.

'Who is it?' I called, making my way down the stairs. 'We need to set off for the hospital in a minute…'

I saw Ursula's platinum hair a second before she spotted me. Her scarlet mouth became a sneer of fury.

'You!' She jabbed her finger in my direction. 'If you come near my daughter again, I'm getting an injunction against you!'

'Hold on a second. Will someone tell me what's going on?' demanded Jacob.

'I'm sorry, Ursula. But you know how protective you are about your daughter right now? Imagine how I feel with Beth in hospital. I don't even know if she'll ever wake up.' The words came out at machine-gun speed. I'd felt good making peace with Chloe, but Ursula throwing her weight around reignited the fury that seemed to burn in me permanently these days.

'What have you done, Mel?' Jacob asked again.

'I'll tell you what she's done. She's upset my daughter. And I'm not having it!'

'Ursula, Chloe and I sorted it out. Chloe kept a secret about Beth and James Harvey, so I had every right to ask her about it. But we're fine now.'

'No. No way. I'm not having you going near her again. What's happened to Beth is dreadful, but it's my duty to protect Chloe.' Ursula was white as she spoke. A fleck of spittle flew with the force of her words. Wiggins gave a small growl. 'You come near her again and I'll get Steve to get an injunction against you.'

'I thought you and he had split up,' I said, confused.

'We've decided we're stronger together. You made us realise that, just now. I mean it, Melanie, Jacob: stay away from Chloe or you'll regret it.'

Jacob stepped towards her, placating, arms wide in a gesture of openness. 'I've no idea what Mel's done, but I'm so sorry if it's upset Chloe. I'm sure that was the last thing she wanted. Wasn't it, Mel?'

'Yes, yes, of course,' I spluttered. 'And she's not upset!'

But Ursula wasn't listening to me, Beth. She flounced away, wiggling inappropriately in her cobalt-blue skinny jeans and high-heeled boots. Climbed into her white BMW and gunned it.

*

Tears stung the raw skin beneath my eyes. I was all cried out, stretched thin and hung out to dry after everything that had happened. After Ursula left, I had expected your dad to hold me tight and comfort me. Despite what he'd been up to, I still wanted that. Instead…

'Christ, Mel, I'm sick of you having a go at people all the time. You're upsetting our friends! We need all the support we can get right now, and you're stirring stuff up.'

Gobsmacked, I watched him pace back and forth. 'But Jacob—'

'No. That's the end of this. Now that James Harvey has been arrested, just concentrate on getting Beth better.'

'But that's the point!' I exploded. 'Nothing we can do will make any difference to Beth's health. Now, though, we can rest easy knowing that I've done something useful in all of this. I've found the person who put Beth in hospital. She doesn't have to be scared any more; she can wake up!'

He stopped pacing so he could rub his face in despair. 'It's great news that James is being questioned – and you're right, that is thanks to you. But you know catching Beth's attacker isn't going to make any difference to her prognosis, don't you?'

'I know—'

'Good. Because God knows, I wish it did, but it doesn't. And I'm worried that you've linked the two in your head.'

'I think I preferred it when you were having a go at me for upsetting friends,' I muttered.

He'd been reaching towards me. But his hand dropped to his sides. 'You know what? Whatever. We need to get going. We're already late.'

I've always said that the family stubbornness skipped a generation and passed direct from my dad to you. But I'm ashamed to admit, Beth, that at that moment I'd have been willing to cut my nose off to spite my face – in fact, I did something even worse.

'Well, if you're going to be so sanctimonious, you can go to the hospital alone,' I said.

I thought he would back down, especially after what he had done, the secret I knew. Give me a hug. Tell me I was being a tit but that he still loved me. Instead he picked up his keys without a word, threw me a remorseful look, waiting for me to say something conciliatory. I almost did. This was ridiculous. More than anything in the world, I needed to see you, Beth. But somehow it was easier to hurt myself than face time in the car while your dad judged me.

As soon as he drove away, I regretted it. Snatched up my phone and unlocked it, ready to dial.

But it wasn't your dad I called.

Instead of being with my family, I sat in Glenn's van in the dark car park of the marsh. Listened to crap music on a local radio station. He pulled out a big flask filled with whisky. I had a slug, grateful, then passed it back. He shook his head.

'Can't, driving. But you help yourself.'

So I did. A lot. Glenn sat beside me, stone-cold sober, writing notes in his silly pink notebook. Updating our investigation, presumably. I snatched it from under his nose before he had the chance to react, possessed with that fluid speed that only drunks seem to achieve. Jumped from the vehicle.

'Give it back, Melanie.' He leapt out too. Silhouetted in the headlights, hands on hips.

'I want to write in it: "Case closed".' Eurgh, I was slurring.

'You're drunk. You'll ruin it. Give it back, Melanie.'

I danced out of the way, stumbling in a direction I hadn't anticipated. Clearly neither had Glenn, as his charge completely missed me.

I opened up the book triumphantly.

'Let me write… Hey, what's this?'

The first two pages were covered not in Glenn's spider scrawl; instead it looked like the neat, rounded script of a teenage girl. In one corner sprouted a doodle of a flower growing from a stack of books. A drawing of a bird with a long, plumed tail, like a peacock or something, dominated the opposite corner. Both were beautiful. They were only a couple of lines, but clearly done by someone artistic. While Glenn had many talents, artistry almost certainly wasn't one of them.

I peered closer when – ouch! Glenn snatched the notebook from my grasp so quickly, my fingertips burned from the friction.

'Flipping heck, Glenn, no need to have a cow! Mardy arse. I only wanted to write in it. Someone else already has, so what's the big deal?'

He hugged it to him. 'Look, you know this was my daughter's, Mel. This is all I've got of hers. I grabbed the nearest thing I could without Marcie noticing, pocketed this book. Writing in it makes me feel closer to my kid.'

Even in my drunken state, shame gripped me. Of course! Sometimes I was so busy thinking about the loss of my daughter that I forgot Glenn had his own loss to deal with.

'Sorry. Some friend, eh?' I took a staggering step and wrapped him in a loose hug. It was nice. Plus it helped keep me steady.

''S'okay.' His voice was small. He clearly hadn't quite forgiven me.

'Look, tomorrow we'll forget about all my problems and do whatever you want. Yeah?'

'Yeah?' He held my shoulders, pushing me back to arm's length so that he could look at me properly. 'Well, you know what I want to do?'

I shook my head, and if it weren't for him holding me up I would have fallen over. 'Whoops,' I giggled.

He laughed and shook his head too. 'I want you to have a lie-in and get over the hangover you're bound to have tomorrow.'

'Yay!' I flung my arms up in celebration. 'I want to see James Harvey get sent down for a very long time.'

'Okay, well, we'll see what we can do.'

We stood in companionable silence. I couldn't face going home. Not quite yet. My head lolled back against Glenn's shoulder as I looked at the stars.

'I could never live in a city,' I murmured.

'Hmm?' He grunted, clearly in his own world.

'I could never live in a city or town. Well, for one, it's too noisy, but... I'd miss the stars. You can only see a handful of the brightest ones there, but here, with no light pollution, wow. It's like someone has sprinkled diamonds across the sky.'

An infinite number glittered, some small, some large, all so bright against the huge black night.

'Yeah. It's funny, when I lived in Nottingham I didn't notice it. But now I'm back, I look up at the sky and it really is incredible how much more you can see. I did see that amazing red moon, though – that was cool.'

I wrinkled my nose. 'I thought you were travelling in September.'

'Huh?'

'September last year. I thought you were travelling.'

'I was. Australia.'

'But the blood moon was in September.' I turned to him, making sure to hold onto his parka for steadiness. He was finally wearing it as a concession to its being well below freezing tonight.

'Yeah. I saw it there,' he replied, still looking at the sky. 'Bloody great red moon. In Sydney, Australia. In September. Supercool.'

'Supercool. Supercool!'

'Come on, let's get you home,' he sighed, and gently led me back to the van.

'Supercool.'

I didn't know what I'd done to deserve such a good friend, but I was so glad Glenn had come along just when I needed him.

CHAPTER 46

At midday the following day, the police arrived at the house. DS Devonport looked as immaculate as ever. This particular day she wore a three-quarter-length black coat that, despite being plain, was clearly expensive. Either wool or cashmere or some kind of mix, it exuded quality.

I exuded booze – from every pore.

'Is Mr Oak here?'

'He's had to go to work. But I can fill him in.' No need to tell her that I hadn't set eyes on him so far that day. I'd been asleep by the time he arrived home from the hospital, and hadn't even stirred when he rose for work. The joy of being in an alcohol-induced coma.

'May I take a seat?' DS Devonport asked. She was a cold fish, that one. Her gaze always appraising; her every move carefully considered. I wondered what you would have made of her; imagined you doing a pretty accurate impression of her husky voice and stiff manner. 'We have news.'

Yes!

'You've charged James Harvey?'

'We have released him. He has an alibi for the night your daughter was injured.'

My stomach lurched. 'He claims to have been with Alison Daughtrey-Drew, I know. But, obviously, she's lying for some reason.'

'We've absolutely no evidence of that, Mrs Oak, and—'

'Come on! It's the only thing that makes sense. James Harvey was taking advantage of our daughter, and, I don't know, perhaps she realised, said no, fought back as he tried to force himself on her.'

'Melanie—'

'No, it has to be said,' I insisted. 'He gets angry that his advances have been rejected at last, and he's scared that she'll tell someone what's been going on. So he hits her. Hits her to shut her up. Or maybe even just to scare her, and goes too far. Whatever – it's clearly him who's responsible.'

The detective took a breath before speaking slowly, calmly. Enunciating each word as if talking to an imbecile.

'Mrs Oak, there's something else. The medical examination of Beth that you agreed to shows that she is still a virgin.'

Relief flooded through me.

The detective continued. 'We've also looked into the dates mentioned in Beth's diary. Dates where she claims to have met Mr Harvey. He has alibis for virtually all of them – he was at practice sessions of a church choir for most of them. Other dates you yourself have said Beth was with you. I'm afraid there is no easy way of saying this, but it appears the book was a work of fiction. A child psychologist has also studied the writings, and reached the same conclusion we have. Apparently the language used is innocent; there is a lot of talk of kissing and love, but only hints of more.'

The silence stretched as I tried to take this in. She reached out to pat my hand. I moved it out of the way.

'Beth developed an attachment to James Harvey, and created a fantasy relationship?' I murmured.

'That's what the evidence points to, yes. I'm sorry.'

The clothes, the secrets and lies, the fantasy world you had woven... Had I known my little girl at all, Beth?

CHAPTER 47

The. Biggest. Smile. Ever.

That's what Beth had plastered on her face as she walked home from Decoy Wood. Watching nature always did that to her. She had seen a hare racing across the dark brown fertile fields, then a little later a fox trotting along, following the scent before finding something more interesting that took it off in a different direction. Presumably something more likely to fill its belly. There had been redwings and fieldfares, crows and starlings, as well as several robins. Not too bad a haul to note in her journal.

The sightings had made Beth lose track of time, though, and she was forced to hurry home. She knew her mum fretted if she were late.

Almost there.

She scurried past the Picky Person's Pop In—

'Oh!'

Beth bumped into Alison Daughtrey-Drew. The woman's handbag flew from her shoulder, spilling contents as it dropped to the ground. Both scrambled to pick everything up. Beth picked up a clear plastic bag stuffed with pastel-coloured pills that looked like sweeties. Almost.

Alison snatched at them.

They looked at each other, neither knowing what to do. Like a rabbit and a fox spotting each other, and that moment of stillness before they ran.

'I, er, I better go.'

'Wait. Keep quiet, and I'll make it worth your while.'

Mum always said Alison had a face like a horse. It was definitely long, but so was the rest of her – Beth only came up to her shoulder. But Alison didn't have the vibe of a horse. Although she'd had very little to do with the older girl, Beth knew her as well as the next person in the village and had always been reminded more of a weasel. Lithe, intelligent, quick, with a ruthless streak beneath the kindly exterior and cut-glass accent.

'I'm quiet. Nothing to tell!' the teen squeaked.

Alison gave her an appraising look. Then a gentle laugh. 'It's Beth, isn't it? Listen, Beth, this really isn't a big deal. I'm holding onto them for a friend, and I'd hate my stupidity to get them in trouble—'

'Seriously, Alison. I'm cool – but I'm running late. Got to go.'

As she walked away, she truly did try to be cool, but her eyes were wide with shock. She knew those tablets were Ecstasy – the school had given them an anti-drugs talk recently. Still, she decided to keep quiet about Alison's haul. She didn't want people thinking she was a grass.

*

Guilt gnawed at her at home, though. She felt that somehow her parents would know she had seen something she shouldn't.

'You okay?' asked Mum, as if reading her mind.

'Yeah! 'Course.'

'Sure? Only you're chewing at your thumb, and that normally means you're worrying about something.'

'I've got something to take your mind off whatever it is,' Dad chimed. 'My new camera's arrived! You can borrow it sometimes for a bit of nature photography. Long as you're careful.'

'Oh, wow, Dad!'

Soon they were mucking about, troubles forgotten. Pulling stupid expressions at the camera and smushing their faces together. Mum couldn't stop laughing, and insisted Dad print one off to put on the noticeboard.

'My gorgeous family!' she grinned, stepping back to admire the bug-eyed image.

Beth stood behind her, looking at the image, her smile fading. In the photograph she looked the same as ever: innocent, happy, carefree. She didn't understand how the truth couldn't show. Her innocence was being shattered; she was weighed down with secrets.

CHAPTER 48

After DS Devonport left, I didn't call Jacob. I didn't want his hope shattered until it had to be. Let him stay at work. Not knowing was better than realising the person who hurt our daughter had been released – although the bad news would, of course, be tempered with relief that the test proved you hadn't been interfered with sexually. Besides, with James Harvey exonerated, thanks to a fictitious alibi, Jacob's own missing hour was bound to come under scrutiny again.

Once more, I instinctively turned to my new friend.

'How's the hangover?' Glenn quipped when he answered his phone. But he fell silent as I explained everything.

'The police might have given up on James Harvey, but I'm still not entirely convinced,' I finished.

'Beth must have had some encouragement from him to weave such elaborate lies.'

'Too right. She's an intelligent, sensitive girl. He took advantage somehow.' I picked at the skin on my thumb while speaking. A bead of blood appeared and grew; the light shining on it as it bulged until it could no longer contain its shape and began to trickle.

'What about confronting him? A mother's anger, and all that? He might cave when faced with what he's done.'

'You know what? That's a bloody good point.'

'Want me there, for moral support?'

'I can handle that pond scum on my own, thanks.'

*

Before that day, I'd have described James Harvey's flat as neat, tidy, clean and modern. Pale blue walls, minimalist IKEA furniture and stylish, neutral striped throws. It had felt like a safe place to bring my daughter for private guitar lessons. Now it felt grubby, seedy, tainted with what the owner had been doing there.

James had seemed such a squeaky-clean, polite, nice young man. Talented and artistic, he had reminded me slightly of Jacob, though they looked nothing alike, apart from being the same height. Where Jacob was blond, and his shorn hair showed off his fine bone structure, James was more hirsute: wavy brown hair shot with auburn and a neat, ruddy beard.

He carried his guitar as though it was the most precious thing in the world. The way he caressed its neck, fingering the struts with the lightest of touches to produce the sweetest sounds, it was obvious how much he loved it. He had fooled me into thinking he would look after you with the same care.

But as he stammered before me, unable to look me in the eye, I felt nothing but contempt for him. Even though he had let me in without so much as a word of protest, he refused to confess to me.

'Tell me the truth, James. You were with Beth that night, weren't you? Maybe you didn't mean to hurt her. Things got out of control.'

'No! No, it wasn't like that.'

'Then what was it like, James? Tell me.'

His eyes darted, hands clutching each other. 'I didn't hurt her. It wasn't anything to do with me, I promise you, Mrs Oak.'

'For God's sake! Why are you lying? When Beth wakes up, she'll tell the truth anyway.'

'I can't… I can't.' Then he straightened, resolved. 'I can't help you. You need to get out or I'll call the police.'

'Fine, call them,' I huffed.

He picked up the phone. As he moved, a cloud of aftershave assaulted my nostrils. Notes of ginger, amber and citrus pushed me back, disgusted. *Smells So Good…*

'Who do you think they'll side with, James? A paedophile, or the mother of an innocent child who has been preyed on?'

He gave his name and address down the phone. I wasn't worried, though.

'You let me in, James. I knocked on the door, and you let me in. I've done nothing wrong.'

'Please… she won't leave. Just make her leave,' he begged the operator.

'They'll arrest you when they get here. Not me.'

When he put the phone down, there was desperation and pleading in his eyes. 'They're on their way. Please, go. I swear to you I didn't hurt Beth. I liked her—'

'Yes, a bit too much.'

Time was running out. I needed a confession out of him before the police arrived, then I'd be able to pass to them what he had done. What could I do to make him tell me the truth?

Beat him senseless.

Turn his well-groomed face into mush.

Snip his penis off with a sharp pair of scissors and hear him scream and cry in agony.

Empty his precious aftershave all over his body, then set fire to him.

Desperation made the fantasies pound in my brain. My world was falling apart, and the only way to stop it was to find your attacker, Beth. James was the only person it could be, and I would be the one to make him face the truth. No matter what.

I snatched up his beloved Taylor acoustic guitar, holding it with both hands by the neck like a baseball bat.

'You hurt my daughter. Now I'm going to hurt you.'

I stepped towards him. He stepped back.

'Tell me the truth, or I'll smash this over your head.'

I wasn't sure how much damage the guitar would do. It was surprisingly light and well balanced, and felt expensive. Smashing it into matchsticks over James's head might not do him loads of damage, but it would hurt him emotionally. He loved that bloody guitar.

Once it was gone, I'd move onto something else. Something heavier. Part of me screamed that I was acting like a crazy woman. The rest of me yelled back that doing whatever it took to uncover the truth was the only sane option.

'I didn't—'

'How long were you grooming her?'

'Listen, please—'

'The diary isn't graphic, but she loved you, you sick bastard. She thought you were going to marry her! What did you do to her?'

'Nothing! I… I wouldn't! I'd never… !'

Everything about him pleaded with me, trying to keep me at bay. His body hunched, hands stretching towards me, fingers spread. Those fingers which had caressed my little girl.

I'd break them to get a confession.

'Tell me!'

I lifted the guitar high over my head. Slammed it on the ground. James gave a horrified gasp. I hefted it again, destruction making me smile in satisfaction. The splintered wreck crackled and crunched beneath my feet as I jumped up and down.

'I mean business, James. That's all that'll be left of you if you don't confess.'

I grabbed a glass vase, its thick bottom giving it impressive weight.

'This will crack your skull.'

'Please, no! She – I didn't – we shouldn't—'

'What did you make her do to you?' My voice was a horrified moan. The vase sagged towards the floor for a moment. But then I raised it higher. Up above my head, ready to smash in the brains of this man, just as he had smashed my daughter's head.

'I'll kill you, you bastard! Confess—'

'I'm gay!'

His scream was barely heard above the crashing sound.

CHAPTER 49

The crashing bang on the front door came again.

'Police! Open up!'

James, still half-crouched, was braced for my blow. I lowered the vase slightly.

'You're gay? You're lying…'

His eyes didn't leave mine as he called out. 'I'm fine, we're fine. The door is open, so let yourself in.'

He made a lowering gesture with his outstretched hands. 'Put the vase down, or they'll arrest you.'

Confused, I found myself doing as I was told. The two officers who walked in could immediately sense the tension in the room, though.

'What's going on?' one asked. I'd seen him before, and he nodded at me. 'Mrs Oak, is everything okay?'

James jumped in. 'Mrs Oak came round for a chat, but now we've cleared the air, haven't we?'

'No, it's not cleared up. If you're gay, what's the deal with your alibi with Alison? Why did you both lie?'

'I really would like you to leave now, though,' James talked over me.

The anger flared back again. 'Who are you, to tell me what to do? To tell me lies?'

I wielded the vase again. The stocky officer who had recognised me stepped between us, his body a wall.

'He's just told me he's gay. If he's gay, why did he and Alison Daughtrey-Drew—'

'I didn't say any such thing,' James laughed. 'I'm not gay. I'm *not* gay.'

'Oh my God, you'd say anything, wouldn't you? Anything to make sure I don't hit you!' I lunged forward, but the stocky officer moved with me, blocking me effortlessly.

'That bastard groomed my daughter, then tried to kill her. Why am I the only one who can see it?' I screamed in frustration.

The officer kept his eyes on me, his expression sympathetic.

'It would be wise if you left,' he said in a low, firm voice, as if speaking to me confidentially. Leaning in so that I got a good look at the painful red razor rash on his neck and the yellow-headed spots it had caused. 'I don't want to have to make you. Not after everything you've been through. But…'

But he'd have to if I didn't do as I was told. The implication was clear.

I hesitated, thinking. I might still be able to smash the vase over that conniving, slimy bastard's head before the officers had time to react. It probably wouldn't do any permanent damage, though, and would almost certainly end with me jailed. Which wasn't so bad, but I wouldn't be able to see you, Beth.

Better to retreat and fight another day. I'd see James went down for what he had done.

For a few minutes I drove aimlessly, unsure of what to do, where to go. I headed down Low Road, a long, straight but incredibly narrow lane that locals tend to floor their cars on, even though the surface is rutted. On either side are dykes deep enough to be lethal if a car careered into them. I put my foot down, not caring if I lived or died.

Wanting the questions whirling around my head to slow.

Wanting peace.

Wanting to go back in time so that this had never happened and you were still my lively, gorgeous little girl, jumping out at me to say boo, or telling me a new fact you had just learned about some animal or other.

40 mph… 50 mph… 60 mph…

The whole car bounced along. Rocking and rolling, almost taking off. I'd once attended an inquest where a seventeen-year-old had gone so fast along the uneven surface that the car had flown off the road. Maybe that would happen to me, if I were lucky.

A thought. I slammed my foot on the brake. The tyres squealed, my body was flung forward, seat belt straining across my chest. I rocked back into the seat suddenly, as the car came to a standstill.

Talking to James Harvey again would probably result in me being arrested, and he was such a slippery bastard that he'd say anything that popped into his head to keep me off track. But there was another way of exposing his lies: by speaking to Alison Daughtrey-Drew.

She knew the truth. Had she really had a one-night stand with him? Or did he have something on her, and was blackmailing her into covering for him?

Hang on…

That Saturday when you had bumped into her flashed into my mind again. I remembered how I had watched you from your bedroom window because I was worried you were late. I'd seen you send her handbag flying, the contents spilling.

That clear plastic bag of pastel sweeties.

Oh, how stupid was I? They weren't sweets. The Picky Person's Pop In didn't sell things in clear bags; everything was branded. They must have been drugs. But what kind? I pulled out my phone, googled images of MDMA pills. They looked pretty similar to

what I'd seen, but then again, I had been a long way off. Too far
to be even remotely certain.

But you had been in such a strange mood when you first got
home. Had Alison threatened you? Had she offered you drugs
in exchange for silence? Were she and James working together?

Perhaps James knew about the drugs – *if there were any drugs,
if it wasn't my imagination*, I told myself – and had blackmailed
Alison into giving him a false alibi. If I could just get her to admit it.

Unable to do a three-point turn on such a thin strip of road, I
carried on until I reached a turn-off and made my way to Alison's
home.

CHAPTER 50

The Daughtrey-Drews are the closest thing to posh that we have in Fenmere. Their family, like many in the area, went back generations. But rather than farmers and farmhands in their ancestry, they could trace their lineage back to Norman nobility. In fact, their great-great, however many greats, had helped to fund the building of the village's square-towered church about a century after the 1066 conquest.

The family may not have that kind of cash to throw around any more, but they still live in the biggest house in the village. An old manor, with windows peeping through trimmed ivy, a thatched roof – something rare for the area – and a huge walled garden behind the sweeping drive. They used to host a summer garden party that was open to the whole village, back in the day when I was growing up, but that stopped about twenty or so years ago.

My dusty Ford Focus looked slightly out of place on the drive beside two sparkling champagne-coloured Mercedes, a brand-spanking-new silver Range Rover and a black Audi I could have seen my face in. With slight trepidation in case the police were also called here, and I wound up arrested, I made my way towards the front porch. A round, heavy metal knocker matched the huge black brackets that stretched across the ancient dark wood door.

I was reaching for it when the portal opened and Alison slipped out.

'Thought I'd save you the job,' she smiled apologetically. 'I guess you've come to talk to me?'

'That's right,' I replied, aware of my local twang sounding harsh against her more plummy tones. Alison didn't have a local accent. Instead she spoke like someone from *Made in Chelsea*, which I put down to her private education. While locals said 'grass' to rhyme with 'ass', she rhymed it with 'arse'. When she said 'hour' it sounded exactly the same as 'our', unlike Fenmere people who pronounced it 'ow-wer'. Instead of 'yes', she said 'yah'. She and her parents were the only people in the entire world, surely, who actually said 'yah'; it seemed such a cliché.

She was thin to the point of almost-but-not-quite bony, and her legs were slightly bowed from hours spent riding a horse from an early age. Her clothes were expensive, but then, she had always been spoiled rotten. I remembered again about how her parents had made her speeding ticket disappear, thanks to a few words in the right ear. I couldn't even get my daughter's attack investigated properly.

Still, I tried to appeal to her good nature.

'I won't beat about the bush. Alison. Please, I'm begging you, if you weren't with James Harvey, you have to tell the truth. He's got to be punished for what he did.'

Alison's eye contact was strong and steady. She didn't seem in the least bit nervous.

'I'm just a mother trying to get to the truth,' I added desperately.

One hand rested on her hip, the other beneath her chin, as if considering.

'Mrs Oak, I'm so terribly sorry to hear what happened to Beth. But, truly, this is nothing to do with me. I have no clue who hurt her – they hit her head, is that correct?'

I nodded, helpless in the face of her composure. A long finger lightly caressed her bottom lip, a thick silver ring glinting in the weak sunlight. I could make out the words 'Tiffany & Co' running around its base.

'You insist you were with James?'

'I *was* with him. Mrs Oak, it's bad enough I've had to make a statement about my sex life. Why on earth would I lie?'

That was true. I had no idea why she would pretend to be with James Harvey if she wasn't. It wasn't as if they were in a relationship, and she might be tempted to cover for him.

'All I know is that he is the only person who had a reason to attack Beth. Nothing else makes sense. Maybe he sneaked out while you slept, then sneaked back again for an alibi?'

She shook her head. 'I wish I could help you. But I can't.'

Despite the natural drawl that could make her sound insincere, she looked genuinely sorry about that, and I appreciated it. Her glossy caramel hair, with perfect highlights, hung around her long face, and she tucked one side behind her ear.

'Look, I didn't know Beth well. You know, with her being so much younger than I, different friends and my only returning to Fenmere recently…' A crazy decision of hers to drop out of university, in my opinion, but I had little doubt Alison's parents would sort out a good job for her, with their connections. 'But she seemed a lovely girl. She was growing up into a beautiful young lady.'

'She *is* growing into a beautiful young lady.'

'Is. Yes, is, of course. She's, er, shooting up, too, is as tall as me in her heels. She truly is a beautiful girl…' She cleared her throat awkwardly. 'I suppose what I'm trying to say is that if I could help you, I would. But I can't, Mrs Oak.'

'Can't? Or won't? James Harvey was grooming my daughter. The police may not be able to find proof of that, but I will. And then it's only a matter of time before his alibi is proved to be lies.'

She looked away, bored. Stood up straight, no longer leaning against the porch frame.

'Look, today he even told me he was gay. He's a liar!' I snapped. 'Is he blackmailing you? Is it something to do with drugs?'

Alison looked as if she had been slapped.

'James must have been desperate to get you off his case; and no wonder, if you're going to make such ugly, baseless accusations,' she recovered. 'Well, I've told you all I can. I really must go now.'

Rhally mast go.

I stepped back to let her by, not knowing what to think.

When I got home, I noticed Alison's Mercedes parked outside the Picky Person's Pop In. Right, so her urgent appointment had been to buy some bits and bobs. That showed how high you were on her list of priorities, Beth.

I flopped onto the sofa and waited, half-suspecting that I might get a visit from either Flo or DS Devonport.

I'd been dozing for about two hours when they both arrived.

Flo was all sympathetic looks and soft noises, something her round face and equally round eyes seemed built for. What did Jacob see in her?

The detective's tight lips looked as if they were struggling to keep angry words in. When she finally spoke, her voice was even lower than normal.

'You need to keep away from James Harvey. You're impeding the investigation with your actions. I'm sure that's the last thing you want to do. New information has come to light which we are looking into.'

'What new information?' Hope flew like a kite.

'I'm not in a position to say at the moment. But rest assured, we are following every possible lead in connection with your daughter's attack.'

'Well, you'll forgive me for thinking that sounds like a load of excuses,' I snapped, as hope crashed and burned.

The front door opened and Jacob called out, 'Are the police here?' He walked into the living room and stopped. 'Have you charged him?'

I closed my eyes. Oh God, he still thought that James Harvey was being held. I hadn't yet told him otherwise.

The DS seemed quick on the uptake though. She explained everything to him that she had told me earlier – and added in the bit about me visiting James. Jacob didn't say a word, just looked at me, stunned, eyebrows raised.

'Well, he's not made a complaint about me, has he?' *Which was suspicious.*

'No, Mrs Oak. In fact, he has been at great pains to tell us there is nothing to complain about,' the detective replied. From the way her eyebrows went up, she clearly wasn't convinced. 'I can't stress enough that Mr Harvey's alibi has now been corroborated.'

DS Devonport spotted my mouth opening to give a retort, and raised her voice slightly to bulldoze over me. 'Not only by Alison Daughtrey-Drew. Jill Young has come forward to say that apparently she saw Alison dropping him off at 5 a.m., and that they were kissing passionately before he got out of the car. She'd been going into the shop to see to the newspapers at the time.'

I slumped back on the sofa, beaten. If James Harvey was innocent, then who attacked you, Beth?

As I tried to sift through what I had heard, Jacob saw the police out. I wandered to the window and watched him, deep in conversation with Flo as they stood on the drive. Their heads were bowed together as my husband spoke urgently. The young officer's pudgy hand was on his arm and her mouth crinkled into a line of sympathy. In the evening light they were cupped in the orange of the street lamp. They looked far closer than he and I had been for weeks.

CHAPTER 51

The crow caught in my trap seemed to know what I was as soon as it saw me. Its intelligent eyes held my gaze for a second, then it gave a deep-throated caw and began to flap and tug desperately.

It was more intelligent than the people who surrounded me every day. It recognised a predator when it saw one.

Take Melanie. My plan was working perfectly, right under her nose, and she had absolutely no idea. What a stupid cow. I was virtually parading before her, and she was too blind to see it. It seemed laughable now that I had, at first, been wary of her.

At one point she had seemed to be trying to pull herself together. Just because your daughter's in a coma is no excuse to let yourself go. But her good intentions hadn't lasted. She was a disgrace. Better her daughter died so she couldn't see the mess her mum was.

She was constantly drunk lately too. In that state no one would take her seriously, no matter what she said. Good. For all my games, the last thing I needed was for Melanie to start putting two and two together.

But in that state, I could make use of her to cover my tracks.

Chuckling at the thought of the fun to come, I took hold of the crow. Killing it would not be the same as snuffing out a human life, but the bloodlust was becoming worryingly difficult to ignore. My kicks needed to be got somehow. I needed my fix.

As I looked deep into the crow's eyes, I was reminded of my elemental power. It struggled, tried to peck and maim me, but I was too strong for it, fully prepared for its every strike, because I was all-powerful. I drank in its panic and terror. Wonderful.

Eventually, I snapped its neck. But not before entertaining myself.

CHAPTER 52

If Jacob's jaw got any lower he could use his mouth as a flytrap.

'Have you heard yourself?' he asked, stunned.

The argument had started almost as soon as he'd come back through the door after his cosy conversation with Flo. A ceasefire had been called long enough for us to get into the car to travel to the hospital for the weekend. But the engine had barely turned over before the bickering began again.

I should have shut up. Of course, I didn't, Beth.

'James Harvey has to be the one that did it. I don't understand why Alison is lying. And somehow she's got Jill in on the act too. What if it's something to do with drugs?'

'You're losing the plot, Mel,' Jacob groaned, slumping over the wheel as if he wanted to bang his head against it in despair.

'No, listen. Who else could it be? James has to be the one! Although I still feel that Aleksy Jachowski knows more than he's letting on. Maybe it's worth talking to him again. Maybe he saw Beth and James together, or – oh, I don't know. But I've got to figure out why Alison and Jill would cover for James.'

'Or maybe they're telling the truth.'

We sank into sullen silence. I stared out of the passenger window, looking at my own reflection in the darkness. My jaw was set, eyes narrowed, arms folded. Laser beam glare threatening to melt the glass. I couldn't let it lie.

'I'm sure Chloe is hiding something too. Which means Ursula is. Maybe I can get to the truth once I corner Davy again...'

'So now Davy Young is involved in this grand conspiracy? Or did he do it? For goodness' sake, Melanie, what are you doing? Leave this to the police.'

I tugged at the seat belt and turned to face Jacob again.

'What's your problem? I'm not getting in their way, I'm helping. I'm looking at things they might have overlooked. As a villager, I might be able to spot things they'll miss in an official investigation. People might open up to me more.'

'Have you heard yourself? Leave this to the experts, okay? Don't you have enough on your plate without going round pointing the finger at all and sundry?'

'At least I'm doing something, Jacob. Unlike you, sitting back and letting the police get away with letting their investigation slide.'

'They're the experts. Not us,' he snapped.

I turned back to the window, resentment festering. God, I wanted a drink. I wanted to beg Jacob to drop me back home so I could talk things through with Glenn. He'd listen; he'd understand and not judge me. What was the point of going to the hospital so that we could stare at your corpse-like body, when I could be doing something far more productive? Something that would actually help you?

Love hearts covered the entrance to the children's ICU, and I realised with a jolt that Sunday would be Valentine's Day. Time was passing; it was three weeks to the day since you had been attacked, and you weren't showing any signs of improvement.

The ventilator still breathed for you.

The monitor showing your heart rate, respiratory rate, oxygen saturation percentage and blood pressure were all as constant as Lincolnshire's horizon.

Your MRI scans showed no change.

A nasogastric tube still fed you.

There had been a time when those words meant nothing to me. Learned by rote, I could now recite them.

Likewise, the team of people looking after you had felt over-whelming at first, but now I knew the difference between the ward consultant and the neurological consultant surgeon. I understood the differing roles they had in your care, and the duties of the nurses, whom I had got to know and become friendly with over the past weeks. We often brought a cake for the team, as a thank you for their continuing hard work caring for you. Sometimes I baked it, but I'll admit it, Beth, a lot of the time I bought them from Seagull's Outlook Café. Ursula probably wouldn't want my custom any more, though; not after threatening legal action on me the day before.

When were you going to wake up, Beth? I wanted to shake you, shout at you, do whatever it took to rouse you. I wanted to take a chunk of my soul and gift it to you, to give you the strength to fight.

'Take whatever you have to take from me,' I begged. 'Take it all, everything I have. Just get better.'

There was no gentle squeeze of my fingers in reply. No flutter of eyelids. Only the usual *beep, beep, beep* that made me want to throw the machines out of the window.

You weren't in the hospital room, were you, Beth? You'd gone. You were on the marsh.

My only child. Every ounce of love in my body and soul had been poured into you, my sweetheart, my Beans. More love than I'd thought a person was capable of feeling. To bits and whole again.

Please get better, Beth. Please, please, please…

I wanted to scream. I wanted to run. All I could do was sit and watch the ventilator filling my daughter's chest with air, making it rise and fall. Hold your limp hand. Watch your face, so pale that even the freckles seemed to have faded.

You know, sometimes I used to catch myself with a soppy grin on my face, just from watching you walk into the room and flop on the sofa. The wonder of you, Beth Oak. Seeing your face glowing with enthusiasm as you spoke about a bird you had spotted. The look of delight at Christmas when you realised we'd bought you those ridiculous platform boots, and you had paraded around in them still wearing your pyjamas. I'd almost got a crick in my neck looking up at you, they made you so tall!

Thinking about those good times made me feel I was teetering on the edge of a cliff. Any second the pain might make me decide to jump.

Think of something else. Anything else.

So I considered the conundrum of who hurt you.

Something about my conversation with Alison bugged me, but I couldn't think what. I kept replaying it, sure I'd missed something, but whatever was wrong wouldn't come to me. Like trying to remember a dream, the more I tried the less substantial it became.

I'd talk it over with Glenn, I decided.

Glenn. Talk about cometh the hour, cometh the man. His reappearance in my life had been perfectly timed. I owed him so much.

Looking at you and thinking of Glenn made me imagine the pain he must be suffering at losing his own daughter. But it didn't have to be like that for him; something could be done to get his daughter back. It was time for me to start repaying him for the kindness, patience and support he had shown me. Speaking selfishly, solving someone's problem might give me a little respite from my own too. Maybe I'd get a step closer to the kind, thoughtful person I'd been before anger and frustration chipped away at me.

Resolved on a plan of action, I stood, my chair making a scraping noise that seemed horribly loud in the quiet hospital room.

Jacob looked up. 'Where are you going?'

'Just nipping to the loo. Thought I'd give Mum and Dad a quick call, too; see how they are, and if Wiggins is okay.'

He nodded. 'Give them my love.'

*

Finding a quiet table to sit at in one of the hospital's cafés, I pulled out my smartphone and got to work. I had a few journalist's tricks up my sleeve. Piecing together the bits and bobs that Glenn had mentioned about his former life, I pinpointed the area he used to live: Dunkirk, Nottingham.

It took mere seconds on a website, using the newspaper's password, to access the electoral register and discover his exact former address. A simple cross reference using his wife's name, Marcie, ensured it was correct. Another tap to get her landline number.

It had taken about five minutes. Jacob wouldn't be getting suspicious yet.

Dialling the number, I held my breath.

A woman with a strong Nottingham accent and a thin, reedy voice answered the phone. She didn't sound like a strident bitch, but that meant nothing.

There was no subtle way of doing this; I'd have to come right out with it.

'Oh, hi, is that Marcie Baker? My name's Melanie Oak. Umm, you don't know me, but me and my husband,' I was careful to add that so she knew I wasn't a threat, 'are friends of your ex, Glenn Baker.'

'You know where he is? Is he okay?'

'Er, yes, he's fine.' Not the reaction I'd expected. Perhaps Marcie had calmed down and would welcome hearing from him. 'I wanted to let you know what an amazing thing he has been doing for us. You see, my daughter was attacked a few weeks ago. She's in a coma, and Glenn has been such a pillar of strength for us…'

'Well, good for him. It's a shame he can't be the same for me – he just upped and left, you know. Barely an explanation—'

'The thing is, I know this has nothing to do with me, but I think he's really missing his daughter.'

Silence.

'He hasn't got a daughter.'

Oh, the old 'he's dead to us' routine.

'I know you and he have your problems, and that's nothing to do with anyone but the two of you. But, well, I can't talk to my daughter, and it's killing me. There's nothing anyone can do about that. Being without his daughter is killing Glenn. Please, let him see Katie. Or at least let him call her.'

'Katie? She's next door's kid.'

What?

'I'm telling you, love. Me and Glenn don't have kids. I always wanted them, and he's so great with them, but…'

'I… I'm so sorry. There's been a mix-up. Sorry,' I repeated, ending the call hurriedly.

What the hell? Why would Glenn lie about something like that? He was yet another bloody person who was lying to me! A person I thought I could trust, but clearly couldn't. But…

As I thought, I calmed down. And started feeling pity.

Glenn and his wife had wanted kids but couldn't have them. It could be an emasculating thing for a man; your dad had felt that, briefly, when we'd tried for another baby and failed. That was one of the reasons we'd agreed not to bother with tests, but instead simply to relax, make the most of what we had and be philosophical.

When Glenn talked about the loss of a child, that was what he was referring to.

Still, why lie? Why pretend that his neighbour's child was his?

My shoulders slumped with the realisation. He'd done it for me. So that I wouldn't feel so alone when talking about you, Beth. I'd thought he was different, that he didn't look at me with pity, but all this time he had.

Walking slowly back along the maze of corridors to the paediatric ICU, I resolved to speak to him about it.

CHAPTER 53

Eyes glittered in the darkness. Skewering Beth in place.

'Things wouldn't go well for you if you told the police.'

This far out of her depth, she only had one option left. Brazen it out.

CHAPTER 54

Hope filled my heart as I woke. The world was normal and wonderful. Then reality punched in, and my face scrunched up as tears leaked down the sides to wet my pillow.

My dream had felt so real. Hugging you, talking to you. I'd felt you, warm and solid. Smelled your perfume as you drew closer, and your minty breath as you planted a kiss on my cheek.

The dream made me crave a drink. That sounded terrible, didn't it, Beth? But drinking to excess made me pass out, so that I no longer had these vivid encounters with you; encounters that felt so real the loss of you was fresh when I woke. A whole weekend without alcohol had taken its toll, the dreams particularly lifelike.

It was just gone 5 a.m. Monday morning. Jacob lay beside me, sleeping through sheer exhaustion. I didn't know how he found the strength to keep going. He was amazing, inspirational… and made me feel ashamed because I lacked those qualities. No wonder he sought comfort elsewhere.

My left hand started to cramp. I had the duvet clutched in a death grip that pulled it taut between my body and my husband's; a physical metaphor for the atmosphere in our marriage. Between Jacob and I lay a mattress no man's land that neither of us would stray into for fear of attack; the exact boundaries were sorted out without words passing between us. Jacob balanced on approximately five inches of bed on the extreme left, and I did the same on the right.

My right side ached from sleeping in one position for too long. As I slid from under the duvet and onto the floor, Jacob shifted slightly in bed, his foot straying across to forbidden territory, but he didn't wake. Opening and closing my left hand repeatedly, trying to get the blood flowing round it properly again, I crept silently into the bathroom, where I dressed quickly. This was my routine, and I was adept at moving around in the dark these days.

Once downstairs, a softened thud, thud, thud from the kitchen, a pattering sound, then something wet and cold pushing against my skin.

'Hello, Wiggins. Yes, all right,' I soothed. My voice less than a whisper as my hands ran over the furry head.

More gentle thuds as he wagged, then a warm, wet tongue found my fingers before I pulled them away and felt for the torch. By its light I also grabbed a tatty rucksack, once olive green, now camouflaged with years of grime because it was used to gather wood for our stove. Into the rucksack I pushed an axe, kept handily beside the fire in the living room.

CHAPTER 55

The only light came from the stars, the crescent moon and the bobbing circle made by the torch. I'd visited the marsh so many times recently I barely needed the faint illumination, instead relying on the familiar changes in smell: from cabbages, to rich earth, to brine. Once onto the sea bank, I watched the tide beating a retreat, uncovering rich pickings for the wading birds and revealing the hardy plants that survived a regular soaking.

The tatty rucksack hung low and awkward on me, and it bounced against the small of my back in rhythm with my stride. Wiggins surged ahead, confident of his footing, while I crunched through frozen puddles.

Finally we reached the sycamore, stunted by the constant wind. Stepping over the bedraggled teddy bear abandoned at its base, I reached out and touched the trunk.

Nothing. No connection.

I yanked off my glove and clutched the rough bark so tightly it hurt. Better. Maybe it would make me bleed. Drip and mingle with the blood already in the earth. But I still couldn't feel a connection with you.

Something ruffled audibly in the wind. It danced along my hand, tickling then fleeing. Caressing. I couldn't see them properly, but I knew it was one of the ribbons tied to the tree, making it look as overdressed as an ugly girl ready for her first date.

This marked the spot where you were attacked.

A blow to the skull. A scream for help, cut short.

Scenes flickered through my mind, numbing me far more than the cold.

Terror. Panic. Confusion.

I could barely feel my extremities now. You must have felt like that. It made me feel closer to you.

Running. Feet won't go fast enough. Silently begging for Mum to come to the rescue. Then…

I screamed my rage into the night. The wind took up the war cry.

I would never forgive myself for not protecting you, Beth. I was sleeping when it happened. Safe, warm, cosy at home. There had been no shiver of fear. No eerie mother's intuition that my daughter needed help. The first time it was obvious something was wrong was in the morning.

'Oh, Beth, you must have been so cold out here,' I said aloud. You always hated being cold.

Trying to share my daughter's suffering was what held me in place as the sky slowly paled to mother-of-pearl with the rising sun. I refused to move despite the wind cutting through my clothing as if it didn't exist, slicing through flesh until it hit bone and chilled me to the marrow.

*

With the sun finally up, I could see properly the landscape I knew off by heart. The land squeezed into a couple of inches; the rest of the view taken up solely by a huge sky. Squatting in the distance, a mere speck, stood the old RAF lookout tower.

I drank it all in, defying the feeling it gave me of insignificance. Then anger twisted my stomach.

Now or never.

Wiggins was leaning against me, warming me with his body and no doubt leeching a little warmth from mine too. I grabbed his collar and led him a couple of feet away, moving stiffly after being frozen with cold.

'Stay.'

His head cocked on one side. The second I stepped away he moved towards me.

'Stay!'

This time, he listened.

I tugged at the rucksack's drawstring. *Come on, come on. Yes!* The knot gave beneath my unfeeling fingers. Then I pulled out the small axe Jacob used to chop firewood.

The balance of it felt alien to me, the heavy head pulling earthward. But I gripped it with both hands and made experimental swings through the air.

Should I use one hand or two? Two.

The axe made an impressive whooshing sound as it cut through the air.

I turned to the tree.

The pathetic sycamore.

Stunted and twisted from the wind bullying it every day.

The soiled ribbons festooning it fluttered towards me, imploring. I swung back my arm then let it fly. The helplessness of your situation; the frustration of James Harvey being released; the betrayal by your father; the bittersweet agony of my dream that morning – they were all behind that blow. It landed with a satisfying thunk, the sharp blade biting into wood; the impact reverberating up my bones.

I tugged the axe free. Swung again. A strangled sob escaped my lips.

The third blow bounced off the bark.

No more sound from me, just the wind whistling in my ears, egging me on as I thought of bone cracking beneath my blows, of blood running rather than sap. I'm not a violent person, God knows, Beth, but anyone with a child would understand my dreams of parting flesh with my axe.

Missing the tree altogether, my next blow sank into the frost-hardened ground, splitting it open to reveal the clay beneath. Sweat mingled with tears. My arms burned.

I didn't feel any better.

Why don't I feel any better?

The scrawny tree stood firm. I couldn't even get that right.

Still I swung. Feet sliding in the mud created from the thawing of the ground where I stood. Another blow, another, another... My feet slithered from beneath me and I landed heavily beside the axe, which sheared the teddy bear in two.

Wiggins gave a bark of distress and rushed forward, nosing through my balled-up body to plant feverish licks on my face. I wrapped my arms around his neck gratefully and buried myself in his fur. Let the sobs come.

Maybe I was having a breakdown, Beth. Maybe I'd welcome one, to escape reality.

Back at home, it was only just gone 8 a.m. There was no note from Jacob, who had left for work.

Feeling dissatisfied and unsettled, I had no idea what to do with myself. So opened a bottle of wine to help me relax. After two glasses, boredom hit. It was a little after 9 a.m.

I stumbled from the house again. Wiggins by my side, as ever. We crossed the road and went down by the paddocks, along a little walkway that ran from the churchyard through to open fields.

Davy was stroking the neck of one of the horses.

He knew something. Whether about James Harvey or someone else, I wasn't sure. That look he had given me. The way Jill came over all protective. The fact that he hadn't been seen at the store since our chat. Call it a mother's intuition, but

I knew he held another piece of the jigsaw. I needed to talk to him again, this time when there was no chance of being interrupted by his mum.

He didn't notice me until Wiggins ran up and danced around his feet.

'I'm sorry if I made you feel uncomfortable the other day,' I said.

'Don't be daft. You got a lot on, Mel.'

'I just want the truth. Beth's my only child, and someone hurt her. I need to understand why. If it was deliberate then that person could be a potential danger to others. And if it was an accident, well, that could be understandable. They should get it off their chest; it will make them feel so much better.'

Luckily I'd been running through what to say to Davy for days, while he'd been busy avoiding me, so my speech was all prepared. Even though the lies almost stuck in my throat, the alcohol lubricated them until they slipped out easily. I'd no intention of forgiving anyone who hurt you, Beth, accident or not. But I'd do or say anything to get them brought to justice.

'It's nothing to do with me or Mam,' Davy protested. Despite his bulging muscles, he looked like a worried child.

'I'm not the police. I'm simply a mother trying to find out what happened to her baby. If you do know anything, even a tiny thing that might help me… please, let me know.'

He shook his head, eyes wide, tiny potato nose reddening. 'Mel, I didn't have anything to do with this. I were with my mam when Beth were hurt – I told the police that.'

Something about the way he moved clicked into place. 'Davy, why were you watching me on the marsh the other day? Have you been following me?'

'Just keeping you safe.'

Keeping me safe, or keeping tabs on me?

'Safe from who?'

'Whoever hurt Beth.'

'Why do you feel responsible for keeping me safe? Come on, Davy, you're a good guy. Please tell me the truth – because I know you're hiding something.'

The damn booze meant my emotions were all on the surface. To my horror, I started to cry. This was stupid. Maybe I'd just imagined the look of guilt he had thrown when I'd spoken to him and Jill the other day. Something kept me pushing on, though. I tried to stem my tears and speak, but they kept on.

'Don't cry!' begged Davy.

'You and your mum, you both know something, don't you?'

'Mam's got nothing to do with this, I promise, Mel. She knows nothing.'

'What about you? Do you know who did it? Was it you? Are you lying about being with your mum? Promise you know nothing about what happened to her!'

He hesitated, drowning in my swimming eyes.

'Please, Davy. The truth will come out in the end. Better now than later. Help me! Promise you don't know anything!'

'I… I can't promise, because…'

Davy did this. Why? Why would Davy hurt you?

My heart hammered against my chest, as if trying to break free and punch him. My hands were curled tight.

'I were with Ursula Clarke,' he finished.

It took a second before words would come, and when they did all I could manage was, 'What?'

'I were with Ursula Clarke.'

'You're having an affair?'

'We are.'

So that was his big secret. That was why he looked so shifty.

'You gave the police a false alibi, saying you were with your mum, because you didn't want your affair to come out? And your mum backed you up?' I checked, my voice weak. I was stunned. Not by the revelation, but by how petty it was.

'I were with Ursula till late, about two in the morning, then she got a phone call and I went home. Her husband were away, so—'

'Okay, well, that's none of my business. But thanks for being so honest,' I snapped.

Disappointed, I trudged away. Wiggins bounded after me, giving an excited bark at being on our way once more.

Another dead end. I was never going to get to the bottom of who hurt you – and why. Not until you woke and told us yourself. If you remembered.

'Mel!' shouted Davy. I didn't bother turning. 'Talk to Ursula.'

But I'd no interest in hearing her confirm his tawdry alibi.

It was only as I got home and lay down on the sofa that a thought occurred in my drink-slowed mind. If Davy lied about his alibi because he was with Ursula, then Ursula lied too – about her cosy night in with Chloe.

CHAPTER 56

If Glenn was surprised he could smell alcohol on me at ten o'clock on a Monday morning when we met at the marsh, Beth, he didn't express it. Instead he listened as I filled him in on what Davy had told me earlier.

While talking, I paced up and down the sea bank, beneath a sky filled with clouds as black as my mood. Gusts of wind tattooed my face with fine needles of icy rain. Far in the distance a weather front moved in, bringing with it a nasty cloudburst. But we had a while before it would arrive – the flat landscape did strange things to perspective, making distant things seem closer and close things seem distant. I kept talking and walking, telling Glenn everything.

'Yeah, but Ursula only lied so that her affair wouldn't be discovered, didn't she?' he asked. 'There's nothing more sinister to it than that, is there?'

'No, listen. Davy was adamant I talk to Ursula, and I think I know why. If Ursula was busy with her fancy man, then where was Chloe? They've given statements saying she was at home with Ursula, but what if she was with Beth? What if she witnessed who attacked her?'

Glenn frowned. Bent down and picked a blade of rough grass, then pulled it apart slowly, letting the pieces flutter away in the wind. I watched them, achingly sad. Bits of me were being blown away on the breeze too. I was disappearing; the person I had been a month earlier was gone, replaced with someone I wasn't certain of.

'Come on, then.' He gave me the softest punch on my arm. 'Let's go and interrogate Ursula. I mean, pose a few *friendly questions.*'

'Right now? You'll come with me?' I asked hopefully.

He winked his reply, and we walked back to the van arm in arm.

Five minutes later, we pulled up at the Seagull's Outlook.

'Hey, what about her threat to get an injunction if you go near her or Chloe?' Glenn said suddenly, pulling me back.

'Come on, she's not going to turn custom away from her café, is she? I'm just a paying customer who has come in for a nice hot cuppa on a cold day. Brrrrr.'

On cue, the rain went from being on the wind to a drizzle. Glenn rolled his eyes and grinned, then opened the door.

With a cheery *ting*, the bell announced our arrival.

Seagull's Outlook Café was virtually deserted at this time of year, apart from the odd dedicated birder and twitcher, and the occasional local. A couple, retired I'd guess, had taken the table at the centre of the small tea room. Sensible walking shoes, outfits in neutral colours. The man, tall and thin, with hair so white it almost didn't look natural, sitting on top of an angular face with friendly eyes. His wife the opposite, all soft curves and nervous glances. Judging by the impressive binoculars that sat on a chair beside them, they were birdwatchers.

The café was done up like a posh beach hut. Limewashed wood ran across the bottom half of the walls, to match the tables and chairs and the counter. A faded blue was used here and there on the striped curtains, the cushions and the floor. The cups, saucers and dishes were white with a blue stripe. Decorative rope knots on the walls continued the nautical theme, and the toilets had rope signs above them which spelled out 'Buoys' and 'Gulls'. The home-baked cakes were displayed on pretty, tiered, glass cake stands from yesteryear. Everything was sparkling, clean and bright – perfect, just the way Ursula wanted them to be.

I ruined the room's perfection. Muddy walking boots. Jeans that needed washing, a sensible but shapeless jumper that, now I came to think of it, I'd been putting on for over a week. It probably smelled a bit. My hair was pulled back into a ponytail that may or may not have been messy – I had no idea, as I hadn't been looking in the mirror when doing it.

Ursula was busy serving someone. As she leaned over the counter to chat, the V-neck of the duck-egg blue cashmere jumper she wore sagged down to show off her cleavage. Her bottom half was hidden behind the counter, but I had no doubt she was wearing something glamorous.

'What can I do you for?' she asked, as always. Cue titter. 'See anything you fancy?'

'Only you, duck,' came the inevitable seaside postcard reply. 'Eh, if I were ten years younger.' Mr Langton was ninety-one. He leaned on his walking stick as he lurched forward to smile.

'Ooh, cheeky! Good job I'm a happily married woman, or I'd take you up on your offer!'

She had always been good at banter, had Ursula. But the comment about being happily married was by far the funniest thing she had said, Beth.

As she handed Mr Langton his cup of tea, she glanced up at her next customer. Me. There was the slightest stutter in her movement. Her sparkling smile was suddenly accessorised with wet spaniel eyes, which darted away from my gaze. On the plus side, she had clearly forgiven our last argument.

'How is Beth?' she asked. 'If only she'd knocked on my door that night…'

'But if she'd knocked on your door she'd have seen something she shouldn't, wouldn't she, Ursula?' There was no question in

Glenn's voice, merely a statement. I was glad he'd spoken up – I hadn't a clue what to say to broach the subject.

She bit her frosted-pink lip, then picked up a cloth and started scrubbing industriously at some invisible dirt on the counter. Glenn elbowed me.

'Beth would have seen you with Davy, wouldn't she, Ursula, if she had knocked on your door that night. Caught you at it.'

My voice was louder than Glenn's had been. The birdwatching couple looked up. Ursula threw the dishcloth down and looked at me, horror-struck.

'For God's sake, Melanie, I've got customers in here. I don't want everyone knowing.'

'Knowing you were having an affair with Davy Young? Is that why you and Steve split, because he found out?'

'None of your damn business.'

'What other secrets have you kept? I need to speak with Chloe again. I need to see if she's remembered anything else about who Beth might have been meeting. Where was Chloe when Davy was at your place? Was she out with Beth?'

She paled. Walked around the counter, narrow-lipped, and grabbed my elbow, leading me to a table in the corner. Glenn followed, silent, and we all sat down.

Ursula leaned forward. Conspiratorial, low-voiced. 'If you must know, Davy didn't come round until later. After Chloe had gone to bed. Having an affair while my daughter sleeps upstairs isn't something I'm particularly proud of. So yes, I have been trying to keep it quiet! But, well, I was lonely, and we were used to snatching what brief chances we had to be together.'

'So Chloe was in the house the whole time?' I checked.

'We had a girls' night in, watched crappy films, ate popcorn. Then she went to bed, none the wiser that I'd be staying up for a bit longer.'

Beth, she didn't even look ashamed of what she had done. Just worried people might overhear and discover her dirty secret. I've known Ursula all my life. She has always worried about what other people thought – caring too much about appearances instead of substance, that was her problem. As long as her life looked perfect, who cared what crap was going on behind the scenes? That was her mindset. But I'd thought she was a nicer person than to cheat on her husband; she had always struck me as fiercely loyal.

'So Steve knows all of this? No wonder you split up,' I said, disgusted.

Ursula had been holding my forearm urgently, but she let go and sat back in her chair. Tossed her glamorous hair and held her chin high. Less spaniel, more Dobermann.

'You don't go anywhere near Steve. He knows everything. Everything. And he doesn't need it rubbed in his face. The same goes for Chloe; you stay away from her. I'll do whatever it takes to protect my family, Melanie. And if that means getting that injunction out against you, then that's what I'll do.'

'Handy, having a lawyer for a husband,' I scoffed. 'Mind you, if you divorce, you'll get screwed over, I'd imagine.'

'As an adulterer,' Glenn added.

A huff of surprise from Ursula. She soon gathered her thoughts, though.

'Melanie, I meant it about that injunction. Leave my family alone. I've put up with today's visit because of our history and what's happened to Beth, but this is your final warning. Keep away from me and mine.'

CHAPTER 57

I watched Melanie as she stomped from Seagull's Outlook Café. Oh, dear. It was so funny seeing her running around, accusing people, pointing the finger left, right and centre. The fool. She had no idea what was going on.

Maybe I should have held a sign up, then she might have got the message about what was really happening under her own nose.

Even if she did manage to discover the truth, no one would believe her. She had become the woman who had cried wolf too many times, accused too many different people. She was a drunken hysteric.

The police were probably as sick of her as the rest of us. I was sure they loved her calling them every five minutes to tell them her latest theory and advise them on who they should investigate next.

Still, she may have been unpopular with everyone else, but I was enjoying her crazy, drunken performance. It was so entertaining being able to sit back, put my feet up and watch it all play out.

It kept the bloodlust at bay. For the time being. It was becoming increasingly hard to ignore, but I was slowly putting things into place for a big kill.

This one would be so perfect that I'd be able to play it in my mind for all eternity.

CHAPTER 58

'Blimey, you didn't need me there at all,' Glenn laughed, giving a deep belly rumble. 'You more than held your own.'

'Yeah, but having backup there really helped – besides, you didn't exactly sit back and do nothing. You got the ball rolling.'

'Pub for a debrief?'

Tempting, but I fought the urge. We couldn't stay where we were, though. Despite the wind picking up and the drizzle beating a faster tempo, Jill Young was sweeping the pavement outside the store and café and straightening up as if to say something. Something I almost certainly didn't want to hear. Davy lurked down the side of the shop, biting the inside of his cheek. Alison Daughtrey-Drew walked by on the opposite side of the road, glancing at my flushed face curiously. And Ursula glared through the window at me, making my hands itch to slap her.

I made a quick decision. 'Marsh. It's easier to talk out there. Call me paranoid, but it feels like the whole village is watching us.'

We grabbed Wiggins from the house, hurrying out just in time to see Aleksy striding away from James Harvey, who took one look at me and hid inside the shop. Everyone was here in one place, watching me watching them. If I didn't escape from under the microscope I'd go mad.

At the marsh, for ten minutes we simply sat watching the rain pelt down and obliterate the view through the windscreen, listening to it roaring on the van's roof. Finally it eased off and we jumped out. Wiggins gave a joyous bark and bounded ahead, stopping at all his usual places for updates on which other dogs might have passed by this way since his last visit.

As he ran back and forth, Glenn and I brought up the rear, walking at a more relaxed pace, braced against the wind which tried to push us over in gusts. After dissecting Ursula's reaction, and the fact that my temper meant I had well and truly burned my bridges with her, we had to accept that there was no prospect of us getting near Chloe ever again.

'Chances are she doesn't know anything more, anyway,' consoled Glenn.

True. And although what Ursula was doing was morally wrong, it was none of my business. Talk gradually turned from our investigations, which had come to a dead end for now, to childhood memories.

'My dad would go fishing for eels in the huge drainage ditches that criss-cross the fens, you know.'

'What? Even that one over there?' Glenn asked.

'Yeah, all the time. He'd catch loads. And here, on the marsh, he'd roll up his trousers and walk through the shallower creeks with a trident, like this.' I did a funeral march, head down, making a jabbing motion downward every couple of steps. 'It's called butting. There are flatfish that lie hidden on the bottom of the creek because of their camouflaged scales. He'd step slowly along, stabbing blindly down with a trident, and sometimes he got lucky and caught one.'

I laughed. I'd never done it myself, and neither did your Grandpa Mick any more, after one too many lectures from you about how eels were becoming rarer.

'My dad never did that. But he always had a rifle in the car, to shoot rabbits and pheasants.'

'Poaching, you mean?'

Glenn shrugged and grinned. 'Yeah, poaching. Always had a machete, too – for chopping the thick stalks of cauliflowers. He'd often come home with a haul, having raided the farmer's field at night. Now I'm back, I do it myself. Always have a machete in the van, just in case.'

'Flipping heck, Glenn, you want to watch you don't get pulled over by the police. They might wonder why you've got a lethal weapon squirrelled away.'

'Yeah, you've probably got a point.'

Glenn looked at me directly. There was no pity or sorrow or embarrassment in his expression; he simply looked at me with deep interest. Each word I said fascinated him, and he wanted to be there for me every step of this awful journey. He had even lied about having a daughter to make me feel better. I was both annoyed and touched.

For a second I found myself harbouring ideas about running away, Beth. A fresh start, somewhere new with someone new, where my history could be rewritten and people wouldn't know everything about me.

Where I could escape the guilt I felt looking at you.

The idea flared faster than a struck match, then disappeared. I would never, ever leave you. I deserved my guilt over not being there for you. And while a wedge had been driven between Jacob and me, your dad was still my one and only.

I laughed nervously and let my hand drop. 'I'd better go.'

'Do you want a drink?'

'Why not?'

The words popped out before I could think.

And yeah, why not? I could do with a drink right now. Maybe I'd even find the courage to tackle Glenn about his heartache at not having children. Maybe not.

*

Okay, so I drank a little more than I thought I would. I'd only wanted one, but it hadn't taken much arm-twisting on Glenn's part for me to get a second round in. Dale had bought in a new red, a Malbec, and it was really moreish. Two large glasses later, my cheeks were flaming and I felt the tiniest touch giddy.

Well, I needed something to cheer me up. I'd be seeing you that night and had no good news to share with you, Beth. I'd have to face long hours with only beeping machinery to talk to. Hoping and praying you would wake, when in reality my well of hope had run dry.

I missed you so much it hurt. It hurt to be away from you. It hurt even more to be with you and see the shell of you, without the spirit. No laughter. No stupid jokes. No jumping out at me and yelling 'surprise', even though it never was. No lectures on how you would only eat free range eggs, or why you were considering going vegetarian. Discussing the latest book you had read, or listening to you singing Justin Bieber at the top of your voice, or watching you dance around to the latest music videos, or, or, or…

The doctors were starting to make noises about test results not being as good as they had hoped. About you not responding to treatment. About running more tests, and then 'thinking about our options'.

I took a slug of wine, finishing the glass. Felt the alcohol's warmth slide down my body, but it never hit my soul.

'I better get home,' I said, reluctantly. Wiggins's ears flickered and he stood, stretching. Glenn raised a hand in farewell as I walked out, Wiggins at my heel.

It was 4.30 p.m., and Jacob should be home any minute. It was lighter than expected; already the days were getting demonstrably longer as winter loosened its grip and spring approached. Everything changing, my old life with a happy family being left behind, frozen in winter's grip forever.

*

As I headed over the crossroads, Jill was locking up a few doors down. Fridays and Mondays were her early-closing days. She always seemed to be around, every time I looked up. Yet the woman who generally knew everything that happened in this village apparently knew nothing about what had happened to you. It infuriated me.

'Pretty pathetic to lie to the police and give false alibis,' I catcalled.

It was the alcohol. If I were sober, I'd have said nothing. But frustration and booze were a terrible mixture, making me take my mood out on someone else.

Jill put down the A3 sign with the latest newspaper headline on it which she had been carrying inside.

'If you have something to say, say it.'

'Just what I said.' I smiled sweetly. 'It's pretty pathetic to lie to the police and give false alibis.'

Yeah, yeah, I had done the same myself for Jacob, Beth, but that wasn't the point.

Jill said nothing. Simply looked at me. Folded arms, straight mouth, frown. Her characteristic lack of response irritated me further.

'Davy told me the truth. Him having it away with Ursula. Only getting to yours after the time Beth was attacked. And you covering for him, Jill.'

'He had nothing to do with what happened to Beth.'

Her low voice gave a warning I chose to ignore. Nothing scared me in those days. Nothing could, when pretty much the worst thing imaginable had already happened.

'Yeah? Well, if you and he can lie to the police about that, what else are you covering up? We both know the answer to that,' I teased, just for a reaction. Just because I felt bolshie. But Jill's eyes widened, her postbox mouth sagging open, perpetually folded arms hanging loosely at her sides.

'Davy told you about the lookout?' she gasped.

'Lookout for what?' The words were out of my mouth before my drink-addled brain could tell it to shut up. Stupid, stupid, stupid mistake.

At my words, Jill's self-control returned.

'Mel, I'll tell you one thing, and that in't two – you better leave before you hurt people with your accusations. We all feel for you… but enough is enough. Get control over yourself.'

I reeled. '"Enough is enough"? I'm supposed to pull myself together when my daughter lies in hospital?'

'That's enough, lady. Go home and pull yourself together. You can't keep acting like this. You're running around playing at detective so you can avoid being at the hospital. Don't blame others for your shortcomings as a mother.'

The air was knocked out of me.

'I'm… I'm not! I'm…' The protestations were too embarrassed to come out of my mouth, knowing they were lies.

'Come on, Mel. I'm not as green as I am cabbage-looking, and I've seen how you're never there. If you're going to have a go at people, you need to look in the mirror first. Get your priorities straight. Be there for Beth.'

She turned her back on me and picked up the sign again. I wanted to run at her. Pelt her back with blows. Scream at the injustice of her words. Instead I stood there, fish-mouthed.

I was furious, too furious to go home. Stalked back across to the pub, ignoring the confused looks Wiggins threw my way as we retraced our steps.

A dribble of wine trickled down my chin. I wiped at it, hoping Glenn wouldn't notice.

'Old cow.'

He nodded sagely.

'But, right, I keep think… thinking about when Jill got narky with me,' I slurred. 'It was when I implied she was covering something else up. Something besides, besides… her son's affair with a married woman.'

Glenn raised his eyebrows quizzically.

'It was when I'd asked her who the lookout was.'

'Lookout for what?'

'That's the million-dollar question.'

I stared across the half-empty pub. Realised I was once again drinking on a Monday evening. I barely drank before your attack, Beth, remember?

'Thing is, I've b-been thinking,' I hiccuped. 'Did she mean a person, or did she mean the, the, er, the old RAF lookout tower? Hey, did I tell you about Alison Daughtrey-Drew and the pills?'

He whistled as I related what I'd seen.

'Right, well, it happened outside the shop. What if she bought them off Jill?'

'Jill? A drug dealer?' He raised an eyebrow and we both sniggered at the ridiculousness of it. 'But I've had a thought myself.'

'Uh-oh, here comes the dreaded pink pad.'

He ignored me and opened up the notebook. 'Right, yes,' he said, finding his place. 'I think we should look closer at Aleksy.'

'Oh, Glenn. That was just racist nonsense.'

'Yes, the mob's racial slurs were ridiculous, but I can't help wondering. No smoke without fire, and all that. We only abandoned Aleksy as a suspect because of James Harvey.'

He had a point. I conceded with a wobble of my head.

'So many people to consider,' I murmured, picking up my glass to take another glug.

Someone grabbed the stem, lifting it away from my lips.

'Hey!' I flailed after it as it floated beyond my reach. Then focused behind it. 'Jacob! What are you doing here? Ooh, you look kind of frowny… Cheer up, might never happen.' I giggled, but Jacob didn't seem to get the joke.

'You're coming home, Mel. It's six o'clock; I've been waiting for you so we can go to the hospital.'

Cold voice. Barely controlled anger in his blue eyes. I didn't want to go home with that. So I turned away. Tried to catch Dale's eye to order another drink. Jacob's hand on my shoulder pulled me, trying to turn me.

'Get off!' I was louder than I wanted to be. *But so what?* 'I'm not a kid. I'll come home when I'm good and ready.'

'Come on, mate, you're only going to make things worse.' Glenn had leaned over from his bar stool to address your dad.

Uh-oh, that was not going to turn Jacob's frown upside down. He flexed his hands, opening and closing them into fists, as if fighting an urge.

'You're the one making things worse. Keep away from my wife, understand?' His face pushed towards Glenn's.

Glenn stood with glacial speed, but didn't move his face away. He hunched over Jacob, staring right into his eyes, unblinking. His chubby cheeks and boyish grin had taken on an unfamiliar look.

'When Melanie tells me to stay away, I will.'

Then he straightened and sat back down again, still looking right at my husband. Deliberately, he let his eyes slide over to mine.

'Do *you* want to go home, Melanie?' he asked.

Suddenly I felt a lot more sober. 'Think I better had,' I replied quietly.

Jacob put his arm around me. It looked loving, but there was no wriggling from it, no denying the inexorable force he exerted that kept me by his side and propelled me across the room.

The darn step caught me out as we got outside, and I stumbled slightly.

'Look at the state of you. You're wrecked.'

'So what?'

'So, we're meant to be seeing Beth tonight. I'll have to call my parents, get them to go instead.'

'There's no need—'

'There's every need, Mel.'

He shoved the key in the door with more force than necessary. As soon as I was inside, he slammed it shut.

'Ooh, Wiggins…' I remembered, pointing back towards the pub.

'Wiggins is here, look.'

Oh, yes. Jacob let him off his lead. Maybe I was more drunk than I'd thought. It was all Jill Young's fault, the old battleaxe, having a go at me for no reason.

Jacob settled me on the sofa and handed me a glass of water.

'I wish you'd stop drinking so much,' he began.

'I don't drink that much…'

'You do since you started spending time with Glenn Baker. He's a bad influence. Drinking, being paranoid, falling out with neighbours and family friends. You've been different since you started hanging around with him.'

'It's not him that's changed me, it's the fact that our daughter is never going to wake up.'

My hands flew to cover my mouth, to try to shove back the words I'd said. Your dad's jaw clenched, the muscles flexing. Neither of us could believe the betrayal of my words.

'Beth's going to get better,' said Jacob. Stiff. Staring at his hands, fingers knitted together in front of him, rather than at me.

'Of course, of course. But…'

There it was, the terrible thought I'd been running from for all these weeks. The fear I'd been hiding away from. The reason why

I avoided visiting you, Beth. The reason why I drank to forget. I made myself whisper the words, hoping that might soften the blow.

'But what if she doesn't, Jacob?'

'You think you're the only one struggling? The only one hurting? I can't talk to you when you're like this.'

Flinging up his arms in despair, he walked out, slamming the door. It was such an un-Jacob-like thing to do, I was shocked. Wiggins whined uncomfortably at the atmosphere, the sudden shouting, then the absence of sound.

'It's all right,' I whispered.

I reached for him but misjudged and toppled off the sofa onto all fours. He scurried away, into his bed, and looked at me with his ears back. Wouldn't be coaxed out.

Not even my own dog recognised me any more. *What had I become, Beth?*

CHAPTER 59

Some people grew up wanting a fairy-tale ending, but Beth had grown up looking at her parents – and she wanted a marriage like theirs. Her mum and dad were so happy together. Laughing and chatting and enjoying each other's company. They even walked down the street together holding hands, still. Beth's mates were seriously disturbed by the sight; they didn't know anyone else's parents who were like it.

Beth felt sure she had found a soulmate in James Harvey. He was kind, sensitive, intelligent. His eyes didn't glaze over when she talked about wildlife; in fact, he was passionate about saving the environment too. He read loads of books, played guitar beautifully and got on well with her parents. He was the full package, right down to how well groomed he looked.

As they kissed, his hands slid onto Beth's shoulders. For a moment everything was wonderful. Perfect.

Then it all went wrong.

Like dominoes falling, once that first thing had gone awry, it started a chain reaction.

CHAPTER 60

Even with my eyes closed, the sunlight burned brightly on my retinas. I groaned and, with some effort, managed to turn my head away. It gave an extra-hard pound that felt like my eyes might explode from the pressure until I rested it back on the pillow as gently as I could.

Why had I got so drunk again? It was idiotic. Memories from last night kept punching me in the kidneys, kicking me in the head. I'd let everyone down, including you. Poor Jacob, having to deal with me falling apart, on top of everything else.

I couldn't seem to think straight. A hair of the dog, that would sort me out. After several minutes, I managed to get out of bed. Downstairs, I had the tiniest nip of vodka, then drank loads of water and necked some painkillers. Hey presto! The world was a marginally better place.

There was a text waiting for me. From Glenn. Saying he'd meet me at the RAF lookout tower at 11 a.m., as arranged. I didn't remember arranging anything. And was already ten minutes late.

'Stay, Wiggins,' I ordered, hurrying to the car. I was unsure of what I'd find at the tower, so thought it was best not to take him.

The tower had its own dedicated turn-off from the main road, created by the RAF. It was still only a single lane, though, and as straight as the other route that I generally took to the marsh.

At the end, I pulled over behind Glenn's van, careful not to go too far over onto the soft verge for fear of getting stuck. Unlike the lane that we usually came down, there was no car park here apart from the lookout tower's, and that was fenced off.

As soon as I stepped from the car, calm enveloped me. The marsh was more of a home these days than the house. I felt closer to you here, Beth. The wind whistled around me as if greeting an old friend, as if you were with it.

Glenn jumped from his van and did up his coat. His solid frame and open face were a sight for sore – and probably very red – eyes.

'You look perkier than I expected,' he grinned.

'I don't feel it,' I laughed, elbowing him.

We walked over to the seven-foot-high, sturdy chain-link fence that ran around the building and the car park. The chain-link gates were padlocked shut.

'Climb over?' Glenn suggested.

My mouth gaped. 'Er, no, I don't think that's feasible.'

But he went a couple of paces back and took a running jump. He easily grasped the top of the gate, pulled himself up and swung a leg over.

'Blimey, you're more agile than I gave you credit for.'

He sat on top of the fence and held a hand out to me. 'Want help?'

'What if I make it in, but can't get back out?'

He motioned with his foot to the strutting on the back of the gate. 'You can use this for a leg-up. It'll be easier coming out than getting in.'

I wasn't sure, but didn't want to appear a complete wimp and, ultimately, we were doing this for you, Beth. I should be the one to go in there more than Glenn, really. So, shaking my head at the prospect, I did what he'd done: backed up a couple of paces, then a couple more and took a running jump, flinging up my hands. He caught hold of one hand and pulled me up while I grabbed hold of the top and pulled myself up with the other. Somehow I wedged the top of the gate under one armpit while cocking my leg in an ungainly fashion. Glenn hauled at the back of my jacket.

When we both sat straddling the top of the fence, we laughed. I panted like nobody's business and my head pounded, but not as badly as I'd feared, the painkillers working a treat.

Abruptly, Glenn swung a leg over, jumped down and held both hands up to me, inviting me to jump into his arms.

The thought made me feel momentarily uncomfortable. Guilty. I mimicked his movement, but hooked my tiptoes onto the strut then jumped from halfway down the fence.

'Right, let's have a look around.'

We wandered about aimlessly, trying to look businesslike.

'There's quite a lot of muddy tyre tracks.'

'I was surprised by that too. Cars, motorbikes and bicycles. Seems like it's been busy,' he replied.

We wandered around the car park area, first looking down, then gazing up, neither sure what we were looking for. There was an air of recent use about it. A pile of beer bottle tops made me realise: of course, Jill must be getting her lads to start doing the place up for her. Clearly they had been at it for a while, judging by the amount of bottle tops.

'I'm going to see if there's a door open anywhere, or maybe even a window we can squeeze through.'

Glenn disappeared round the corner. He was out of sight for no more than a few seconds when he called out to me. I ran, and there he was, pointing at the ground.

'Does that strike you as a bit odd?' he frowned.

Lying on the ground was a pair of what looked like expensive wireless headphones; the good kind that were noise-cancelling.

'Well... It doesn't seem the sort of thing Jill would use, but it's hardly a clue. Maybe one of her lads uses them while he's doing building work here, and forgot them.'

Glenn shrugged. 'True. It just seems a bit, I don't know, out of place.'

It wasn't the only thing that was out of place. In the corner was a huge stack of empty water bottles. Building was thirsty work, but not that thirsty.

I peered into a window. The place was totally empty, as expected. No cobwebs, though. Turning away, I noticed the thick, heavy blackout curtains; they must have been a leftover from the military.

'Clues are pretty thin on the ground. Non-existent, in fact. Maybe Jill did mean a person when she referred to "lookout". If she did, how the hell are we going to find out who they were and what they were looking out for?' I said.

'What else could the lookout tower be used for?' Glenn wrinkled his brow. 'Could it be a base for smugglers? Just thinking of your theory of Jill as the world's unlikeliest drugs baron.'

I stuck my tongue out. 'Some of the creeks *are* deep enough and wide enough for a shallow boat, maybe, but it would be a squeeze. Maybe... hey, maybe Beth had a clandestine meeting at the tower with James Harvey, or Aleksy Jachowski, or, I don't know, someone else. Look how easy we found it to break in.' A thought occurred, making me gasp. 'What about Davy? His mum owns this place, so it'd be simple for him to get the key; he's got a car, so could meet Beth and drive her here easily enough, for a date; and his involvement would explain Jill's paranoia over me knowing about the lookout tower. You said yourself that he's quite childlike, so...'

'Wouldn't he have his hands full with Ursula?'

'Well, they're not full-time, are they? I wonder how often they manage to hook up? If he was seeing Beth, it would explain him watching me now – he's not looking out for me, he's checking up on me.'

I liked Davy, didn't want to be suspicious of him. But this theory made sense.

'Yeah, you're right, I don't know what's going on and I'm not sure we're getting any closer to the truth. But we've got to treat everyone with suspicion,' Glenn agreed.

We were both floundering in the dark. But I couldn't give up – not when I was convinced that if I stumbled around for long enough, I'd come across the metaphorical light switch.

'You look at Davy. I'm going to have a look at Aleksy,' decided Glenn.

'And how are you going to do that? The Jachowskis won't talk to anyone in the village after that mob the other day.' My eyebrows must have been right beneath my hairline, I was so sceptical.

'I'll find out something, somehow, don't you worry. Best if it's only me, though. If you try to talk to anyone in the Jachowski family they'll probably clam up.'

'Good plan. Now then… let's see if we can find out anything else.'

I pushed at the bottom of the window, trying to force it open. Glenn did the same on the neighbouring pane. I moved onto the next window. Fingertips exploring the underside, sides, corners, tops. There had to be a way in; burglars broke into far more secure houses than this every day. But I couldn't manage it. Glenn and I went from window to window, working in opposite directions until we met again.

'I could get something and smash a pane?' he suggested.

I hesitated, then realised I was actually contemplating breaking and entering. Trespassing was one thing, but that was a bridge too far when we only had hunches leading us on.

'Better not,' I decided hurriedly. 'I'm the law-abiding type.'

Glenn kicked gently at the bottom of the wooden door. 'Probably wouldn't take that much to kick it open…'

'Love your enthusiasm, and it's really tempting.' I went on tiptoes again, cupping my hands around my eyes, the better to see inside. 'But I can't see anything in there that would make it worth getting a criminal record for.'

Disappointment sank through me. Another lead gone, another dead end. Would talking to Davy again be yet another wild goose chase? Probably, but I had to keep going – just in case.

'Right, how are we going to get back over that bloody fence?' I asked, forcing myself to brighten up.

It was actually easier going back. Glenn gave me a boost in his cupped hands. From there, I stepped fairly easily up to the strut across the middle and pulled myself over the fence. This time when I jumped down, though, I landed awkwardly, lurching forward and going down heavily onto my knees and skinning my palms.

'Should have let me catch you,' observed Glenn from the top of the fence, leaping down beside me.

'Smart-arse.'

I hesitated, wondering if it was the right time to speak to him about his imaginary daughter. But didn't have the heart. I needed to think of how exactly to tackle it because it could blow up in my face. If Glenn felt embarrassed, he might just turn his back on me. And that was something I couldn't face at the moment.

We said our farewells, then drove off in single file, me following behind Glenn. I couldn't help once again thanking my lucky stars that he had come into my life. Off we went, chasing up yet another half-baked idea. I ignored the helplessness and doubts stifling me, told myself that each failure must bring me closer to the right track eventually. I was probably fooling myself, I thought, but it was better than giving up.

CHAPTER 61

The café's sign read 'closed', but Beth tried the door anyway. Her mum had sent her out on an urgent mission to buy her Auntie Tricia a birthday card. Mum always forgot her birthday until the last minute, too busy preparing for Christmas. Beth had actually been sent to the Picky Person's Pop In, but she thought their cards were a bit cheap and rubbish. Seagull's Outlook Café had recently started selling some lovely cards, though. A bit expensive, but handmade and really different, and she was sure Ursula Clarke wouldn't mind her daughter's best friend nipping over after closing time.

Mrs Clarke must only just have shut up shop, anyway. It was only a minute or so after 4.30 p.m. 'All I Want For Christmas Is You' still blasted out over the speakers – which was a bit unusual, as Beth knew that Chloe's mum usually preferred to have background music only.

'Hello?' Beth called.

No reply. She moved, hesitantly, further into the café, suddenly feeling like a trespasser. Well, if there was no one around, she would take a card and leave the money along with a note explaining. As she moved over to the stand, she heard a grunt, followed by moaning.

It had come from the kitchen.

'Mrs Clarke? Are you okay?' called Beth.

What if something had happened to her? Perhaps she had fallen. As the teenager hurried round the counter, Mrs Clarke appeared. Dishevelled, not her usual pristine self. Her hair stuck up at the back and her blouse buttons were undone one more than decency demanded.

'Beth! What on earth are you doing here?'

'I just wanted a birthday card. Umm, are you okay? Have you hurt yourself?'

'Hurt... ? No, I'm fine. Fine.'

A cough came from the kitchen. Beth's face flamed scarlet as she realised what she had stumbled on. Mr and Mrs Clarke were at it!

'I'm sorry, I'll go.' She backed away. Then her eyes fell on a jacket. Not the kind of jacket Mr Clarke, a solicitor in Wapentake, would wear. He wore smart three-quarter-length coats over his suits. This was the type of waxed jacket favoured by the farmers in the area.

Mrs Clarke was having an affair.

Shit, shit, shit!

Beth never swore, but this was definitely a sweary moment. Mrs Clarke seemed to realise it too.

'This is grown-up business, and not something you should get involved in. If anyone were to find out, people could get hurt. You wouldn't want people to get hurt, would you, Beth?'

The look on her face was so strange when she said it. Like a crazy woman.

Beth thought of her best friend. She came across as confident, cocky even, but Beth knew that beneath the bluff and bluster hid surprising fragility. There was no way she wanted to share this news with Chloe.

'You know you can trust me, Mrs Clarke. I... I haven't breathed a word of our other secret.'

'Well, yes. You really haven't told anyone, have you?'

Beth shook her head.

'And you won't tell anyone about this, either?'

Another shake.

'Not even your parents?'

'No, not even my parents.'

But she wanted to. As she walked away, she chewed on her thumbnail, scared that Mrs Clarke could tell.

CHAPTER 62

At just gone 1 p.m., I got home. Odd; my parents' Escort was parked on the road outside – they must have come straight from being with you at the hospital. Your dad's Subaru was in the drive too. Something must have happened to you, Beth. The knowledge poleaxed me. It was my fault; I had spoken aloud my fear that you might never wake up, and tempted fate. Now it was coming true.

My legs shook as I clambered from my own vehicle, almost falling, and I feared I would be sick. The key trembled in my fingers, refusing to slide into the lock. It took a couple of goes before I succeeded.

Mum and Dad were sitting on the sofa with Jacob. They looked sombre. My heart thudded.

'Sit down, duck,' began Dad.

'Oh God, no. No. No, no, no!' I backed away, shaking my head, tears spilling.

'Hey, hey, what's happened? It's okay,' soothed Jacob, jumping up. He hugged me.

'You're asking me what happened? I thought you were about to tell me something dreadful about Beth!'

He exchanged a look with my parents. Mum tried to get me to sit down this time. I did as I was told, wiping my face.

'So is everything okay?'

'Well, that's what we'd like to know, duck,' replied Dad, leaning forward, businesslike.

I frowned. Mum reached for my hand and took up the conversation.

'The thing is, we're a bit worried about you. You've been through so much, and I wondered if you fancied a little holiday? Me and your dad would pay. Nothing fancy, just a cottage in Wales or Scotland or something. And of course, we'd keep an eye on Beth for you, see her every night. You need not worry about her – and, well, you'd be close enough to get home quickly if you needed to.'

'Umm, that's a bit of a turn-up for the books, Mum. I thought you were going to say something terrible from the look on your face.'

'No! No, nothing like that. We've been worried, that's all, and we think it'd do you good to get away.'

'I'm all right, Mum, Dad, honest. This is a lovely offer, but I don't think right now is a good time.'

Jacob knelt beside me, resting his hands on my knees and gazing up at me. 'It's the perfect time. Come on, we need a break.'

I considered it. I truly did, Beth. If we had a break together, perhaps your dad would forget all about Flo. But putting our marriage first was selfish when you needed us. I shook my head. 'Jacob, I'm so close to finding out who did this. I can't—'

He'd already erupted onto his feet. 'This again! You see what I'm talking about?'

My parents nodded. I looked from one to the other of them. And realised. 'This is something you've all cooked up together? To stop what I'm doing?'

'We're worried about you,' Mum repeated.

'And you're drinking too much,' Dad growled. 'You smell like a brewery, lass. You'll find no answers at the bottom of a glass.'

'I've had one drink, Dad.' No need to mention it was for breakfast.

'It's not only that,' Mum jumped in, 'though it is worrying. You're getting yourself worked up about trying to figure out who did this, aren't you?'

'Of course I am!'

'Yes, yes, of course. But, well, the police are the experts, they'll get to the bottom of this. If you start suspecting people you've known all your life, you'll drive yourself mad.'

Jacob had been pacing during this exchange, but now he seemed to force himself to be still. He sank down at my feet again.

'I know how horrifying it was when we thought the contents of that book were real. But, thank God, they're not. Beth was just exploring her emotions by using her imagination. That's all. James Harvey didn't hurt her – he didn't do anything to her.'

Absolute clarity radiated from his expression. He had no doubts. Maybe… maybe he was right.

'He's been completely exonerated, hasn't he?' I accepted quietly.

Jacob nodded, his eyes softening but never leaving mine. 'If I thought he was guilty, and the police weren't doing anything about it, I'd kill him.'

'Would you?' I whispered, stunned. But I knew he was simply using the expression everyone does; he didn't actually mean the words. Although he might be moved to beat James Harvey up, on the spur of the moment, he would never go so far as to cause real hurt, let alone kill. He was too good a person.

'But medics have proved Beth is still…' Jacob floundered, not wanting to say the word *virgin*. 'None of the dates add up, because there was never a chance for he and Beth to be together the way she describes. It's just a fantasy.'

'And he has a rock-solid alibi for the night Beth was hurt,' reminded Mum.

I nodded slowly, their words hitting home at last. So why did I feel like the fog was descending on me, instead of lifting?

Why did my mother's intuition scream that James was lying? What about Aleksy, who seemed to know more than he was letting on? What about Jill, and the lookout – was she smuggling drugs and you somehow found out? Why did the conversation with Alison feel like a jigsaw piece? And how much did Davy know? I need to talk to him again.

Am I losing my mind?

Seeing me appear to accept their words, everyone relaxed a little. The tension dissipated. I used my go-to excuse to leave the room to try to clear my head.

'Cup of tea, anyone?'

As per usual, though, my plans were scuppered when Mum followed me into the kitchen.

'Come here,' she said, and went to hug me. I gently pushed her away. The hurt on her face at my rejection was writ large.

'Mum…' I knew there had to be a way of explaining this without hurting your Granny Heather, Beth, but I couldn't think of it at that moment.

'I wish you'd talk to me, Melanie. You used to tell me everything, but since Beth was hurt you've clammed up.'

'Oh, Mum.' I doubled over the counter, hands over my head. It was true. We'd always been best friends – like you and I.

'Please, stop pushing me away, sweetheart.' Her hand rubbed circles on my back, as if I were a child. Just as I used to do for you, Beth.

And that was the problem.

I wanted my mum. I wanted her to nurture me and take away the pain like she had when I was a child. I wanted to lie on the sofa and feel safe and have real, adult life suspended.

But I couldn't be around my mum, because of my jealousy of her.

She had a daughter she could look after. I didn't. So I avoided my mum, to avoid the pain of what I was missing. It felt better to sit alone, longing to be held, but not daring to accept it. How dare I be comforted, when my own child couldn't be held properly in case we dislodged some vital wire? I couldn't tell you that everything would be all right, because you couldn't hear me.

I couldn't fix you.

So I refused to be fixed too.

Trying to put that tangled ball of emotions into words was impossible, though; all I managed was a muffled cry.

Mum made soothing noises, but her hand rubbed my back faster, betraying how frantic she truly felt. She wanted to take my pain on, to spare me. But she couldn't. Just like I couldn't do that for you.

'Oh, Mel. Oh, love. She'll get better. She has to.'

'She must have been so scared,' I sobbed.

Did you look up at the full moon and think of me, Beth? Did you despair, or was there still hope in your heart that me and your dad would do our job to protect you?

There were so many questions, and I'd never find peace until I had answers. James Harvey may or may not be innocent, but someone put you in hospital, and I wouldn't rest until I discovered who.

*

I finally stopped crying and managed to stand up straight after using half the kitchen roll to wipe my face and blow my nose. I felt better for giving in to my emotions for a while. The kettle had boiled and the water gone well and truly cold again in that time, so I really hoped Dad and Jacob hadn't wanted their cuppas too badly. Finally I got myself together enough to make them.

Mum's eyes sparkled with unshed tears as she watched me stirring the milk into their teas.

'You're sure you don't want a holiday?' she checked.

'It's lovely of you. But not right now. You're right, though, I need to prioritise my family, not my DIY detective work.'

It was a blurring of the truth, though. Mum would take it to mean I was giving up my investigation. I had no intention of doing so.

She helped me carry the steaming mugs into the living room and we handed them out. Neither man mentioned the inordinate amount of time we had spent in the kitchen, or the fact that my face was red and puffy.

'I've had an idea,' I announced. 'We should do something special for Beth. She always loves it when we have a girly pamper night – especially when you join in, Jacob.'

He smiled, eyes sad, at the reminder.

'Did you take the whole afternoon off today?'

He nodded.

'Well, we could get the stuff together now and go straight to the hospital.'

He seized the olive branch. Mum and Dad swiftly made their excuses and left their teas so that we could get ready.

'I'm so glad you're feeling better,' Mum whispered in my ear as we hugged goodbye. 'You know you can talk to me any time.'

My heart clenched. 'I know.'

Dad enveloped me in a hug next.

'You'll crack my ribs,' I laughed.

'You stay strong, duck. Beth will get better soon.'

'I know.'

'And no more drinking.'

'Okay, okay. Promise.'

Jacob and I stood on the step, waving them off. Wiggins had his nose pressed against my leg, trying to peer round it, as usual. You would have stood on the ground in front of us, my hands on your shoulders to peer over. That was the way we always stood when bidding farewell…

I tilted my head back and blinked rapidly to disperse the threatening tears.

'You okay?' checked Jacob.

'Yeah, fine. Honestly.'

Maybe I would be. If I tried hard enough. So I rushed around, getting things together, then heard a car door slam shut outside. Peering out, I groaned.

'Great. Flo's here.'

Jacob rolled his eyes. 'Don't call her that. Her name's Britney—'

'I know! But Flo suits her more.'

'Nicknames aren't really appropriate. She's only here to do her job.'

And steal my husband.

Still, I slapped a welcoming rictus on my face and went downstairs to greet her. I wasn't going to give her another opportunity to try to steal my husband, so I'd play nicely for now, because if I kicked off then Jacob would think I was acting crazy again and going back on the peace we had just brokered.

'Thought I'd pop in, see how you are,' she said.

'Oh, you know, all right…' I trailed off, unsure of what else to say. I brandished the handful of hair accessories. 'Going to have a pamper night with Beth.'

Flo made all the right polite noises about how lovely that would be. As she did, Jacob slipped from the room.

'Melanie, I hope you don't mind, but Jacob has mentioned that you've been struggling to deal with everything.'

I silently 'thanked' him for that, Beth, my blood pressure rising. 'I'm fine.' If I said it enough, it might come true.

'Well, I wanted to assure you that the investigation is making progress, and there are several promising leads that are being followed up. Don't give up hope.'

'I won't.' It didn't sound sincere.

'It's also come to our attention that you're conducting some kind of investigation yourself.'

I froze.

'I really would urge you to stop. Without realising it, you could jeopardise what we are doing. I know that's the last thing you would want.'

Unbelievable. The police had done nothing to find your attacker, as far as I could see. The appeal had thrown up absolutely nothing. The only real lead, James Harvey, had come from me. But they expected me to step back so they could let your attacker get away? Not bloody likely!

But if I said all that, it would be obvious I was going to carry on my own investigation.

I stepped into Flo's personal space. 'It's okay, I've stopped.'

Confusion flickered. 'That's good to hear. It's for the best. We don't want any crossed wires.'

What I wanted was to tell her to concentrate on arresting your attacker, Beth, and not to try counselling me and mine. I wanted to give her a good slap and tell her to keep her freakishly small hands the hell off my husband. But I forced down the words and smiled politely.

'Well, I must get on,' I said. Then leaned back and yelled, 'Jacob! Can you come and see Flo, I mean the FLO, out, please?'

Seconds later, he emerged, red-faced, from the kitchen, where he'd clearly been hiding.

Upstairs I watched them chat, her hat under her arm, her round face earnest. Finally she got into her car and drove away.

Five minutes later, Jacob and I grinned at each other sheepishly, then got on our way.

CHAPTER 63

Flicking through your iPad, I found your music 'favourites' list and pressed play. The hospital room filled with the sounds of Stormzy, whoever he was. Your dad tried to do a robotic dance to it. I could just imagine you rolling your eyes at him and begging him to stop, before joining in yourself.

But you didn't move.

I smeared a face mask on myself. Your dad gamely joined in and we giggled self-consciously at the sight.

Your turn. I smoothed the sweet-smelling pale pink cream over your face so carefully, terrified of knocking your breathing tube and nasogastric tube. Then popped cucumber slices on your eyes. Pulled them off again quickly. They had made me think of the large pennies Victorians used to place over the eyes of corpses.

The pamper nights we had shared over the years were filled with fun. We'd try to make each other laugh, to crack the face packs. Do silly dances, tickle each other, make funny noises. We'd giggle at how the dried mask made us look like old crones until we washed it off. There would be noise, chatter, singing. Me and your dad tried our very best to replicate it, but it was a hollow copy.

After wiping the mask off your petal-soft skin, I did your hair. Put a braid in across the top. It looked lovely.

'Which polish do you fancy?' I asked. Trying to be light and playful. Trying to make it sound like any other fun night in together. Trying to pretend that my gorgeous girl wasn't lying there, unresponsive.

'I've got Glitterati Fashion Icon, which is the sort of purple-blue one you like. Remember? Or there's Bedazzle, which has all different kinds of glitter in it. There's reds, blues—'

'I can see some silver bits,' chipped in Jacob.

'Oh, and I love the name of this one: Eyes Like Angels. It's white glitter.'

'Think I'll have that.'

'Right, Dad's volunteered for that one. Oh, no, you said it, so there's no getting out of it!' We smiled, acting out our parts. The tears of clowns behind our jolly masks. 'I think Bedazzle for you, Beth? Hmm? It's your favourite, after all.'

I carefully did your nails, the pear drop smell of varnish filling the room. Glancing at Jacob, I barked out a laugh at the sight of your dad trying to do his. His left hand wasn't too bad, but his right…

'Oh my goodness, your dad looks like he's been attacked by the sparkle monster! You should see the state of him!' I grinned. Then had to turn away because of the tears.

You should have seen him. You should have opened your eyes, Beth.

Those days, the only time I saw your eyes, grey-green as the sea, was when a medic pulled your eyelid up to check pupil response. They were expressionless and unfocused, not full of the bright spark of your personality.

If I thought it would have brought you back, Beth, I'd have killed the whole world. Everyone. If I thought it would have brought you back, I'd have gladly given my own life, without a second's hesitation.

I wiped my face, put my shoulders back and turned again to my family. Jacob gave me a look of understanding, his own eyes reddening. But if I acknowledged it, I'd break down. So instead, I grabbed up a nail polish.

'What's this one? Ah yes, Glitterati Fashion Icon. That's the one for me because, well, I am, aren't I!' I leaned into Beth's ear and stage-whispered: 'Actually, don't even look at what I'm wearing, Beth. Yep, it's my favourite jumper, the comfy one you say makes me look like an abominable snowman.'

You were right; it was a thick cream Arran, but I loved it. It was snuggly and warm and comforting.

'Well, you must be a bit of a fashion icon, because Beth does borrow your clothes sometimes,' Jacob said.

'Good point. Ha! Caught you out there, Beth. You're much slimmer than me, so it's a bit depressing seeing someone so young and gorgeous in my outfits – but then again, it makes me feel I must be a bit trendy still. Still got it, eh? "Like peas in a pod," Granny Heather says, remember? Ha, I wish! Well, I'm not as slim as you, but you're not as tall as me – yet.'

'Yeah, but you'll both always be short-arses.'

'You're not exactly massive yourself, Jacob!'

'Well, neither of you are ever going to get near five ten, not even in your heels,' he teased.

I gasped.

That was it. That was what was strange about what Alison had said to me the other day.

CHAPTER 64

All those times I had tried to work out what was odd about Alison's conversation, but it had eluded me. Then, like trying to remember a word on the tip of my tongue, it had come to me the second I stopped thinking about it. Now I had the answer.

Alison had said you were as tall as she was when you were wearing heels.

But you were short, like me, Beth. Even in heels I wouldn't be able to look Alison right in the eye. She was about five feet nine inches, only around an inch shorter than Jacob. There was no way, even in heels, that you or I were as tall as she was.

Why was this bugging me so much?

Unless…

The last time Alison saw you, you were as tall as each other. Which meant that you were wearing more than heels – you were wearing your brand-new platforms, with the ridiculous two-inch sole and six-inch heels. That would take you up to a relatively towering five feet eight and a half inches.

And the only time you had ever worn those boots was on the night you were attacked.

I gasped again, a drowning woman coming up for air, as the realisation came. Jacob wrapped me in a hug, comforting me, with no idea that I'd just had a breakthrough. But I couldn't tell him. Not tonight, when we'd been the closest we had felt to a family for weeks and weeks. Not when he and my parents had spent time lecturing me on how worried they were with my investigation.

He would think it was my imagination.

But this business with Alison definitely meant something. I buried my face in Jacob's neck, breathing in his wood resin scent, so that he couldn't see my eyes. They weren't sparkling with tears, but excitement. It was a minute before I trusted myself to come out of his embrace.

'Hey, I think I'm about ready for a film now. How about we put *Divergent* on, eh?'

Jacob kissed me on the top of my head and gave a muffled 'good idea' into my hair.

But as we watched, my mind raced.

Alison saw you the night you were attacked.

That meant James had been there too.

I knew it! I'd been right in thinking I could find clues the police were missing. Thank God I hadn't listened to everyone telling me to stop. Glenn had been the only person to have faith in me.

Perhaps Alison and James had ambushed you, like some modern-day Myra Hindley and Ian Brady. Perhaps she and James were running some kind of paedophile ring together. Drugging young girls and taking pictures and videos of them? I'd read a lot worse in the newspapers. It seemed crazy that something so depraved could be happening right under my nose, though, here in sleepy little Fenmere. Perhaps Alison had simply discovered your crush on James and had hit out in a fit of jealousy.

The credits rolled. As Jacob put *Frozen* on, I chewed over the riddle that Jill posed. Although Glenn and I had found nothing suspicious at the RAF lookout tower, something about that place worried her. That was why she had chosen to demolish me with a few choice words. She could be stern, but cruelty was not her usual style.

Running repeatedly through the confrontation the night before, searching for clues, I stroked your hand and silently begged you for inspiration.

*

When Jacob nipped out to the loo, I hurriedly whispered all my suspicions and questions to you, Beth. Did you hear me? I hoped hearing that I was edging closer to the truth would spur you on to come round again. Give you the extra impetus you needed.

The breathing machine held as steady as ever. The heart rate monitor remained constant.

'If you can understand me, squeeze my hand. Did Alison hurt you?'

Nothing.

'James?'

Nothing.

'Jill? Aleksy?'

Not even a twitch.

I leaned closer.

'Dad?'

I was appalled that I'd let my paranoia reach this height.

Jacob was virtually chivvied from the house as soon as he got up. We'd got home from the hospital at about 2.30 a.m., and he had managed to snatch some sleep before heading off to work. Although tired, he looked so much happier than he had the morning before. Just from the way he carried himself, the set of his shoulders was less tense; he positively radiated relief, convinced that he and my parents, along with a nudge from Flo and Jill, had got through to me.

He was so relieved he didn't seem to notice my feverish desperation to shove him out the door. I forced myself to wait five whole minutes before getting into my own car.

*

The journey to Wapentake along the winding main road should only have taken ten or fifteen minutes, but I got stuck behind a tractor that threw chunks of mud off its wheels and onto my car. The landscape either side of the road was identical: a deep drainage dyke; fields of rich earth with strips of some kind of membrane or plastic over the top that looked like stripes of water; the odd hedge or cluster of trees; and an occasional huddle of houses around a church. Everything monotonously flat. I couldn't imagine living anywhere where I couldn't see what was coming from miles away.

At the police station, I asked to see DS Devonport. After ten long minutes or more she finally came down and led me to a quiet side room.

I leaned forward, febrile enthusiasm radiating off me while relating the whole conversation I'd had with Alison Daughtrey-Drew.

'Don't you see?' I finished. 'It means she's lied about her whereabouts that night. It means she saw my daughter, and must have been close by, too, not from a distance.'

DS Devonport looked perplexed by my logic, so I spelled it out for her. The whole huge platform thing – that was the only way you could have been tall enough to look Alison in the eye. The fact that you had never worn those bloody stupid boots before.

'To your knowledge,' the detective said.

'Excuse me?'

'To your knowledge, Beth had never worn those boots before. But, Mrs Oak, Melanie, you didn't realise she was wearing them that night, either.' She was doing her special *leaning forward at an angle* thing again, her head on one side in just the right place to be sincere and not patronising. Which made it all the more patronising.

I spluttered, trying to think of a reply. 'That's... not... the point. The soles weren't worn, so that night must have been the first time Beth had put them on.'

'You must stop telling us what to do, Mrs Oak. You're upset. You need to concentrate on Beth.'

'Don't tell me how to be a parent!' I jumped up, the chair's legs screaming their own protest across the floor.

DS Devonport smoothed her skirt then met me with her steady gaze again. 'We will look into this. At some point. Right now we're following up some other leads that—'

'Oh, "other leads". You always say that, but nothing ever comes of it, does it? As far as I can tell you're twiddling your thumbs,' I shouted, and stormed from the room.

No matter what anyone said, I knew I was on the right track at last. After that conversation it was clear no one, not even the police, could be trusted to find your attacker, Beth. It was down to me. I would never listen to anyone who told me to stop. I would never give up.

CHAPTER 65

The frenzy grew inside me. The only thing keeping me under control was how well my plans were advancing. My next target was lined up; it was simply a matter of time.

My previous victim had run like a frightened rabbit, but there had been nowhere for her to hide beneath that huge moon. Chasing her down had been exhilarating. She had been well worth the long months I had invested in coming up with the perfect plan, the time spent carefully putting everything into place beforehand, grooming my unsuspecting little helper. My mask of normality hadn't slipped once the entire time.

I needed to feel that power, for someone to stare into my eyes and know they were about to die. Not much longer now. Just a tiny bit more patience.

CHAPTER 66

I couldn't go home. I was too furious, too desperate to prove I was right and the police were wrong. Tears threatened to overwhelm me, but I smashed my fist against the steering wheel until they subsided, the car wobbling dangerously across the road. There was too much to do to give in to my emotions and fears. I would do that once you were better and this nightmare was over.

With no clue of what to do next, I found myself driving once more past James Harvey's house. Let the car crawl along the crescent of road, rounding the corner just in time to see Alison getting out of her car and opening her boot. She must be going to see her boyfriend; so she really had been telling the truth about that. Rooting around in the boot, she didn't see me edging by, but I craned my neck to take a good look at her. She was rearranging a bag. An overnight bag? No, a plastic one. Stuffing a coat into it. A black, padded coat with distinctive reflective chevrons on the front and back.

Your coat, Beth.

Adrenaline punched through me, making me shake as I put the car into gear. In my eagerness, I stamped on the accelerator harder than I should have. As I sped away, in my rear-view mirror I saw Alison turn and watch me go.

Racing along the streets, I was barely keeping to the speed limit, screaming in frustration at red lights. Finally I was back at the police station, sprinting up the steps, then demanding to see DS

Devonport again. When she appeared, her eyes were hard, but I didn't pause to let her get a word in.

'I've got proof that Alison Daughtrey-Drew and James Harvey hurt Beth. You've never found my daughter's coat, have you? That's because Alison has it in her car. If you go now, right now, to James's house, you'll find it in her boot.'

'Are you certain?'

'Absolutely!'

My heart was pounding as the detective grabbed another member of her team and sped to her car. I followed behind, feeling as if I were flying. At last, we were getting somewhere! I'd get justice for you, Beth, and everything would be okay.

At the flat, there was no sign of Alison's car, though. And no answer from James's flat. I shrieked my frustration into the air.

'Mrs Oak, go home. We're going to Alison's house,' DS Devonport ordered.

No chance. I hung back for ten minutes, then followed. I wanted to be there to see Alison and James arrested.

A smile played on my face as I pulled over onto the verge and crept up the Daughtrey-Drew's sweeping drive.

Alison doubled over in tears. James in handcuffs, face ashen. DS Devonport reading them their rights.

That was the tableau of my imagination. Instead, Alison looked furious, the detective apologetic. There was no sign at all of James.

'What's going on?' I demanded.

Ellen Devonport didn't appear surprised to see me, but from the way she ran her hand through her hair and sighed, she was exasperated.

I didn't care.

'Well? Why haven't you arrested her?' My finger impaled the air in front of Alison.

'Mrs Oak, calm down. We've checked the coat in Miss Daughtrey-Drew's car. It isn't Beth's.'

'I saw it. It's identical to my daughter's.'

'Mrs Oak!' Alison's voice cut the air. 'Here. Take a look yourself.' She held up a jacket. Black, padded.

I took it, shaking my head.

'No, this isn't the one I saw. It had chevrons on it. Reflective strips. It was Beth's coat.'

'It was this coat, Mrs Oak.' Her long nose crinkled in sympathy that didn't quite reach her eyes.

I whirled on the detective. 'She saw me drive away. She must have realised I'd seen the coat and dumped it before you got to her. Don't look at me like I'm mad! I'm telling you the truth!'

A firm grip on my elbow pulled me away, and after a few paces Ellen Devonport glared at me and spoke. 'If you don't let us do our job, you're going to get yourself into a lot of trouble. You're upset. You're seeing things you want to see.'

'It's not my imagination.' But the force behind my words was burning away like mist in sunshine. Perhaps I was imagining things…

As I was led back to my car and ordered away, I glanced over at Alison to apologise. She bit her lip. But not fast enough to hide the small smile of relief that had been there a second earlier.

Back at home, I was still furious. I paced up and down, Wiggins following me at first, then lying down with his head between his paws, big brown eyes so sad.

The house felt claustrophobic. Tendrils of sorrow escaped from under your closed bedroom door, trickling down the stairs, then curling around my ankles, ready to trip me up. I couldn't breathe.

Throwing open the front door, I called Wiggins to heel and strode towards my usual haunt, the marsh. I slowed as I approached the old council houses, spotting Glenn talking to little Roza Jachowski. Why wasn't she at school? Then I realised, of course, that it was half-term. Already I was losing touch with such things. The world carried on as normal, but I was separated from it by my own bubble of horror.

Glenn must have been talking to Roza to try to get information on Aleksy for me, just as we'd discussed on the marsh yesterday. Damn, I was supposed to have tracked down Davy for another chat, but had been sidetracked by the intervention staged by my parents, then my revelation about Alison. I didn't want to stalk past Glenn, especially not in the state I was in. It might distract him. Instead, I hid behind Bob Thornby's overgrown hedge.

I peered through the foliage, praying no one would spot me – particularly not Phyllis Blakecroft, because she would give me a lecture on the disgraceful state of the hedge and how Bob should trim it. I wasn't in the mood to face that.

Roza was a pretty little thing of seven, with olive skin and dark brown hair, who spent most of her time upside down against the front wall of her semi-detached home doing handstands, or practising dance moves on her own. I'd always thought she must prefer her own company, but for the first time it suddenly hit me that there might be something more sinister going on. Perhaps the poor girl was finding it hard to make friends because of village bigotry.

She looked happy talking to Glenn, though.

Watching them together, I could see how great he was with kids. Just like his ex, Marcie, had said. He had an easy charm around them that he kept more hidden when with people his own age. Glenn didn't let many people in, except me.

As they spoke, Roza showed him something on her phone. He put his arm around her to have a closer look. Mrs Jachowski opened the door and called to her daughter. Glenn looked up and beckoned her over, showing her his phone. She shook her head, bemused, while Roza chatted away again, all smiles that gave her the cutest dimple on one side. She pointed at her phone, and Glenn nodded. Mrs Jachowski made a dismissive gesture with her hands, laughing and shaking her head as she went back into the house and shut the door.

Tears stood on my eyes, threatening to spill once more. It was such a huge shame that Glenn couldn't have children.

He took Roza's phone, tapping on its screen and his own a few times. After a minute he showed her both, and she nodded vigorously and took hers back. What on earth were they doing?

They chatted on for a little longer, and I was half-amazed that her parents hadn't come back out again. Then I realised Glenn and Roza were being watched from the window, a shadow behind the net curtain giving the game away. Glenn clearly realised, too, because as he walked away, he turned and waved cheerily towards the house.

He strode briskly, gazing down at his phone as he approached me, beaming. Excitement positively thrummed from him.

'Glenn,' I hissed, pulling my sleeve over my hand to dab my face dry. 'Glenn!'

He looked up. His expression was ugly with anger, little eyes cold and glaring. I flinched. Next second the look had disappeared, replaced with his boyish smile.

'Christ, you made me jump!' he laughed. Then he clocked my expression. 'What? Is something wrong?'

'No, no, it's nothing. I'll tell you about it later.' I couldn't face talking about the morning's events at that moment. Glenn didn't look convinced.

'Okay… if you're sure. Well, I've got some news that might make you smile.'

I doubted that, Beth. But I forced one anyway. 'Great. Tell all.'

'I was just chatting to Roza – don't know if you saw me. She told me something very interesting. I was telling her about my daughter, and asking her advice on some books I might buy for her. I thought it might get her to open up a bit. And it worked! She was soon boasting to me about how Aleksy always reads her a bedtime story now – you remember?'

The reference to his fabricated daughter made me cringe. I should pull him up on it, but curiosity got the better of me. I nodded, wondering where this tale was leading.

'He's had to read her stories ever since she started blackmailing him!' Glenn said with a triumphant flourish.

'Blackmail?'

'Yep! She overheard him talking to a friend about going to a secret party. Once she heard the bit about how their parents could never know or they'd string him up, Roza starting demanding bedtime stories in exchange for her silence.'

'Right…' I still wasn't sure where this was going.

'So I asked her if she knew where it had taken place. Melanie, it was somewhere on the marsh. On the night Beth was attacked.'

'The old lookout tower,' I breathed.

But a party was a noisy affair. The tower might possibly be far enough away from everyone for the noise not to travel, but it was a risk in this flat country. Sound tended to travel far, especially if blown along on the wind. Unless…

'It was a silent rave!' I grabbed Glenn's arm in excitement.

'What the bloody hell is a "silent rave"?'

'I've never been to one but I've heard of them. Instead of the music blaring out, everyone is given headphones. They get the same experience as at a normal rave, but it means venues don't get complaints about noise. They've been around for years; they're really popular. Some even have different channels, so you can choose the music you listen to – a load of people all dancing to different songs. Beth and me once watched a feature on them on *The One Show* on the BBC.'

Glenn shook his head in a 'kids today' way. I'd always thought they sounded a laugh, Beth.

'Think about it,' I urged him. 'Those wireless headphones we found, and the blackout curtains? I reckon someone held a silent dance at the RAF tower, and used blackout curtains to eliminate any lights. With no noise and no light, no one would suspect a thing out there – it's not like anyone is going to pass by and spot the revellers. They could shout at the tops of their voices, too, as it's too far for that sound to travel to the village. It's perfect.'

'If we're right, then that means Jill Young knew about this.'

I nodded eagerly. 'She's definitely lying. I knew it! And it means there must have been someone who witnessed what happened to Beth. Surely!'

'Why wouldn't they come forward?'

'It's an illegal rave, Glenn. No one is going to admit to breaking the law. And I bet half the people attending were underage, like Beth, and the other half were doing drugs. Not the sort of thing you'd want to tell the police about. That's why Beth was so dressed up – she was there too.'

'Along with Aleksy.'

That made sense – that would be why he'd got so freaked out about me pushing him when he'd mentioned dancing.

'And Alison Daughtrey-Drew,' I realised, pieces falling into place. 'That must have been where she was when she saw Beth. And I bet James Harvey was there, and that's how he and Alison hooked up. So he's back in the picture. Maybe she really was selling drugs, and that's why she has lied for him.' I chewed my lip, thinking. 'But how would word be spread about this do without parents finding out about it?'

Glenn pondered. He clicked his fingers. 'Did Beth use Snapchat?'

'Umm, yeah, name rings a bell. I don't understand what it is, though.'

'It's images that can be sent between users, and they only last for ten seconds. Could be the perfect way to communicate a secret.'

'Bloody hell!'

This was it; this was the reason why everyone was lying. Now we knew what the connection was, it was only a matter of time before we discovered who had hurt you. All thanks to Glenn's detective work. I could have kissed him.

'So how come Roza told you all this, anyway?'

'Kids love me. Besides, I can be very persuasive. I told her I'd get her a sparkly cover for her phone, in exchange for her showing me how to download a ringtone from it. After that it was easy enough to chat to her. Mind you, working out how to Bluetooth the ringtone was a nightmare; it took ages to figure out how to do it. I'm such a technophobe!'

He played his new ringtone, which sounded like echoing, villainous laughter. 'Cool, eh?'

'Hang on, how come you know about Snapchat, but don't understand Bluetooth?'

'Looks like we're getting somewhere,' Glenn said, rubbing his hands together and ignoring my dig. 'The question now is whether we tell the police what we've discovered. Or do some more investigating ourselves?'

'After the run-in I had earlier with the police, I'm not inclined to go to them until I have something solid. Otherwise they'll have another go at me and probably accuse me of being a hysterical mother.'

'So our next move is… ?'

'Fancy anything from the shop?' I asked, giving him a smile made of iron.

CHAPTER 67

The Picky Person's Pop In was empty. That seemed to be the norm lately, for which I thanked my lucky stars. Jill stood behind the counter, hands on hips hidden behind a blindingly white apron. I looked at her, then slowly, deliberately, locked the door and turned the sign hanging on it to 'closed'. Glenn stood in front of it like a bouncer, his arms folded.

'Hey, lady,' she blustered.

But I cut across her.

'I think we need to have a little chat about the lookout tower. And the rave that was held there.'

She slumped forward, holding onto the counter. Jill had always seemed like the puppetmaster, in control of everything. Now she looked like a marionette with her strings cut. You wouldn't have recognised her.

'That's why Beth was on the marsh that night,' I whispered, my voice full of malice. 'So I want you to tell me everything. Right now.'

She nodded. Stumbled back and pulled a stool over to rest on, then looked at me sadly.

'I'm so, so sorry.'

Then she sat up straighter, seemed to pull herself together. 'You want to know everything? I'll do my best, but it's hard to know where to start...

'I bought the old RAF lookout tower back in 2005. It had taken a long time for the property bubble to reach these parts, but finally it had. Prices had been going up and up and up. So when the RAF decided to stop using the marsh for bombing practice, and sell the tower, I snapped it up. I thought I couldn't go wrong. I'd wait a couple of months, give it a lick of paint, then sell it on to a property developer for a tidy sum.

'Just weeks later, the credit crunch hit. World recession, banks teetering on the edge. The value of the property plummeted overnight. The bank changed the terms of the mortgage on me, and I wasn't in a position to argue, was I? Everyone was panicking.'

Jill stared down at the counter as if she could see it all playing out there. I barely breathed, impatient to get to the relevant part of the story, but not wanting to urge her on for fear of breaking the flow. This was, after all, the most I had ever heard the normally laconic Jill say in one go.

'I almost lost everything; it's taken all I've got to keep my head above water. I tried to auction the tower off, rid myself of the millstone around my neck, but no one would touch it. Only one offer was made, and it was so far below what I'd paid for it that I'd have been in negative equity. So I had no choice but to hang onto it and hope...'

Her head snapped up, desperate eyes meeting mine. 'Look at this place. It's so quiet, with everyone getting their shopping from the supermarkets. Even the café is taking trade now they're selling cards. Things have got better since I started selling some farmer's market produce: local cheeses, vegetables, meat. But the money isn't coming in fast enough, and property prices are still nowhere near where they use to be. I went to the bank to ask for a loan, showing them how the shop's books have improved – I wanted to use the money to do the tower up as best I could myself, then sell it. But the bank turned me down. I've too much debt, thanks to the tower's mortgage.

'In desperation I went, cap in hand, to the Daughtrey-Drews. I had a stupid idea that the old ways might survive, that they'd feel it their duty to help a villager out, the way their ancestors would have. Of course, they didn't.'

The bitterness in her voice was evident. Her shoulders rounded again, and Jill's eyes slid away to the counter once more as she continued.

'As I left the house, their kid, Alison, came after me. Said she had a business idea that could help both of us. She'd organise a disco at the tower, promised me it would make a fortune and that no one would ever find out. Reckoned kids these days liked to dance with headphones on. She offered to organise the whole thing for a fifty-fifty split in profits. So I agreed. What was the harm? She had big ideas about holding a few of them, then going to London with the money and staging legitimate ones there, launching merchandising. It all sounded a bit pie in the sky, but I thought, why not let her have a go?'

'I've spent my whole life scrimping and saving, Melanie. You know what my background is. I grew up in squalor, doing home-work to the sound of Mum and a punter in the next room. What little money she made prostituting herself went on booze – you know she was an alcoholic.'

A statement rather than a question, but I nodded.

'I vowed I'd work hard and never, ever have to live a life of poverty. And I've done it. Then to come so close to losing it all…' That desperate look again. 'I need to leave an inheritance for my boys. Even my own kids don't know about all this, Melanie. I had to protect them from how desperate things are financially. As a mum, you understand that, surely?'

That was too much, and from the way her face paled, she knew it. I stepped forward, trembling with fury.

'You knew why my daughter was out on that marsh – to be at the rave. To help pay off your debts. And you created a conspiracy of silence, stopping possible eyewitnesses from coming forward,' I spat.

She shook her head vehemently.

'No, no, I asked around. Got Martin to, as well. No one saw anything, I promise you – if they had, I'd have come forward with the information. But what's the point of you going to the police with this, and me being arrested? I've done nothing wrong, not really. I'm certainly not responsible for what happened to Beth. Think of my family…'

'What about *mine?*' I roared the words. My chest was going to explode from the beating of my heart. 'Alison and James got you to lie to the police about seeing them together, didn't they?'

The nod she gave was tiny.

I pulled my phone from my jacket pocket and dialled Detective Sergeant Devonport. My eyes never left Jill's.

The police were quick to arrive. Glenn made himself scarce as soon as they did. After DS Devonport had read Jill her rights, she took me to one side while a uniformed officer handcuffed the woman. I almost felt sorry for her.

The detective sergeant scrutinised me from beneath her heavy fringe, hands in the pockets of her expensive black coat.

'Mrs Oak, I really do need to ask you to leave your detective work to the experts.' One hand appeared, briefly, to run through her hair. I couldn't believe what she was saying. I'd just given her a criminal – two, in fact – on a plate.

She sighed. 'This must be exceptionally difficult for you, but there are things going on right now that you're unaware of. We're close to a breakthrough in your daughter's case, and you don't want to blunder into the middle of things and blow them apart.'

'What are you talking about?'

'I can't say right now, but' – she held up a placatory hand as I opened my mouth – 'but please, be patient for a few more hours. We're on the same side, Mrs Oak. I'll be able to tell you everything very soon.'

Slowly and grudgingly, I nodded. She was right: the last thing I wanted to do was to stop the person who had hurt you from facing justice.

The truth would all come tumbling out now. How James Harvey had blackmailed Alison Daughtrey-Drew into providing him with an alibi for the entire night, otherwise he would have reported her to the police for staging the illegal event and selling drugs. He'd got her to get rid of your coat – the evidence that tied him to the crime. Alison had then dragged Jill into the lie; because, if the truth about the rave had come out, they would both have been in trouble.

James must have been at the rave that night and seen you, Beth. He had pounced, like the predator he was. Why couldn't anyone see it but me? He sickened me. Intense pain made me look at my hands in astonishment. They were curled into such tight fists that my nails had drawn crescents of blood on my palms.

Jill was ready to be taken away for questioning. I threw her one more look of disdain before leaving the shop. On the opposite side of the road was Davy, rushing at the sight of police cars outside his mum's business. Remembering that Jill had told me her children had no idea of her financial dire straits, and that only Martin had known about the rave, I jogged over to him.

'Davy, your mum—' I began.

'What's happened?' he demanded, surging forward.

I tried to hold him back. Went flying. He was far too strong.

'Son, it'll be all right,' Jill called to him.

He stopped, stunned at the sight of an officer putting a hand on her head, fingers splayed around that high, pewter ponytail and guiding her into the back of the squad car. As the vehicle pulled away Jill gave Davy a firm look through the window, her mouth a grim line that echoed the horizon.

He spun round to look at me. 'Mel, do you know what's going on?'

'Your mum has been arrested. She allowed an illegal rave to be held at the lookout. I think that's where Beth went before she was attacked,' I sighed.

He stood still, processing the news. Frown deepening. 'That must have been where Chloe was,' he murmured.

Where Chloe was?

'She was upstairs in bed the night Beth was hurt, wasn't she? While you and her mum were…' I trailed off, not sure how to phrase what they were doing.

Puzzlement clouded his face further. 'Eh? Did you talk to Ursula?'

'Yes. She told me how you waited until Chloe had gone to bed, then sneaked in and the pair of you, well, you know. Isn't that what happened?' Realisation dawned on me. And I had thought Davy was slow. 'Was Chloe out? Was… was she with Beth?'

'Did you ask Ursula what she did that night, Mel? All night? Did she mention the phone call?'

'What phone call?'

He plucked at my sleeve like a child. Fretful. 'Mel, she didn't tell you the truth.'

I started to go cold. 'What am I missing, Davy?'

'Chloe were out when I went over. She were supposed to be staying at yours, with Beth. Then Ursula got a call from her, and told me I had to leave because she had to go out and get her.'

'Chloe was with Beth?'

'I don't know… but I think so. The call came about 2 a.m., and I didn't hear what were said. But I could hear the tone of it, you know? Chloe sounded hysterical. And I swear I heard Beth's name shouted.'

'Davy, you have to tell the police.'

'I've been trying to get Ursula to go. I've told her that if Chloe can point the finger at who did this, I'll protect them. They don't need to worry about the attacker hurting them. Even if she stays with Steve, I'll protect them. She won't listen to me, though.'

Poor, poor Chloe. She was a victim of James Harvey's, too. I wanted to rush round there and hold her, tell her that everything would be all right. And that she had to inform the authorities what had happened. Clearly the police had managed to get evidence against James, and an arrest was imminent, but it would be even better if I could persuade an eyewitness to come forward.

CHAPTER 68

Beth sat cross-legged on the bed, skipping through her music, looking for something decent to play. But her mind wasn't on what she was doing.

'You really think we'll get away with it?'

'Of course! Like, when was the last time your mum called mine to check you were staying?' Chloe's voice was confident, strident. She always seemed so sure of herself.

'Not in ages and ages. At least a year,' Beth conceded.

'And the last time my mum called yours to check?'

'Umm, dunno.'

'Ages! Exactly! So if I tell Mum I'm staying here, and you tell your parents you're staying with me…'

'We'll be free to stay out all night and no one will know.' Beth shivered, but not with fear. With excitement.

But a thought occurred to her. 'What about our clothes? And Mum won't let me out of the house with make-up on.'

'Got it totally covered. We can get changed in the cricket pavilion. Mum's got a copy of the key from doing the refreshments every summer. Then we can be out all night, and get changed again before we go home. Oh, and no dumping me to spend time with James bloody Harvey, if he's there.'

'I wouldn't!'

'Oh, come off it. I know how much you *love* him. Don't know what you see in him, myself. He gives me the creeps. It's like he's hiding something.'

'You and your overactive imagination,' Beth teased.

'This is so cool. I can't believe you managed to score free tickets to this!'

Beth warmed at the praise. All the teenagers at school were talking about the rave; the older ones looking forward to it, the younger ones wishing they could go. It was all the cooler because no adults knew, and everyone with an invite through Snapchat was sworn to secrecy. Beth and Chloe would be the only ones there in their year – they were the envy of all their friends.

So the plan was set. The girls moved on to hair and make-up, without a second thought for the deception they were weaving.

The next morning, Beth asked her mum if she could stay with her BFF that night.

CHAPTER 69

'Ursula, I'm sorry, I know you told me to stay away,' I gabbled, the second the Clarkes' front door opened. It rapidly started to close again.

'I know!' I shouted.

The crack widened. Ursula stood in her immaculate cream hallway, her perfectly made-up face looking tired and drawn beneath the foundation. Her hand seemed to fall in slow motion, the door opening wide. We stood looking at each other for ten long seconds. I didn't know what to do; she stood as though inviting me in, but wasn't saying anything.

Finally, I walked in. Murmured, 'Thanks.'

As I entered the hallway, Chloe walked down the stairs. She rubbed her face with her hands, shoulders hunched. I knew instinctively she had heard what I'd said.

When we were all in the living room, I sat down on the red sofa, which stood out like a bloodstain against the cream surroundings. I tried to smile, tried to radiate calm into the tension of the room. Ursula and her daughter stood looking at me as if I had a loaded weapon trained on them.

'I've pieced it together,' I said. 'You were with Beth when she was attacked.'

There was a low moan of despair, whether from Chloe or her mum I couldn't tell.

'You don't need to be afraid of anyone – but please, you have to go to the police.'

'No, no, no!' The same moan. Chloe. She shook her body from side to side.

'No. No!' Her voice louder now, a scream of terror. Fists flying. She hit herself, beating at her body.

Her mum rushed forward, making frantic soothing noises. Trying to wrap her arms around her daughter and stop her from hurting herself. She fell back, knocked away. Wisps of burgundy hair floated to the ground, torn from your best friend's scalp. Ursula flung herself forward again, wrapping her in a bear hug that pinned her arms against her sides.

'What did he do to you?' I whispered, horrified. 'What did James Harvey do?'

'No. No. No. No,' sobbed Chloe.

Her mum hushed her in a lullaby voice. They rocked together.

The front door opening made me jump, but Ursula didn't flinch, simply carried on soothing.

'Hush, my love, hush now.'

'What's going on?' Steve's voice was sharp.

Ursula looked at him over Chloe's shoulder and said nothing, simply shook her head.

I walked over to him and lowered my voice to a reassuring pitch.

'I came over because I wanted to try to persuade Chloe to go to the police. I know she was there when—'

He grabbed hold of the top of my arm and I gasped in pain. His fingers were like a vice, sinking into my flesh even through my padded jacket. He lowered his face to mine, his breath blasting my face. His chocolate-brown eyes were bloodshot, and sweat blossomed on his forehead.

'What do you want? Money? I'll give you money. If it will stop you going to the police.'

'What? I... I don't want money, Steve. I want justice for both our girls.'

He gave a hollow laugh. The despair in it terrified me. I twisted, trying to pull free, and he seemed to come to his senses, suddenly letting me go so that I stumbled backward, towards the front door.

Something in his eyes scared me, Beth. I fumbled for the lock and flung the door open. Ran to my car and drove away as quickly as possible, shaking like a leaf.

CHAPTER 70

The full moon lit the way for them, along with the torch apps on their phones, but it was a miserable walk along the narrow lane that ran from outside the village to the marsh. It made Beth wonder if she should call an end to the plan and go home.

Chloe seemed to sense her friend's dissatisfaction, but instead of providing encouragement, they bickered.

'So, why are you carrying your new boots instead of wearing them? I mean, we've left our rucksacks hidden in the cricket pavilion, and then you insist on bringing a carrier bag? And you look such a loser in those flat boots.'

'Because there's no way I could have walked all the way from the village to the marsh in those platforms!'

Besides, Beth didn't want to get them covered in mud and ruin them. She knew they had been expensive, that her parents would have had to struggle to scrape the money together for them, especially after paying for guitar lessons for her too. So she was walking in her flat boots, and would change when they got to the lookout tower.

It was all right for Chloe, her parents had loads of money, thanks to her dad being a solicitor. If she ruined the high-heeled boots she was wearing, she could get more the next day. Her mum spoiled her rotten, always wanted her to look nice. Beth thought all of that, but didn't say a word. She knew it would lead to an argument, and she couldn't be bothered.

'You're so sensible. You're totally like an old woman, sometimes!' Her friend laughed at her stoic silence.

'Ooh, look, a barn owl!' said Beth, to change the subject. She pointed at the bird that swept low over the deep indigo sky. Silent as a ghost, its wings barely moved. Its flat, oval face turned towards them, then it banked, giving a flash of buff stomach. In the silvery light it looked as pale as the moon, a sliver fallen to earth and trying to find its way back. Beth turned to her friend and beamed. Chloe shook her head.

'Mental,' she muttered. 'Anyway… So Aleksy is defo going to be there tonight?'

'That's what he said!'

Lately, Beth felt as if she and Chloe were growing apart. Talking about boys and music and bitching about other people was all well and good, but Beth needed more. She wasn't sure Chloe would ever feel that urge.

As they grew closer to their destination, though, Beth's excitement built. Especially as the occasional car went by, packed to the gunnels with people they recognised from years above them at school. When Aleksy and a bunch of his pals cycled past on BMXs, he called out a casual 'hi' to them, but didn't slow down.

'This is going to be so amazing,' Chloe gushed. 'Like, all our friends will be well jell when we tell them about tonight. So come on, how did you hear about this? Why all the secrecy?'

Time to tell the truth. No harm in letting one little secret go, to her best friend.

'Right, okay, you can't repeat a word of this to anyone. On Saturday I bumped into Alison Daughtrey-Drew. Like, literally. And she dropped a bag full of Ecstasy! Well, I think they were; they looked like the photos we've seen in the anti-drugs lessons…

They must have been, anyway, because she was really weird with me, saying she was carrying them for a friend.'

'OMG, this is fucking amazing! Did you, like, blackmail her or something?'

'No! God, no. But on Monday she was waiting for me when I got off the school bus and was just chatting to me – but totally with an agenda, you know? I think she was worried I'd tell someone about what I'd seen.'

'Well, you're so trustworthy, Beth. Like, you'd never tell anyone anything if someone wanted it kept a secret.' Chloe stopped and hugged her. 'So what happened next?'

'Like I said, she seemed to be creeping around me a bit. Asking me how I was, and all that. Then she said that "as we're friends now", she'd like me to come to this silent rave she's organised.'

'She said "as we're friends"?!'

'Yeah. I know – mad, right? But anyway, I asked if you could come too—'

'Ah, thanks BFF!'

'No problem, BFF! She said we can get in free, so we're sorted.' Beth shrugged. 'It's totally to buy my silence, but I've no intention of telling anyone anyway – anyone but you.'

The conversation had brought them to the grounds of the tower, which glowered over the marsh. There was barely a sign of anyone outside.

'I don't know why you had to wear your coat,' hissed Chloe. 'It so makes you look dead young.'

'First you tell me I'm an old woman, now I look too young. Make up your mind.'

Beth kept her voice light, even though she was a bit annoyed by her pal's fresh nagging. Chloe shivered against the wintery wind in a thin denim jacket, her arms folded and her teeth almost chattering. She looked as if she had goosebumps on her goosebumps. Beth decided that giving up her coat wasn't worth the risk of hypothermia. But while the coat stayed firmly in place, Beth did change into her new boots, balancing on them expertly. All those hours of practising walking up and down in her bedroom had paid off.

'Seriously, do I look all right? Do I look older?' she asked Chloe.

She wore smoky eyeshadow, dramatic eyeliner and false lashes, which felt strange when she blinked. Her lips were a hot fuchsia. Her long, golden-blonde hair was a backcombed and hairsprayed mane.

'You look, like, totally gorgeous – and you'd easy pass for eighteen,' replied her pal. Chloe's black-and-white stripy playsuit only just skimmed her bottom, showing off her legs in sheer tights and the long boots that she'd nicked from her mum's wardrobe. Her heavy make-up made her virtually unrecognisable. She didn't ask how she looked, such was her confidence.

One more hug, and the two girls strutted into the compound, linking arms to hide their nerves.

Despite there being cars, motorbikes and bicycles in the car park, there was no sign of anyone other than a trio huddled under a single security light by the large, single-storey rectangular building attached to the tower. Two huge men stood at the doorway, wearing big padded jackets. They dwarfed the coltish form of Alison in her skinny jeans and form-fitting North Face jacket to keep the cold and wind at bay.

Chloe's face fell a little when she saw how stylish but sensible the older woman looked. The teenagers pulled up short. The security light illuminating the area went off, plunging them into darkness. Beth gave a little shriek, clutching Chloe's arm tighter.

'It's okay,' Alison called, sounding bored. As she spoke the light flicked on again, and she seemed to be waving her hand. 'Bloody sensor. It's motion-activated, so I have to keep waving my hand.'

Chloe prodded Beth with a finger in the ribs, so she stepped forward. Her heart thudded so hard against her chest she was sure people would see it. Her hands were slick with perspiration despite the freezing temperature, and she wiped them on her coat, hoping no one would notice. She did not belong in this world of raves and drugs and lying to her parents in order to stay out all night. This was wrong. She worried that Alison might change her mind and send her home – and half-hoped that she would.

'Umm, hi, Alison. It's Beth, Beth Oak. Umm, you said it would be okay for me…'

'Beth! Of course! Let me take your jacket and that bag. I'll look after them for you,' smiled Alison, urging the girls forward. Beth thought of a predator eyeing up prey as she looked at the calculating eyes and perfect white teeth behind the blood-red lipstick.

'Go on, then,' Chloe whispered. 'You'll look a total pillock taking that lot in there.'

'I'll pop them in the office,' said Alison. She grabbed them from Beth, then opened the door and pulled back a heavy black curtain. Lights strobed and flickered like will-o'-the-wisps, luring the teenagers forward.

The sight before them was eerie. A huge crowd of people danced feverishly, their bodies a heaving, sweating mass. But there was no music. No sound but jumping feet, swishing material, the occasional whoop. One person burst suddenly into song at the top of their voice, tone-deaf and pumping their hands to a silent beat. The atmosphere was euphoric, the club lights flickering over upturned faces lit from within with the fervour of an evangelist preacher.

'Here, put these on,' said Alison, giving them a pair of wireless headphones each.

As soon as the girls put them on, they were blasted with dance music. Grinning, they gave each other the thumbs up, then pushed a little way into the crowd and started to dance.

It was like nothing Beth had ever experienced. Tightly packed, the crowd moved almost as one. Normally it might have made her panic a bit, as she would only have been chest-height to most people, and that could feel claustrophobic. But in her new boots, she was elevated. She felt more confident, stood taller. Beth planted her feet and started to move to the pulsing beat. After a couple of minutes, Chloe tapped her shoulder and pulled the headphones away from her ear. It was bizarre suddenly to be pitched into silence again.

'Aleksy is over there. Let's head towards him,' she said.

Beth nodded. Headphones back in place, they slowly wound their way closer. Bodies pushing against the girls, lads gave them hungry glances that Beth had never seen thrown her way before. Strangers' hands curled around her waist, but she carried on moving, slipping away like an eel.

They stopped beside Aleksy and his friends, but didn't say anything. Instead they played it cool, dancing beside them, pretending they didn't realise their proximity, waiting for him to make the first move. It didn't take long for the tap on the shoulder and the friendly wave to come. Aleksy was beaming at Beth.

Damn. It was exactly what she had feared would happen.

Chloe shot her a look that had more stopping power than a well-aimed half-brick. She'd been banging on for weeks now about how gorgeous Aleksy was, about how he must surely fancy her because he always talked to them on the bus. Beth had had to keep quiet, knowing how much her best friend would hurt if she realised that her heart's desire had actually asked Beth out.

He flicked his long fringe out of his eyes, glossy dark hair reflecting the ever-changing lights. Pulling his headphones down, he never took his eyes off Beth.

'Hey, you came,' he grinned.

'We sure did. Hey yourself.' Chloe placed herself slightly in front of Beth, pushing her chest out. She met Aleksy's eye confidently.

His gaze slid over her and back to Beth, in her white crop top, black miniskirt and thick black tights. Her legs long and lean in her super-high boots. 'You look great.'

'Thanks, so do you,' replied Chloe before Beth could react.

She put a hand on his arm. He sniggered. His eyes were glassy and red, and he smelled kind of weird. So did all his pals. Beth twigged suddenly.

'You been smoking weed?' she blurted.

A beatific smile spread across his face and he nodded slowly. Four or five of his pals circled the girls and laughed. For a second, Beth thought of sharks circling. Then they all slid the headphones back on and started dancing.

*

Hours passed. Beth was having a brilliant time. The music, the lights, the sweaty atmosphere, the bodies so tight against each other, pushing, surging, shoving, sticky skin against sticky skin. They only paused occasionally to sip bottled water.

Aleksy's arm wrapped around Beth's shoulder and pulled at her headphones.

'We're going to get something to make things a bit more interesting. Want to join us?'

Before Beth could answer, Aleksy took her hand in his. Gentle but insistent as they weaved through the crowd back towards the door. Chloe came with them, still determined to get her man. Aleksy didn't look impressed. Despite the quiet, he bowed his head so that only Beth could hear his whisper.

'I'm really glad you came. Maybe later we could go somewhere alone, and just chat?'

'Oh, I'm not sure…'

'It would only be to talk. Come on, ditch your mate. Chloe, is it?'

Beth knew damn well he knew Chloe's name.

'We'll see,' she replied firmly. It was the line her mum always gave her whenever Beth asked for something and she meant no but didn't actually want to say it.

The little gang stopped beside Alison, she and Aleksy forming a huddle. Money and goods were exchanged almost invisibly.

'Sorted.' He smiled, grabbing Beth's hand again. It was soft and warm, and Beth quite liked the feel of it. He was incredibly handsome. But he wasn't James, and she was definitely in love with James. She was almost sure of it.

'Do you want some, Beth?'

The question cut through the teenager's thoughts. She looked at Alison in amazement, who gave her a charming smile. 'A free sample – for a friend. There's no harm.'

'Great! Thanks!' Chloe gave Aleksy a knowing look as she stepped towards Alison, hand out.

'Chloe, no. I don't think this is a very—' Beth began.

'Oh, grow up, Beth. It's no big deal.' She rolled her eyes, the performance put on for Aleksy's benefit.

He and Alison ignored her, looking only at Beth. She and Alison were almost eye to eye, thanks to Beth's platform heels. Alison gave a viperlike flash of her smile.

'It's up to you, of course. If you don't want it, you don't have to. It's just a gift, from one friend to another.'

But Beth wasn't stupid. She guessed what the older woman was thinking: that once the teen had sampled the drugs, she would no longer be a threat to Alison because her silence was guaranteed. She gnawed on her thumb, trying to think of what to do, what to say.

Alison's pupils contracted; her smile became more fixed. 'If you're uncomfortable, you can always leave. Perhaps you are too young for all this.' She unfurled a small plastic ziplock bag of pills in front of them, then lifted it out of reach, teasing.

'I've got money—' Chloe surged forward to get closer to Alison, to prove how terribly grown-up she was. But Beth grabbed her arm. 'God, what, Beth? Chill, for fuck's sake!'

'I don't think you should be here,' Alison decided. 'Look, you're kids, this is a bit… full on for you, don't you think? Besides, don't you have to be in bed soon? I mean, you're still sucking your thumbs…'

Beth yanked her digit from her mouth, mortified. She was chewing her nail, not sucking her thumb. Now everyone would think she was a baby! Around her, the row raged on.

'We've every right to be here. We'll be partying all night long. Our parents are totally cool with it,' said Chloe.

Alison raised an eyebrow.

'What? You going to throw us out of an illegal rave because we're underage? That's mental!' Chloe stropped, flinging her arms in the air. Her hip jutted out sharply to one side, emphasising how bent out of shape she felt by the injustice.

'Yeah, maybe we should call the police, report that you're breaking the law,' joked Beth. That would teach Alison for making that crack about sucking her thumb.

Alison threw her a look that skewered the rest of her words in her throat.

'I wouldn't joke about calling the police if I were you. Things wouldn't go well for you if you told the police.'

'Beth, what is your problem? Do you want to stay here, or go running back to Mummy and Daddy?' Chloe added.

Aleksy stepped between them. 'Hey, chill out. Beth, you don't have to do anything you don't want to.'

He was only trying to help, but his involvement made things worse. Chloe looked ready to flip out completely, her mouth narrowing to a mean little hole, her eyes flashing. Beth made a snap decision.

'Alison, I'm so sorry for making a big deal of this. I know you're just trying to be nice. Thanks for the offer; we'll take a tablet.'

A single lilac pill with the shape of a flower pressed into one side dropped into her outstretched hand.

'Enjoy,' Alison smiled, turning away with a smirk on her face.

Beth, Chloe and Aleksy stared at the pill.

'Maybe we could take it later?' Beth suggested weakly.

She looked around, as if searching to be rescued. And sweeping through the crowd came the answer to all her prayers. SSG, James Harvey, the love of Beth's life, was headed straight towards her.

She had daydreamed about this moment countless times. Tonight was the night he would see her for what she truly was, not some kid he taught guitar to. She'd dance with him and they would kiss. A proper kiss. Not the stupid close-mouthed stuff she had done with Oliver Reece last year, behind the cricket pavilion, accompanied by the smack of willow against leather and the muffled cheers of the crowd. This would be the real deal.

Who needed drugs when there was true love?

CHAPTER 71

I parked on the drive at home and didn't move from my seat, not knowing what to do next. Shaken by what I had seen at the Clarkes' house, from Chloe's hysteria to Steve's desperation, I went to call your dad, Beth. Then saw the time. It was only lunchtime; Jacob would still be at work. I longed to tell him everything that had happened, though, and realised it had been a good while since I had felt that urge. Shutting him out like that had been unfair of me. No wonder he had turned to someone else for comfort. I would call him, despite the time, I decided.

But what was there, really, to tell him? Jill had been arrested; but that didn't have anything directly to do with your attack. Something terrible had obviously happened to Chloe as well as you; but once again I had no real proof.

No; best to wait until there was concrete evidence.

Instead I called Detective Sergeant Devonport. She sounded distracted and stressed – something hard to picture as she was such an ice queen generally. She didn't have time to talk, she informed me. But when I told her I had been talking to Chloe about James, she snapped.

'Mrs Oak, for the last time, I need you to stay away from this investigation. It is imperative that you do nothing else. Go home and wait.'

I felt so stupid. Only hours earlier I'd given her my word that I would do just that, and had gone back on it almost immediately. I gave my word again, realising that something big was in the offing.

'You're about to make an arrest?' I asked.

'Yes. And you could endanger everything.'

Once they had got James Harvey, they would have time to persuade Chloe to testify, I was sure. It was hard to take in. Once charges were made, once the person who had shattered my family was properly identified and facing justice, it would surely be the push you needed to wake, Beth. We could get back to normal: no affairs, no investigations, no useless police. We could pretend none of this had ever happened. Couldn't we?

All the hope I had been sitting on for so long, trying to crush it because it hurt too much to acknowledge, came flooding back. Overwhelming, joyous, suffocating. I could hardly catch my breath, and sobs caught me, heaving at my chest. I folded over the steering wheel and, for the first time since this nightmare had started, I truly gave in to the tears at last and allowed myself to hope.

It won't be long until we see your smile again, Beth. Not long, Beans.

CHAPTER 72

'What the hell are you doing?' SSG snarled. Only he didn't look like SSG any more. The man of her dreams. He looked like Mr James Harvey, who got annoyed with her when she mixed up her sharps and flats and made her drill chord changes until her fingers were almost bleeding.

'What? Just having a laugh. I'm old enough to be here,' she said. Jutted her chin out like Chloe did. Born to rule.

It didn't work.

'I saw you buying drugs. Are you insane? If you don't go home right now, I'll tell your parents.'

What was he so riled about? He must really care about her to be so upset, she decided.

The music, the euphoric atmosphere, hope and a dash of desperation made her fling her arms around his neck and plant a kiss on his lips. She felt them give way beneath hers, his hands slide onto her shoulders; smelled his aftershave. This was the first kiss she had been waiting for, hoping for.

A shove on her shoulders pushed her stumbling backwards, hitting some dancers. They turned and pushed her back again, a pinball heading back towards James's mortified face.

'Beth. I'm sorry, I… I don't feel that way about you,' he said.

Stuttered, in fact. That was what hurt her more than anything: the fact that he was clearly so embarrassed he couldn't speak properly.

'You kissed me back,' she insisted. 'You love me, like I love you.'

He shook his head. 'Love? No, I care about you. You're my pupil, of course I care about you. You're a nice girl.'

Her eyes widened. Nice?

'But I certainly don't love you, Beth. You have to tell people that you kissed me but I wasn't interested – you must tell them the truth! People saw! This could ruin me, destroy my chance to become a teacher.'

She ran from the building. From the crowd. From Chloe, who screamed her name. She threw a quick glance over her shoulder before she went through the door. Everyone seemed frozen in place, like a film on pause. Alison giving her a calculating stare, ever the clever weasel. Chloe's face twisted in disappointment. Aleksy's angry humiliation, arms hanging loose at his sides; the intensity of his eyes making her tremble once more. His mates grinning and circling like sharks behind his back. And James Harvey holding his head in his hands, fingers clutching his hair, mouth slack, looking as if his entire world had come to an end.

Beth had never felt so embarrassed in her entire life. How would she ever face any of them again?

CHAPTER 73

The prospect of sitting at home waiting for a development with only Wiggins to talk to was too much. So I sent Glenn a text. He was over in The Poacher, and asked me to join him.

He sat at his favourite table, tucked in the corner furthest away from the fire. It was the darkest corner, too, and gave him a good vantage point from which to see everyone coming and going, so as soon as I came in, he stood to get my attention.

'Want a drink?'

'It should be me getting you one, after everything you've done.'

'Well, when you put it like that, I'll let you,' he joked, posing in a mock-hero stance. 'But seriously, let me get you one.'

After the day I'd had, I could have done with a stiff drink. But my parents had made me promise; and the look of concern on their faces when they had spoken to me made it impossible for me to break my word.

'I'll have an orange juice, please.'

'Nothing stronger? Go on!'

'No, honestly, orange juice is fine for me.'

He came back a couple of minutes later cradling a pint, an OJ and a glass of red wine between his hands. 'In case you change your mind,' he winked.

I gave a single huff of laughter and shook my head.

'You're incorrigible. Listen, I've got loads to tell you.'

He leaned forward, elbows on the table, taking in all the new information. Saying nothing, simply nodding or shaking his head at bits in the tale. When I told him of Chloe's reaction, he seemed stunned. Made me go over it again and again, unable to believe it.

'She must be totally traumatised,' I sighed.

'How do you feel about things, then? About James getting arrested again soon? You really never had any clue what James was like before all this?'

'Of course not! Otherwise I'd never have let him near my daughter. He's lying, perverted scum. I mean, look at the way he even pretended to be gay.'

'Some people will say or do anything when backed into a corner,' Glenn said sagely, taking a slurp of his pint. 'You must want to kill him after what he's done to your girl.'

The breath that escaped my lips was shaky. 'The thought of him targeting Beth. He must have befriended her and winkled his way under her defences so slowly, so carefully. You should have seen Chloe's reaction – she's utterly terrified. Oh, Glenn, when he hurt Beth, she must have cried out for me. I wish I could kill him.'

Silence passed as he patted my hand. Then he nodded at my drinks. 'You're not going to let that wine go to waste, are you?'

'Sorry, I don't fancy it.'

I felt bad that he'd bought it. Then again, I hadn't asked for it. Glenn was always so generous, buying me drinks; I felt I owed him an explanation.

'Thing is, my parents and Jacob staged a bit of an intervention yesterday. They're worried about my drinking, so I made a promise.'

'What! Bit of an overreaction, isn't it?'

'Well…' I picked at the cardboard of my beer mat. 'I have been drinking a bit much lately.'

'You've been through a lot. One little drink's not going to hurt – I won't tell anyone.' He grinned at me, that cheeky twinkle in his eyes, that boyish charm working overtime. But today I found myself feeling annoyed.

'Flipping heck, Glenn, give it a rest, eh? I don't want a drink.'

He sat back, shocked. Face fallen. 'Sorry.'

We chatted some more, whiling away the time. But with nothing left to investigate, I was struck by how little we actually had in common. Talk of the good old days seemed ridiculous right now, when any minute I hoped to hear from the police, but we did it anyway. It felt as if we had been over everything already.

At 4.30 p.m. I started to make noises about leaving, because Jacob would be home soon. Then Flo walked in. She spotted us in seconds.

'Melanie, Jacob said you might be here. I asked him to wait at home while I came to get you. Could you come with me now, please?'

Wordlessly I stood, pulling my coat on while trembling with nerves and excitement. This had to be it. I was too keyed up even to care that it was my husband's mistress who would be breaking the good news – she'd be out of our lives for good soon, I was sure.

Glenn's eyes stayed on me all the way out of the door, silently wishing me luck.

I followed Flo in silence across the road. Tempting as it was to question, I wanted to be with Jacob when we heard the news that your attacker would finally be facing justice, Beth.

Inside the house, Jacob sat on the sofa with Wiggins, whole body tensed. He had killed time by making cups of tea for us all, and they sat steaming on the coffee table, no one touching them. I sat beside him, so close I could feel his body heat.

'Melanie, Jacob, there's been an important development,' Flo began.

Jacob's hands were clenched, and I brushed my fingertips over the back of one. It uncurled and my fingers slid along his palm until they were woven together with his.

'We've made a number of arrests relating both directly and indirectly to Beth's attack. We've also arrested and charged the person responsible for putting her in hospital.'

Jacob gave a laugh of relief. We looked at each other, smiling.

Flo held one hand out. Why was she looking at us like that?

'You need to prepare yourselves for what I'm about to tell you. What happened is…' She stopped, searching for the words. Unable to find them.

Beth, what the hell had happened to you and Chloe?

CHAPTER 74

It had all gone wrong. Beth shivered out on the marsh, having run as far as she could and as fast as she could in her stupid platform boots, *thump, thump thump*ing through the frozen mud. Rather than going straight down the RAF road, she had, instead, headed along the sea bank, where she planned eventually to use her more usual route to Fenmere via the other lane. She was too ashamed of bumping into people if she went back the way she and Chloe had come earlier. They would recognise her as the girl who had just made a complete and utter fool of herself. People at school were bound to have seen; they'd all be gossiping on Monday.

Eurgh! She wished she were dead!

She wrapped her arms around herself and trudged on. She was freezing cold, had left her coat and flat boots back with Alison at the rave. The wind picked up. It eddied, as if trying to turn her round. But she wouldn't go back. At least on the marsh she was safe from people judging her and laughing.

The tide had started to go out, but it was still close enough that she could hear the sound of gentle waves occasionally blowing towards her on the wind, and the infrequent cry of a goose disturbed from its slumber.

The thirteen-year-old had never felt so alone.

She would go home, she decided. Her mum and dad would be furious with her and probably ground her for eternity, but with all her heart she longed to be in her own bed. She wasn't ready yet for this adult world of secrets and lies, drugs and romance.

Tears streaked down Beth's face, and she wiped at them quickly, fearing what would happen to her make-up. Bad enough that she looked like a stupid little baby, crying like this, but to have panda eyes too would really finish her off.

In the brilliant light of the gibbous moon, which hung large in the sky, she could see a shape rising up from the endless flat of the fens. Her heart thudded momentarily, terror seizing her. Then she laughed. Stupid; it was the stunted sycamore that grew on the marsh side of the sea bank. That meant she had another twenty minutes to walk before she even reached the lane.

A voice called her, making her whirl round.

'Wait! Beth, wait a minute!'

Her best friend jogged as best she could in her heels along the top of the sea bank, tracing Beth's footsteps. When Chloe reached her, she was out of breath – but still angry, from the look on her face.

'What the hell are you playing at? I can't believe you left me like that. And what the fuck are we going to do now? We can't go home!'

'It's not my f-fault,' Beth sniffed. 'I was so h-h-humiliated. I couldn't have stayed there!'

'Well, I've got no chance with Aleksy now, have I? The whole night's ruined because of you.' Chloe's hands were going nuts again, leaping all over the place as she spoke. She hadn't even bothered asking how Beth felt.

'Yeah, well, you're the one who wanted drugs!'

'Shit, Beth, want to say that a bit louder? Someone might hear you, for fuck's sake. We're not at the fucking rave any more.'

'Oh, stop swearing. It doesn't make you sound older, you just sound like an idiot.'

'God, you're such a child!'

'Drama queen!'

'Mardy bitch!'

'Right, well, if I'm such a mardy bitch, I'm going home.'

'Don't you dare, Beth. You'll drop me in shit.'

'Don't care.'

Beth turned her back and started to walk. Her boots were beginning to rub, and their weight hurt her ankles. She couldn't wait to get home.

For a moment she thought she heard someone out in the darkness, but no, it was the wind rustling the grass… wasn't it?

Chloe ran in front of her and planted herself firmly. Hands on hips, head cocked to one side. 'You've ruined things between me and Aleksy. You don't even want him, you want that old fart, James Harvey! So why ruin things between me and Aleksy?'

'I didn't ruin anything. I've never shown him any interest, Chloe! I don't care about Aleksy; he's nice, but he's not my type. Have him!'

'Have him? So, like, take your fucking cast-offs? I don't think so.'

'Oh my God, it's like arguing with a brick wall! Have him, don't have him, be my friend, don't be my friend, I don't give a toss.'

Chloe got a look in her eyes of pure fury. Her hand flew back and she slapped at Beth, hard. But Beth caught her hand. She was used to dodging Chloe, lately. Her friend got so angry sometimes, her temper out of control, flashing like lightning then disappearing equally fast.

The first time Chloe had hit her, about four months earlier, she'd been mortified afterwards. She had apologised over and over. Promised it would never happen again. She was Beth's Best Friend Forever, so of course the girl had forgiven her. But then the same thing had happened. Several times.

Beth hadn't told anyone about these uncontrollable rages. The bruises were easy to hide; most of the blows were landed on her body, and Chloe was always so embarrassed afterwards that Beth didn't have the heart to get her into trouble.

Mrs Clarke had once caught her daughter punching Beth in the kidneys, and assured Beth that she was going to arrange for a counsellor – until then they had agreed it was best if it were kept a secret. Chloe had made her pinkie-promise.

There had been times over the last four months when Beth had almost confessed to her parents. But it sounded so stupid saying that Chloe had a bad temper. As for the promised counselling, Mrs Clarke kept making excuses about why it still hadn't been sorted. Sometimes Beth suspected Chloe's mother was worried about what people would think if it got out that she had a violent daughter.

Out on the marsh, though, Beth had had enough. She wouldn't be someone's punchbag any more. Glaring at Chloe and, never flinching, she threw her friend's arm away from her.

'Don't you dare touch me,' she said, voice steady, despite the blood thumping in her ears. Then she turned and walked away.

'Beth. Beth! Get back here.'

But she refused to listen to her Best Friend Forever. It was a long way home, she thought, so she had better get going. Once there, she decided, she would break her pinkie promise and let her parents in on her secret. She would tell the truth, and get her best friend the help she needed. She felt bad, but keeping secrets from her parents made her feel uncomfortable. While she was at it, she would throw away that stupid make-believe book about her and James flipping Harvey. She was so over him.

Beth had had enough of secrets and lies to last her a lifetime.

The wind rose to a howl, the sycamore's branches rattling. The brent geese took off with loud cries of consternation. Beth didn't hear Chloe behind her. The blow, when it came, was totally unexpected.

CHAPTER 75

Flo's eyes were brimming with sadness as, finally, she spoke.

'I have to tell you that Chloe Clarke has been charged with assaulting Beth.'

Little Chloe? Your best friend?

'That can't be right.' Each word was slow, as if dragged from the depths. I felt heavy, numbed. Each movement, each blink, seemed to take forever. I noticed the ticking of the clock. Flo's hands falling open, palms up, apologetic. Her agonised stare, tears sparkling then blinking away rapidly.

I turned to Jacob, convinced I had heard wrong. His Adam's apple bobbed up and down as he swallowed repeatedly, trying to digest the news that a child had caused so much damage to our child.

Oh God, Beth. All the people I had suspected. All the people I'd accused. But I hadn't seen the one person who was guilty.

'How?' My voice rough and quiet. I cleared my throat, tried again. 'I don't understand… There has to have been a mistake.'

We had taught you about stranger danger, Beth. We'd never taught you not to trust your best friend.

'Did Ursula know?' I asked.

As Flo nodded, I jumped up, sprinting towards the loo. Veering off at the last second to grab the wastebasket as the contents of my stomach poured out. I spat out the last of the vomit, and swore shakily.

When Ursula hurried over with the casserole, had she hoped you were dead, so she and her daughter could be in the clear? All the times she asked how you were, had she really cared – or only asked for fear you had woken and spilled her and her daughter's ugly secret? That bloody teddy they had left at the sycamore shrine beside the mere they had thrown you into, with the note saying they missed you. *Missed you?!* They were the reason you were in hospital.

Flo talked to your dad and I for over an hour, explaining the police investigation. I had thought they were useless, sitting back and doing nothing, when all the time they had been working tirelessly to catch your attacker.

As Flo talked, there were times when either Jacob or I jumped up in a sudden fury, or paced like a caged animal around our living room, but on the whole we listened calmly. We questioned surprisingly little. Shock seemed to have robbed us of our voices. I thought the truth would have made me rant and scream, but everything seemed to have shut down and I felt as if I was in a bubble, removed from this awful scene and watching it play out rather than being a part of it.

After speaking with me, Davy had apparently gone straight to the police, figuring that he had waited long enough for Ursula to persuade Chloe to come forward. He had thought he was protecting them – mum and daughter – from a potential future attack from whoever had hurt you. He'd had no idea that Chloe was the one who had struck the blow, and that her parents were feverishly trying to cover her tracks.

Poor bloke; he must have loved Ursula, but she would never have risked leaving Steve and the comfortable lifestyle he provided for her. Once Ursula had told her husband what Chloe had done, they had been tied together forever by their dreadful family secret. She'd probably only kept stringing Davy along for fear that if she broke up with him, he might manage to figure out the truth about Chloe.

'I saw the Clarkes earlier, suggested they went to the police,' I told Flo and Jacob at one point. 'They must have thought I was trying to blackmail them or something. Chloe must have gone crazy because she was scared of being arrested for what she'd done. I thought it was because she was traumatised by what James had done to her.'

I sounded almost matter-of-fact as I spoke, Beth. *Please don't think I was.* It was more that there were too many emotions to compute, so my body and brain had shut down, a bit like when a computer overloads and gets that spinning wheel. That was me; I was frozen, haunted by the memory of Chloe lashing out at herself.

'Apparently, according to what has come out in our interview with Chloe's parents, Chloe has had a problem with her temper since hitting puberty. She can't even remember the details of her argument with Beth, just that Beth had annoyed her,' said Flo, her eyes full of sympathy.

When the red mist of rage descended, your best friend had snatched up a branch that had fallen from the sycamore nearby, and she had lashed out. I could just imagine it…

The thud of wood connecting with your skull. Your head snapping back. Falling to the frozen ground. Perhaps you tried to stand, tried to cry out for help. Fingers twitching in the dirt.

You didn't see it coming, Beth, you didn't stand a chance. She was your best friend! My stomach contracted painfully, but there was nothing left to bring up.

Afterwards, Chloe had called her mum in a panic. That's what had alerted the police – they had got hold of Chloe's mobile records and been able to pinpoint her to the location at the time of your attack. Davy coming forward was the extra piece of proof they needed to make the arrest.

After receiving the call from Chloe, Ursula had come running, of course. Unable to find a pulse, she and your best friend had carried your fragile body to the mere and thrown you in, hoping it was deep enough that you would sink and never be found.

They had tossed you aside like a piece of rubbish. My beautiful little girl; intelligent, funny, caring.

Ursula would have done anything to protect her daughter. Just like I'd have done anything to protect you. Apparently she hadn't told Steve what had happened, not at first, but when he got back from his golfing weekend he'd quickly picked up on the atmosphere at home and guessed Chloe was somehow involved in Beth's attack. When Ursula had confessed to him, he had been so shocked that he'd left them. But when I had started sniffing around, he had returned so that he could protect his family from the truth coming out.

But now he and Ursula had been charged with assisting an offender and perverting the course of justice. Whatever, it wouldn't be enough. That cow Ursula had cooked me a casserole in exchange for almost killing my little girl. She had looked at me with her wet spaniel eyes, all full of fake sympathy.

I wanted to kill her.

Jill Young would face charges of her own for staging the illegal gathering on her property, and knowingly allowing alcohol to be sold to underage people on those premises.

Alison Daughtrey-Drew was in even more trouble. She had been selling drugs. The police had been on to her quickly, finding out about the rave when they had looked more closely at Alison and James because of the allegations against him. By looking at her bank details, they had discovered that Alison had hired a couple of hundred silent disco headphones from a company and had them delivered to her home. Once the police started digging around, they had soon uncovered rumours of the event – someone can't stage something that large and keep it totally quiet, no matter what precautions are taken. In addition, Aleksy Jachowski had come forward to tell the authorities about it, and that he had seen you there, after being scared he would get the blame for what had happened to you. So at least the mob had been useful for something.

After that, the police's case against Alison had quickly started to take shape, but they had been biding their time to find out if she had been your attacker. She hadn't – but Beth, she had seen your seemingly lifeless body in the water while walking to her car after the rave. Assuming you had taken drugs and had a reaction to them, she hadn't called the police or an ambulance for fear of getting herself into trouble.

The cowardly bitch. But the fury inside me didn't explode into ranting and raving. It burned white hot, turning my pain into something hard, implacable and dangerously calm.

'By the time Alison discovered Beth had been hit, she'd had time to come up with an idea of how to cover her tracks. She'd set up a fake alibi by roping in James Harvey's help,' explained Flo.

'But why did he go along with it?' I asked.

'According to Alison, Beth had kissed James that night at the rave – and he had pushed her away. Alison blackmailed him, saying that if he didn't give them both an alibi, she would go to the police and give a statement saying that she'd seen him later that night, hurting Beth.'

'And he was telling the truth when he said he was gay?' I breathed.

Flo nodded, ginger bob swinging. 'He hasn't come out yet to his parents, and is anxious to keep that quiet for now.'

So many people with petty worries about themselves. Not giving a thought to my daughter, left fighting for her life.

CHAPTER 76

Suddenly Jacob and I were a couple again, united by the news we had received. Moving as one, automatically. Side by side we let Flo out, Jacob holding my hand tightly as we said our goodbyes. The news had shifted something fundamental between us, as natural and huge as an earthquake.

'Let's get to Beth and tell her the news,' I said.

I wanted to apologise for not realising the secrets you were carrying, Beans. I needed to let you know that now the truth was finally out and the lies were over, I would find my courage and spend every spare second with you until you were better.

Excitement fizzed through me too. I was convinced you would react once you heard you were safe and justice was being done. There would be a twitch of an eyelid, a squeeze of my hand, and it would mark the start of your journey back to us. I'd do anything I could until you were the happy girl you had been a month ago. I would never allow myself to give up hope again. I would do whatever it took to fight for this family.

As we hurried along the warren of hospital corridors, your dad and I held hands. Everything felt sorted, and it could only be a matter of time before you came home and we were a proper family again.

Outside your room, we stopped and washed our hands with the obligatory sanitiser. I was rinsing, lips quirking at the thought of seeing your own smile again one day soon, when I heard it.

An alarm. Harsh, ear-splitting in the quiet.

Jacob ran two steps ahead of me. He stopped so suddenly I almost crashed into the back of him.

Your monitors were flashing like a cheap disco. Your face was a delicate grey. Then you disappeared behind a horde of nurses who bolted into your room. Your dad and I flattened ourselves against the wall, not daring to get in the way.

'We're taking Beth for a CT scan,' someone called as they whisked you away.

We were left alone. Eyes huge, faces drawn, punch-drunk from emotional blow after emotional blow. How long we stood like that, I couldn't tell you. We didn't move until the consultant came back in and took us to a quiet room just off the corridor that led to yours.

When he sat down, he gave a sigh. Tiny, involuntary, but enough for me to brace myself.

'As you know, a month ago Beth suffered an epidural haematoma due to a blunt impact to the head. When she first arrived here, she had a build-up of blood between the brain and skull. That's why we operated, to stop it.'

Jacob and I nodded. We didn't need this recap; it was something we would never forget.

'Well, now the brain has haemorrhaged again. Beth is suffering severe intracranial pressure – so severe that the brain is being crushed against the skull.'

'You're going to operate again?' questioned Jacob.

The doctor's mouth gave a sad little twist. 'I'm afraid that this time there is no point. I'm sorry, Mr and Mrs Oak.'

I groaned at the blow, my body folding over. Vision darkening at the edges as I fought not to pass out. The thing I had feared most was finally coming true.

Oh, Beth, my beautiful girl. How could we live without you?

'Why won't you operate this time?' Jacob asked eventually, his voice brittle.

'The bleeding is so severe that there's virtually no chance we could stop it. Even if we could, signals from Beth's brain to her heart are no longer getting through properly. She's dying. There's nothing we can do; nothing anyone can do.

'When her heart stops beating, we don't think it would be appropriate treatment for the team to give Beth chest compressions. We have tried everything to make her better, and it isn't working.'

'So, what...' My lips were stuck to my teeth. I licked them. Tried to make my mouth work properly. 'What happens now? How long... ?'

'Do you have friends and family you would like to call to say goodbye to Beth?'

'Everyone in the family will want to be here,' replied Jacob.

'Then you need to call them right now. Are there any religious ceremonies that you would like to have arranged before she goes?'

I shook my head.

'Have you ever considered organ donation?'

We flinched simultaneously. I looked at Jacob. He looked at me.

'She, umm, she... Beth would like that,' he managed. 'She's always liked to help people.'

He threw his head into his hands then, shoulders jerking, with dry sobs wracking his body.

CHAPTER 77

The nurses worked quickly and efficiently around each other, as if in a dance. They pulled the endotracheal tube from down your throat. The nasogastric tube from up your nose. The conduit from the intracranial pressure bolt in your head. The cannula at your wrist.

They wheeled away machinery, and all manner of things, until finally all that was left was you, Beth.

Already you looked more peaceful.

I stroked your long blonde hair. Trying to burn the feel of it into my memory forever, terrified that one day its exact texture couldn't be recalled. The wiriness of the red hairs; the silken gloss of the golds. I arranged it to cover the shaved part of your head and fanned it across the pillow. You looked like a Pre-Raphaelite painting.

Your breathing sounded shallow and laboured.

'Beth? Please, Beans, wake up. Squeeze my hand if you can hear me.' Jacob leaned over you as he spoke, staring at your eyes intently. His hand rested in your loose, open palm.

You didn't respond, my love.

My own hand slid across your dad's back, back and forth in an oval motion, comforting him as I used to comfort you when you were tiny.

Can you remember that, Beth? Can you remember my touch? Can you remember our love?

I looked across at a nurse, standing awkwardly to one side, taking in the futile scene of a father trying to save a daughter through sheer force of will. I cleared my throat, aware of each sound, each movement.

'Could we have some time alone, please?'

The nurse stirred into action. 'Certainly.'

As soon as he had left the room, my arms wrapped around Jacob's sinewy body and I leaned my face on his back as he gazed, immovable, at you. His whole body tensed against me, then quaked with silent tears.

'Oh, Jacob, honey.' There was nothing I could say. No words of comfort I could give when my own heart was breaking too.

'How can I let her go?' he sobbed, sinking to his knees, still clinging to your hand. I went with him, kneeling by his side and taking his face in my hands.

'We'll do it together, Jacob.' My voice was soft but steady. I was amazed by the certainty that I felt, despite the pain. But even that was a facade, and suddenly I was shaking too. My face was soaked, the words choking me. 'We'll draw strength from each other, for Beth. We… we have to do this right. We can't let her suffer any longer, because God knows she has suffered enough already.'

He held me then. Kissed the top of my head and stroked my hair. When you were tiny, he'd stroked your hair to help you go to sleep. But every time he had tried to stop, you had stirred and woken. Sometimes he had been at it for hours. At the memory, my hands fisted in his jumper, pulling him even closer.

'Do you think she is suffering?' His voice was so tiny that only I, with my ear so close to his mouth, would hear it.

'I'm scared she is. I can't stand that thought. We need to set her free.'

'What, to be on the marsh?' He asked with no recrimination.

'If that's what she wants. Her soul can, I don't know, go on. Go to something better. I truly believe that.'

'But she might improve…' There was no hope in his voice.

I pulled back and looked into his eyes, at a soul as broken as my own.

'I'd kill for her if I thought it would bring her back. But nothing will.'

Minutes passed. Jacob wiped his eyes with his sleeve. Lifted us both off the floor, then sat down and took your hand again.

Suddenly I had an idea. I climbed up onto the bed and lay alongside you, carefully hugging you. A proper, full hug, only possible now that all of the machinery, wires and tubes had gone.

'Oh, I've been longing to do this for a month. You love your hugs, don't you, eh? Yeah…' I sighed, breathing you in, marvelling at how soft your cheek was. Would I always be able to remember the exact feel of it? 'Beth, my love, we've called everyone – your aunts and uncles, and your grandparents – they're all on their way. But if you can't hold on for them, don't worry. Don't be afraid. It's okay to let go.'

Your chest trembled rather than rose and fell.

'We're here, so there's no need to be afraid. We'll always, always be here for you, my love. But it's time for you to leave us.'

Jacob lay his head on your chest. 'All the pain will be over soon. And you'll be free.' His voice gave the slightest hitch at this last. 'Don't you worry about us. We've got each other, and we'll think of you every single day. Every day.'

'We love you to bits and whole again,' I whispered.

*

Time slipped by. Relatives came and went. Shuffling past, bending over you, crying, whispering farewells, patting us. Your dad and I didn't move, too hypnotised by your breathing.

We were alone when Jacob lifted his head from your chest. His eyes were devastated hollows, his pupils huge. I cupped my trembling hand under his chin and nodded.

You had gone.

I settled back to holding you. I didn't want you to get cold. You always hated the cold.

CHAPTER 78

BETH
FRIDAY 22 JANUARY

The pain in her head shattered through her whole body. Her teeth chattering with it. Her legs gave way. Body folding.

Starbursts of information broke through the agony.

Chloe leaning over her. 'Shit, fuck, shit, I'm sorry. I didn't mean… Fuck it, Beth. Get up!'

Blink.

Chloe lit up by the light of her mobile phone. 'Help me! I… I don't know what to do! I'm so s-s-sorry. She isn't moving, Mum!'

Blink.

Ursula's perfectly manicured hand trembling as it touched Beth's neck. Voice floating towards her on treacle.

'… can't find a pulse. Nothing…' Swearing. Crying.

Blink.

A sensation of movement. The sound of grunting and tears.

Blink.

She was so, so cold.

The full moon looked down on her, all-seeing, all-knowing, timeless and patient. The wind caressed her skin, as gentle as her mother when she used to check for fever.

Hush, hush, everything will be all right. You'll feel better soon.

Let go.

I love you to bits and whole again.

Bits.

Beth could feel herself breaking apart and floating away on the wind. Cradled. Loved. Warmed. Cherished.

Gone.

CHAPTER 79

The village grapevine was fast and efficient. News of the arrests spread quickly. People pretending to be in shock when secretly they had known at least part of it all along. Bunch of lying bastards – they deserved to have someone like me living among them.

The criminals got their comeuppance, though. They were amateurs, with no idea they had a professional in their midst.

I'd have to wait a little while for the furore to die down, but then I'd be free to strike again. These country bumpkins were no match for me.

Not long before I could finally kill.

The smash of a skull. The huff of breath. The mottling of skin.

I couldn't wait.

CHAPTER 80

Beth, you died at 5.03 a.m. on Thursday 18 February. I will hate that date, that time, for the rest of my life.

There should be a special word to describe the weariness of the bereaved. It was far beyond exhaustion, yet I couldn't rest. No sleep would come, apart from snatched moments which left me fuzzier-headed and more exhausted than before. Eyes hurt, muscles ached, stomach churned.

Time meant nothing. Doing the simplest of tasks, such as making tea or cleaning my teeth, seemed to take an eternity. Other times I stared out of the window and realised that a couple of hours had disappeared in a blink. People came to visit, talking in low voices, patting my hand.

Mostly, Jacob held me, and I held Wiggins. Our little family of three, no longer four. But together we had more strength than apart, and it was a revelation to me. How had I managed for so many weeks without my husband?

The rare times I did glance at the clock I found myself thinking: *this time yesterday Beth was still alive. This time last month Beth was up and about and… what?* What exactly were you doing? I didn't even remember, and panic flooded through me. You see, I hadn't realised I needed to memorise every second. I'd had no clue that time with you was running out.

Did you know, Beth?

I ran to the calendar on the wall, and flipped back to the date exactly one month ago: 18 January. A Monday. The Monday before you were hurt…

Think, think, think!

All that came was routine: getting you up; you getting ready for school and running across the road for the bus out of the village and into Wapentake; you coming home at night. Nothing special. Nothing out of the ordinary.

Was that the night you ranted about how people should make holes in their fences, to help hedgehogs?

'It's so easy. Just a tiny five-inch hole so that the hedgehog can travel around. Why don't people do that, Mum? It wouldn't make any difference to them, and they could help save hedgehogs. They're dying out, you know!'

You had emanated fury at the injustice of it.

'Well, maybe they don't realise…' I'd offered, reasonably.

Your eyes had boggled at me. 'Well, I'm going to make a hole in our fence right now.'

I'd laughed, watching you grab the torch then stomp outside in the dark and carefully make a hole on one side. Then the torchlight bobbing up and down as you trudged across to the other side of the garden to make one in that fence too.

But maybe that hadn't happened in that final week of normality. Perhaps it was the week before. The more I tried to be certain, the more ambivalent I became.

Friday morning dawned bright and cold. You seemed reflected back at me in each twinkle of frost, then you hung in the air with the mist as it melted, enveloping me. Daffodils nodded their heads in the gentle breeze, reminding me of your golden hair. I would never see you again.

I clutched my stomach and ran to the loo, only just making it before the breakfast Jacob had cajoled me to eat made a return visit. Ever since your death, I had barely been able to keep anything down. You might think I had turned to booze again, but the smell of it was enough to put me off.

Wiggins, Jacob and I went for a long walk. We passed the Seagull's Outlook and the Picky Person's Pop In, which were both closed and looked forlorn. On the marsh, even the wind seemed quieted in grief, and the huge sky wept light tears for you in a constant patter. But I didn't feel you, Beth. Not in the shifting of the tide. Not in the susurration of the long grasses, or the splash of water, or even in the haunting cry of a lone seagull wheeling above. We walked around the creeks I knew off by heart; the ones that stayed permanent, and the ones that shifted subtly day by day. There was no sign of you.

Please don't leave me, Beth.

When we got home from the walk, we started to arrange your funeral. The numbing pain lifted for a while then, because I got angry. I welcomed it back like an old friend. No parent should ever have to arrange their child's funeral.

And it was another child's fault. It didn't seem possible. I wanted to hurt Chloe, or steal her away from her mother so that Ursula would know exactly how I felt. Instead, I chose a coffin and music and what you should wear.

'I'd like Beth to be buried with this. What do you think?' Jacob asked, hesitant. He held the wooden egret he had carved for your birthday; the one you'd never seen.

It took a couple of deep breaths before I trusted myself to speak. 'Perfect.' A little bit of nature to fly with you on your journey.

'Oh, darling.' Jacob's mum enveloped him in a hug. My mum did the same with me. It felt good, comforting.

'That Chloe should burn in hell for what she's done,' Mum sobbed.

In his mother's arms, Jacob stiffened but said nothing. He and my parents had already agreed to disagree on this subject. A knock at the door saved reopening that can of worms.

'I'll get it,' sighed Jacob.

'Another person come to give their condolences,' Mum said.

There was a hint of pride in her voice that your tragically short life had touched so many people. Despite the steady stream of cards and flowers, Jacob and I had already agreed that we wanted family only at your funeral. No one else in the village could be trusted. So many people must have known about that rave. Parents covering for their children, teenagers covering their own backs, the DJ, the bouncers, innumerable liars and hypocrites. The Daughtrey-Drews had already sent a huge bouquet of flowers and offered to write a cheque to Beth's favourite charity. I wouldn't be bothering to reply to that.

Jacob traipsed back into the room. 'It's for you, Mel.'

'Who is it?'

Jacob's face clearly wasn't keen, but he looked resigned to his fate.

'Glenn.'

Ah; that one name explained everything.

My friend waited outside, dancing from one foot to the other as if to keep warm, even though the day was relatively mild now beneath the bleak blanket of clouds. He glanced at me shyly.

'I didn't know whether to come or not. I'm so sorry.'

'You can come in, if you want.' I held the door wider, gestured. He shook his head.

'I don't want to intrude; I just wanted you to know I'm thinking of you – of you all. If there's anything I can do…'

Bone-weariness robbed me of the strength to speak. But for him I made the effort.

'Thank you. And Glenn, I'm so, so grateful for all you've done to support me and help me. I couldn't have got through this without you.'

He held his hands up. 'Happy to help. Least I could do. So... bloody stupid question, I know, but how are you feeling?'

I heaved a sigh as I tried to describe my emotions.

'You know, after Beth died I stood outside the hospital for some fresh air before going back to sign paperwork. So much paperwork. There was a woman visiting her elderly mother, and I simply let her words wash over me. It was comforting not to have to think for a while, you know? To pretend that I was a normal woman, chatting.'

Glenn nodded. Settled against the door frame to listen closer.

'So we did the usual getting-to-know-you questions: where do you live, what do you do, are you married... do you have children? When she asked that I just stood there, opening and closing my mouth like a goldfish, no idea what to say.

'I ran the whole future conversation in my head. If I said yes, she was bound to ask details: what's Beth's name, how old, where is she tonight? You know the kind of thing. My options were to spare her feelings and lie; pretend everything was fine with Beth, that she was at home, practising the guitar or learning about animals. Or say that my daughter was fourteen, and would stay that age forever because she was dead. Or say, no, I don't have children. Because that's technically the truth now – but saying no simply isn't an option.'

'No matter what you say, it's wrong,' muttered Glenn. 'I'm so, so sorry for your loss. God knows how you're feeling right now. I mean, I miss Katie like crazy, but at least I know that she's out there somewhere, enjoying life.'

That again. His fake daughter. I looked at Glenn; really looked at him. And even though I knew he was lying, I still couldn't see any hint of it. Not in his steady gaze, not in his confident posture, leaning against the door frame. His round face appeared as open as ever, only a frown of concern marring it.

Confusion pierced my grief. Who was this person I'd allowed to become so intimate with my life? All in the space of less than a fortnight? Yes, I had known him as a kid, but we hadn't been friends. He hadn't truly been friends with anyone.

I rubbed my face, sighing deeply. I couldn't be bothered with any more lies, no matter how well intentioned. I could have called him out, told him that I knew there was no daughter. In gratitude for all he had done for me, I spared him the embarrassment. But I was done with liars.

Without a word, I closed the door and walked back to what was left of my family. They were poring over the laptop, looking at photographs of you. I joined them. Holiday snaps, birthdays, Christmases, school plays, special occasions and everyday life – we lost ourselves in them for a few hours. Let laughter mingle with tears at the memories, jarred occasionally when your killer made an appearance here and there. There you and Chloe were, arms wrapped round each other, beaming identical smiles. She had taken your life. Another brick slotted into my wall of bitterness and anger.

CHAPTER 81

DS Devonport looked tired and brittle when she came over on Saturday afternoon. Her hands went in and out of the pockets of her coat, as if she didn't know how casual or official she should look. It was quite good to know that even the generally together Devonport had been knocked by your passing. I felt bad for not warming to her, though, when she had worked so hard to untangle the village's conspiracy and identify your killer.

'Good to see you. Thank you for coming,' acknowledged Jacob.

'Mr and Mrs Oak. I'm so very sorry for your loss.'

Wiggins put his silken head in the officer's lap, and sighed in contentment as his ears were fondled.

'I've come to let you know that Chloe Clarke has been charged with murder.'

Murder. I hadn't expected that. I felt a surge of triumph.

'Is there any chance of it being plea-bargained down to manslaughter?'

'Possibly. It's possible she will offer to plead guilty to voluntary manslaughter, but deny murder. In which case…' The detective made a flip-flop gesture with her hand. 'But we're confident murder can be proved, so we'd be disappointed if that happened. Although there was no malice aforethought – the attack wasn't premeditated in any way – by her own admission Chloe deliberately hit Beth with the branch to hurt her. She then left her out in the cold, and didn't call for an ambulance. These are calculating acts. Even when you called her and spoke with her asking about Beth's whereabouts, she didn't tell you. Circumstantial evidence definitely corroborates murder.'

'What sort of sentence will she most likely get if she's found guilty?'

DS Devonport pulled a face. 'It's not my job.' She took in our expressions. 'But, if pushed… Chloe is fourteen, and therefore deemed above the age of criminal responsibility. She knows right from wrong. The maximum sentence for manslaughter is life, but the term is at the judge's discretion. It's highly likely Chloe will receive a custodial sentence in a young offender institution until she is eighteen, when she will be moved to a prison to serve out the remainder of her sentence. I'd hazard a guess that she'll get between three and ten years.'

I should have felt happy. Justice was being done. Punishment meted out. But it wasn't enough. Three measly years for killing you, Beth. For extinguishing the light in my life. That was it?

Jacob looked stunned. 'It doesn't seem right. But… then again… I don't know.'

'Know what?'

Although I had a feeling I knew.

'Well, she's a kid. She's got to live her entire life knowing that a fit of temper caused the death of her best friend. It was a stupid, tragic mistake, and she'll be punished for it her entire life. She's a good kid, she just…' He shrugged, the words failing him.

'She's a good kid?'

I ducked from under his arm. Stood and grabbed the photograph that he had printed the night before. There you were, a six-year-old with sunshine glowing through your golden hair. A butterfly net in your hand, on the marsh, lips pouting with determination, eyes full of hope as you scanned the grasses for insects. I brandished the photograph now, like a weapon.

'Chloe took this beautiful, perfect child away from us. She hit our daughter because of a stupid row, then left her to die. If she or her mother had called an ambulance, then Beth would have got treatment quicker. Maybe she wouldn't have died!'

'But Chloe did what a lot of teenagers do. Overreact, lash out, then panic,' said Jacob.

He looked so reasonable. So calm and dignified in the face of everything that had been thrown at him. I wished to find that peace in forgiveness, but there was no way. This wasn't some case we had watched unfold on television, then calmly discussed with no emotional involvement. This was our little girl. We would never have the bathroom hogged for so long it caused a row. Never hear you singing at the top of your voice. Never hear you come down the stairs like a herd of elephants. The hugeness of it took my breath away.

No punishment could be enough to pay for that.

'I'll never forgive Chloe. I hate her,' Jacob added. 'But… I also feel sort of sorry for her. Two young lives with bright futures ahead of them were destroyed that night.'

I sat back down and folded my arms. 'I'm glad her life is destroyed. I'm glad she'll be haunted by her actions, find it hard to get a job, to *move on* and live the life she would have lived if she hadn't killed our daughter.'

Jacob's eyes were soft with kindness beneath the heat of my anger. I couldn't go back to the happy, forgiving woman I'd been before.

When you died, Beth, the best of me died too.

The clearing of a throat reminded Jacob and I that we weren't alone.

'There is one more thing,' DS Devonport added. Each word weighed and measured. 'All three of the Clarkes have received bail to their home.'

There was every chance we would bump into each other.

Jacob – solid, warm, dependable – wrapped an arm around my shoulder once again. A show of solidarity. 'Thank you for everything, detective sergeant. Now, if you don't mind, we'd like to be alone.'

DS Devonport stood. 'Yes, I'd better be going; I just wanted to give you this update myself.'

'Of course.' Jacob held out a hand. 'Goodbye, detective sergeant.'

Once we'd seen her out, Jacob gave me a hug.

'It's not right, but Ursula and Steve were only trying to protect their daughter. Wouldn't we have done the same?'

'Oh, Jacob,' I despaired. 'You want too much from me just now.'

I slid from under his arm and stood, shaking my head. 'I can't deal with this right now.'

I wasn't sure if I'd ever be able to deal with it. Not with so much anger and bitterness clawing at my soul. I wanted the world to stop, for it to cry tears of blood, for every single person to mourn. But even that wouldn't be enough.

CHAPTER 82

On Sunday morning, my broken sleep ended at 5.03 a.m. As usual. I slipped away from Jacob's embrace and into the bathroom. Looked at my face in the mirror. Tired, grey, thin and lank-haired.

'I'm no longer a mother,' I told myself.

The reflection disagreed. Your physical presence wasn't needed for me still to be your mother, Beth.

I felt bone-tired of everything, but the anger that had fuelled me for so many weeks kept me going. One day soon I was bound to see the Clarkes. I couldn't wait.

I wandered past your bedroom, still too cowardly to face it. I hadn't been in there since discovering the 'diary' the week before when, in my panic, I had interpreted your innocent fantasies about James Harvey so wrongly.

Where my feet led me was inevitable. To the coat hooks. Wiggins appeared instantly by my side, pressing against me with a forlorn whine that seemed to say, 'Don't forget me'. He'd been extra protective of me since your death.

Quickly wrapping myself up, I stepped out into the unseasonably mild early morning to make my way to the marsh once more. My true home in those days.

*

The familiar *twit-twoo* of a tawny owl heading home after a night's hunting sounded somewhere close by, flying on silent wings. I gazed out into the greying darkness, searching for you. But there was no sign.

'Is it because I'm so angry?' I asked out loud. 'Do you want me to forgive Chloe? You're so full of forgiveness, just like your father. You wanted to make the world a better place. But that's why I'm so bloody angry. Beth, you didn't deserve this!'

A harsh intake of breath. God alone knew what I looked like, in the middle of nowhere, talking to myself, tears tracking my face. I didn't care. I couldn't sense you out there any more. Desperation raked at my soul; I needed to get you back. Somehow.

I walked down the sea embankment and further into the marsh. Eyes straining to see you beneath an almost full moon which taunted me like a pregnant belly.

'Sweetheart, I know Chloe was your BFF, but… I'm not sure I can do it, Beth. If it's what you truly want, I'll try, though. Promise. I'll really try to forgive her.'

I walked on in the dark, towards the glow of light appearing above the dully sparkling line of sea in the distance. I didn't bother checking where I stepped, too concerned with scanning the horizon for signs of you, with listening to the wind for your whisper, concentrating on its touch to see if it contained your caress.

Around me, birds began to call. Brent geese stirred restlessly, moving around to feed in their flocks, giving their constant, gossipy call.

After half an hour, the sun peered over the horizon, announcing the start of a new day. I faced the wind, calling your name. A pale ghost rose in front of me. Looming large in the gloom, making me gasp and stumble back momentarily, before it fled ponderously across the land, straight as an arrow. It was a little egret. It was a sign from you.

I turned to watch it disappear, long legs trailing straight behind it, its brilliant white plumage making it easy to spot in the ever-increasing sunlight. That's when I saw how far I had come. In a trance of grief, I had navigated far into the marsh, impossibly avoiding falling into any creeks. Where the little egret had scared me, I had been brought to a standstill right beside a deep creek, hidden beneath springy foliage. I peered down, both scared and relieved, because resting at the bottom, half-hidden in the water, lay a rusting oil drum and a snarl of barbed wire. If I had stepped into that, I could have been seriously injured – and out on the marsh, no one would have heard my cries for help.

That's when I realised.

You had guided me through the maze of creeks. You had saved me from harm. You had sent the egret to stop me taking another step forward. Beth, even as I'd searched for you, you had been beside me every step of the way.

The glow of knowing you hadn't left me kept me cosy-warm all through the walk home.

*

Waiting on the doorstep were more flowers, left by an early riser. I checked the card. They were from Jill Young. They got tossed into the wheelie bin, the slamming lid loud in the Sunday-morning silence, jarring against the birdsong.

I went inside and made my weary way upstairs with a cup of tea, Wiggins at my heels. The pair of us climbed into bed with Jacob, and we lay tangled together. We barely moved for the rest of the day.

CHAPTER 83

We lay below the plaque Jacob had carved as a teenager – *I will always love you* – foreheads touching, legs twisted together like vines. The space in between us formed a heart, in which Wiggins was curled.

'I love you to bits and whole again,' Jacob whispered, blue eyes an ocean of sadness. I traced the delicate lines around them with a gentle finger.

'We can survive this. Together,' I said. 'But…'

Time to get rid of the last secret plaguing us. I'd been putting off talking about this for so long, but nothing would ever seem a big deal again after losing you, Beth.

'But only if you stop seeing Flo, Britney, whatever you want to call her.'

'What? Why would I see her again?'

He sounded so confused that my old bitterness flared.

'I saw you, Jacob. You and Flo, snogging like a couple of kids while your family fell apart.'

Eyes widened, pupils contracted. 'Mel… shit, I… I…' His hands flew up to his blond stubble of hair, running over it. 'Christ, I'm so sorry. It should never, ever have happened. But… Melanie, I swear to you that what you saw was all that happened. There was no affair, nothing more than a kiss.'

'I don't want details; I don't care. Not any more—'

'No, just – please listen a moment. You know how I can prove what I say is true? I can tell you exactly when you saw what you saw, because it was the only time it happened. It was exactly ten days ago. It was the day James Harvey was arrested and we thought he'd, you know, done things. To Beth.

'I was in a panic, and you… you were starting to change, to give up. I should have been stronger for you, but I wasn't. You're my best friend, always have been, always will be, and suddenly I couldn't talk to you. But that wasn't your fault, it was mine. I… I felt so helpless, so useless, and there was so much going on inside me that I didn't even know where to begin identifying it myself, much less talk about it to you. I wanted to run away. To be someone else. Besides, I should have been able to do more. I should have protected Beth—'

'You couldn't. Neither of us could.' I felt that way myself, but hearing him say it made me realise how foolish it was. Neither of us were to blame for this.

He shook his head, heavy with regret, refusing to listen.

'Britney, I mean Flo, well, she understood – it's her job to understand. We kissed as we stood in the hall just that once, after you and I had given consent for those tests on Beth. I'll never forget it because it was one of the worst moments of my life. That kiss proves how weak and pathetic I am, and I'm ashamed of myself. I let you and Beth down. And I will never, ever do that again.'

There were tears in his eyes now. He let go of one hand and wiped at them with his knuckles, childlike. His eyes so wide and innocent, desperately seeking absolution.

I knew then that he was telling the truth. This was the man I had grown up with, the man I would trust with my life. He had made a stupid mistake, but he had not betrayed me, and he hadn't changed throughout all this mess.

Still, I checked. 'It was only a kiss?'

'Nothing else happened.' He shook his head. 'But it's bad enough. If… if you can't forgive me, I understand. But I'll never do anything like it again. As soon as it happened, we both realised how wrong it was. We've been avoiding each other ever since; it's been so awkward. When we did talk, it was to assure each other that neither of us would ever tell anyone. We knew it wouldn't happen again, so we just left things.'

A kiss. Only a kiss. It churned my stomach, but after losing you, it was nothing. We could get past this.

CHAPTER 84

Monday dawned; 5.03 a.m. You had been dead for four days. The numbness and anger were giving way to constant tears. We shuffled along, hunched, broken. Jacob's bosses had told him to take as long as he needed. We told our parents not to come over. Each of them had taken over a task for the funeral, now that it had been decided what we wanted. My life was in jagged shards, thoughts slashing me and making me gasp. I wanted to bleed.

Upstairs, Jacob stirred. I heard his gentle footsteps, then a door opening and closing softly. He had gone to your room, Beth. I sensed by the fact he had closed the door that he wanted to be alone.

So with nothing to do but grieve, I found myself flipping aimlessly through the Sunday newspaper Jill had left on the step the day before. My eyes roamed over the words but not long enough to take anything in.

Suddenly they stopped. Widened.

'TIFFANY'S MURDER IS KILLING ME,' SAYS TRAGIC MUM

Read the headline running across two pages. Below sat a picture of a woman whose eyes were as haunted and angry as my own.

I leaned over the print. It was an interview with the mother of the girl who was killed a few months before you were attacked. The one who stole our publicity from us. At the time I was so furious, but now the words of the article resonated with my own agony. At least our mystery had been solved, and I knew who was responsible for your death; this poor woman, Angela Jones, 34, had no clue. I felt her pain alongside my own.

Fleetingly I wondered if I should contact her. Perhaps we could offer each other comfort.

There were the briefest details of the crime. I didn't dwell on those, remembering them instead from the initial coverage. How twelve-year-old Tiffany had disappeared on 27 September 2015, the night of the blood moon, from her home in Clifton, Nottingham. Her body had been found weeks later, her head caved in. She'd been sexually assaulted after death, then dumped in some undergrowth by the side of the M1.

The police had initially looked closely at her family, mainly because Tiffany had apparently half-heartedly tried to run away a few months before her death, going walkabout in the middle of the night. When the newspapers got wind, there had been some pretty unsavoury reports, sneering at her relatives, seemingly because they lived on a large council estate. Her mum's boyfriend, Bear – who the hell had a name like Bear? – had been given a particularly hard time. He had looked the part of a pervert, to be honest: slightly dishevelled, with uneven eyes that gave him a permanent leer. But looks aren't everything, are they?

When it became clear the family (and Bear) were innocent, the police worked on the assumption that Tiffany had run away again and been taken by an opportunist who had spotted her in the night. The A453 ran fairly near her home, and connected to the M1. It was a busy road, and police reckoned someone passing by in a car may have spotted the girl and snatched her. Dumped her before making his escape along the busy motorway.

All that had stopped when Tiffany's phone had been found in bushes near where her body was dumped. Text messages showed she had been lured from her home by someone posing as a teenage lad her age. Police believed this 'Justin' was actually a paedophile who had deliberately targeted her. How he had got her number remained a mystery.

The media had then launched a charm offensive to make up for the hatchet job they'd done on the family earlier. They were on a crusade to make the family look good – and to catch 'Justin'. That was one of the reasons why her story ran while your attack didn't make the news, Beth.

That, and the fact that the moniker the 'Blood Moon Murder' had a great ring to it.

Your attack didn't have that. Apart from your dad smoking a joint, which had been splashed briefly over the front pages of the nationals, there was nothing juicy about this case that could be reported. The fact that your attacker was a young girl meant restrictions imposed by the court were in place over what could be printed. Chloe's identity was legally protected – and because of that, so were her parents'. As a result, your death had been the smallest of paragraphs, buried in the back half of the national newspapers. Easily missed.

Unlike this huge report on Tiffany's murder. So far, there were no new leads in the case.

I had to stand for a moment. To distance myself physically from the arctic glare of the article on the kitchen table. Not because I was sobbing in sympathy. No; it was because I was so bloody furious at the injustice of yet another young girl's life snuffed out. I knew exactly the hell this mother was going through.

CHAPTER 85

School crap, friends crap, life crap, Tiffany thought to herself.

Her mum sat downstairs, watching *Gogglebox* on catch-up, by the sound of her laughing to herself. Let her laugh. At least it was better than the sound of her crying after yet another bust-up with her butt-ugly boyfriend, Bear. Who the hell had a name like Bear? That alone should have given her mum warning that he was well peak. The latest in a long line of crap, butt-ugly blokes.

Tiffany should have been sleeping, but the students next door were all up, so she'd got no chance. The walls were so thin she could tell from the music that the bloke in the bedroom beside hers was playing *World of Warcraft*. And swearing a lot.

With a sigh, the twelve-year-old turned her bedside light on, put on her round specs, dug out her notebook and started writing. She wrote constantly. Tiffany could lose herself, block out the shitty reality of her life and create a whole new world. One with dank vampires, and werewolves, and she was thinking about introducing a talking dragon. But not a crap one. One that was dark and a bit evil and, like, totally sick.

Her mobile phone lit up, buzzing like an angry wasp had climbed inside it. She almost didn't bother looking at it. Curiosity got the better of her, though, as she wondered who the hell would be sending her texts at just gone midnight on a Sunday.

It was from a number she didn't recognise.

Hey, Tiffany, seen u round. Want 2 chat?

And get scammed by someone? Not likely. Knowing her name wasn't enough to gain her trust.

Loser

She typed back.
Seconds later, it buzzed again.

Hey, c'mon, Tiff. Jus tryin' 2 b mates. I seen u round.

Yeah, yeah, they had already said that.

Who r u?

Aside from a loser.

Name's Justin. Just moved here. In year above u @ school.

Justin. Justin? She didn't remember anyone new at school. But it was big, so hard to keep track. Plus, she tended to live in her own world. Which was why she didn't get many texts, let alone at midnight.

Buzz.

Be gr8 to get 2 know u better. U r gorgeous. So peng.

At the bottom was the most loser-ish emoticon, with eyes bugging out of its head.

Tiffany huffed. Put the phone down, turned off the light and closed her eyes. No way was she going to reply. The compliment had infuriated her, sarcastic thoughts ricocheting round her brain. Gorgeous? Peng? Yeah, right. With her puppy fat still clinging to her like a rabid Rottweiler, and acne that Clearasil struggled to cope with, she reckoned she was a real catch.

The waspish buzz of her phone came again. She ignored it. Screwed her eyes shut even tighter, trying to block out *World of Warcraft* too. At least the television was silent downstairs; her mum must have gone to bed.

Another buzz.

'Grrr! Go away!' she huffed. Then threw off the duvet and turned her bedside lamp back on. Read the two messages.

Hey, where'd u go?

Please, I only want 2 chat. Wots the harm? Tell me 'bout yourself.

Yeah, what was the harm? Wasn't like she'd be getting any sleep anyway. And how often did anyone ever ask her about herself?

Right, you might regret asking that. What you want to know?

It wasn't long before the phone went again. Tiffany laughed at the image Justin had sent. One of the Minions, dancing for joy.

Yeah, funny guy. I prefer vampires.

She shot back.

Soon they were batting texts back and forth. In between, Tiffany doodled idly. A phoenix with a long plumed tail. A stack of books, with a flower growing out of the top. She didn't know why she liked that image so much, but she did, and drew it in all her notebooks. It gave her something else to think about as she tried to play it cool with Justin, almost kidding herself that she wasn't interested in trying to make a new friend. Even in a large school, people like her were few and far between.

CHAPTER 86

The newspaper article lured me back again. I was drawn to this mother's pain, so similar to my own, although the circumstances were very different.

There were some photos of Tiffany clustered together at the far left of the page. As a toddler, all gorgeous rolls of flesh and cherub-faced. Older, on her bike, posing awkwardly. Then the school photo, obligatory and now made famous because it was the one which was used to accompany every news report on television and in print. This girl looked more serious. Her round glasses gave her a slightly owlish and studious look, but they suited her. Glossy dark brown hair was centre-parted and fell to her shoulders.

She was pretty, but clearly wasn't aware of it; she had that hunch-shouldered, slightly apologetic set to her body that gave it away. A couple of spots marked her face, but nothing more than the average teen.

Almost despite myself, I read on.

'She always had her head in a book,' Tiffany's mother told the reporter. This girl sounded a lot like you, Beth.

'Her dream was to be an author, and she was constantly scribbling ideas in her notebooks. They had to be the same brand, too; bright pink Moleskine ones. Reading her stories gives comfort to me. But the one she had just started was never found. The killer must have taken her notebook from her – she wouldn't go anywhere without it.

It probably only had a couple of pages of her story in it, but I hate the idea of him stealing her dreams along with her life.'

A bright pink Moleskine notebook. Like yours. Like the kind Glenn incongruously always wrote in.

I pulled the bottom of the newspaper closer to me to stare at a photograph in the far bottom right of the article. There was a little pile of Tiffany's pink notebooks, one of which lay open, showing her neat, round writing. Tucked away at the top of the notebook's page sprouted a funny doodle of a flower growing from a pile of books.

The same doodle I'd seen so recently in another bright pink notebook.

The room seemed to tilt, and I sat down hurriedly. Wrapped my arms around myself to keep out the sudden cold. I was imagining things. If I had Glenn's notebook to compare, I would see that his doodle looked entirely different.

Only…

It wasn't his doodle, was it? It wasn't his handwriting, either. He'd told me it was his daughter's… but he didn't have a daughter. Katie was the child of his former neighbour.

Shivers ran through me.

Suddenly a memory of a drunken conversation burst into my mind. Me clinging to Glenn to stay upright as we stared at the stars on the marsh. Him saying how he had seen September's blood moon while travelling in Sydney, and thought it incredible.

Bloody great red moon. In Australia. In September. Supercool.

Those had been his exact words; I was sure of it. He couldn't have been more adamant than that.

But now I was recalling the conversation, stone-cold sober, I realised the lie in it. Glenn couldn't have seen the blood moon in Australia. Remember the research we did into it, Beth? The blood moon couldn't even be partially seen in that part of the globe.

Glenn had lied; he had clearly been in this country at the time of the blood moon – when Tiffany was killed. And where had she lived? Feverishly, I scanned the newspaper article. There! Clifton, in Nottingham. Wasn't that near where Glenn had lived? I grabbed my tablet and looked online. According to the map, Dunkirk and Clifton were next to each other.

I forced myself to breathe steadily. To slow my thoughts.

Perhaps Glenn had innocently stumbled across this notebook. Found it lying in the street, or something. If that were the case, then he needed to hand it in. It was probably way too late for forensics to get anything from it, but they could work miracles nowadays, couldn't they, so it was worth a shot.

Giving him the benefit of the doubt, this was the first time the notebooks had been mentioned by the press. There was no reason why Glenn would know about it. No doubt the police had been holding back the fact they suspected the killer had kept it as a trophy, and had only just given permission for the information to be released.

But what about Glenn's lies? I'd thought they were for my sake, a misguided attempt to help me, or because he fancied me. Suddenly I looked at them in a whole different light.

A crazy idea grew in my mind.

Grabbing my car keys, I rushed upstairs to Jacob. Knocked on your bedroom door. Jacob called me in. He was sitting on your bed, hugging your teddy bear.

'You all right?' I checked.

He sniffed, nodding. His red, puffy eyes told the truth, though.

This was stupid; I couldn't abandon my husband because of some daft idea. I was obviously trying to find something to occupy my mind other than my own grief. Needing another puzzle to solve; imagining mysteries where there were none.

I would stay home with my husband. No more wild goose chases.

'Want a cuppa?' I asked.

'You going out?' Jacob tilted his head to one side and indicated with his chin towards the car keys dangling from my hand.

'No. Well, I'd been thinking about going for a drive, just to get away from here for a while, you know? But I'd rather stay here, keep you company.'

'I'll be fine,' he protested.

He reached towards me and I stepped forward, allowing him to wrap his arms around my hips and rest his head against my stomach. I ran my fingers over the stubble of his head. After a minute, he spoke again.

'I know we deal with things differently. I know you like to have your own space. If you want to go out, go. I want to sit here for a while.'

Bless him, I understood instantly. Jacob didn't want to say as much, but he needed to be alone for a while. He found solace in your room, the way I found it on the marsh. I think it was your way of ensuring we both got time alone with you.

'Well, in that case… If you're sure.'

'I'm sure. Go on, get gone.'

As I closed the door, he curled up on your bed, Jesus by his side.

CHAPTER 87

The keys were getting warm in my hand, I'd been gripping them for so long as I sat in my car, trying to decide what to do.

I could stop this silly paranoia, grab Wiggins and go to the marsh.

Or… I could nip over to Glenn's flat in Wapentake, though I wasn't exactly sure which number he lived at because I'd never been there.

Or… I could text Glenn and meet up with him somewhere, ask to see the notebook. But I didn't want to sound like I was accusing him of keeping something back from a murder investigation, when he was the person who had kept me sane the last few weeks. Although sick of his lies, I didn't seriously think he knew who the killer was. There was no way.

Making a decision, I set off.

It felt so good to have something to think about other than you, Beth. When I thought of you, all my breath left my body and I felt so weak I simply wanted to curl up and die. But this mystery kept me going. I needed it.

For the entire journey I batted facts back and forth in my head.

The doodle in the newspaper looked identical to my memory of the one in Glenn's notebook.

The stupid doodle probably wasn't anything like Tiffany's. I had a lot on my plate, and was remembering wrong.

Had he pretended to be out of the country during the blood moon so that I wouldn't suspect him?

But why would he even think that I would suspect him? No, he'd simply wanted to impress me with his well-travelled-man act because he fancied me.

Why had he pretended to have a daughter?

Again, to impress me. To bond with me and help me. There was absolutely no other reason that offered itself.

But I kept coming back to the same fact.

The doodle in the newspaper looked identical to my memory of the one in Glenn's notebook…

CHAPTER 88

TIFFANY
SUNDAY 27 SEPTEMBER

The second the minicab pulled up, Tiffany slipped out of her home. She had warned Justin to tell the driver not to beep its horn, for fear of waking her mum. Though Mum had taken sleeping tablets ever since she and Dad split, and generally the twelve-year-old could make enough noise to wake the dead and her mum would remain snoring. But Tiffany didn't want to take the risk – and definitely didn't want neighbours twitching their curtains at 3 a.m.

Justin had assured her that he would pass the message on to the taxi driver, and clearly he had. It comforted Tiffany, as it showed Justin was trustworthy. He had even told her not to bother bringing money, as he would pay the fare. In fact, he had organised the whole thing, taking her address so he could sort the pick-up.

With a taxi, u know u will be safe, he had texted. That was nice of him.

His parents were away, leaving him alone for the night. He reckoned he had cadged her number off someone at school, and decided to text her.

Tiffany felt flattered, but worried. Last time she had got caught sneaking out, her poor mum had been interviewed by social services. They had told her they would put Tiffany into care if she ran away again. Idiots. She had kept trying to explain that she hadn't been running away, she simply liked being out. The students next door never seemed to sleep, and she got antsy trying to block out their noise. It helped her to go for a walk. Of course, her mum kept warning her that some pervert was going to try to whisk her away and take advantage of her in the middle of the night. Yeah, 'cos she was that dumb, Mum. If some weirdo came anywhere near Tiffany, then she would just scoot – simple as that. Honestly, her mum thought she was so *unaware*.

Anyway, sneaking out was no big deal. She would only stay an hour at Justin's. She'd be back home before anyone realised she was gone. The students might be in bed by then, and she would finally get some sleep before school.

Tiffany couldn't quite believe her luck at Justin getting in contact with her. Turned out he was into all the same stuff she was. Telling stories and stuff. He wasn't like anyone else she had ever met. When he'd sent her a photo of himself, wow, he was buff. Dark hair, brooding eyes, like a vampire hero from one of her stories.

She clutched her pink notebook in her hand as she walked towards the cab. It had been a last-minute decision to bring it, to show Justin the latest story she had started. It was only a few pages, but he'd get the idea. Vampires. Werewolves. Dragons. It had got everything in it they both loved.

He was so utterly sick. Bare dank – or 'cool', as her mum would say. God, she was old.

Tiffany felt a bit nervous as she opened the cab door. The light didn't come on inside, but the street light illuminated enough for her to see what she was doing as she clambered in.

'The person who booked you gave you the address, right?' she checked.

'That's right,' said the driver.

He turned towards her slightly, but he had a soft, low voice that made her crane forward. In the dark she only had a vague impression of a round face and tight curls, slightly balding. He looked like an overgrown baby.

Then they were off, into the darkness, towards Justin's house.

CHAPTER 89

I was reminded of the poem by Mary Howitt as I sat in my innocuous dark blue Ford Escort, the engine running. We'd studied it at school, and it had always stuck with me. "'Will you walk into my parlour?" said the spider to the fly', that was how it went. When the door opened and the girl climbed inside – voluntarily – the fly came right into my web.

It was her fault for being such a gullible kid.

Justin, my alter ego, had informed her that she would be picked up by a taxi; and my car could pass for one if no one looked too closely. And what twelve-year-old did look closely? The idiot hadn't even asked for Justin's address, so had no clue where I was taking her.

Now, there she was, the aptly named Tiffany. Mummy's little jewel, stolen away. She sat in the back of my car, staring out of the window or thumbing through her notebook as I drove. No idea what lay ahead of her. Didn't appear worried until I pulled over in a lay-by near a wood, driving through a pothole full of water and smashing the reflection of the moon.

CHAPTER 90

Parking was a bit of a nightmare on Glenn's old street in Nottingham, as it was bumper-to-bumper. I had decided to visit his ex, Marcie. Glenn would never find out because they didn't have anything to do with each other. That would allow me to find out a bit more about his background, put my overactive imagination at rest once and for all. I had to park round the corner from his house, but walking to it gave me a chance to get a feel for the area.

The narrow road had been built for Victorian foot traffic, with no room to be widened. It was easy to imagine it cobbled, as it must have originally been. This was no tree-lined avenue. The terraced cottages faced each other, almost looking into one another. They didn't have gardens, the front door opening straight on to a narrow pavement.

Some of the streets seemed quite affluent, but not this one. It had been missed for some reason by the changes that had swept through much of the area. The cars were rust buckets, the newest fifteen years old. Wooden window frames sported peeling paint. On the sill of one house, someone had left a used nappy. Open, so the contents could be fully appreciated.

Luckily Marcie did not live at that house, but a few doors down, at the opposite end to the one I had entered at. It was one of the better kept properties, the yellow paint on the door so new that it still smelled slightly.

I gave a timid knock at the door, cursing myself for this stupid idea. What the hell was I going to say? I hadn't even rehearsed it first.

I'd just have to wing it.

After a minute I knocked again, harder. I started to have second thoughts. But what was the alternative? Let a murderer go free? Drive home and cry over the gaping hole in my life?

I'd knock once more. If no one answered, then I'd give it up as a bad job. Then I realised: of course, it was a Monday. Marcie was probably at work. Like normal people were on normal days. It was hard to get my head around the fact that the world was still functioning as usual, despite your death, Beth.

'Just a minute,' called a voice from inside. Thin and reedy, I recognised it from the phone. The door opened, revealing Glenn's ex. She hung onto the door, a hint of wariness in her deep-set, ice-blue eyes.

'Hi, umm, hello. We spoke the other day?' My voice rose, as if I'd asked her a question. 'I'm Melanie Oak.'

She looked blank. Then her mouth formed an 'oh' as realisation hit. 'The lady whose daughter is in hospital?'

Don't cry. Do not cry. I nodded furiously to try to disguise the rapid blinking of my eyelids.

'How's she doing?'

'She's fine.' My voice sounded high-pitched and alien even to my own ears. Clearly Marcie had missed the tiny paragraph the national newspapers had written about your death. And I hadn't said the words aloud yet, Beth; I'd never had to tell anyone that my beautiful daughter was dead. To say it for the first time would be a massive step, and one I wasn't willing to take at that moment.

'Come in,' Marcie gestured.

Her thin face and sharp chin were transformed when she smiled. Everything about her was thin, in fact – her lips, the slightly beaky nose, the wispy blonde hair, feather-cut down to her shoulders.

She had a startlingly high forehead, the pale skin covered in faint freckles. But that smile brought a lightness to her, making her eyes sparkle from beneath the heavy black kohl lining them top and bottom.

I found myself smiling back in spite of myself, warming to her as my nerves dissipated.

*

I stepped inside, straight into the lounge, as there was no hall, and sat on the squishy pink floral sofa, sinking lower than expected. I pulled myself forward a bit more, in danger of drowning in cushions.

'Sorry to disturb you. Thought you might be at work, so it was a bit of a gamble.'

'Ooh, I don't work. Not with my back. Spondylitis. Would you like a drink? Kettle's just boiled, so you've perfect timing.'

Was it awkwardness making me feel hot and cold all at once? Or was it because the electric heater was on full but the windows let in a nasty draught around my neck and ankles?

'Ah, er, a coffee would be lovely, thanks.'

She bustled into the kitchen. I took the opportunity to have a nose round from my seat. The place was tiny, the furniture tired, but it was clean, tidy and clearly well looked after. The ancient brown carpet had threadbare whorls here and there, which Marcie had tried to hide beneath a large purple rug. A huge television took up most of the space on the wall opposite the window I sat beneath. Marcie's lounge was too small for any other seats apart from the sofa.

A photo in a silver frame on the mantelpiece caught my eye. It was of Marcie and Glenn, laughing at the camera. Her angular face looked tiny beside his round one.

Marcie reappeared and handed me a mug.

'Right, what can I do for you? Is it something to do with Glenn?' As she asked, she perched on the edge of the sofa, her body turned towards me, our knees almost touching.

I took her in, trying to get a sense of her, trying to figure out how best to broach the subject of Glenn and the notebook. She wore a pale denim shirt, untucked, over black leggings, and on her feet were fluffy slippers with cat faces on. It was the slippers that did it, along with the photo of her and Glenn; this was a nice woman, I decided. There was an air of desperation about her, too; she wanted to be liked. She was so utterly different from the hard-faced bitch Glenn had painted. Well, he might not have any feelings for her any more, but judging from the photo on display, Marcie was still in love with him.

Going on my gut, I suddenly decided how I'd tackle this problem. I'd try to charm the information from her. I smiled my best 'I'm a journalist and want to win you over' smile, and popped the mug down.

'Well, Glenn's done so much for us, and we want to do something nice for him, you know? He talks about you, a lot.' I almost winced at that blatant lie. Marcie tilted her head to one side, curious as a cat. Pink splotches of colour bloomed up her pale neck and cheeks as she blushed in surprise and pleasure. 'So I wondered if there was anything I could do, to help smooth things between the two of you…'

Marcie bit her lip then looked at me, shaking her head.

'Is that what he wants? Really?'

Her voice was a whisper, but the hope in it shouted. I felt dreadful, but told myself this was to help another mother, desperate for answers. A mother like me, who had lost her child. Eventually I'd just have to find a way of letting Marcie down gently after needlessly building her hopes up.

'Of course that's what he wants,' I soothed.

'But Glenn just walked out one day. He'd been in a funny mood for months before. Distant. And picking rows with me all the time. Then suddenly things seemed to improve. They were great for a few weeks, until…' She shrugged. Her eyes were wide, appealing to me desperately. 'He just walked out on me. Packed a bag and said he was leaving and wouldn't ever be coming back.'

A tear balanced on the black rim of her eye, then tumbled down her cheek. She wiped at it, clearly embarrassed.

'Sorry,' she sniffed.

'No, I'm the one who should apologise. I'm sticking my nose in where it's got no business. I wanted to help.' I took a calculated gamble, moved as if to stand.

'No, it's lovely of you,' she sniffed again. 'But… are you sure it's what Glenn wants? What's he said?'

'Oh, well, he's told me a lot about how much he misses you, but that he feels too ashamed to come back after the way he walked out.' The lies flew out of my mouth.

She gave a watery smile, sat a little straighter.

'Honestly? I mean, I know he's not perfect, and, well, he'd have to make some changes, not take me for granted so much, maybe take me out once in a while, but, well, I might be willing to forgive him.'

'So, do you mind me asking… What exactly happened between the two of you? It was back in September, is that right?'

'January,' she corrected.

'He didn't leave you until January? I must have got my wires crossed. I thought he went in September. To go travelling?'

'Travelling! That takes money. We haven't even travelled to Skegness for a day trip in years.'

My mind raced at her answer. So Glenn had definitely been lying about being in Australia. I knew it! He had moved straight to Wapentake after leaving his wife in January.

Marcie gave a sad sigh, collecting herself.

'He'd been out of sorts for about six months. But then there was all that terrible business. You've seen it in the news, you know, about that little girl, Tiffany Jones, getting snatched off the street in the middle of the night? Horribly murdered.' She shuddered. I did too. Another poor girl meeting a violent end. But I couldn't allow myself to get upset about it, or connect with it emotionally – to do so would give the game away, and it was too important for that. So I forced myself to keep my journalist head on, pleased the subject had come up so easily. Marcie had presented it to me on a plate.

She leaned closer, lowering her voice as if worried she might be overheard.

'Our neighbour's girl was mates with the poor mite, you know. Terrible business. Well, she and Glenn have always got on well. Honest, he's like an uncle to her, buys her presents, gets through to her when her parents can't; it's a gift. He even helps her with her phone and computers and stuff – he's good that way.'

'Is this Katie? Your neighbour's girl's name is Katie?'

'That's right! The one you got confused about; thought she was Glenn's daughter!' She chuckled at my foolish 'mistake'. 'Thing is, Katie was devastated by Tiffany's murder. I mean, they weren't close, but they knew each other, texted sometimes, and something like that's bound to upset a child, isn't it? So Katie's parents asked Glenn to keep an eye on her, too, and it seemed to snap him out of his mood. He was like a different person for a while. Couldn't do enough for me. But then one night he just upped and left me. Out of the blue. Said he couldn't stand to live here any more. Couldn't stand *me* any more.'

She hunched in on herself again. Her hair fell around her face, but I could hear her crying. I took her hand.

'I'm so sorry.' I hesitated. 'Did Glenn know Tiffany? Had he ever met her?'

Marcie shook her head, high forehead crinkled at the question.

'I thought he might be upset about her death, and that had made him act out of character, leaving you,' I improvised. 'He's, er, really good with kids, isn't he?'

Her bottom lip quivered as she nodded her reply. 'Loves them. Has a real way with them, you know? It's such a shame we never had any. We tried, but we couldn't. My fault,' she added hastily. 'My fault.'

This was all well and good, but how the hell was I going to ask about the notebook, Beth? As I thought, I ran over the conversation, buying time by sipping my coffee. Suddenly a fragment of the conversation floated up. Something that didn't fit.

'Did you say Glenn helped Katie with her phone?'

'He's a whizz at stuff like that.' Marcie looked proud. I looked confused.

'Glenn's useless with phones, it took him forever to get the ringtone off Roza's mobile,' I muttered to myself.

'Oh, he's still nicking ringtones, is he?' Marcie smiled. Shook her head indulgently. 'He did that with Katie too. Downloaded her ringtone to cheer himself up. Something to do with Bluetooth or something. Oh, I did laugh at him, wanting the same ringtone as a twelve-year-old kid.'

For some reason, that made me go cold. I felt as if I was missing something vital, just at the tip of my fingers. All I had to do was stretch, and I'd be there.

What if Glenn had got Tiffany's number from Katie's phone?

'Did Tiffany come round much? To visit Katie?' I asked.

'Don't know. Got the impression she'd never been round, actually. Like I say, they weren't close, but close enough for Katie to be hit hard. Don't expect anyone you know to die, not at that age, do you?'

I blinked rapidly at the inadvertent reminder of your own tragically short life. Chewed hard on the side of my cheek to stop the tears and made myself concentrate on Tiffany. I wouldn't – couldn't – think about you.

If Glenn had never seen Tiffany, why would he target her? Then again, maybe Marcie was confused, and the girl had often visited

Katie. Maybe Glenn had simply found the notebook on the street and had no idea it belonged to a murdered child. Maybe he knew the person who had hurt her.

That was a whole load of maybes.

Frustration built; I needed to know more.

'What about the notebook? Glenn's pink notebook?' I blurted. Marcie looked at me like I was mad.

'The bright pink Moleskine notebook that he always carries with him?' My voice was urgent now. 'Do you know where he got it from? When did he start carrying it? It was after Tiffany disappeared, wasn't it?'

She flicked her yellow hair off her shoulders suddenly. Her eyebrows, so pale they were almost invisible, pulled together sharply.

'What are you on about? Why are you asking all this? I don't know anything about a notebook.'

She stood. 'I've, er, just remembered that I've got to nip out now. Sorry. Tell Glenn he can call me any time. And, er, I hope your girl gets well soon.'

Damn! I had completely freaked her out with my strange questions. I made myself calm.

'Thank you,' I murmured, standing too. 'I'll pass the message on to Glenn.'

Marcie opened the door. Reached up and patted my shoulder hesitantly as I walked past her.

'You must be under a terrible strain with your girl being so ill. I'll keep everything crossed for her. Being a mother is such a blessing.'

I hurried away, tears threatening again. I couldn't think about you, Beth. Not yet. Wouldn't think about never seeing you again. Never hearing you. Never holding you… Much easier to pretend you were still in hospital, and that I'd visit you later.

Instead, I jumped into my car and popped to a chemist, then started the journey home, my head exploding with thoughts.

CHAPTER 91

When I had lived in Dunkirk, Nottingham, my neighbour's teenager, Katie, had been the perfect patsy.

I was good with kids, and her parents often came to me, begging me to speak to her when they had problems. They called me 'the voice of reason', and were always amazed that she listened when I talked to her. But manipulating children and adults was something I had studied from an early age.

For years I had been satisfied with torturing innocent animals, but ever since my teens a fresh longing had been building inside me. I wanted to prove my power over life by killing a child. They are so treasured by the world, such a symbol of hope and purity.

But I didn't want to just do it once, and then get jailed. If I were to be able to do it again and again, I would have to be careful. So I had taken my time, perfecting my plan. Watching people and their complicated, pointless emotions, so that I could insinuate my way into their lives and gain access to their treasures with their blessing. Building up to the point where I could pull off my project.

My second wife, Vicki, had got in the way last time I had got close to my goal. I'd made a stupid mistake, using my home computer to look at some interesting photographs on a very secret and specialised site. When Vicki had found them, she had thrown me out, but been too embarrassed to call the police for fear of what people would think of her, married to a man like me.

Annoying, but it had taught me a valuable lesson.

Marcie had not been as sharp. And I had been smarter this time. Hidden my tracks better, and slowly got to know young Katie's parents. When they asked me to babysit her or be her 'voice of reason' when she was playing up, she had no clue they were encouraging their daughter to talk to a monster. They had no idea how often I fantasised about squeezing the life from her.

Chatting to her helped me refine my plan.

I'd been speaking to Katie's parents one day when I heard an unusual ringtone. It was my big chance, and I seized it.

'That's really cool – or do I sound like a big kid myself?' I asked Katie. 'Where can I get a ringtone like that?'

She had grinned, glowing at the attention, as usual. I got the impression she didn't get much at home – kids like that were easy targets for people like me.

''S'off the internet. There's a site,' she shrugged.

'Hmm, I'm not very good with technology. Could I get it off your phone instead? Download it somehow? That way, if I have any problems, you're here to help.'

No one seemed to find it odd that I apparently couldn't figure out a website but knew enough about technology to transfer the ringtone from one phone to the other. Idiots.

'Sure.' She offered her phone to me, and I looked at her mum to make sure everything was above board. When she gave me the go-ahead, not even remotely interested in what I was doing, I almost laughed out loud.

'Do you want to do it?' I double-checked, proffering her child's phone.

'Oh no, I'm probably worse than you at that sort of thing!' she chuckled. Just as I'd hoped.

That's the thing about people: the more open you are about what you're doing, the less they ask questions. If I had tried to be sneaky about getting my hands on her daughter's phone, she would have been instantly suspicious, but because I was doing it right in front of her, she couldn't have cared less.

Fingers working quickly, expertly, I got started. I opened up Katie's contacts and quickly Bluetoothed the lot over to my phone.

'Hang on, I'm in the wrong place,' I lied to cover myself, not that anyone was looking closely. 'Here we go. Have I… Have I managed it?'

I looked round at the blank, stupid, unsuspicious faces as I showed them my screen. Shrugs all round.

'Could one of you call me to check?'

Katie did that. My phone rang with that ridiculous new tone. Proof that I had done what I had said I'd done. No one was suspicious.

Stupid sheep. Never realising there was a wolf among them.

As I walked away, I couldn't stop the smile spreading across my face. I had a huge cache of children's numbers, thanks to my cunning. I was spoiled for choice over who to target with my text messages.

While deciding, I bought a disposable phone and transferred the numbers to that before deleting them from my usual phone. To make extra sure nothing could ever be traced back to me, I made it known to everyone that I had 'lost' my old phone and got a different one, same number, when in reality I'd stamped on it until there was nothing usable left of it, then chucked the bits in various bins scattered around town. Now I had my new phone, free of any evidence, and my new burner phone that had the youngsters' phone numbers on.

A few days later, at around 11 p.m., I decided to start my experiment. I wanted someone vulnerable, bored, easily hoodwinked. And once I got the ball rolling, I knew I'd have to act fast, so sent texts to several different numbers at once.

Who would get back to me first? I'd no idea what any of them looked like, but it didn't matter. One girl was as good as another.

CHAPTER 92

In the car, the miles home barely existed. The horror grew inside me as I thought of Glenn. Thoughts flashed past me faster than the white lines on the road.

He'd lied about Marcie being a bitch.

He'd lied about having a daughter.

He'd lied about the notebook.

He'd lied about being out of the country when Tiffany was murdered.

He'd lied about being useless with technology.

I'd thought it was odd when such a self-confessed technophobe made the connection between Snapchat and spreading the word about the raves. It didn't fit with the Glenn I knew at all. But it fitted the person Marcie knew: the technical whizz.

Everything was circumstantial. But now I knew there was a connection between Glenn and Tiffany. He had been close by when she was killed. He had her notebook. He was a liar, a manipulator.

But was he a murderer?

I warned myself to calm down. Possibly I was adding two and two and making five, as I had with James Harvey. Perhaps I was convincing myself there was evidence of Glenn being a killer when in fact he was a totally innocent man.

For the past two weeks I had spent countless hours with him. We had worked side by side, become so close. Never once had I picked up anything sinister from him.

The doodles probably looked nothing like Tiffany's, I told myself once again. But there was only one way to be sure. I'd have to get a look at that notebook. Then I'd know for certain. My foot pressed down on the accelerator and I urged the miles to disappear.

As much as I tried to think of Glenn, you were smashing through the wall of questions I hid behind, Beth. A fever flash of grief made me tremble, blurring the cars in front of me dangerously. I shook with it, forcing my hands to grip the wheel tighter, to try to blink the tears away so that I could see. They fell faster than I could clear them. I put my trust in you that you would either keep me safe or let me crash and burn so that we could be together.

Was I losing my mind? Had your death pushed me over the edge, Beth?

'Just let me solve this last mystery,' I begged you. 'Just let me get justice for this girl, like I got it for you. Then I don't care what happens.'

CHAPTER 93

The kid was as fast as a striking snake, I had to hand it to her. From the edge of the pothole I picked up a lump of loose tarmac the size of a grapefruit. Raced after her, exhilarated.

Adrenaline flowed as I gave chase. These were the bits I loved to replay in my mind over and over.

Feet running. Screaming for her mother. Begging for mercy. The sound of a watermelon smashing. A huff of breath. Legs giving way.

I straddled her and got to work. And watched her skin slowly, slowly changing colour.

When it was done, I threw my head back, elated. Above me the huge moon hung red in the sky. Even the heavens had arranged themselves to acknowledge my greatness. The blood moon was mine for the world to see.

All those years of longing and planning, patience and cunning had been worth it. I was a god.

I laughed and wiped the sweat off my face. Grabbed the kid's phone and tossed it into some bushes. In her hand she clutched a bright pink notebook. I took it from her and, on a whim, pocketed it. My treasure. Each time I wrote in it, I felt again the rush I had experienced at that moment.

CHAPTER 94

By the time I got home, it was 3 p.m. Outside the primary school, children streamed out towards their parents, who were eager and harried in equal measure. I wanted to scream at them to cherish every second, tell them how lucky they were to have their children.

Instead I parked the car and ran inside. Jacob snoozed on the sofa, still clutching Jesus and now also Wiggins. Only the dog stirred, tail wagging in greeting, then slowly settled again as I backed out of the house.

Perfect. I pulled my phone out and sent a text to Glenn.

Where are you? Fancy a drink?

Always, came the reply. *Already in pub. Join me.*

My heart thumped in time with my steps as I crossed the short distance over the road and into The Poacher. It was virtually empty, but the conversation stuttered when the handful of people saw me. Many moved towards me, murmuring their condolences, saying what a terrible business it was with the Clarkes. Hypocrites. But I nodded, unable to respond, scared one of the waves of grief would sweep me away again.

Not now. Not when I had to do this first.

Eventually I broke free and made my way over to Glenn, who sat at his favourite table, tucked in a corner.

So he could watch people coming and going, like a hunter. See, without being seen himself.

The thought flashed through me like lightning. I shuddered, told myself I had been in this paranoid place before, with James Harvey. I had felt a burning conviction that he was responsible for killing you, when all along he had been innocent.

'How you doing?' Glenn asked me, not bothering to stand up to greet me. Instead he kicked out a chair towards me, smiling that cherubic smile of his. 'You okay? Bloody stupid question. I got you a drink.'

I forced a smile, which felt more like a rictus. That was okay, though; I could get away with acting strangely, given the circumstances. You were my cloak, Beth. I hid behind you.

Glenn leaned towards me, eyes earnest. 'So, how are you doing? How are you feeling?'

This was ridiculous. Glenn was always so concerned with how I felt. He allowed me to share with him my deepest, darkest, most hurtful thoughts. Without him letting me offload, I'd have gone mad the last few weeks. He knew just when to stay quiet and let me speak, and when to probe, asking me incredible questions that got right down to the horrifying pain in me.

I was suddenly so weary.

'Oh, I don't want to talk about me. Not right now,' I deflected. 'Tell me about your day instead. I need to take my mind off things. I want to hear something stupid and mundane. Please.'

'All right,' he smiled. That boyish grin. 'Well, I've mostly been helping Dale out with his bloody crossword. Not very exciting! Silly sod didn't know that baby eels were called elvers.'

The minutes slipped by, and Glenn talked nonsense. I took the tiniest sip of my wine, encouraged by him.

'It'll help you forget about things,' he said.

That wasn't possible. Besides, he hadn't got me my usual brand, and this had a strange taste to it. Everything did now. I blinked back tears. Now was not the time to lose it.

'You be all right if I leave you for a minute? Need the loo,' Glenn announced, setting down his half-empty pint glass.

I watched him walk away. And knew what had to be done to halt the confusion tearing at me.

Feverish, I ran my hands over his jacket, which was slung over the back of his chair. The notebook was in his inside pocket, as always. I flicked it open.

The handwriting looked similar to Tiffany's. Rounded. Neat. A high bar above the lower case 't', which almost missed the top sometimes. But it wasn't enough to make me certain.

The doodle did that. A stack of books, a flower sprouting from it. The same lines; the same confidence; the same way of going over the petals again and again.

The wine came rushing into my mouth. I had to swallow down the acrid taste of it mixed with bile.

Oh my God, Glenn had Tiffany's notebook.

Perhaps he knew who had killed her.

Perhaps he had done it himself.

Or perhaps he had simply found the notebook, and this was all a coincidence.

I needed more than just this notebook. I looked around. No one so much as glanced in my direction. For once I was glad people couldn't bring themselves to look at me, thanks to my grief-induced invisibility. Still, I only had seconds more to find out all I could. I'd check Glenn's phone, see if there were any incriminating texts to the killer, or something.

There it was, in his outer pocket. Pulling it out, I quickly scrutinised the contacts and messages. There was nothing suspicious at all. Feeling like an idiot, I put it back in his pocket – and felt a buzz. It wasn't coming from that phone. Dread froze me for a heartbeat. Then I tugged again at the pockets and found the second phone. Cheaper, simpler, not even a touchscreen. The kind people have and chuck away. A burner phone.

Did I have time to check it? Glenn would be back any moment. My fingers were at sixes and sevens in my haste.

Come on! Come on!

There were loads of contacts. I flashed through them, and realised with growing horror that I recognised almost every single name. They were the names of children in the village.

The wine churned in my stomach. A rushing pounded through my head as if I were being enclosed by a tsunami wave. But I forced my shaking fingers to move over the plastic buttons. Find the messages, open them.

Hey, seen u about. My name's Justin. Want 2 chat?

The message had been sent last night to a little girl called Sally-Mae. You know, Susan and Colin Winston's youngest. She was only seven, the same age as Roza. She hadn't replied, thank God.

She hadn't replied yet.

Yet.

I shoved the phone back into its hiding place. Jumped from my seat and ran to the ladies' toilets just as Glenn came out of the gents'.

'Hey, are you… ?'

But he didn't have time to finish. I slammed the door in his face and vomited into the sink, no time to make it to a cubicle. I heaved and heaved and heaved, bringing up every last thing I'd eaten and drunk that day.

CHAPTER 95

For a moment I didn't know what to do as I stood in the door of the gents and watched Mel go through my pockets. It seemed she had finally figured out that I couldn't be trusted. Which was both disappointing, that she had seen through me, and also made me think, what took you so long, you stupid bitch?

I was going to have to do something about her. The faster, the better. Luckily I was good at thinking on my feet. I'd get her drunk. Everyone was used to her getting paralytic, then being walked home by me. Good old reliable Glenn. Only instead of our going home, I'd take her to the marsh and dump her corpse far out in one of the deep, hidden creeks. Even if the body were found, people would assume she was so grief-stricken that she had done something stupid. No one would ask questions. And I'd play the grieving friend, berating myself for not looking after her properly. I could just imagine it…

'If only I'd watched her go inside her house. I walked her right up to the door, but sh… she insisted she was fine and I left her. I should have known better,' I'd tell people.

I would cry, too, if I could manage it. Sometimes I could. Villagers would rush to reassure me that it wasn't my fault, that I had done all I could.

But what if she refused to have a drink with me? Became hysterical and told everyone in the pub what she had found?

No one would take any notice. She had been accusing people of all sorts for weeks now. People were sick of listening to her, even though they felt sorry for her. She was pathetic. And I could still play the gent and insist on walking her home; my poor, sad friend who was clearly having a breakdown… Then I'd punch her once we were outside, and carry her to the van. Similar plan as before, same outcome. Anyone who saw me would simply assume she was off her face, as usual.

Perfect. Melanie Oak was good and vulnerable and ripe for the plucking. No matter what she did, I would win.

CHAPTER 96

It took me a good five minutes to pull myself together, Beth. To wash my face, rinse my mouth clean and gather my courage. I had no idea how to face Glenn again now that I knew what a monster he was.

In the mirror, my eyes stared from my ashen face. I visibly quaked with convulsive shivers. Hopefully it would be excused as grief.

Eventually I took a deep breath, forced my shoulders back and walked out of the loo and back into the cheery, gentle chatter of the pub. Glenn sat at the table, smiling that cherubic smile of his. Lolling back in the chair, relaxed, no tension in his body at all as he looked at me.

He didn't suspect a thing.

I walked over to my chair on legs as wobbly as a toddler's and gathered up my things.

'I'm not feeling very well,' I chuntered, forcing myself to look at him but aware that my eyes kept sliding away.

'Oh, no! That's awful – but not surprising after everything you've been through.' He stood, concerned, solicitous, extending an arm towards me as if afraid I would fall. 'Here, let me walk you home.'

'I'll… I'll… honestly, I'll be fine.' The blood whooshed in my head again, and I started to feel weak at the knees.

'Mel, you look dreadful. I insist. I wouldn't be much of a friend if I didn't see you were safe.'

'You're all right, Glenn, I've got this.'

I had never been so glad to hear Jacob's voice. I turned and gave him a dazzling smile that must have seemed totally out of place. Grabbed onto his hand as if he could pull me from my nightmare.

'You got my text, then?'

'Yeah. I'm glad you asked me to come and get you – you don't look well at all. Okay, hon, let's go home.'

Your dad let go of my hand, but only to put his arm around me.

I saw Glenn's jaw tighten for a second, but only because I was looking for it. Then the mask slid back into place. He nodded, patting my arm with a concerned frown.

'You're in safe hands now, Mel. Feel better soon.'

'See you, Glenn,' replied Jacob.

But I remained silent. I clung to my husband and allowed myself to be walked home.

With each step, a killer's eyes bored into my back.

CHAPTER 97

Befriending Melanie had been a master stroke. Without her, I have to admit, I couldn't have coped. My need to murder might have overwhelmed me during the past couple of weeks, as the flush of thinking about my first kill wore off.

I had needed a fresh hit of pain and despair, and the only way I could see of getting that was to take another life. There was nothing like that power to give me the ultimate rush. But instinct had warned me not to hurry into another kill. After all, I wanted this next one to be perfect. I wanted to be able to take more time and have more fun – there was so much I had learned from that first time. So, sadly, an immediate murder could not be the solution to my problem.

Then I had read about that idiot, Jacob Oak, smoking marijuana while his daughter was being put in a coma. I remembered him from school. The good-looking, popular newcomer who everyone seemed to adore. Lads wanted to be his friend; girls wanted to date him. I never could stand him. Wanker.

Then I'd remembered he was married to Melanie. I had always had a soft spot for her, had often thought what it would be like to have a bit of sport with her. There was something so sweet and innocent about her that it would be a laugh to despoil. Even as a kid of eight, I'd picked her to play football because she smelled good enough to take a bite out of. Watching her made me think of the delicate birds I would trap and whose skulls I loved to smash.

I hadn't been back to Fenmere in years. Why the hell would I? But reading about Jacob Oak had given me an idea. I could return to my childhood home and live vicariously on Melanie Oak's pain.

Leaving Marcie had been no hardship. She was a whiny, pathetic woman I never should have saddled myself with. But it was easier for a married man to befriend people with kids than a single bloke; that's why I'd been married three times. I had stayed around long enough after Tiffany's murder to avert suspicion, and had sold the car – putting its real number plates back on first, of course – and bought the van straight after the attack. There was no longer a reason to stick around, and when I left Nottingham it was with a clear conscience.

It had been so easy to become Melanie's friend. She had been desperate for someone to understand her. All I needed to do was listen – and I'd been more than happy to do that. What a rich seam of pain I had struck! Melanie was full of rage, and so articulate that it was a joy to listen to her. When I probed, she gave up her secrets willingly, spilling her deepest, darkest, most raw feelings to me. Looking into her eyes, brimming with horror, had been wonderful. When she had imagined herself in the place of her child... my God, it had almost been as good as being there.

She was clearly cracking up, though. All that talk of being able to feel Beth when she was on the marsh was nuts.

I didn't particularly care who had hurt her kid, of course, I was just bloody grateful they had. But it hadn't taken a genius to ask the right questions, watch the body language and put two and two together. After years of studying people in order to manipulate them, it was easy to see the whole village was covering something up, but that Chloe was clearly guilty as hell. I could have told Melanie that, but why bother? It was so much more entertaining to wind her up and point her in the wrong direction – and hell, sometimes the right one, just to see how she would muck it up.

Making her into a pitiful laughing stock had been easy, as I encouraged her to drink more and more. Sometimes I slipped a little top-up into her glass from my hip flask, when no one was looking. It had never required much effort to get her to have a go at people, point the finger or even call the police with her suspicions.

She had been my little lab rat, trapped in a maze of my creation. Thinking about it, sometimes, in the privacy of my own home, I'd laughed so hard I had tears in my eyes.

CHAPTER 98

I saw Glenn through fresh eyes. Like a glass in a pub that looked clean until the sunlight hit it, and abruptly the smears were in plain view. He was something grubby that needed to be scrubbed off the face of the earth.

A moan escaped my lips as my stomach clenched again, trying to eject the disgust I felt at this man. I held the rim of the loo a little tighter, and spat bile into the white bowl.

'Mel, are you okay? Should I call a doctor?' asked Jacob.

'I'll be fine in a minute. Honestly.' My voice sounded weak, but I stood on wobbly feet and ushered your dad from the room. Some things required privacy.

After shooting the bolt across, I grabbed my handbag and rifled through it. What I searched for lay at the bottom. The pregnancy test that I had bought earlier, after leaving Marcie's house.

Since you had been found a month earlier, I had been nauseous every day, which I had written off as stress. Marcie's talk of wanting children had made me realise, though, how late my period was – about five weeks. Everything tasted strange to me; I was tired all the time, and my emotions were all over the place. Grief was one explanation. But there was another.

Sitting on the loo, I did what had to be done. And waited for the answers to come. There was so much to think about, Beth. Too much. Jumbled and disjointed thoughts twisted and clashed in my mind. You. Chloe. Pregnancy. Glenn. Tiffany. Roza. Fenmere's lying residents. Everything created a whirlwind in my mind.

Glenn was the person who had lured Tiffany from her home by posing as a boy through a series of texts. He had brutally murdered a twelve-year-old child. Now he was looking to do the same with a girl from Fenmere. His next target was either Roza or Sally-Mae. Time was running out for them.

The look on his face when he'd been talking to Roza while I spied through the hedge haunted me. He'd looked so happy, so triumphant. He'd positively glowed. Then when he'd seen me his expression, for a second, had been one of fury. I had had a glimpse into the abyss.

My heart thumped like a rabbit's caught in a fox's gaze. I could not let him kill again. Poor Tiffany. Her body touched and mucked about with after death. I heaved but nothing came up. Nothing was left any more.

Little Chloe Clarke may have smashed the life out of you, Beth, but she was in a different league to Glenn. He was pure evil.

I'd let him get close to me. I'd told him my deepest, darkest feelings; told him things I would never even admit to Jacob. Why had he befriended me?

The answer made me clutch the pregnancy testing stick so tight that it almost snapped. He was like one of those murderers who insert themselves into an investigation of a crime they themselves have committed, so they could relive the thrill. Only he had been living off the thrill of my pain. My investigation.

Beth, I knew now that Glenn had sullied your memory by using your attack for his own twisted purposes.

I could go to the police and tell them what I suspected he had done to Tiffany. Chances were they wouldn't believe me, though, not after all the calls I had made about you, Beth. They would think I was going crazy, seeing crimes where none existed. If he got wind that they were investigating him, he might throw away the notebook and his burner phone, destroying what little evidence there was. Evidence was everything, and without it, he would get off scot-free.

I hung my head in despair. Looking back up at me, the test stick announced one word.

Pregnant

Beth, you were going to be a big sister! The laugh I gave was a blade of both joy and pain. You should have been around for this. You would have been such an incredible sister.

The knowledge that I was bringing another life into the world hardened something in me. Suddenly I knew that I must do whatever it took to make the world a safer place for my unborn baby. Even if it meant briefly placing myself and my child in danger. I would never let her down the way I had you.

A plan began to form.

I would have to be careful. To my knowledge, Glenn had already killed once, and was planning to do it again. What's more, he kept a machete and a shotgun in the back of his van. He probably wouldn't hesitate to use either of them on me and my unborn child.

But doing nothing wasn't an option. I had to protect my family and other innocent kids. I had to stop another mother suffering the pain of my grief.

CHAPTER 99

I had got too cocky, that was the problem. Melanie had broken free of the maze of lies and misdirection I had created around her, and suddenly my lab rat had the potential to bite me. I couldn't give her time to go to the police. It wasn't simply that I didn't want to get caught, it was that I was so close to completing my beautiful work of art.

Melanie had provided me with the ideal way of befriending little Roza Jachowski. The kid's parents loved me because I'd gone round to warn them about the mob coming over before they arrived.

Of course, what the stupid Poles didn't realise was that I was the one who had whipped the villagers up in the first place. It hadn't taken much. Merely a few comments about 'pikeys coming to the village and suddenly there was a pretty teenage girl hurt'. Telling the yokels in the pub about Melanie's suspicions of Aleksy and making them sound a bit worse than they were.

It had been easy, when everyone was so suspicious of foreigners anyway, and so eager to find an obvious scapegoat for Beth's attack.

So after nipping round to warn the Jachowskis that trouble was brewing, I'd just sat back and watched the entertainment unfold. It meant the parents trusted me around Roza – after all, I was the only good guy in the village, as far as they were concerned. Getting the kid to give me her phone so that I could Bluetooth all of her contacts to my new burner was easy too. Little brat thought I was simply getting a stupid ringtone.

Of course, I would never be so stupid as to hurt Roza. She was safe, because otherwise suspicion might fall on me. Instead, I would target her pals. Send a text, do a spot of fishing, see who replied. Then reel them in, just like I'd done with Tiffany. I had sent loads of texts out that night to the numbers I'd got from Katie's phone. Hadn't been able to believe my luck when a girl had got back to me so quickly. Things weren't working quite so well with the Sally-Mae kid, but I would win her over in the end.

When I finally got to be alone with her, I would be more careful of the memento I would take. Keeping Tiffany's notebook had been a stupid indulgence, I realised. Clearly that was what had made Melanie suspicious. It was the only explanation. I raged against myself for my stupidity and arrogance. I had thought it fun to use my little souvenir in front of her. The notebook of a murdered child right under the nose of a mother losing her own daughter. It had seemed hilarious and poetic.

Now I was left with the problem of how to get at Melanie – and quickly.

The only thing I could think of was to call her and persuade her to join me. But how?

She was still vulnerable, and that made people stupid. I'd appeal to that overweening maternal instinct of hers. I would tell her I'd had awful news about my daughter. Good job Melanie had no idea who Katie actually was; it had been a genius idea to pretend I had a kid. Made Melanie trust me all the more. Two parents missing their kids, aww, how tragic.

*

I wandered outside to make the call. Didn't want to risk being over-heard in the pub. It was almost 7 p.m. and the cloudless night made it cold and bright. The wind was getting up too. I shivered, but didn't bother putting my coat on. I wouldn't be outside long.

I unlocked my phone and it lit up in the darkness. Scrolling quickly, I found Melanie's number and dialled.

A shout came from the other side of the road. Someone hurried towards me. Just for a moment, I felt completely and utterly nonplussed.

CHAPTER 100

Over an hour had flashed by after I had emerged from my bathroom hiding place. In that time I had confirmed a few things online and firmed up my plan. It wasn't much, but it would have to do.

Jacob had fussed around me, trying to get me to eat. In the end, I had forced down a bowl of cereal to keep him happy. My stomach was still churning.

Your dad still didn't know why I was being ill, Beth. I would tell him everything – almost everything – eventually. Once I told him I was expecting a baby I knew he wouldn't let me out of his sight.

So when Jacob disappeared up to your room for a while, I had felt a guilty relief.

Then I had switched the living room lights off and stared out of the window, across the road to The Poacher.

Coat on, ready, I waited impatiently for Glenn. If my plan were to work, I needed a lucky break. I prayed to all the gods that had so badly let me down when I had appealed to them over you, Beth.

Glenn stepped outside. His face illuminated from below made him look like a devil in a spooky story as he scrolled through his phone.

Hurrying towards the front door, I took one last look around my little home, which used to be full of noise and laughter. There was a strong chance that I would never see it again. Glenn might well kill both me and the life of a child who no one even knew existed yet but me. Was I making a terrible mistake, gambling that way?

I laid my hand on my stomach and felt strength flow through me. The gamble was the only way to ensure that little life stayed safe.

I didn't shout anything to Jacob; I'd no idea how to say goodbye, and didn't want to risk losing my courage.

'Stay,' I whispered to Wiggins.

I slipped from the house, knowing I might not return.

Glenn looked confused for a second as I ran over to him, shouting his name. That innocent smile was skilfully slipped on, though; his eyes so wide, so blue, so twinkly. No one would ever guess his truth by looking at him.

'Are you okay?' he asked.

Now I could hear the slightly guarded nature of the question, could see the tiniest tension in the corners of his boyish grin. 'You still look really pale, a bit feverish.'

'Yes, that's why I thought I'd get another breath of fresh air. Do you fancy going to the marsh? It's a beautiful clear night.'

As I spoke, my breath floated into the air before me. It was a freezing night, not a cloud in the sky. A full moon gazed down to watch my fate unfold, as it had watched yours. It felt serendipitous, as if you were somehow backing me up, Beth.

I had rehearsed my excuse, trying to make it sound as natural as possible. After all, Glenn had no reason to suspect that I was up to anything. Still, I held my breath while waiting for his reply.

Glenn raised his eyebrows and positively beamed at me. 'Of course I'll come to the marsh.'

I shivered as we walked towards his van, and it wasn't simply from the cold.

CHAPTER 101

How stupid was Melanie? I almost laughed in her face. She was clearly up to something, but that was fine because she equally didn't realise that I knew. She had no clue that I'd spotted her going through my things.

As we walked to my van, I glanced around, pretending to look at her to see if she was okay. In reality I was making sure there were no witnesses. But it was a cold, dark Monday night. Everyone was at home, curtains drawn. No one to see Melanie Oak jump into the passenger seat of my van. No one to see us drive off in the direction of the marsh.

We didn't speak much on the journey. I put the radio on loud to drown out any noise and give me a chance to think, uninterrupted.

I definitely wouldn't use the shotgun, I decided. Too noisy. Too messy. Too easy to trace back to me.

Perhaps I could somehow set her death up to look like suicide. People would totally buy that. If she caused me trouble once we were on the marsh, though, I could still just bash her head in, strangle her, whatever it took. Even if she were obviously murdered, it didn't really matter. Suspicion would fall on others well before me. After all, Melanie had annoyed a lot of people. The Youngs, the Clarkes, the Daughtrey-Drews, even that James Harvey bloke – though he seemed to lack any bottle at all. All of them appeared to have a lot more reason than I to kill Melanie Oak.

Murdering Mel had never been part of my plan, but now it was happening, I was looking forward to it. It wouldn't be as big a prize as killing a child, but it was way better than an animal. The longing that had been growing inside me these last months was finally going to be sated. My heart started to thrum, my blood singing with anticipation. I could barely keep the smile off my face.

   Step into my parlour, little fly.

CHAPTER 102

As usual, Glenn had chucked his coat onto the passenger seat rather than wear it. I pulled it over me like a blanket. This was crazy. Was I really going to face down a killer? But I thought of Tiffany, so casually murdered by this man. I thought of you, tossed aside like rubbish by your best friend. I thought of my unborn child.

I had to go through with this.

'It's freezing!' I gasped. 'Look at me, I'm shivering!'

I pulled it up under my chin, too busy doing that to bother with my seat belt for such a short journey.

'Help yourself,' laughed Glenn, watching me wriggling and trying to get warm despite my own coat, hat and gloves.

The weight of both phones in his inside pocket bumped against my body. Yes! It was the pocket on the side furthest from Glenn. Blindly, I slid my hands inside, hoping he wouldn't spot my fingers wriggling.

'Could you pop the heaters on full blast, please?' I asked.

He turned the ignition, the engine roaring immediately. We plunged into darkness as the cab light went out. Glenn leaned over towards me – I fought the urge to lash out, to scream in panic – and pointed the air vents at me.

'Better?'

'Hmm, much. Thank you.'

He flipped the radio on too. Good – the noise would stop any conversation. The local station blared out tunes for lovers as we headed into the inky night. No time for nerves. I used the cover of darkness to get hold of the phones and slide them down towards my own pocket.

My heart was hammering. If Glenn saw me, anything could happen. A punch to the head to knock me out. Chopped into pieces with the machete, my dismembered corpse scattered across the marsh for the animals and birds to feast on, and the tide to steal my bones.

I thought of the police. I thought of the evidence they would need to convict a child killer. I thought of my plan.

The phones slid closer to my pockets. I fumbled at them, hands clumsy in my woollen gloves. In the dark, the mobiles slithered from my frantic grasp, skated down my leg onto the floor. If they made a thud it couldn't be heard over the sound of the fans going full blast and the radio station's advert jingles. I shuffled my feet desperately. The phones got pushed further under the seat.

That was my only shot.

My heart seemed to thud in my throat now. I reached for the notebook with frenetic fingers. Managed to hook it into my pocket and told myself that it was enough. That everything would work. It had to.

There were no tears. Only steely resolve. I was resigned to my fate now. No turning back.

CHAPTER 103

As I drove over the hump of the sea bank and pulled into the car park, my stomach rumbled. I'd have pizza and chips for tea, and there was a film on television later that I fancied watching, once I'd dealt with Melanie's body. This really was turning into the perfect night.

How best to kill her, though? My last kill had been planned for years, and now this one had sneaked up on me. It was a wonderful gift the world had decided to give me, in recognition of my power.

Keep things simple, I resolved.

I couldn't be bothered with the hassle of trying to set things up cleverly to look like suicide. Not when I was this excited. I was like a child, eager to tear the wrapping off my present. My blood was pounding; my fingers twitching for the kill.

I was going to punch Mel, strangle her, then dump her in a creek. Not one of the meres, like those idiots the Clarkes had used for Beth; they were too shallow for the purpose. But the hidden fissures of the creeks were perfect. Overgrown. No one would notice her body. And if they did, well, hopefully she would have decomposed a bit by then; enough to disguise her injuries and confuse any possible forensic evidence. It would be particularly handy if some wildlife had a nibble at her.

Oh, to hear that last exhalation of breath as life slipped away. To feel the pulse quivering beneath my fingers, then stilling. To look into eyes begging me for mercy, and not to give an inch.

Melanie's pale skin would turn a beautiful shade of blue, I decided, stealing a glance at her as I pulled into the car park. I bit my lip in delight at the joys to come.

CHAPTER 104

When Glenn turned the van's engine off, the silence was infinite. The isolation of the marsh was hammered home to me.

No one came here at night. No one would hear any screams for help.

Glenn shifted in his seat and turned to me. Hooked his coat away, exposing my body, and pulled it on. Then rested one elbow nonchalantly on the top of the steering wheel.

'Well, I'm ready for anything. So, what now?' he smiled.

It was not his usual boyish grin. It was slower, more calculated, and cold enough to freeze my bones. *He knew.* Oh God, Beth, he knew.

I was not ready to die. I would not let him take my child's life the way he had stolen Tiffany Jones's.

I glanced at the clock on the dashboard. It was 7.02 p.m. Time was running out.

Closer, closer, closer crept death.

I yanked at the door handle, just as I heard the central locking sliding into place. I was trapped.

A movement in the corner of my eye. I flung my body forward, thanking God I hadn't done up my seat belt, and threw up my arm to ward off the expected blow. I struck out. Years ago I'd done a brief self-defence course, and had always remembered that instead of trying to hit a man where it obviously hurt, the best place to thump an attacker was his throat. My fist connected. Not hard, but enough to draw a gasp, a desperate struggle for breath.

I grappled for the lock, yanked it up and burst from the van, falling on all fours to the ground. The wind whistled a welcome that I ignored.

I only had minutes left. I knew that, Beth. I had to make them count.

Up on my feet I jumped, pelting straight out across the marsh. The ground firm at first, as I crashed through long, soft grass, giving way to low, coarse blades. Next was springy vegetation, up around my calves, trying to trip me up. The land got wetter. I slipped off a hummock, ankle turning, but kept going, the full moon lighting my way.

Must get away!

A splash of water as I hit boggy ground, feeling the ground sink beneath me in other parts. But I was swift, too swift for the sucking mud to grab me.

Still not swift enough, though.

There were footsteps behind me. Rapid, wheezing breath. Glenn had longer legs than me, and a killer instinct.

I forced myself to go faster. I was no gym bunny, but the endless walking of the past weeks had made me stronger and fitter. I carried less weight. And fear for my unborn child lent me wings, despite the headwind coming from the ocean trying to hold me back.

Throat burning with effort. Adrenaline pushing me forward. The ground was more uneven now, the hummocks twisting my ankles. I couldn't see clearly enough to leap from one to the other; all I could do was run, despite the pain. Ahead of me, the sea looked like mercury in the distance, out on the mudflats.

I ran for my life. I ran for my child's. I ran for Jacob. I ran for you, Beth.

The footsteps, the breathing, they were catching up. Then fingers of steel would grab me. Choke the life from me. I would look up at the huge, remorseless sky, and it would be the last thing I would ever see.

Just a little bit further. Please, just a few more seconds of life.
Any. Minute. Now.

I hit a hummock; flew into the air, limbs flailing. Landed with a thud, helpless on the cold ground, the breath knocked from me. Twisting where I lay, I looked up into Glenn's face. The friendly mask was gone, replaced with something as hard as metal in the cold moonlight.

'Argh!' I heard a cry of shock and pain.

Glenn had disappeared. Tumbled into a hidden creek. He gave a second roar, only the top of his head showing. I lay frozen, unable to tear my eyes away from his hands grasping at the vegetation as he tried to pull himself up. Another agonised yowl echoed high into the air, but the wind caught it before it could reach the unflinching moon.

I crawled forward, panting. Glenn's enraged eyes met mine. He looked like a rat caught in a trap. He lashed out, but he couldn't reach me.

He was in the creek you had led me to the other day, Beth. The one with the rusted oil drum and the barbed wire at the bottom of it. The one I almost fell into myself, until the egret you sent flew up and stopped me.

Glenn's eyes changed as he looked at me.

'Help me. My leg's trapped,' he gasped. He bent down, pulling desperately at his leg. When his hands came up again they were black with blood in the monochrome landscape. It trickled down his arm.

'Look! I'm bleeding! Mel, please… I know you're in a mess right now. Your life is falling apart, and that's why you lashed out at me for no reason. You scared me when you ran. I thought you were going to hurt yourself – that's why I came after you. Please, you have to help me.'

He pleaded, confusion clouding his soft features.

'Your leg's gone right through the rusted drum?'

'Yeah, it's—' He looked down, gasped in horror and pain. 'Oh God, it's bad, Mel. The metal's slashed me almost to the bone.'

My smiled reply was as brilliant and cold as the sky above me. There were tears in his eyes.

'Come on, Mel.'

I didn't move. Didn't speak.

'Call for help. You're not a killer. You're not cruel. You're better than this.'

Was he right, Beth? I thought about my life and everything that had brought me to this point. All the laughter and warmth and good things I had enjoyed, thanks to you. And how all that had been stolen from me by a silly argument, so silly that Chloe couldn't even remember the details properly. I thought about how much that hurt; the supernova of pain that had now whited out everything else in my life. Then I thought about the secrets, the lies and deception of everyone around me – and the biggest liar of all, Glenn. He had done so much evil, of that I was absolutely certain.

Any minute now. The countdown was almost done.

I sidestepped away from Glenn, then peered over the edge of the creek. His leg did look terrible. The gash flapped wide and gaping, and with each tiny shift of his body, the metal sawed further into flesh. His other leg was tangled in barbed wire.

'You're stuck fast. There's nothing I can do.'

'You can call an ambulance!'

I patted my pockets, then held my hands out, palms open. 'Left my phone at home.'

'Bitch. You fucking bitch!'

CHAPTER 105

'Bitch. You fucking bitch!'

I spat the words with fury. When I got out of the creek – and I would, eventually – I was going to make her pay. It wouldn't be a fast kill. I'd torture her, like I'd done with the animals and birds I'd trapped as a kid.

Just you wait, Melanie Oak.

I must have instinctively leaned forward towards my intended target. The metal sawed deeper into my flesh, jarring against bone. The pain! I was wild with it, couldn't bite back the screams.

Somehow I found the inner steel to still myself. I didn't need Melanie to call for help; I would do it myself. My feverish hands ran over my body.

No, no, no…

My phones weren't in my coat pockets. Neither of them. What the hell?

The agony of my right leg formed a vice for my mind. My calm control was shredded; pain was all I could think of. I shook my head. I needed to keep it together. Assess my situation calmly.

With only the light of the moon to see by, it was hard to get an exact idea of what was going on. Although I couldn't see, it felt as if the skin had been sheared from the front of the leg as it had plummeted through the rusted oil drum. I kept thinking of the cakes in Ursula Clarke's café, with their curled shavings of chocolate on top, and imagining my flesh now looked the same. Far worse, there was a massive gash across the inside of my thigh that was impossible to miss.

When I plunged through the metal, it had sliced into me as deep as a butcher's cleaver. With each beat of my heart, a traitorous pump of blood soaked the material of my trousers.

I needed medical help. Fast.

I forced my mask back on and gave Melanie an innocent, bewildered look.

'I'm sorry I swore, Mel. But I'm scared… and I think you're having a breakdown; it's the only explanation for your behaviour.' Tears started to fall. 'I'm begging you, call for help. Come on, Mel, after everything I've done for you!'

I knew she would give in to her weak, finer feelings and get me help. And once I was back to full strength, I would make her pay and pay and pay for this.

There were spots in front of my eyes. Blood loss would soon make me pass out. The realisation made me desperate enough to try something different. The tears fell faster – I was a good actor.

'Okay, Mel, I know you know what I did to Tiffany. But I didn't mean to. I… I don't know what's wrong with me. I need help, psychiatric help, I know that. You're my friend; you know the goodness in me; you know I'm not a bad person; I just did a bad thing. I think it was losing my mum at such an early age. It broke something in me. My dad used to beat me. He did terrible things to me…'

It was all rubbish, but would get a reaction. Sure enough, she crouched down so that she could see into my eyes better.

*

His small, bright blue eyes begged me. Pleading. He had never really known a mother's love, he said. His father had abused him.

As I crouched down the wind blasted my face, making my eyes water with crocodile tears.

'Glenn, even if I called for help, it wouldn't arrive in time. Look at the water level. The tide is coming in.'

*

I knew then. I recognised the look in her eyes as she crouched in front of me, because it was the look I have given to my victims: no mercy.

All that time spent with her, laughing, manipulating, and I never once realised the real reason I had been drawn to her. She was a kindred spirit. There was a streak of something diamond-hard inside Melanie Oak.

Still I pleaded and begged. Perhaps she would pity me. I was an animal caught in a trap, and I would do anything to survive. Anything. If it meant gnawing my own leg off, I'd do it. If it meant supplicating before Melanie Oak, I would.

But she stood. Gazed down at me. Started walking away. Slow, nonchalant, no hesitation in her step.

'Come back. Melanie, come back!'

She was right. The tide was coming in faster than a man could walk. Its distant rush grew closer, the water level rising around me. I was knee-deep now. I didn't have long. Once I got out of the creek, how long would it take me to crawl across the boggy land? For a second I allowed myself to picture the sea closing over my head, not in a series of waves but one continuous, unstoppable, inescapable motion.

No, I would not die that way.

I pulled at my leg again. Rusty metal carved flesh, ground bone. The pain was agonising, but the will to live was stronger. I yanked at my limb, gritting my teeth and roaring. Already I was weakening, the black spots in front of my eyes growing bigger, my head spinning dizzily. I wouldn't be able to stand for much longer.

I could not die here, at the hands of a mother. A housewife.

I was a god.

I was all-powerful.

I controlled life and death.

I was as relentless as the tide…

'Help me! Please help me!'

The full moon was an all-seeing eye gazing down at me, unable to help. I would not give up until I had breathed my last. I would kill Melanie Oak. I would annihilate her family. I would…

The water was rising. It was at the top of my thighs now. My heart pounded, and there was an unfamiliar feeling taking me over, making me splutter and gasp. I had seen it in the eyes of others but never felt it myself.

I was terrified.

CHAPTER 106

When I stood and looked down at him, no pity stirred my blood. Yes, there were tears in his eyes, and genuine fear. But I was pleased, because all I could think of were the countless children who would be saved from a horrifying death at his hands. He would never have shown them a drop of mercy.

Are you shocked, Beth? I've told you everything that happened from the moment you disappeared, because you need to understand what brought me to this moment. What I had done was for you and your father – and now for your little sister or brother. Although I had changed from the person you knew, nothing would ever change how much I love my family. You and your father always wanted to make the world a better place. I had done that by ridding it of Glenn Baker.

I was no longer the woman who'd run around the village a month earlier, panicking and placing my trust in others. I had learned from the liars and manipulators who surrounded me and took advantage. Now I knew that I could only truly trust myself, because anyone else would let me down.

So when I found out about Glenn, there had never been any chance of me going to the police. Collecting evidence had not been my plan, Beth.

If he went to prison, his punishment would never be enough for the pain he had meted out to his victim and her family. He would get out in a few years' time, and be free to kill again. No one would be safe from him. Not unless I took action.

So I lured him to the marsh. This place of peace and war, of life and death, that had been bombed and machine-gunned by the RAF, then reclaimed by nature. A place of extremes. It seemed fitting.

When I took both his mobiles from his pocket, it was not in order to give them to the police. I had deliberately let them slide onto the floor so that he wouldn't be able to call for help as I murdered him. I'd been careful to wear my woollen gloves, and rubbed them over the phones as much as possible to smear my fingerprints, should the police choose to check them. But it was doubtful that they would – why would they, when everything had been set up to point to Glenn's death being a tragic accident? Everyone was familiar with his habit of chucking his coat onto the passenger seat, and it was feasible his phones had fallen from his pockets as he did that.

I had realised he was bound to attack me, though I'd thought it would be when we were out in the open. The plan had always been to run, Beth, knowing you would show me the path across the marsh. Thanks to you, I knew just where to go, and exactly where to leap over the creek so that Glenn would fall into it and go through the rusted drum. I knew you would keep me safe.

I'd even gone online earlier in the evening to double-check what time the tide would be coming in. With the full moon, the spring high tide due in would be a big one, strong and sudden. If blood loss didn't kill Glenn, drowning would.

It would appear as though he had wandered onto the marsh and been caught out by a tragic set of circumstances. After all, who would want to kill a caring, pleasant guy like him?

There was nothing to link me to any of it. Witnesses at the pub had seen me leave with Jacob; no one had spotted me returning. I was fairly certain I'd get away with murder. And if I didn't, well, a mum sent mad with grief would receive a lighter sentence, particularly as I was pregnant – I had googled that too.

I'll admit, Beth, that I surprised myself with how cold and calculating I was. But I had learned from some of the best.

When his screams stopped, I would feel no more than the stars did as they looked down on the scene. He had used your death for his own horrifying ends, and I had stolen the notebook because nothing of you – or Tiffany – should be left with that evil man.

I wasn't sure what I'd do about the Clarkes yet. I disagreed with your dad. He always was a better person than me. You and he made me the happy person I was, but that had all been shattered. You see, I thought that Chloe should pay for what she had done to you. Maybe your death *was* an accident, a lashing out in a violent temper. I didn't care. Chloe took your life; that was all that mattered. She extinguished the light of my life, and took you from me forever. Since that moment, darkness had spread across my soul like a storm cloud over the moon.

Dispensing justice might not bring you back, but it felt right.

I had years yet to make a plan. I would see what happened. Perhaps I'd feel differently when the baby arrived. For now, I stood beneath the full moon, listening to Glenn's shouts get more desperate. I thought of how I had saved children from screaming by obliterating his life. In the distance the sea was rushing towards me. It was a long way off yet, but it came in faster than a person could walk. I couldn't hang around to watch Glenn drown. Which was a shame, really.

*

I turned. Walked away towards the distant lights of the village as the wind roared its approval and tugged at my clothes. Or was it you, Beth? I swear I heard you whisper to me as I smiled.

'I love you to bits and whole again.'

EPILOGUE

The cry for help is ragged and desperate, the voice hitching. There is no one to hear it.

A moon hangs so fat that it oozes an aura into the sky that almost blots out the stars surrounding it. It looks down on land as flat as an open palm, and as unforgiving as a clenched fist, and gives no answer to the screams of fear and rage that float up to it.

This is the wind's playground. It races across the North Sea and hits the land full force. There is nothing to slow it; no hills, few trees or hedges here on land reclaimed from the water to create the marshes and fertile flats of Lincolnshire. It screams ecstatically, punching the handful of houses it comes across, revelling in its unfettered freedom as it rattles windows. On its journey it picks up the entreaties for help that are echoing into the sky. Hurls them across the landscape, as gleeful as a toddler with a toy.

'Help me! Please! Help!'

There is no one to catch the words.

No one, except a lone figure, turning, walking away towards lights in the far-off distance.

AUTHOR LETTER

Thank you for reading *The Darkest Lies*. There are some difficult subjects and emotions covered in it, which were sometimes tough to write, and I hope you feel they were done justice. It would be wonderful to hear your thoughts – and if you have the time to leave a review it would be very much appreciated.

Your support means the world to me, because without readers what is an author? It is you who recommends books you've enjoyed to friends, you who leaves reviews that help other people decide whether or not to buy, and you who push me on to keep writing.

If you want to get in touch, or find out the latest on what I'm up to, there are lots of ways: Facebook, Twitter, my blog and website, as well as Goodreads. I'd love to hear from you! And if you'd like to keep up-to-date with all my latest releases, just sign up at the following link. Your email address will never be shared and you can unsubscribe at any time http://www.bookouture.com/barbara-copperthwaite.

Thank you for your continuing support and enthusiasm.
Barbara Copperthwaite

AuthorBarbaraCopperthwaite/

BCopperthwait

barbaracopperthwaite.wordpress.com

www.barbaracopperthwaite.com

ACKNOWLEDGMENTS

Writing a book is a strange thing. It is a lonely undertaking, and I have spent hours every day holed up on my own as I wrote feverishly. But without the help of others, I wouldn't be lucky enough to now see my book being published. I owe so many people a debt of thanks.

First and foremost is my partner, Paul, because I couldn't do any of this without his support. A man of few words, Paul has listened to me when I've worried, brought me endless cups of fruit tea, and taken over so many practical things, so that I could wander around with my head almost permanently in a make-believe world from which he was excluded. Thank you for giving me that freedom, and for joining me on this publishing adventure.

My mum also puts up with non-stop phone calls where the only subject I am capable of talking about is my latest book. Luckily, she loves crime (it's where I get it from!). I couldn't have done this without her.

Sarah Ward had a sneak peek at the first 20,000 words of a very rough draft of this book. Her encouragement at that stage was key to me keeping going with it, and I'm eternally grateful for her kindness. Neats Wilson, Joanne Robertson, Shell Baker and Anne Williams all cast their expert eyes over the finished product, and their thumbs up meant the world to me, giving me the courage to submit it to Bookouture. I owe you!

Thanks to my agent, Jane Gregory, for all her work behind the scenes, and to Bookouture for having the faith in me to take my book on – particularly to my editor, Keshini Naidoo. She not only commissioned me, but has already turned into someone I trust absolutely to push my work to be better. Bookouture consider themselves a family, and I have to echo that. From the wonderful Kim Nash, who works tirelessly on publicity, to my fellow authors who are always there with advice, commiserations and celebrations, I feel very lucky to have been adopted by them!

I must mention the incredible blogging community, who are some of the most dedicated people I have ever met. For no personal or financial gain whatsoever, they share their passion for books with people. Their enthusiasm for my previous novels helped to keep me going when times got tough. I'd particularly like to thank Book Connectors, a fabulous Facebook group which has been a massive help, along with Crime Book Club, Crime Fiction Addict and UK Crime Book Club. Last but by no mean least, the mighty Facebook group that is THE Book Club (TBC) has been a huge help.

Through TBC, I was able to contact Sara Bain, whose advice on legal matters was invaluable to the novel. The fabulous blogger Linda Hill also consulted with a former judge on my behalf. Massive thanks, too, to Kim Pocklington, who was incredibly generous in taking time from her busy role as a nurse to help me with my questions about head injuries and the like. It was so lovely of you, Kim!

Finally, I'd like to thank the village of Friskney, in Lincolnshire, for lending itself as a geographic basis for my story. Luckily, the people actually living there are nothing like my fictional characters in Fenmere, and I enjoyed a happy and peaceful childhood growing up there! This is my homage to the beauty and atmosphere of that place.

CPSIA information can be obtained
at www.ICGtesting.com
Printed in the USA
LVOW05s1510060717
540470LV00016B/1156/P